Graham,
Hope you en

GW00546563

The Devil Y

A Scott Lee Mystery Novel

by Peter Gregoire

Peter J Grégoire

To Nick's Dad, Hope you enjoy it as
much as the last one!

Peter Gregoire is the bestselling author of *Article 109*, the legal thriller set in Hong Kong and joint-winner of the international Proverse Prize 2011. He works as a legal counsel in the Hong Kong financial services industry and is an Honorary Lecturer at the University of Hong Kong.

Peter's website address is: www.peter-gregoire.com

The Devil You Know
A pressing need for income tempts Scott Lee to take on media tycoon, Rufus Lam's case. It seems like a straightforward enough missing person's search. Find out what happened to Rufus Lam's friend and close business partner, Terence Auyeung. Take the money and move on. That's the aim. A nice distraction too, from the growing malaise into which Hong Kong, the once vibrant city which has been Scott's home for the past ten years, is slowly sinking. Sure, it's 2017 and the city is about to elect its new Chief Executive. But not with the election system Hong Kong people want, Beijing has seen to that. The dream of democracy – true democracy – ended in 2014 when the initial exhilaration of the Umbrella Protests petered into nothing. But as Scott digs deeper in his search for Auyeung, he soon discovers that the Umbrella Generation never dissipated. It just went into hibernation, waiting for the right leader and the right time, to take up the cause once more. That leader is none other than Scott's client, Rufus Lam.
That time is now. And Scott's caught right in the middle of it.

The Devil You Know is Peter Gregoire's blistering follow-up to his prize-winning first novel *Article 109* which reached Number One on the Dymocks list of best-sellers.

The Devil You Know

A Scott Lee Mystery Novel

by Peter Gregoire

Proverse Hong Kong

The Devil You Know
by Peter Gregoire.
1st published in Hong Kong by Proverse Hong Kong, 22 December 2014.
Copyright © Proverse Hong Kong, 22 December 2014.
ISBN: 978-988-8227-63-1

Distribution (Hong Kong and worldwide):
The Chinese University Press of Hong Kong, The Chinese University of Hong Kong,
Shatin, New Territories, Hong Kong SAR.
E-mail: cup-bus@cuhk.edu.hk; Web: www.chineseupress.com
Tel: [INT+852] 3943-9800; Fax: [INT+852] 2603-7355
Distribution (United Kingdom):
Christine Penney, Stratford-upon-Avon, Warwickshire CV37 6DN, England.
Email: <chrisp@proversepublishing.com>

Distribution and other enquiries to:
Proverse Hong Kong, P.O. Box 259, Tung Chung Post Office, Tung Chung,
Lantau Island, NT, Hong Kong SAR, China.
E-mail: proverse@netvigator.com; Web: www.proversepublishing.com

Printed in Hong Kong by Artist Hong Kong Company, Unit D3, G/F,
Phase 3, Kwun Tong Industrial Centre, 448-458 Kwun Tong Road,
Kowloon, Hong Kong.
Cover design by LOL Design Ltd.
Page design by Proverse Hong Kong.

British Library Cataloguing in Publication Data.
A catalogue record for this book is available
from the British Library.

CHAPTER ONE

People say first impressions last. If that's so, it wasn't good news for Napoleon Wong.

He had waspish eyes and a stocky build which tapered off into the kind of superior mannerisms deliberately deployed to wind people up. Right now he was steepling his fingers and looking down his nose at me. Arrogance dripped off him like oil from a spit roast. Many people took leadership in their stride. Napoleon wore it as comfortably as a fifty-year old would his graduation tuxedo.

It wasn't the fact that a man like Napoleon could become CEO of Gadgetech which irritated me. It was the way he was so at pains to make sure everyone knew it, all of it just a little too forced. The Gadgetech brochure with his carefully photo-shopped picture in reception; the 'me' shelf replete with photos of him glad-handing district councilors and business big-wigs and a series of those tacky bought-and-paid-for industry awards. Then there was the desk itself. Planes had launched themselves from aircraft carriers half its size.

The little act he was giving me now, switching from the steeple to drumming his fingers on the Mahogany veneer, aimed for an image of vast intelligence. All I saw was a man with a serious inferiority complex which probably manifested itself in periodic tantrums, constant put downs, and other inordinate compensatory measures, the size of that desk being case in point.

So what the hell was I doing here, asking this man for a job?

I was about to recognize this for the mistake it plainly was, call proceedings to a halt and make a swift exit, when Napoleon paused his little finger drub and looked at me like he had just thought of the most impressive opening question in the history of job-interviewing.

Somewhere, I could have sworn I heard a drum roll.

"So tell me," he said. "Who is Scott Lee?"

If Gadgetech's fawning HR people had been witnessing this, they would have broken out the high-fives.

"That would be me," I said.

Stupid question, stupid answer. Then remembering the reason for my being here, I threw in a chuckle to make sure he got that I was joking and quickly launched into my pitch. "I'm Scott Lee, Mr Wong. I'm a lawyer. Been in the profession for over ten years. Corporate and commercial law is my specialty, but I do most things. Litigated more cases than I care to remember. Even drafted a few wills. An all-rounder with a specialty, you might say. Right now, I'm freelancing."

"Freelancing?" Napoleon said the words like he'd just sucked on a lemon.

"It's a new way of selling legal services, Mr Wong," I soldiered on. "And there's a gap in the market for lawyers like me in companies like yours."

"Is that so?"

"It certainly is. Under your leadership, Gadgetech has been a highly successful private operation, right? Its turnover and staff size mean it's outgrown its humble beginnings as an SME. But it's not quite got the scale yet to fund a permanent in-house legal department of its own. So here's the question. What happens when you need legal advice? And, trust me, a company as successful as Gadgetech is gonna need professional legal advice sooner or later. Answer. You go to a law firm. And what do you get? A caveated unclear recommendation and a big invoice. In a word, 'dissatisfaction'. Well, I offer something different. You hire me in-house on a short-term basis, I provide you with the advice you need at far lower cost. In a word, 'satisfaction'."

Napoleon Wong screwed up his eyes in thought. He didn't like me, I could tell, but that didn't bother me. I'd been around long enough to know that men like Napoleon Wong didn't like anyone.

"What makes you think I need any legal work done, Mr Lee?"

I choked down my gag reflex. Here I was offering my services to Gadgetech. Here was Napoleon Wong taking the offer as having been made personally to him. As if he was to Gadgetech, what Jobs was to Apple or Gates was to Microsoft. Took some ego to see yourself in that league. Napoleon was evidently built for it. Still, the question afforded me the opportunity to deploy my strategy which, simply put, was to flatter the hell out of him and offer him something he needed for as cheap as he could get it.

"I think there's a need for my services because, thanks to you, Mr Wong, Gadgetech has reached that golden stage, the one which all start-ups dream of." I laid it on in spades. "Based on the number of

6

outlets you've got across Hong Kong, I would put you, what, second or third largest electronics retailer in the market?"

Yeah, he sure liked where I was heading with this little ego-stroke.

"But Gadgetech's still a private company," I continued. "So right about now, I'm guessing the management here....you, Mr Wong...are deciding on which one of three options to take."

"And what might they be?"

I listed them off on my fingers. "One, you keep Gadgetech private and your existing investors pump in more capital to grow the business to the next level. Two, again, you stay private but add in one or two more investors, retaining overall control with your current shareholders. Or three, you take it public and go straight for the initial public offering. The big IPO!"

Napoleon's pencil-thin eyebrows flicked north. No greater compliment could you pay a CEO than to suggest their company was ready to be listed. Even if it wasn't part of his plans, it was a badge of honour my recognizing it as an alternative at his disposal.

"Whichever option you settle on," I continued, "at some stage soon you're going to want to make sure Gadgetech has all the necessary legal and compliance systems in place to be ready for, say, the additional listing disclosure requirements. That's where I come in. Hire me as a contractor short-term, and I work full-time to sort out all your legal needs. Trust me, it's far cheaper than just throwing it out to a law firm. Plus I will be right here, within sight, so any legal questions you have I'll be here to answer in real time. You won't be left waiting for some expensive partner to return your call when he deigns to do so."

Napoleon sat there in a look of deep thought. Either that, or he was constipated. Eventually he put on his reading-glasses and picked up my curriculum vitae. I had handed it to him at the get-go, but right up until that moment it had sat there on his desk, undeserving of his attention.

"Do you have any particular experience of handling management buy-outs?" he asked.

There it was: the question I'd been waiting for. I made a show of puffing out my cheeks and looking skywards as if reaching into the darkest recesses of my memory to tease out an answer.

"Yes," I eventually replied. "I do. I forget if it's two or three I've worked on. They're on page two of my CV."

He flipped over a little too enthusiastically, his thick lips moving as he read. When he was done, he looked up. "I confess that I have never heard of any of the law firms you have worked for. Are they well known?"

So beautifully condescending. One of Napoleon's evident strengths. Why didn't that surprise me?

"Jackson, Weiss MacDonald is currently number five in the world," I answered. "Yip & Siu is a local partnership. It's relatively well known in Hong Kong."

"And yet," his mouth creased into something between a grimace and a smile, "You were a partner in neither firm."

Ouch!

"That is correct."

He acted like he had won a point in tennis. I let him have his moment before moving to destroy it.

"I turned down an offer of partnership from Yip & Siu."

Wong's eyes turned sceptical. "You turned down the offer of partnership to become a freelancer? And they will verify this if I ask them about it?"

"They'll verify the bit about my turning down partnership, sure. But I didn't tell them I was going to start this gig. Anyway, you can contact Philip Yip, the senior partner there. His details are at the end of my CV, in the references section." I decided to add a little sparkle for the hell of it. "I don't think he has a council meeting today."

"Council meeting?"

"The governing council of the Hong Kong Law Society. Phil was elected President earlier on this year. He's spokesperson for the profession now."

Napoleon nodded. "And who are you freelancing for now?"

"Right now, I'm inbetween things. I recently finished my last contract and haven't found my next one yet. That's the honest truth, Mr Wong. It means I can start whenever you want me to, if you feel that you need me, that is." I tried to make it sound a little desperate, make him think he could really get me on the cheap.

He bit his lip, then asked. "How much would you be expecting me to pay you?"

Finally we were talking turkey. I told him the monthly figure I wanted. It blew his socks off, I could tell. He was already counting the savings against the budget for his precious management buy-out. But a man like Napoleon wouldn't have got where he was, if he didn't try and knock me down some more. When he did, I discounted my figure by ten percent. He seemed content enough with that.

Right then my mobile phone rang. Usually, at job interviews you're supposed to make sure your phone is turned off, and if you forget, it's considered the height of rudeness to answer it. But this was all part of my play. "Excuse me, one second," I said.

Napoleon's thick neck flushed red with anger as I answered. But when I started to carry on my conversation in fluent Cantonese, he almost lost colour. That's the thing with being a non-Chinese in Hong Kong. Mandarin, maybe, but definitely not Cantonese, a dialect with nine tones laced with slang and flexible rules of grammar too hard for most Westerners to pin down. Thankfully, my mum emanated from these parts, you might say, and drummed it into me and my brother during our English upbringing. It's always an impressive sight to see a *gweilo* speaking it. And where better to impress than a job interview?

After two minutes, I finished the call and apologized. Napoleon didn't say anything, but I could tell I'd scored big. He flicked through my CV some more.

"You didn't say who your last contract was with?"

I smiled. Another gift. "It was with AsiaRisk, the insurance subsidiary of Kwan Holdings? Helped them implement their anti-money laundering compliance system."

He asked me some follow-ups about my experience there, but I knew that the mere mention of Kwan Holdings, the company currently fifth in market capitalization on the Hang Seng Index, had got him over the line.

A comfortable silence hung between us, the cogs whirring in Napoleon Wong's brain, as he convinced himself this was a good idea.

"Well, Scott," he eventually said. "This is your lucky day! I think I could put your services to good use. Work out the rest of the details with our head of human resources, but consider yourself hired. Congratulations!"

"Thank you so much, Mr Wong, you won't regret this."

He stayed seated while giving me a moist handshake.

"We're not quite in Kwan Holdings league here," he said with a smile that sent a slither of trepidation down my spine. "But I do like things done properly and in a disciplined manner. And you will find me very hands on. I expect you to keep me fully informed of everything you are working on."

"Of course," I said.

But the thought of having this odious man breathing down my neck was hardly a gratifying one.

Still, I thought, if Napoleon Wong did have anything to do with Terence Auyeung's disappearance, I was going to find out. And then I'd wipe that self-satisfied, reptilian grin from his lips once and for all.

CHAPTER TWO

After signing the necessary paperwork, I walked back to Quarry Bay Mass Transit Railway subway station and jumped on to the first train to Causeway Bay.

It had just gone four o'clock, knocking-off time at the schools. The carriage was a cacophony of gossip and giggling school-kids letting off steam, playing games on their iPhones and trading What'sApp messages. I didn't begrudge them. Being a school-kid in Hong Kong was a tough, never-ending round of brutal homework and ridiculous CV-enhancing hobbies. Travel time in between was probably the only opportunity they got to blow the cobwebs off and be themselves without parental or teacher intervention. I took a seat in the corner of the carriage, shut my eyes and let them go at it.

Philip Yip had invited me to join his family for dinner at their home that evening, so I killed time by picking up some emergency provisions at Jason's supermarket before going back to the five-hundred-square-foot apartment I currently called home. Happy Valley was an exclusive area, what with the racecourse at its feet and the Jockey Club on the hill. Although in the heart of the city, the district retained a village feel for which the residents were prepared to pay top whack. Like the rest of Hong Kong though, property owners round the Valley right now were feeling the pinch. Prices were stratospheric, pushed there by Mainland Chinese money which had poured in from the north. It had created bitter resentment from locals, angered about being kept off the property ladder because it was too expensive.

Those local owners who had managed to ride the property wave were beginning to get jittery, trying to get out at the top of the market before the inevitable downward spiral began. One of them was my landlord, a doctor who had made a bundle flipping properties. He had been advertising the flat I was staying in for the last three months. No-one was biting. He was happy enough for me to stay there month-to-month at a fractional rent, just so the place looked lived in to potential purchasers. That summed up Hong Kong. Everyone had an angle, everyone was on the make.

Everyone, that was, apart from me. A while back, I had stepped off my less than stellar career path at Yip & Siu solicitors, following a case which had forced me to take a good long hard look at myself and ask some serious questions about where I was going in life. Two years on, the answers were as elusive as ever, but I was in no hurry. My savings weren't much, but as a single guy who had eschewed alcohol having found out early on that, like my father, I had too unhealthy a liking for it, neither were my expenses. I had taken monthly contract jobs here and there with law firms looking to even out the cycle of their workloads without adding to headcount. I also got paid for contributing the odd article to an online legal magazine. But mostly, I just hung out, read, paused, and thought. It was a way of life I enjoyed and what had started as a sabbatical was slowly petering into something more permanent. I didn't mind. Not having a plan or any pressures suited me fine.

When I made it back to my flat, I checked my share portfolio and flipped through the *South China Morning Post*. The news was replete with uninspiring stories on the latest goings on in the Hong Kong Chief Executive election. In any other country in the world, a political race to be the head of government would have galvanized heated debate and held the attention of the electorate for months. Not in Hong Kong. Not any more. Not since the government, through a mixture of broken promises and sheer blind-eye stubbornness had forced its sham election procedure down our throats in the face of massive public protest and discontent.

For the forthcoming election, sure, there was a new voting system which allowed people to vote directly for the candidates for the first time. Universal suffrage had finally come to Hong Kong, the government was telling us, just like the Basic Law – Hong Kong's constitution – had promised. Problem was, the only candidates permitted to throw their hat into the ring were two 'yes' men vetted by a shadowy nominating committee controlled by the Central People's Government up in Beijing. So who did the electorate end up getting to choose between? The current Financial Secretary, Jeremy Lau and the current Chief Secretary, Ronnie Wu.

The procedural farce had become even more absurd when two days after the call for candidates closed, Ronnie Wu dropped out of the race, leaving the Hong Kong electorate with Jeremy Lau, a 'technoprat' with the personality of a plank of wood and spine made of jelly, as the only name on the ballot paper.

Real Democracy. Proper universal suffrage, it was never going to happen, not for Hong Kong. The city had fought the fight and had lost. Lost to a government who didn't give a damn what people thought, so long as Beijing's agenda got rolled out. HongKongers weren't so much accepting of the situation, now. They were just exhausted. So exhausted, they had given up and gone back to doing what they were best at: making money for the here and now and working on an exit plan for tomorrow.

I spent more time on the back-pages of the paper, catching up on the latest sport. The latest transfer news in the English Premiership and the mystery of American sports, with its countless innings, time-outs and quarters, were able to absorb my attention until it came time for me to head out again.

Phil Yip had told me to keep this evening informal, but I knew what that meant to a man born wearing an Italian-tailored suit. I dug out my one lightweight blazer and checked out how I looked in the mirror. The blazer was blue and fading at the cuffs, not unlike its owner. Still I was pleased with what I was looking at. Having the time to exercise everyday had produced good results. My stomach was tight, my shoulders broad and my jaw-line was still a long way from turning soft. Sure, there was some white creeping in at the edges of my hair, which I liked to wear at a Bohemian length nowadays, but I was okay with that. The bags under my eyes were still evident, years of looking at legal documents late into the night had left an indelible toll, but they were less prominent than they used to be. I looked my age, but I was comfortable in my skin.

At five o'clock, I headed down to the minibus rank at the back of Times Square. The heat was off its height, the humidity still a few weeks away from taking the city in its moist grasp. Causeway Bay was its energetic self, swamped with Mainland tourists fighting for position on its cramped pavements. I was used to doing the jay-walk hustle these days to get wherever I wanted to go.

Eventually, I jumped on a mini-bus and headed south. The driver was the usual type of nutcase they put in charge of these contraptions. It was as if lobotomizing that part of the brain which felt fear was part of a mini-bus-driver's job description. We pitched and swerved like an Ocean Park roller-coaster without the safety features. As we ducked and weaved through Repulse Bay, I was glad I hadn't eaten a big lunch.

Eventually, the driver let me out near Stanley Market. I took a moment to settle myself down. The air was always cleaner on the south side of the island. A nice breeze was coming in off the sea. I liked coming to Stanley. A village on its own little peninsula, it had a distinct irreverent feel to it, compared to the rest of the bustling island. The beaches were great, the run of cosmopolitan bars and restaurants on its picturesque waterfront promenade even better. But the market which spread like octopus tentacles through its back alley-ways, was Stanley's stand-out feature. It was a cross between a modern day bazaar and the pirate's lair which Stanley once used to be. You could root around for hours in there and never get bored.

The Yips lived in a house down one of the leafy back-roads where only the uber-wealthy resided. A house in Hong Kong cost a fortune. A house in Stanley cost double that. Philip Yip had come a long way from the time he'd pulled up a seat next to me in the Law Library at Durham University and asked me to explain *Donoghue v Stephenson* to him. We'd been students together, but our paths had diverged. He was Senior Partner at Yip & Siu and Law Society President. I was his ex-employee.

I was met at the door by a Filipino maid who called me 'sir' and showed me through to a massive kitchen, which was a picture of the kind of frenetic activity that only a Hong Kong family preparing to eat can produce. I waited a moment before making my presence known, taking in the scene.

Phil was at the head of the table, his top button undone, tie loosened, the sleeves on his white shirt rolled up to just below the elbow. Next to him was his son, Peter, tuning out the whole world to concentrate on some gaming device he was busily working with his thumbs. Phil's father, whom I had only ever known as 'Mr Yip', sat opposite, barking orders to his broker on his blue-tooth while his wife buzzed around him directing the maid as to where the dishes should be placed.

"You know the rule, Peter. No games at the table please," Phil chastised.

"What about Grandpa? He's using his mobile."

"Grandpa should know better." Phil glanced at his dad who held up his finger as if to say he was almost done. "Now put the game away. And where's your sister?"

Peter gave a sulky exhale like only a hard-done-by ten-year-old can. "Probably in her room talking to Jonathan?"

"Jonathan? Who's Jonathan?" This from Phil's mum, as she popped vegetables into everyone's bowls with her chopsticks. She was five-foot two, in her seventies, but the kind of lady you never messed with. "Do you know about this Jonathan, Philip?" She always called her son 'Philip'.

"He's one of her classmates, Ma. Good at football apparently. Wants to be a doctor."

"A doctor! Isn't that good!" The way she said it, she was already making wedding plans.

"A doctor?" Mr Yip was finally off the phone, and as ever, always ready with an opinion. "One doctor in the family is enough. She should marry a lawyer." He was a large man with a cheerful face and a head of wiry, grey hair. The "Yip" in Yip & Siu had come from him, the co-founder of the firm. He had bred Phil to follow in his footsteps. Evidently, he was already looking out for the next generation.

"Joanna's sixteen, Dad. I don't want any talk about marriage for the next twenty years."

"Good point! You won't let me down, will you, Peter?" Mr Yip ruffled his son's hair as he passed by. "Hong Kong needs good lawyers. You know why, because its greatest strength is…."

"…..the rule of law." Peter rolled his eyes. "Yes, granddad, we know."

"That's my boy."

"But, Grandad, my friend Tiger says being a lawyer is borrrring! He wants to be an astronaut." This, Peter's final remark before leaving the room to fetch his sister.

"Tiger? What would this Tiger know, with a name like that?"

"He's winding you up, Dad!" Phil said. "Now can we eat, please?"

I shook my head. Philip Yip, always the mediator, whether at work or at home. Seeing the Yip family in full flight made me momentarily nostalgic. It had been a while since I had visited my brother in the UK. I wondered for a moment how he and my nephews were doing.

"Welcome to chaos!" someone whispered in my ear. I half-turned to see Alison Yip, Phil's wife, sidling up to me. She was the picture of elegance, with a glass of chardonnay in her hand and a smile that could shatter hearts.

"Hard day at the clinic?" I asked, as we kissed each other on the cheek, and I enjoyed a delicate waft of Chanel.

"Not any harder than your average family meal in this household."

"Come on, you love it," I said; and as we stood there admiring her family, I could see from her face that I was right. Alison Yip had long, wavy, black hair and a face with sharp standout features that wouldn't have been out of place on a catwalk. She was the doctor in the family to whom Mr Yip had referred. Her job was to treat refugees whose claims for asylum were being managed by the UNHCR sub-office in Hong Kong.

"Let's get this over with."

She led me over to the table.

"Well, look what the cat dragged in!" Phil jumped to his feet and gave me a hearty hand-shake and a look which thanked me for rescuing him. "Scott, you remember my parents?"

"Of course, I do."

"Scott!" Mrs Yip hugged me like a hostage being released from captivity. "Wah! So thin. Come, come, eat something!"

"Mr Yip, how are you?" My handshake with Phil's Dad was pure permafrost. He still hadn't forgiven me for leaving what he still referred to as 'his' firm.

"Good, thanks."

There was a moment of awkward silence, thankfully broken by Peter and Joanna Yip entering the room.

"Hey, Uncle Scott!" Peter came over and high-fived me.

"Hey kiddo! Still giving your dad a hard time?"

"Nah, I leave that to Sis."

"Shut up, Dai Lung!"

"Mum, tell her not to call me that!"

"Both of you sit down!"

I waited for a moment before nodding at Joanna, who was a dead-ringer for her mother and no doubt, with those dynamite looks, a popular girl at school. Boy, were they going to have a handful with her!

As we got stuck into the meal, Phil's mum probed Joanna about Jonathan, Peter regaled me with a knowledge of dinosaurs that would have put a paleantologist to shame, and Phil and his dad swapped stock-market tips. I couldn't help but feel infected by the Yip family's warmth. Phil and Alison had done a good job with their kids. All they wanted was for Peter and Joanna to be happy. Phil had confided to me once how difficult that was in Hong Kong, especially with his dad, who hadn't given him the kind of breaks he was giving Peter, and was not happy with Phil being so soft. But Phil had always been his own man and was more than satisfied when Joanna came home getting ninety-two percent on her maths exam, when for other kids that would have been the prelude to a beating.

But it was only a matter of time before Phil's dad turned his attention to the subject that was taboo between us.

"You ready to come back and work for the firm yet, Scott? Or are you still 'finding yourself'? As Mr Yip added the sarcastic quote marks with this fingers, sweat broke out under my collar. I took a deep calming breath.

"Dad, it's called a sabbatical," Phil jumped to my defence.

"A sabbatical? We didn't take sabbaticals in my day."

"Dad, I don't think this is any of your business?"

"It's not my business when one of the solicitors in the firm I built just ups and leaves in the prime of their career? Especially when he has just landed Cyrus Kwan as a client? Explain that, please, because this old man cannot understand it."

Oh boy!

"Scott has no obligation to explain anything to you or me, Dad. And if you hadn't noticed, you are no longer a partner in Yip & Siu! It's not *your* firm! And it's not for you to tell anyone where they should work. Not Scott, not Peter and not...."

"It's okay, Phil." I put a palm up to stop Phil before he said something he regretted. Blazing rows and family gatherings went together like chocolate and strawberries, but I had no intention of being the cause of this one. "Mr Yip, to answer your question, my sabbatical comes to an end first thing Monday morning."

Silence hit the room like a bucket of ice. Mr Yip opened and closed his mouth. Phil looked at me askance. Alison raised the amused eyebrow of a spectator. Peter picked his nose and got his hand slapped by his Grandma. Joanna looked like she wanted to be some place else.

"It does?"

"I got a new job today. But I'm afraid I'm not coming back to the firm, Mr Yip. I'm moving in-house. I am the new legal counsel for Gadgetech."

"In-house?" The words must have tasted like vinegar coming out of Mr Yip's mouth.

"Gadgetech?" Phil weighed in. "Scott, are you kidding! What the hell have you gone and done this time!"

"Philip!" Alison chastised.

Phil leant back in his chair and shook his head in disbelief.

"Hmmm," Mr Yip pondered. "Could be good for the firm, Philip. This Gadgetech could be a new client for you."

"Dad, shut up!" Phil wasn't in the mood and I could tell I was in for some explaining.

He stared me down like a boxer called to the middle of the ring by a referee. "Let's take this out on the patio, shall we?" he said to me, already up off his chair.

"Well, okay then!"

CHAPTER THREE

It was a perfect evening, balmy and warm with the mix of scented flowers and sea-salt drifting in on a light breeze. Lights from the restaurants along Stanley water-front illuminated the night. Over to the left, rugged peaks stenciled the sky with their black, harsh outlines; a line of cars and buses crawling round them at waist height, their headlights tracing the winding road back to the other side of the island like ants hard at work.

Seemed a shame to ruin an evening like this, but the mood Phil was in, I could tell I was going to have my work cut out. Part of me thought it best to allow him to let off steam for a moment, encourage him to take a few deep breaths. But then Phil had always been a bit of a drama queen. Used to get all het up the night before exams. It was just his way. As his friend, I knew there was no getting round it, so I braced myself and dived straight in.

"What's with the mood, Phil? You look like someone stole your favourite pair of cuff-links. I got a job, so what? Thought you might even be pleased for me."

He looked at me, his features contorting with incredulity.

"Pleased? This is Rufus Lam we are talking about, Scott. I can't mess around with people like him!"

He looked out to sea again, shoving his hands deep in his pockets, rocking back on his heels, the very picture of a man with the responsibility of the world on his shoulders.

"How about you stop acting like a schoolgirl for one second and let me explain how this works?" I said. My response didn't go down too well. Phil looked ready to hit me when he swung back round. I put my palms up in a calm-down gesture.

"Let's just wind back a week, shall we?" I said. "You came to me and asked me to help this Rufus Lam guy, remember?"

"This Rufus Lam guy? Scott, he's one of the richest men in Hong Kong!"

"Whatever."

"No," he held a finger up to me. "Not whatever, Scott. You know what it could do to the firm if we screw this up?"

"We? Don't see you doing much here, Phil, apart from getting me to do your dirty work, so you can set me adrift if things go wrong."

He pouted for a second. "It's not like that."

"It's exactly like that," I shrugged. "And I don't mind. Makes perfect sense. You're President of the Law Society. You've got a family, a reputation. I can understand your wanting to protect that. Me, I've got nothing. Which means I've got nothing to lose. That's why you came to me, right? Plus my not working for Yip & Siu any more gives you perfect deniability if it doesn't go as planned."

I watched my words twist through his mind, taking his temper down notch by notch. "But in return for giving you deniability, Phil, you don't get to question my methods, understand?"

He nodded. "I hope you know what you're doing!"

"All I'm doing so far is getting a job at Gadgetech. I start Monday as its temporary in-house counsel. Turns out Napoleon Wong wants some help with his management buy-out."

"You told Napoleon Wong you knew about him buying-out Rufus Lam's investment?"

"Relax, Phil. I just used it as an 'in'. Wong's going to need legal services. I pitched up at the right time offering them on the cheap. It was him who brought up the buy-out, not me. Oh and he said nothing about Rufus Lam. I'll act suitably surprised when he lets that little gem slip."

Phil looked a little impressed with me. "Okay, so how does this work?"

"Well, Rufus Lam asked you for help in finding out why Terence Auyeung disappeared. He wants to know whether there was any connection between Auyeung's disappearance and him being the Chief Finance Officer at Gadgetech, right?"

"Right."

"So I start work on Monday as Gadgetech's in-house counsel, helping Wong with his MBO. But whilst I'm in there, I can also see what I can find on Auyeung. May take a few days, but I should get the access to the files I need. And then when I'm done, you can give Rufus Lam the answers he wants and I can either see out the contract, or just up and leave."

Phil frowned. "You don't think a quick departure would raise suspicion?"

"Come on, Phil, this is Hong Kong. People change jobs faster than it takes the Star Ferry to cross the harbour."

He tapped his lips with his forefinger, doing what he always did, thinking of what could go wrong, thinking of every reason he could to play it safe and not take risks.

"You have full deniability, Phil."

"That's not the point!" Phil sighed and shot me a half smile. "You're my friend, Scott. Damn it, you're Peter's godfather. If something happened to you, and Alison found out it had something to do with me, you know what she'll do to me?"

"Phil, it's just an in-house job. What could possibly happen?"

He bit his lip in a way I didn't like and for the first time I realized he was holding something back from me. "Phil?"

"You're probably right," he said after a while. "Is there anything I can do to help?"

He'd skated away from my question a bit too fast. A nagging sense of foreboding ignited somewhere deep down inside of me. I decided to let it fester and circle back to it later.

"Two things, actually,'" I said. "Some guidance on how to handle a management buy-out would help. I told Napoleon Wong I had done at least three, but the truth is I haven't got a clue. I'm a litigator, not a corporate lawyer. Oh, and by the way, if someone from Gadgetech rings you asking for a reference, you'll need to confirm it. I'll send you a copy of the CV I gave him, just so we're singing from the same hymn sheet."

"You lied at a job interview?"

"Yeah, Phil, me and the rest of the eight million people in Hong Kong. So, can you help me out with the MBO? Maybe get someone to do me a cheat sheet and be on hand to look over any draft documents? It'll free my time up to find out what happened to Auyeung."

Phil nodded. "I'll put someone on it first thing. What's the second thing?"

"I want to meet Rufus Lam."

"What? Why?"

I knew he wasn't going to like that and for a moment I thought of letting it go. But the way Phil had avoided my question just now had set my antennae buzzing. He was holding something back, which meant the demand I was about to make was no longer optional.

"A face-to-face meeting with a client is always best practice."

"Rufus Lam is not a client," Phil argued. "He's just someone we're helping out."

"We, Phil? Really? Way I see it, it's me doing the heavy lifting here. Plus, I'm getting paid for this, right? At least that's the way I recall our conversation going the other night."

"Of course, but…."

"Then that makes Rufus Lam my client and I want to meet him. Are you going to make it happen or not? Because if not, I won't waste any more time on this."

Phil blew wind through his cheeks before reluctantly conceding. "I'll see what I can do."

"Do you two want any coffee?" Alison's gorgeous head popped round the patio door. The coffee offer was a mask for her checking up to see we hadn't killed each other.

"No thanks. It's getting late. I'd better be heading off," I said.

She came over and kissed me on both cheeks. The waft of Chanel made me go warm inside. "Don't be a stranger," she said.

I told her to say 'bye to the kids for me as she sashayed away.

When Phil and I were on our own again, he waited a moment before holding out his hand for me to shake. "I guess I should say good luck then."

"Thanks," I said. Then still gripping his palm, I followed up with, "Phil, is there anything else you need to tell me here?"

He shook his head and pinched his nose.

"Everything I know, you know already."

After we said our farewells I headed back to the bus-stop. With every step I took, that uneasy feeling inside me started to grow. It could have been because the wind was starting to get up, or that I wasn't used to eating that much for dinner and the food was sitting heavy in my stomach.

Or it could have been that my best friend of twenty years had just looked me in the eye and told me a big fat lie.

I knew which one was most probable and I didn't like it one bit.

CHAPTER FOUR

That weekend I spent finishing up some items of work which had been burning a hole in my desk for a while: an article for the *Hong Kong Lawyer* magazine, and a case I was working on pro-bono. I managed to get the article done and out to the editor on Saturday morning. The case wasn't that simple. It required me to attend a meeting on Sunday afternoon, which left me kicking my heels the rest of Saturday. So I killed time by doing some more research on Rufus Lam, the man for whom I was about to jump back into the job-market.

Rufus Lam was a real rags-to-riches story. Age eight, he had come to Hong Kong as an illegal, crossing the Lo Wu river on his brother's back from the Mainland, one of many families risking it all to escape the chaos of the Cultural Revolution that Chairman Mao had unleashed. During the ensuing five decades Lam had worked his way up from nothing to become the Hong Kong dream, the epitome of money and respect.

He had started out by hustling magazines on street corners, graduating to picking them up wholesale from the publishers and distributing them direct to the shops. The thing which set Lam apart from your average pamphleteer, however, was his voracious appetite for reading. Everything he delivered, he would read first, devouring page after page until he had a sixth sense for predicting your average HongKonger's appetites and desires. As assets went, that wasn't a bad one to have and boy, did Lam exploit it.

His first step up was convincing one of the editors of the papers he delivered to give him a job as a journalist. Before long, Lam was combining writing hit stories with analyzing the paper's business model. Realizing there was room for improvement on the latter, he convinced the owner to give him free rein to try out his ideas. Sales quadrupled, the owner was happy and Lam was put in charge. A few years later, Lam had enough to buy the company.

And Lam hadn't stopped there. He bought other papers and magazines too, mainly competitors, shedding drab publications, refreshing the ones he thought had legs and bringing out a few new ones of his own. By the time he was fifty, Rufus Lam had his very own media empire.

Like you'd expect of a media tycoon, Rufus Lam wasn't shy of self-publicity. He was tall and thin, but physically imposing with it. Handsome too, with a serious face and a head of dyed blonde hair that disguised his true age. But most of all, he dressed the part of eccentric billionaire. His penchant for brightly coloured shirts, lime-green, yellow and orange, was well known. He favoured cravattes over ties. But his trade mark was the silver-topped cane he always carried around with him, like he was Fred Astaire in a fifties' musical. It was a pure prop that made him one of the most recognizable figures in Hong Kong. With the kind of money Lam had, he could get away with it. Not bad for a kid who had started out with nothing.

According to Phil, it was three years ago when Rufus Lam had first hooked up with Napoleon Wong by buying into Gadgetech. Back then, Gadgetech was nothing; just one of the many hundreds of enterprises trying to make its way in the snake-pit of the Hong Kong business world. Under Napoleon Wong, Gadgetech was just about surviving. But when Lam stepped in with an equity investment, Gadgetech grew wings and soared.

For Lam, the investment proved inspired. He had seen the writing on the wall for the hard-copy newspapers and magazines that were his bread and butter. Like the dinosaurs, they were on the verge of extinction. One day soon, Lam realized, HongKongers would be reading news on the mobile-phones and tablets through which they were increasingly living their lives. So he decided to sell these hand-held gadgets himself, only with his publications preloaded onto them. It was vertical integration, pure and simple.

To make sure his money would be used in the right way, Lam insisted on putting his own man inside in Gadgetech. That was part of the deal he shook on with Napoleon Wong. And that's how Terence Auyeung came to be appointed as Gadgetech's new Chief Financial Officer. Napoleon Wong hadn't liked Terence Auyeung's appointment one bit, but the promise of Lam's money was enough to make him agree to the shot-gun wedding. And it had worked like a charm. Under Wong, with Auyeung's guidance, Gadgetech grew in three years to become the third largest electronics retailer in the Hong Kong market. As rises went, that was pretty meteoric, helped out, of course, by the kick start Lam gave it by loading free six-month subscriptions to his publications onto all mobile phones and tablets which Gadgetech sold. An inspired move from an entrepreneur with his finger on the pulse.

Everything with Gadgetech appeared to be going swimmingly.

Until Terence Auyeung disappeared.

It had happened two weeks ago. Terence Auyeung just didn't turn up for work one day and he hadn't turned up since. For a man like Auyeung, it was unheard of. But there was no sign of him and no tracks either. His wife didn't know where he was, nor did his family or friends. He had just vanished, like a puff of smoke through a key-hole.

The police hadn't so far shown much interest, Auyeung was a grown man after all. Rufus Lam had tried to look into it as far as he could, but as yet his people had drawn a complete blank. And with no-one watching over his investment any more, he wanted out of Gadgetech, fast, which said a lot about the faith he had in Napoleon Wong. But Wong seemed happy enough at the proposal that he buy Lam out.

Before Lam pushed the eject button, however, he wanted to find out what had happened, only he wanted it done below the radar screen. In particular, he didn't want Napoleon Wong knowing what he was doing. Which was why Lam had approached my buddy Philip Yip. And Phil had approached me.

Why me? Because I was someone with nothing to lose and someone like that could push the boundaries of the possible to get the job done. I wasn't sure whether to be flattered or insulted that Phil thought of me in that way, but I didn't dwell on it that much. The truth was, after over a year out, my funds were overdue a decent boost, plus being out of the job market had slowed my instincts. Here was something that could sharpen me up again. And as I looked through the print-outs on my research, I felt those instincts flickering into life.

Two things were bothering me about the story of Gadgetech and Auyeung's disappearance.

First was the fact that, for all his fame and fortune, Lam's investment in Gadgetech simply hadn't made it into the public domain. Everything I had learned had come from documents which Phil had fed me. Lam had managed to keep the whole thing secret by hiding his capital injections into Gadgetech through a series of companies registered in the Caymans and British Virgin Islands, jurisdictions well known for their sun, sea and secrecy. But there was more than one way to skin a cat like this and, given Lam's fame, I was surprised that no paparazzi had found a way through the corporate veil.

Second was the question why Lam was looking to exit Gadgetech so fast? I got it that Auyeung had been overlooking his investment. But couldn't Lam just have appointed a replacement, rather than selling out to Napoleon Wong just like that?

These questions – and others – needed answering, but at the beginning of a case, questions are all you have. So whilst they bothered me, they didn't bother me that much. Certainly not as much as the way Phil had lied to my face last night. Phil probably thought he had got away with it too, but I had news for him.

All these thoughts and more were spinning through my head during the course of that Saturday until 7pm my brain was a complete quagmire. I decided to go for a run. Four laps of the Happy Valley race track proved to be the perfect antidote, just what I needed to clear out the rubbish. It certainly did the job in calming my mind and after getting something to eat I was pretty much ready for bed.

Saturday nights certainly weren't what they used to be. But that was no bad thing.

CHAPTER FIVE

Sunday was a different story.

I put all thoughts about Rufus Lam, Philip Yip, Napoleon Wong and Gadgetech on hold to concentrate on my pro-bono case. It was a classic underdog fight, complete with a feisty client looking to take on the system, and yes, a dog.

The feisty client was Mrs Lo; the dog, her fifty-pound basset hound, Combo, named after Combo Menu C at the local Tsa-Tsan-Teng, which Combo could finish in two bites. Apart from being able to eat his own weight in food, Combo was the perfect pet. He was company for Mrs Lo, slept eighteen hours a day and when he was awake had a temperament so docile you could be forgiven for thinking he was dosed up to his big ears on Prozac. Mrs Lo volunteered Combo as a Dr Dog at the local hospital, where kids petted him and pulled his ears and tail as part of their recuperation. All Combo would do was raise his head occasionally, just in case there were any treats on offer.

Unfortunately, the public housing estate in Tseung Kwan O, where Mrs Lo lived, took a dim view of dogs. The Deed of Mutual Covenant, the document setting out the rules by which all residents agreed to abide, made it a "no pet" estate. It was a rule which many ignored. There were cats and dogs all over the place and usually the management company for the estate turned a blind eye. But it could only do that as long as no other tenant complained. If there was a complaint, the management's hands were tied and they went into full bureaucrat mode, enforcing the law to its fullest extent with threatening letters, hounding phone calls and tight dead-lines to be abided by.

And, yes, someone had launched a complaint against Combo; a police officer, no less, who lived two doors down from Mrs Lo. Combo was unhygienic, according to the complaint, and kept the officer awake when he had come back from night-shifts protecting his community.

It was complete bull. The way Mrs Lo looked after Combo, he was probably the healthiest thing on that estate. And it would have taken a brass band with Chinese fire crackers to have roused Combo from his eighteen-hour-a-day slumber.

The real cause of the trouble was Mrs Lo's son, Tak Ming, a brute of a man who happened to work for one of the local gangs as a debt-collector. The officer down the hall had tried to bust Tak Ming once, only for the case to get kicked out on a technicality. Police don't like getting embarrassed like that, so he had evidently decided to get his own back against Tak Ming's mum – or his mum's dog, more to the point – by filing this nonsense complaint.

The case had come to me from Philip Yip last year, this time from the pro-bono scheme Yip & Siu ran. He had begged me to take it on because none of his associates could find a way round the Deed of Mutual Covenant, at least that's what Phil had told me. But I knew that the true reason Phil wanted the case off his firm's books had more to do with the waft of street-level crime and the anti-police position which the case forced the defendant to take. Once again, I had become Phil's dust bin.

I didn't mind too much. I loved dogs and the underhand way this policeman was going about using Combo to settle a score didn't sit well with me.

So I had made life difficult for him. For about a year, I had been running stalling tactics, responding to every letter with a lengthy answer that took issue with every fact asserted. But now, finally, the policeman had become serious, calling an incorporated owners meeting for Sunday evening to try to get solicitors appointed so that formal court proceedings could be commenced against Mrs Lo.

I was going along to see what I could do to stop them.

An hour before the meeting, I met Mrs Lo at her flat. It was a five-hundred-square-foot space, living-room and kitchen combined into one. I sat on the sofa with Combo's big head on my lap. Tak Ming sat opposite me, not saying a word, while his mum bustled in the kitchen area, making tea.

"That man! He is not a man! He is a bastard!" Mrs Lo barked, as she poured out the hot water. She was four-foot eight with silver hair and a face etched with the battle-lines of experience. Her Cantonese was like gun-fire. As she banged a tea-cup down in front of me, I wondered whether leaving her in the same room with the policeman for five minutes would be the best way of resolving the matter in her favour. "Why he do this to Combo! He's just a dog. Never harm any one. Big strong policeman scared of a dog. I give him something to be scared of!"

I didn't doubt it for a second.

Combo shuffled up closer onto my lap. He had evidently seen his owner in these sorts of moods before and knew it was best to take cover.

"This your fault! Why you have to get arrested by him? Why not some other cop? Why my neighbour?"

"I didn't mean to get busted at all, Mum!" This came from Tak Ming, six foot four, black singlet, elbows on his jiggling knees, his tattooed muscles dancing around like there were rats under his skin. Every inch of him would have intimidated the hell out of me, had it not been for the fact that he was taking a heated salvo from his mum. "If I wasn't on probation, I'd go over there right now and...."

"And what? Threaten a policeman in his home? You make things worse for poor Combo. I bring you up to be this stupid, yes or no?"

Tak Ming's knees jiggled faster. He looked at me, then at Combo with contrition. Combo groaned his understanding. I sipped my tea and checked my watch, wanting to make sure we weren't going to be late.

"No more talk from you!" Mrs Lo pointed a veiny finger at her son before moving it on to me. "You leave it to Lawyer Lee. He save Combo from that policeman, not you!"

Despite my always telling her it was 'Scott', Mrs Lo preferred calling me 'Lawyer Lee'. Made me sound about a hundred years old, but, hey, she was the client.

I held up my watch. "Mrs Lo. I think we should go. Otherwise we will be late." She didn't look too impressed with that, so I added, "The plan is to play to our strengths. Tak Ming stays here and looks after Combo. You and I attend the meeting. Just introduce me as a family friend and leave the rest to me. Oh, and it may help if you took some tissue."

"Tissue?"

"So your neighbours can see you dabbing your eyes. At how upset you are at the prospect of losing Combo." As if on cue Combo raised his head. Mrs Lo looked down at him and her face softened.

"Poor Combo," she said, the machine-gun fire turning into a quake, and yes, her eyes filled with tears. The very picture of an old woman trying to save her dog from a jackbooted bully. I wanted to say 'perfect', but didn't think it would go down too well. Instead I got up and led her to the door, trying to keep her in the moment before Tak Ming said something to set her off again.

She picked up her handbag, took out a biscuit and threw it to Combo. Combo caught it in his mouth and crunched it down in one bite. Combo could be lightning quick when it suited.

We walked to the lift and waited with everyone else on the floor, heading down to the same meeting. The policeman was there. He stood ramrod straight as if on patrol, staring straight ahead down his aquiline nose, apart from the odd glance in my direction, wondering who the hell this *gweilo* was and working out quickly that I was there to try to spoil his party.

There were three other couples waiting too, all in their forties or early fifties and all going to the meeting, partly out of civic duty and partly for the sheer entertainment. Nothing a housing-estate likes more than a dispute between neighbours. Stories would flow, alliances would form and change on the back of what was about to happen. Each of them nodded to both Mrs Lo and the policemen, as if to show their neutrality, for the time being at least.

On seeing the policeman, Mrs Lo puffed out her chest in defiance every inch of her looking ready for the fight. It wasn't what I wanted. But I bided my time until the lift arrived and we all got in.

The atmosphere was tense with awkwardness. Standing elbow to elbow with Mrs Lo, I gave her a nudge and held out a small pack of tissues as my first play. She twigged immediately and went straight into victim-mode, dabbing her eyes and sniffing. Perfect. The very image of an old lady about to be bullied by someone who was abusing his power and status. I could feel the policeman squirming and the other couples feel embarrassed for even thinking this was a fight in which they should remain neutral.

When the lift arrived the policeman had the good grace to let Mrs Lo and me out first. We turned the corner into the hallway outside the management's office where the meeting was being held. I realized then that Mrs Lo and I had our work cut out. The hallway was crowded, probably about fifty people had turned up to see the show, and what was worse, many of them shook the policeman's hand as he made his way to an empty seat. He had evidently done his homework packing the place with his own supporters.

"How many other policemen live in the building?" I whispered in Mrs Lo's ear.

"Lots."

Oh boy! Things weren't looking good for Combo.

And so it went.

Mrs Lo had done her best to rouse her fellow retirees' support. Her mahjohng partners had turned up in force. But five minutes in, I knew it wouldn't be enough.

PC Chong – the anti-Combo policeman – was introduced by a man in a tie and an elbow-patched sports jacket from the management company, as the owner responsible for calling the special meeting and the floor was turned over to him. Chong was good, I'll give him that. His speech was the perfect pre-emptive strike, tugging at the heart-strings just like he knew Mrs Lo's would have to. He talked about the stress of his work, the long hours, the need to be sharp because as a policeman you never knew what would be waiting every time you walked up to a door or knocked on a car window. Sleep was vital, a matter of life and death in his job. He had nothing against dogs, apart from when they interrupted his sleep between midnight and six am. Last week, Combo's barking had kept him awake, he said. The next day he had to confront a drug-dealer wielding a knife. He hadn't felt at his best, and it was luck more than anything which had accounted for the take-down. So he was sorry. Clause 6.2.1 of the Deed of Mutual Covenant said what it said. He needed his sleep and the citizens of Hong Kong needed him to have it too, which meant Combo had to go, otherwise the mutt could be responsible for a crime-wave.

That last part was a bit of a reach. Combo causing a crimewave? Come on! To me the whole display wasn't worthy of a man who was supposed to be in the front-line defending us citizens, which made me think this officer had pretensions above his station. Maybe once in a while he'd face down real crime, sure, but most of the time he was probably directing traffic, organizing crowd control or walking a beat. But it didn't matter. The impassioned speech had hit the spot and I could see the vote was lost before Mrs Lo even had a chance to say her piece.

Not that it stopped the old girl from trying. She laid on the sob-story thick like she was cementing bricks. Combo had come from the government kennels, she explained, having been abandoned as a puppy. She had picked him out twenty-four hours before he was scheduled to be destroyed. He was skinny, just a bag of bones, so on the way home she had stopped at the local Tsa-tsan Teng and ordered the biggest dish on the menu; the Combo. He had wolfed it down in two gulps and the name had stuck. Mrs Lo had lost her husband when she was only sixty after forty years of marriage. She never thought she could survive on her own. But that was it, she said, her eyes glassing over with tears. She wasn't on her own. She had Combo. A dog who had shown human beings nothing but love. And in return what were we about do? Vote to destroy him. It was wrong, just plain wrong. And as for the barking, well it wasn't for her to cast doubt on PC Chong's sense of hearing, but the only thing Combo did after ten at night was snore. It was pretty loud snoring, sure, but no way could you hear it two flats down.

By the time Mrs Lo wound it up, there wasn't a dry eye in the place and the vote would have been a tough call if that damn rep from the management agent hadn't reminded everyone of what the Deed of Mutual Covenant said and of their duty as owners to uphold the provisions in that document.

And that was the way it went. Fifty-five votes in total. Thirty-two for PC Chong's motion, nineteen against, and four abstaining.

"I am sorry, Mrs Lo," the rep was all heart. "You are to remove Combo from your home."

"I won't do it!"

"If you don't, we will have to commence proceedings to gain entry to your flat and remove Combo."

"What? You have no right…."

"The Deed of Mutual Covenant gives us that right, Mrs Lo!"

And that was when I struck.

"Actually, it doesn't!" I was on my feet.

The silence which followed my intervention was louder than a thunder clap and had the same shocking effect. The rep's mouth formed a perfect 'o'. He opened and closed it guppy-like, before finding his feet.

"I am sorry, but only incorporated owners are allowed to speak at meetings…"

"Again," I cut him off, "Not true. Clause five two of the Deed of Mutual Covenant says that any incorporated owner 'or their appointed representative' may be present at a meeting. My name is Mr Scott Lee and Mrs Lo will confirm that I am appointed as her representative."

Mrs Lo nodded. "And if you don't mind, I will ask you to read the clause on which you are relying to suggest that the dog named Combo can be forcibly removed from the estate."

The representative looked stunned for a moment, but then he cleared his throat and said. "Clause six point two point one reads: 'any pet who, in the reasonable opinion of the manager, causes a sustained nuisance must be removed from the estate'."

"Well there you are," I said. "We have heard PC Chong's views as to why Combo should be removed from the estate. We have also received the vote of the incorporated owners. But none of this is important. The question is whether the manager is of the reasonable opinion that Combo has caused a sustained nuisance. So," I addressed the rep, "As the representative of the managing agent, please inform us what is the opinion of the manager?"

The representative took a deep breath: "Well I believe the managing agent's opinion is that Combo has caused a...." he looked down at the document, "a sustained nuisance."

"I see. Then please explain why that opinion is reasonable."

"I'm sorry?"

"The opinion reached by the manager. The Deed of Mutual Covenant indicates that to be operative, it has to be reasonable. How is his opinion reasonable? How was it reached? On what evidence is it based? On what advice?"

"Why, we received written advice from a law firm. Wang & Lam is the name of the solicitors."

I held up my hand. "Are you telling us you instructed solicitors?"

"Why yes."

"Would you please refer to clause eight point thirteen of the Deed of Mutual Covenant."

"Eight point thirteen?"

"To save time, perhaps you would permit me to read it." I did not wait for permission. "Clause eight point thirteen is headed 'Tender Policy' and reads, 'To appoint a contractor or other professional to carry on work at or on behalf of the estate, the manager shall seek at least three quotes from different contractors or professionals, as the case may be, and present them to the incorporated owners at a special meeting before proceeding with the selection'. Now, did you follow this tender process before appointing the law firm from whom you obtained the advice?"

"Well I......the firm is the usual one instructed by the incorporated owners. We have used them on many occasions in the past."

"I am sorry, but it is a simple yes or no question. Before you instructed the law firm on this issue, did you follow the tender policy in the Deed of Mutual covenant. Yes or no?"

Silence.

I turned towards the audience. "Then, on behalf of Mrs Lo, I say that the vote you have taken this evening is void, as the opinion of the managing agent on which it was based relied on a legal opinion obtained in breach of the Deed of Mutual Covenant."

"This is nonsense." This from PC Chong who could see me swaying the crowd. "We are all here and know the situation. The dog has to go!"

"PC Chong, you have sought to rely on a provision in the Deed of Mutual Covenant to bring about this vote. I put it to you and your fellow-owners that it is hardly fair to rely on one term of the Deed to get rid of Combo, yet ignore an admitted breach of another term which suggests the vote taken to get rid of him is void. This is an important matter. We are not talking about a piece of property here, but Mrs Lo's companion. Your insistence that procedure should be followed is correct. It has not been followed in this case."

The policeman's face flushed with anger. He stood there eye-balling me with the kind of hatred that reaches down and fills your gut with bile.

"Then what do you suggest? That we have wasted our Sunday evening?" His voice was like the wisp that follows a match-strike.

"The vote does not stand," I said, "But the evening has not been wasted. We have clarified that the next step is for the managing agent to go through the tender process to confirm the appointment of the solicitors they want to use. Then they can deal with your complaint and assess whether it is reasonable. In that regard, we have learned from your own mouth, PC Chong, that it is the alleged barking of Combo between the hours of midnight and 6am that keeps you awake. So we have installed a sound measure in Mrs Lo's flat with a timer on it, which will tell us the decibels of the noise coming from her home in those hours. We invite the managing agent to inspect it and indeed every day for the next three weeks, Mrs Lo will be happy to report its record levels. That would assist, we believe, in helping the managing agent to decide whether your complaint is reasonable and indeed in helping the owners to decide which way to vote, should you choose to bring this matter before them again."

There it was. Check-mate. Not only had I invalidated the vote, but I'd pushed PC Chong into a corner. If he didn't accept the proposal, it would make him look like a liar. At least if he accepted it, he could save his face in the meeting and let the matter die quietly, which I hoped he would. If he didn't I had plenty more provisions in the Deed of Mutual Covenant which could spin the process out. Whatever, Combo was staying put.

After the meeting broke up, we went back to Mrs Lo's flat. Combo showed his gratitude by getting back on my lap and letting me scratch his ears for a bit, while Mrs Lo recounted our victory to Tak Ming. Then I made my excuses. I had my first day of work tomorrow and needed a good night's sleep. Mrs Lo insisted on my taking something by way of payment and threw together some stir-fried noodles and beef which she put in a Styrofoam box for me to eat when I got home. I told Combo to keep quiet at night, but he didn't hear me. He was already asleep.

Tak Ming walked me back to the MTR station.

"Lawyer Lee, thank you. Really thank you," he kept repeating

"Don't need to keep thanking me, TM. This isn't the end of the matter. These managing agents are known to play dirty."

TM stuck out his chest and banged his thumb against it. "I play dirty too."

I didn't doubt it.

"You want to help your mum, you stay out of trouble, you hear me?" I said.

We walked on. Then a thought struck me. "TM, are you any good with computers?"

"Not bad. I play games, use the internet."

Good enough.

"There's something you can do to help your mum, but you may not want to tell her you're doing it, if you know what I mean. For her own good."

His forehead creased into a Neanderthal frown. "What do you mean?"

When I told him what I had in mind, the frown disappeared and was replaced by an out of place beatific smile. "You think we need to do this, Lawyer Lee? Really?"

"I think we do. Just to be safe."

He banged his chest with his thumb again. "Then I will do it."

As we walked on, he kept on thanking me intermittently and I kept telling him it was no problem. Then when we were just about to part ways, he shook my hand.

"If ever there is something that I can help you with, Lawyer Lee, you just ask, okay? You just ask."

One saved dog, a free meal and a standing favour from a street gang enforcer.

Not a bad tally for my last evening of leisure.

CHAPTER SIX

Eight-thirty next morning, a lady named Tabitha Yan was waiting for me in Gadgetech's reception. She was slim, late forties with fierce glasses and the professional mannerisms of an administrator. With a slightly nervous smile, but a firm enough handshake which gave me her measure, she introduced herself as my new secretary and led me on a tour of the offices.

She did her best to make it interesting, but it was a thankless task. The only room for deviation between one Hong Kong office and another is the colour of the partitions between the work booths (in this case purple) and how high they are (a socially disruptive five-foot). I did my best to feign interest, but honestly the only thing I retained was that Gadgetech had two floors in the building, the twenty-first and twenty-second. Napoleon Wong's palatial office, where I had been interviewed, was on the twenty-second along with the purchasing staff. Hardly a surprise there. Purchasers were the income generators for Gadgetech, negotiating hard on price with wholesalers to maximize mark-ups on the product when it came to be sold through the fifty Gadgetech outlets round the territory. Most of the purchasing staff were already at their desks when Tabitha led me round, phones pinned to their ears, shamelessly asking for discounts and clicking away at computers. Wong himself, however, had yet to put in an appearance. Boss's prerogative, I guessed.

The lower floor, the twenty-first, was where the support services were situated: finance, operations and now legal, the kind of functions which to management were just necessary overheads and not worthy of a place in the limelight. Being well into the second decade of my legal career, I was used to being treated like that, so when Tabitha showed me to my new office, an internal hutch with a window wall that overlooked Tabitha's work booth, it came as no surprise. Much worse had befallen me before, so I was satisfied enough. To Tabitha, however, I could see it was a disappointment.

As I settled into the creaking chair behind the desk, she stayed in the door-way casting round a distasteful glance. "Is the temperature okay for you, Mr Lee?"

"It's fine. Oh and Tabitha?"

"Yes, Mr Lee?"

"To the Inland Revenue, I'm Mr Lee because I don't like them very much. The rest of the world, however – and I would include you in that – calls me Scott."

"Yes, Mr….." she stopped herself on my raised eyebrow.

"I don't expect you to make me coffee and I promise that I will never use you to do any of my personal stuff."

She nodded, taking my comments as instructions rather than as the ice-breakers they were intended to be. "Human resources will be around in five minutes to arrange your security pass. And Mr Wong has asked that you join him for lunch at his club at twelve-thirty, since it's your first day."

"His club?"

"Channings. It's in the basement of this building. Take the lift down and ask for Mr Wong at the concierge desk. If you have any other questions, I sit right outside. My extension is zero three three six and if you want to dial an outside line, you have to press nine."

She made to leave, but I stopped her.

"Hang on a minute, Tabitha. I want to talk to you."

"But your appointment with HR?" She looked at her watch.

"It can wait." I gave a wave of contempt. "Please. Shut the door and take a seat. We're going to be working together, so there's a few things we need to cover."

She hesitated, obviously the kind of gal who liked to maintain a respectful barrier between boss and secretary. Eventually she did as I asked, but perched herself right on the edge of the chair, as if in protest.

"How long have you worked as a secretary, Tabitha?"

"Fifteen years."

I figured as much.

"Then how come you've been assigned to me, the new guy, the temp?" Her head moved awkwardly to one side, betraying nervousness at the territory I was threatening to stray into. "Fifteen years of experience in a company like this is priceless. I'm glad to have someone with that kind of experience showing me the ropes, don't get me wrong. I'm just interested as to why I'm the lucky one."

The silence which followed stretched out like an unwelcome shadow across a sunny day. I let it. Discomfort and directness were the fastest way to the truth. A truth which had me guessing that by appointing Tabitha here as my secretary, Napoleon Wong was putting in place one of his longest serving loyalists to watch every move I made. If that was the case, I wanted the message passed back up the chain that I was nobody's fool.

As it turned out, my bout of paranoia was as wrong as it possibly could be. The answer was much more obvious and when she served it up, it hit me hard in the gut.

"I worked for Mr Auyeung," Tabitha said.

Terence Auyeung, the man whose disappearance I was there to uncover the truth about. Obviously his secretary would be at a loose end now, so I was the short-straw Tabitha had drawn. A temp lawyer. A poor consolation prize for someone used to working for a CFO. But it did give me an opportunity to do some prying. "You came with Mr Auyeung to Gadgetech when Rufus Lam bought into the company?"

She nodded.

"How long did you work for Mr Auyeung before Gadgetech?"

"Thirteen years."

I knitted my fingers on the desk. The secretary-boss relationship was like a marriage, so the saying went. During the week most bosses spent more time in the company of their secretaries than their spouses. Which meant, when it came to bosses, secretaries knew the secrets which were dirtiest and darkest. Problem was, they also guarded those secrets closer than Cerberus did the gates of hell.

Charm had never really been my thing, so I went for straightforward instead.

"Do you know why I have been hired to work here, Tabitha?"

She shrugged. "You are a lawyer. I would guess Mr Wong requires legal advice."

Stupid question, stupid answer. Fair enough.

"I assume you know about Mr Wong's intention to buy Mr Lam out of Gadgetech?"

The fleeting widening of Tabitha's eyes behind those vicious glasses, told me she had no idea. Her face quickly went back to ice, but there was no disguising the permutations now going on in that head of hers as she tried to work out the implications for her own future.

"Mr Lam is selling his shares in Gadgetech to Mr Wong," I said. "So Mr Wong needs a lawyer to advise on the documentation. That's my job."

Her lips parted then closed, as if she was about to say something but then thought better of it.

"You want to ask me something Tabitha?"

"I just……what about Mr Auyeung? What happens to him when he comes back?"

I leaned back in my chair and pondered the question. Loyalty. It was a priceless commodity in this day and age. Terence Auyeung was not on a business trip. He had not taken a leave of absence or gone on holiday. He had disappeared without a trace or a word to anyone. Yet to Tabitha Yan, his imminent return wasn't even in question. I didn't have the heart to tell her how unlikely that was, how the whole reason Rufus Lam had decided to exit Gadgetech was because Auyeung, his inside man, was gone. Instead I said: "I expect Mr Lam will ask him to take up another position in his organization."

My words seemed to provide some comfort. I decided to plough on.

"The thing about the legal aspects of management buyouts, Tabitha, is that there's a big cross over between the legal work and the company's financial position. Mr Auyeung was Gadgetech's Chief Financial Officer. You were his secretary. That would be why Mr Wong has assigned you to work for me. To get myself up to speed, I'm going to need to see all Mr Auyeung's books and records. And I need to see them now, so I can understand Gadgetech's financials before my lunch with Napoleon Wong. Can you get me access, please?"

Her eyebrows locked into a frown. "Well, I'm not sure that's appropriate. Mr Wong said..."

"As the lawyer for this company, I can assure you that it's very much appropriate," I said, lacing my words with a bit of steel.

Tabitha bit her lip in debate a moment before reneging. "No-one has been into Mr Auyeung's office since he…" she paused a moment searching for the right phrase. "Since he last came in to work. I keep it locked."

"And where is his office?"

"Over there," she pointed through the window wall to a door the opposite side of the open plan.

I checked my watch. It was coming up to ten o'clock. Two hours before lunch with Wong. "I'd better make a start then. Would you mind opening it up? I'll be over in just a moment. I need to make a phone call first. And would you mind putting off my appointment with HR until this afternoon?"

I picked up the receiver and put it to my ear ensuring that she didn't have a chance to push back on any of my requests.

***

As soon as she was out of the room, I called Phil.

"How's it going?" he asked.

"Just met my new secretary."

"She cute?"

I tutted. "You sure you're President of the Law Society?"

"Scott Lee, the prude. Hmm. Nope, somehow it doesn't quite fit."

"What's with the good mood, Phil? Lane Crawford doing a two for one offer on pink Pringle golf sweaters?"

"Lane Crawford doesn't sell Pringle sweaters."

Phil probably knew his comeback line had bombed and quickly got serious by asking me what was up.

"I need that crib sheet on management buy-outs as soon as. Got lunch with Wong at twelve, so it would be good if I can at least pretend to know what I'm talking about."

"First time for everything, I suppose."

As someone who likes deploying sarcasm as part of his repertoire, I hate it when it's used on me.

"Very funny. Now get me that crib sheet."

"All right, all right, keep your hair on," he chuckled. "How do I get it to you?"

"E-mail it to my Yahoo account. I'll pick it up on my phone as soon as I get a wireless signal. Have you set up my face-to-face with Rufus Lam yet?"

Pause.

"I'm still working on it."

So he was still giving me the run around on Lam. Now wasn't the time to get into it, so I told him to work harder at it and then we rang off.

All through the conversation I had been keeping my eye on Tabitha Yan through the window wall, making sure she did what I had asked. She made one phone call, no doubt to HR, then she bent down to her hand-bag, came up with a bunch of keys and went over to unlock the office she had identified as Auyeung's.

Bingo, I thought to myself.

I was in.

***

Five minutes later I was in Auyeung's office, door closed.

It was the same size as Napoleon Wong's, but without the ego-stroking objets d'art. This was a working office. Desk functionally sized, computer screen and key board pushed off to the left, in-tray shoved off to the right burgeoning with outdated, unread accounting periodicals. To the side, were three wall-mounted shelves. One had books, one had box-files and the third had two photographs.

The photographs caught my eye first. The first was a full family portrait with Auyeung and his wife seated, her hands on his knee, his hands on hers, both smiling lovingly into the lens. It wasn't the first time I had seen Auyeung, but the Auyeung pictured here was different from the hard-faced, silver-haired accountant in the newspaper articles I had dug up on the internet. He was relaxed, happy and smiling, the quintessential family man. Flanking Auyeung and his wife were their kids, one boy, one girl, both grown up, university age I guessed. The son's parted hair resembled his father's style only it was black and it stretched to the front of his forehead. The daughter looked like she studied medicine, an awful stereotype on my part, but no less true.

My eyes lingered a moment on the wife. She wore a white shirt and black skirt, her dark hair neatly coiffeured, her face holding a welcoming chubbiness. Her eyes held that maternal mixture of steel and honey. Like all family portraits this one pictured perfection. With Auyeung missing, the truth had to be different.

I felt bad. Bad that I had to ask Mrs Auyeung some difficult questions. But that was for later. Right now, my starting point was far more obvious and the key lay in the second photo. It was of Auyeung and Rufus Lam. They had been snapped at some glitzy award ceremony. Both were dressed in black tie and laughing at a shared joke. That this was one of only two photos Auyeung had on display said a lot about the closeness of his relationship with Lam.

I bet every time Napoleon Wong came into this office, his eyes would gravitate to that photo and it would twist in his gut. A constant reminder of why Auyeung was here, looking over his shoulder, protecting Lam's investment, shackling that large ego of his.

Auyeung's disappearance had put the prospect of the management buy-out on the table. A buy-out that would enable Wong to break free from his shackles. Some might call that serendipity. I called it a possible motive. I didn't want to rush to judgement, but Napoleon Wong certainly had some explaining to do.

Next, I spent time looking through the box-files on the second shelf. They mainly consisted of holiday request forms from Auyeung's staff and signed expense claims. One of the folders had Auyeung's own expense claims. I went through it twice. It told me that Auyeung was a perfect boy scout. Lunches were either with the chief financial officers of Gadgetech's wholesalers or fellow members of industry bodies. Every penny was accounted for, every receipt attached, every tip explained. No hint of extravagance in the amounts. It was accounting heaven. Pure, damn perfection.

Shaking my head, I placed the box-file back on the shelf with the kind of reverence it seemed to deserve.

Next I found a set of working documents for the preparation of Gadgetech's most recent set of annual accounts. I took time to study the draft balance sheet and profit and loss. As Gadgetech was not a listed company, I had not been able to find these published anywhere, so this was the first time I was becoming acquainted with the company's value and profitability. Not a bad business, from what I could tell. I plugged the figures into the note book section on my phone for later consideration.

As I worked my way down the box-files on the shelf, something piqued my interest. Wedged between two of the files was Auyeung's desk diary for the previous year.

I sat down at the desk and paged through it. By the time I got to June, one recurring item kept jumping out at me. Every Wednesday the words "LKW" were penciled in for 6.30pm.

So who was LKW?

I made a mental note of the initials.

At the front of the diary was a page full of Auyeung's personal information, address, mobile number, office contact details. I paused on the page a moment, then thought 'what the hell' and picked up the receiver to dial Auyeung's mobile. An automated voice told me the phone was turned off and to try again later. Something told me there would be no point.

The door opened then and Tabitha popped her head in. When she saw me looking at the diary she caught a breath. I ignored it and didn't offer any explanation. The need to explain only indicates an acceptance that you've done something wrong.

"Hi." I prodded.

"Er…you'd better go to your lunch with Mr Wong."

I checked my watch.

"I'll head out in a sec. Just want to finish one thing."

She shut the door. I waited a beat of ten.

Then I reached down and ripped out the page with Auyeung's contact information on. The home address would come in handy for later.

Right now, it was time to see if I could give Napoleon Wong a bit of a stir and see what came to the surface.

CHAPTER SEVEN

The private member's club scene in Hong Kong had never been my thing.

Mostly, I found it just plain weird. Weird that, even after the territory had gone back to the Chinese in ninety-seven, clubs of the colonial era still thrived; and not just with Gweilo expats. These days it was new Mainland money keeping them afloat, that stratum of people who had got rich on the back of Deng Xiao Peng's transformation of China from command economy to capitalist free-for-all. Investment immigration, it was called: buying Hong Kong residency by splashing cash. And once these folks had their Hong Kong pied-à-terre (usually some hideously over-priced eight hundred square foot apartment in a Mid-Levels high-rise) they set about acquiring all the trappings of Hong Kong society to match, chief among them, club memberships.

So old colonial clubs remained over-subscribed. New clubs too had sprung up to take up the slack. Housed in slick modern office blocks, they decked themselves out with eighteenth century décor, Mahogony surfaces, green leather chairs, imported libraries, fancy restaurants and burgeoning wine cellars. The veneer of privilege and exclusivity was still in full demand, driven by money from the Mainland, the last existing socialist society in the world bar Cuba and North Korea. Only in Hong Kong could such blatant irony exist without anyone batting an eye-lid.

Channings was the perfect noveau riche fit. Its name came from nowhere, chosen because it sounded sufficiently old English. The portraits and black and white photos had probably been picked up in an antique shop on Hollywood Road. When I told the receptionist I was there to have lunch with Napoleon Wong, a precious waiter in a Mao-collared uniform was summoned and enthusiastically ushered me through to Mr Wong's 'usual table'. Mr Wong liked sparkling Perrier with his lunch, according to the waiter. He produced a chilled bottle with a flourish and poured me out a measure without my even asking.

Napoleon Wong was late, so I killed time by reading through the cheat-sheet on management buy-outs Yip had sent me, making sure to keep my phone below table level. Places like Channings prided themselves on their "no-mobile" policy. I guessed the pristine waiters enforced it more viciously than the Cultural Revolution Red Guards whose uniforms they had ripped off.

When I was done, Wong still hadn't arrived. I asked the waiter if he had today's *South China Morning Post*. He brought it over.

A quick flip through the front page had me wishing I hadn't bothered. Same old, same old. Rumour had it that the Democratic Party was trying to put up a candidate to run against Jeremy Lau for CE. Rumour, my ass. Always, the Democrats were pulling some stunt. The fact that they had lost every battle they'd ever fought here never stopped them coming back for more. How they thought they were going to run a candidate, when the nominating committee had already decided on those the Hong Kong electorate could choose from, was anyone's guess. In any event, I pitied the poor sap who got the Democratic nod. He or she would get their fifteen minutes of fame, spending a month bitching about how the whole process was unfair. At the end of the day nothing would progress, everyone knew that. Jeremy Lau's appointment would be confirmed by the Central People's Government up in Beijing and all the Democratic Party would have succeeded in doing is remind everybody of how Hong Kong's yearning for true democracy had been stifled by bureaucratic intransigence and a steadfast refusal to listen. It was farce bordering on madness. Still, it gave reporters something to write about, even though no-one was really interested any more.

Ten minutes in, Napoleon Wong finally turned up.

He sat down opposite me with a dyspeptic grunt which made me lose my appetite. No apology was offered, nor did he deign to acknowledge my existence until he had taken a long glance round to see if there were any other members in worthy of his note. The heavy sigh which followed told me he came up blank on that score. Eventually he gave me his attention.

"Settling in? Getting up to speed?" He asked, then glugged his Perrier too quickly and let out a distasteful little belch into his fist.

"I'm doing my best," I said.

Wong summoned the Mao waiter with two fingers and opened a book with his palms signaling for a menu. "I want to talk about the buy-out. But let's get some food first."

I ordered a Caesar salad. Wong settled on Singapore noodles with Clam Chowder to start. The waiter was dispatched and we got straight down to business.

"One month," Wong announced. "Four weeks. That's how long I want it to take. Buy-outs can be unsettling for staff and our business partners so I want it over quickly. Do you foresee any problem with that?"

Four weeks? He had no chance. But on my first day the last thing I needed to do was rain on the boss's parade. Plus, I saw this as an opportunity to glean some more information, so I went with displaying some of my new found knowledge.

"Four weeks is on the aggressive side, Napoleon, but it should be do-able. Effectively, we are talking about a transfer of shares in Gadgetech from Rufus Lam to you…"

"Shh….keep your voice down!" He glanced round to see if anyone had heard.

The reaction surprised me. Napoleon Wong, the sensitive type? I made a show of looking around to see where the perceived danger lurked. The nearest occupied table was across the other side of the room. They were deep in their own conversation.

"As I was saying," I continued, forcing the sotto voce, "an MBO is simply a transfer of shares, so it can be effected by a way of a simple sale and purchase agreement to fix the price and then an instrument of transfer to effect the change of ownership. Have you fixed the purchase price yet?"

There was a pause, as Wong debated whether to disclose this piece of information.

"I'll need to know the S&P agreement," I prodded.

He glanced left and right then leaned in: "Fifteen million."

The number slapped me with surprise. "As in one-five?"

He nodded. "Is there a problem?"

I did some mental permutations comparing the purchase price to the value of Gadgetech which I had gleaned from the financial statements in Auyeung's office.

"Could be a possible complication with the stamp duty," I said.

"What complication?"

I leaned in to make clear my effort to keep my voice hushed.

"The purchase price for the shares is quite a bit lower than the equivalent net asset value they represent. Sounds like you struck a great deal with Rufus Lam. But the Stamp Office may view it as an undervalue and want to charge duty based on the higher value. We could be in for a fight."

As I spoke, I saw Napoleon Wong's face darken with a cocktail of anger and annoyance, his eyes narrowing into dark pips of viciousness. Evidently, he didn't like the fact that I had been nosing around the financial information. I'd tweaked a nerve.

He rested his chubby hand on the white linen tablecloth grinding his forefinger against his thumb. "You just concentrate on the legal documents. Get them done as quickly as possible. Let me worry about the price. I know about the stamp duty issues. I have accountants taking care of that. You just get the contracts into shape. Do we understand each other?"

His glare was designed to put the fear of God into me. But I held it. Most of my career had been spent working for partners with egos as big as their wallets and tempers which outdid both. So Napoleon Wong's didn't phase me one bit.

I fixed my diplomatic smile in place. "As you wish."

Just then the waiter returned with Wong's chowder which he slurped down in greedy silence. The conversation only started up again when the main course came and this time we stuck to subjects devoid of controversy. I asked him about his family. He told me his son was currently forging a career for himself in a bank and doing well by the sounds of it. A good apprenticeship for taking over the reins at Gadgetech one day, he said. Napoleon Wong had it all figured out, it seemed.

Keeping the conversation going was hard work and it soon descended into a question and answer session, punctuated with several awkward silences made all the worse by the fact that Channings was pretty quiet that day. It was a relief when the coffee arrived.

"Busy afternoon?" I asked, filling the dead air.

Wong was just about to reply when his mobile phone beeped loudly in his jacket. He pulled it out. None of the Mao waiters batted an eyelid.

Whatever the message said, it certainly left Napoleon Wong in a state of agitation. He said nothing for the rest of the lunch, just fidgeted in his chair, his face locked in a scowl of concern.

"Sorry, I have to go," he said after one sip of his Cappuccino. He fluttered his fingers at the waiter, signaling for the bill with the swish of an imaginary pen. "I have an urgent meeting."

The waiter came, Napoleon signed and then he hurried for the door.

CHAPTER EIGHT

Five minutes later I was in the back of a taxi, heading east. Where, I had no idea.

I took a moment to consider what exactly had triggered my instinctive decision to follow Napoleon Wong. Sure, on reading the text he received, the man had looked like he had swallowed a wasp and had run out of the door faster than a politician from tricky reporter. But it was the apology for having to leave which had really hooked my attention. I may have had only a few encounters with him, but they were enough for me to know that an apology from Napoleon Wong was rarer than a solar eclipse. Which meant the author of the text message, whoever he or she was, had just sent Napoleon's world spinning off its axis.

Interesting.

So I had followed Wong out of Channings, keeping a respectful distance, taking the stairs up to the ground floor so we wouldn't be in the same lift together. Wong's car and driver were waiting by the building entrance. I noted the direction in which they headed off, hailed down a taxi and told the

driver to follow.

Napoleon's car was a black Mercedes, about as common on the Hong Kong roads as sand on a beach. Thankfully the license plate – "GTECH" – made it easy for my taxi guy to keep tabs on it. I sent a message to Tabitha telling her I was at the Law Society library doing some research, then I watched out for road signs trying to work out where we were going. Sai Kung definitely looked like a possibility, but it was only when we exited for Hang Hau that the destination became clear.

Hang Hau was a classic New Territories new town. Created to tackle Hong Kong's housing shortage, it consisted of a series of big public housing estates, each one with fifty-storey concrete towers huddled together in tight quadrangle formation. Full washing rails hung out of every window, it seemed, and the only views on offer were into your neighbour's living-room. Places like Hang Hau had ended the hill-side shanty towns into which illegal immigrants from the Mainland had flowed, back in the fifties and sixties. I had seen the black and white pictures of those things. They were disasters waiting to happen and in the case of the Shek Kip Mei fire in the 1950s, the risk had materialized with a vengeance, killing hundreds. Public housing became the solution and the Hong Kong government was still the territory's biggest landlord because of it.

I had been out this way before, but not for a long time so it took me a while to get my bearings.

Eventually, my driver told me the Mercedes was stopping. I made a note of the street name and told him to go round the corner and drop me off. I handed over two red hundreds and told him to keep the change.

Walking back one street, I kept my stride pattern even, as if I belonged there. It was a wide cul-de-sac, restaurants of all different types lining each side. The lunch rush was over, so the place was quiet. At one end of the street, waiters and cooking staff exchanged gossip over cigarettes and bottles of Pocari Sweat from the nearby Circle K.

I saw the G-Tech Mercedes parked on the opposite side of the road. The driver in the front seat was absorbed in his racing form.

The nearest restaurant to where the Mercedes was parked was a place called Lardo's. It had large glass sliding doors, but from the angle where I was, the glint from the sun meant I couldn't see through to the inside. So I ambled round in an arc until I found a different viewpoint.

I glimpsed Napoleon Wong seated at one of the tables with his back to me.

"Gotcha," I muttered. He didn't look like he was going anywhere for a while, so I popped into the Circle K and picked up a newspaper before returning to position and pretended to read it. A newspaper disguise! The Secret Service had nothing on me.

The heat was high but I found a nice piece of shade in the shadow of a building. The through breeze kept me comfortable and the quiet was enchanting. That was the thing about the New Territories. They offered Hong Kong space to breath, a prospect of tranquility half an hour's drive away from the most densely populated urban jungle on earth. From my position, I now had a good view of Napoleon's back. He looked to be the only customer in Lardo's, sipping an expresso, staring out of the window and every now and then exaggeratedly flicking his arm to pull up his cuff and check his watch. Someone he was waiting for was late. I was glad he knew how it felt.

The street was full to the brim with parked vehicles. Killing time, I made an inventory of them. Fifteen BMWs, ten Mercedes, four Audis, two Lexus and the partridge in a pear tree being a black Range Rover with glistening hubs and blacked out windows. A true car thief would have probably walked away from this lot for the lack of challenge.

Fifteen minutes passed before anything happened.

Then I saw it: another Mercedes, this one silver, ambling leisurely down the road towards me. It pulled to a halt just outside Lardo's.

The back door of the car opened. Out stepped a petite woman dressed in a pink towelling track suit. The top was hooded, the trousers had the word "Juicy" embroidered across her backside. She wore it well, though. Sophia Loren sunglasses and the lid of a red baseball cap masked the top half of her face. A Louis Vuitton clutch completed the ensemble.

After throwing back some instructions to the driver, she jogged over to Lardo's and pulled back the glass door.

Napoleon Wong turned to her.

The look on his face was one I had thought he would never be capable of. A respectful deference is the only way I can describe it. They pecked each other on the cheek. The woman slid gracefully into the opposite seat, her back to the wall, her face so that I could see it. She took of the cap and sun glasses.

Wow!

I could feel myself take a step back. Even from this distance, she was stunning. Perfect round eyes, pert cheeks, gratifying smile, features immaculately proportioned. It had been disguised well by the gaudy get-up. Difficult to put an age on her, but wow!

What the hell was this, I wondered. An affair? Maybe, but the truth was it didn't look like it. There were no affectionate pats or intimate leanings-in between Napoleon and his companion, but that didn't necessarily mean anything. The conversation appeared to switch from serious to amusing. One moment the woman's immaculate face locked in a frown, the next she was shooting a smile that made the whole world light up. The waiter, I could tell, was besotted. Unfortunately with Wong's back to me it was difficult to tell what he was thinking, but the peck on the cheek to start meant this wasn't the first time they had met. A little voice in my head told me I'd hit on something interesting.

Ten minutes went by with me trying to eek out something more, but I was drawing a blank. They just talked and talked, but there was no way I could know what about. I didn't want to leave there empty-handed, though, so I took out my iPhone and zoomed in to get some pictures of her. I had already jotted down the silver Mercedes' license plate. Both were leads I could use to start to piece things together and see where this lady fitted in, if at all.

A glint of light caught me in the eye.

I put my hand up to shield it and turned to see what it was.

The Black Range rover with the pristine hub-caps. The window had just whirred down. There, in the passenger seat was a white, rat-faced, bald man.

He was staring straight at me.

Oh shit!

For a moment I was a deer in headlights, ice snaking through my veins.

My statue impression seemed just the thing the bald man needed. He lifted a camera to his eye, one of those full telescopic lens jobs, pointed the thing straight at me and snapped away.

What the hell.....

The action kicked me back into myself. The decisions came quick then. I broke into a walk, striding fast straight towards the Range Rover. In a tit-for-tat my iPhone was up and I hit record, videoing what was happening. The bald man didn't waste another second. Up the window whirred, the engine ignited and within moments the Range Rover was squealing away round the corner, leaving me wondering what had just happened.

Whatever it was, now was not the time to stick around and put it together.

I had to get out of there.

Fast!

CHAPTER NINE

By four pm, I was back at Gadgetech, the door to my office closed, my computer on but only for effect because I certainly wasn't giving it any attention. In my absence an e-mail had been sent out announcing my temporary appointment and I'd received in my first two pieces of work. One was a confidentiality agreement, the other a draft brochure to sign-off. Both I dealt with in twenty-minutes, thankful for the distraction which enabled me to put some distance between me and the events of that afternoon. But soon my mind drifted back to my predicament and was spinning with the possible implications of what had happened.

Trouble was I had too many questions and too few answers, at least for me to make any sense of what was going on. Sipping a cup of green tea, I shut my eyes and took some deep breaths trying to slow things down. But all I could see was that granite-faced bald man snapping picture after picture of me, catching me doing something I wasn't supposed to be doing.

Not good.

I toyed with the idea of phoning Phil, but decided against it. He would only panic.

The green tea tasted cleansing. Staring down into the cup, I let the logical side of my brain get into gear and quickly a conclusion on my next steps fell into place. Speed was now imperative. Someone had snapped me following Napoleon Wong and his fancy lady, whoever she was, so it was only a matter of time before my cover of in-house legal counsel was blown

On day one.

Like I said, not good.

But then again, whoever had caught me was also following Napoleon Wong. Hardly likely then, that it was Wong to whom the bald man would be reporting back. Maybe I did have time then before I needed to clear out? How much time, I didn't rightly know but like a bomb ticking down, it concentrated the mind. Time-limits were the catalyst for the possible, so if I could move on quickly with my investigation maybe, just maybe, I could find the answers and get out of Gadgetech without anyone noticing. That meant forgetting about the self-analysis for now and using the rest of the day to advance as far as I could down the best lead I had.

I reached into my jacket on the back of the chair and pulled out the page I had ripped from Terence Auyeung's diary. His home number was there.

Secrets always started close to home, I figured, so that was where I needed to head right now.

Bracing myself, I dialed the number and did what every lawyer worth their salt is good at.

I lied.

***

When a person is broken you can tell just by looking at them. And Gladys Auyeung was broken.

No matter she dressed the part of a composed housewife, in a cleanly pressed white blouse and black skirt. No matter, her hair looked like it had been sculpted by Da Vinci. No matter the immaculate make-up. It was all a little too forced, a little too perfect. And then there were her eyes. Dark wells of devastation, the kind of devastation of a family being torn suddenly to shreds. A wife's devastation from a missing husband. A half separated from her other half.

She showed me into a living-room, asked me if I wanted coffee, told the maid to fetch it, then sat down on the edge of the sofa, her legs twisting prettily sideways, her head cocked to one side inquisitively.

"What can I do for you, Mr Lee?"

There was the question.

I had lied to get this appointment, introducing myself as Gadgetech's lawyer in search of some documents I needed as a matter of urgency. Maybe Mr Auyeung had left them at home, I had said.

She had bought it, so here I was.

I was about to extend the lie, had this whole elaborate story ready about a deal with a new wholesaler, but something stopped me. No, not something. Those eyes, that devastation and the attempt to mask it. Who was I to add it?

"Listen, Mrs Auyeung. I am a lawyer and I work for Gadgetech, but that's not why I'm here. The truth is I have been asked to find out what happened to your husband. I have some questions and I need your help."

An expectant but tense silence stretched between us. The maid came in, served the coffee.

"I know who you are and why you are here, Mr Lee," she said as soon as the maid was gone. "After I received your call this afternoon, I called the person who hired you. I knew Rufus would do something like this. He and Terence have been friends for years. He is the reason Terence went to work for Napoleon Wong. But I am sure you know that already."

The revelation surprised me, but I kicked myself for not seeing it. Of course, Auyeung and Lam had been friends both outside and in work although the dividing line between the two areas was probably beyond their ken, such was the world they lived in. Of course, Gladys Auyeung would have turned to Lam when I had called out of the blue with my pathetic back story.

"I am sorry about what I said, but….."

"But nothing, Mr Lee! I understand and I am grateful for your candidness now which, it is noted, came unprompted. What is it that I can help you with?"

The thrusting defiance took me aback. It was a defiance that made clear I was playing on her turf, that she was in control here. But still the fragility was unmistakable, lurking there just beneath the surface, reminding me of the need to tread with care.

"May I ask you about your family name, Mrs Auyeung? It is the same as your husband's."

Taking the husband's surname was a western tradition, so I was curious to know why she had done it in this case.

My inquiry was met with the hint of a smile. "I see you are accustomed to Chinese ways, Mr Lee."

"That's because I'm Chinese," I said. "Well half, anyway. My mum was a local girl. My dad's British."

I don't know why I always felt the need to explain that, when someone mistook me for being a complete foreigner. But I did. Something in me always hated being identified as an outsider, even though part of me knew I could never truly fit in. The Eurasian quandary: it never truly went away.

Gladys Auyeung nodded. "No wonder you know about such things," she said. "But the answer is perhaps not as exciting as you

56

might expcct. My family name is also Auyeung. Our respective families emanated from the same part of China, a long time ago. So I have not, as you say, taken his name. I am just reliant on, what you might call, a happy coincidence."

I nodded. "Can you tell me about the day Mr Auyeung disappeared."

She looked off into the distance a moment, as if weighing her answer. "I don't know what to say. He went to work as usual, left here at seven-thirty like always. We had a dinner appointment in Central that evening with some family friends. He never made it. I tried calling him several times. But….." her voice drifted off into a shrug.

I decided to break it down. "How did your husband get to work?"

"He always took a taxi."

That surprised me.

"Terence insisted. He felt it too much of an unnecessary expense to have a car and a driver, though goodness knows we could afford it. But my husband is an accountant, Mr Lee. Not just by profession, but by nature." Again with the guarded smile.

"And did you phone him that day? In the morning, I mean."

She shook her head. "You may find it strange, but I know never to disturb Terence at work."

"So there's nothing more you can tell me about that day?"

She looked at me and said sharply. "Don't you think I have been over every detail in my mind already? The only thing out of the ordinary was that my husband of over thirty years has disappeared. Out of the blue, just like that. Leaving me and my children on my own!"

There it was. The complete and utter sense of devastation, anger and hopelessness breaking through to the surface. I let the silence hang a moment, let her work her way through it before going on. "How are your children taking it? I believe their names are Chloe and David, have I got that right?"

"You have done your homework," she sighed. "Chloe is devastated. She was always her father's little girl. They were very close. She is a good girl. Calls every day to see how I am and to ask for any updates. It has hit her hard. But she is a doctor and works very long hours. She finds work a comforting distraction. Just like her father does...or did...or…"

Her voice tailed off.

"May I ask what Mr Auyeung found work to be a comforting distraction from?"

She hesitated. Then: "I see you are good at your job, Mr Lee. Taking full advantage of a slip of the tongue."

"If it comes across like that, I apologise. But the task I have been given means I do have to cover some sensitive ground with you. So, if I may be even more blunt, Mrs Auyeung, is there anything about the state of your marriage that you feel I need to know for the purposes of trying to find out what has happened to your husband?"

She took a deep breath, her shoulders rising in defiance.

"A blunt question, deserves a blunt answer. No. Our marriage has had its ups and downs, like any marriage of thirty-three years. Nothing is perfect, Mr Lee. Nothing at all. But make no mistake, Terence and I are a strong couple, a strong partnership. That is all you need to know. I do not know what has happened to my husband, but I do know this. His disappearance has nothing to do with our marriage."

"And yet, he needed to find comfort in his work from something?" I forged on. "According to your own words, Mrs Auyeung."

Her eyes narrowed into black pips of anger. "I don't think I care for this line of interrogation."

I held her steely stare. This wasn't something I was proud of, but it was necessary. Giving the tree a shake, seeing what fell out, hoping it was the truth.

"Do the initials LKW mean anything to you?" I eventually decided to pivot.

She frowned. "Why do you ask?"

"Because your husband's work diary showed he had a meeting with someone with those initials every Wednesday. After work."

In three quick jolts her expression turned from shock, to anger and then to a relieved amusement which manifested itself in a low chuckle. "Perhaps you are right, Mr Lee. Perhaps he was having an affair. But not the kind you are thinking of. My husband's work meant everything to him. His career defined him as much as his family. It was his sole distraction and, yes, his hobby. And LKW was his mistress."

"She was?"

"*He* was, Mr Lee. Lam Kah Wai. Rufus Lam's Chinese name. Rufus and Terence are cut of the same cloth. Both men love their work. We wives are in many ways the distraction that keeps them away from it."

I felt like an idiot and probably deserved to.

"Thanks for clearing that up."

But there was something she wasn't telling me. Something obvious. Something I was missing. I quickly replayed the answers she had given me in my head, analyzing them for weakness. Nothing jumped out. A dutiful daughter, the apple of her father's eye, who rang her mum every day. Terence Auyeung, the family man, accountant, a Rufus Lam loyalist and a fierce workaholic. Gladys Auyeung, the defiant matriarch, the glue that held the family together. Only she hadn't been able to, not this time.

Then it hit me. The missing link.

"Your son David."

She glanced down at her feet. I could tell that I had hit on it. That screwdriver had finally found its way under the lip of the lid. All that was needed was to give it a good prise.

"You've spoken about Chloe, Mrs Auyeung. You've spoken about yourself. Your husband. But you have yet to mention your son? Why is that?"

She raised her face to mine. "It's complicated."

I waited to see if there was more.

"With families, it always is," I prompted after the silence had stretched to breaking point. "So the relationship between David and his father has been a difficult one?"

She nodded.

"Can I ask what David does?"

"He is something in finance. I am not sure what exactly. But he lacks his father's caution, always has done. There are many things they have never seen eye to eye on. Fathers and sons," she shrugged.

I pondered that answer.

"Do you think David may have had something to do with your husband's disappearance?"

"I....", she hesitated. "I don't know, Mr Lee. But then again, it has been over two years since we last saw David. So I doubt it very much."

Although I nodded at the answer, I wasn't so sure I agreed with it.

CHAPTER TEN

That night I tried to sleep but my mind was like a tumble-dryer, spinning my thoughts around too quickly for me to get a grip on any particular one. When I did manage to drift off, it was only into that hinterland that lies just short of true slumber, where dreams never make any sense and always end with an unsettling jolt. Three times, I found my eyes sparking open, my chest drenched in sweat, relieved to hear the rhythm of the air-conditioner's constant drawl.

By 5am I gave up on rest, pulled on some shorts, an old T-shirt and a pair of trustworthy Nikes. Then I hit the streets. Morning running had never been my thing and it was such a shock to my body that the sweat mechanism took a while to kick in. After ten minutes of gentle and lethargic padding, however, I felt the reassuring bathe of perspiration wrinkling my shirt into cling-film across my torso.

I did a slow circuit of Wong Nai Chung Road before taking the under-pass which led to the tarmac track inside Happy Valley race-course. It was there I found my flow, clearing my mind of the clutter through the rhythmical slap of my feet.

I loved the race-course. In a city of contrasts, this was probably Hong Kong's biggest. On Wednesday nights it was here that the gambling-obsessed population indulged its habit, flooding the Jockey Club coffers with cash in a frenzy of quinellas, reverse forecasts and other complex bets that would have made a derivatives trader blush, but were meat and drink to the Ah Bah string-vest brigade who had spent the week debating tips in the Tsa-tsan Tengs. Hong Kong was an international finance centre and Happy Valley racecourse on Wednesday nights was its very soul.

And yet for the rest of week, no better oasis of tranquility could be found in the city than at this track. Many a time I had circled round here and found peace and clarity in the cleansing ritual that was running. Right now, I had the place virtually to myself. Calmness reigned.

By the third lap, I was energized enough to start the day, so I stopped by the asphalt gym area and put myself through a routine of sit-ups, push-ups, chin ups and cool-down stretches. Lying on my back for a moment, I felt cleansed and energized and ready for the seemingly impossible tasks that lay ahead. High above me, the twin turquoise towers of the High-Cliff development sparkled in the morning sky, probably the primest of prime real-estate in Hong Kong. The two tower blocks looked like a victory sign for capitalism, but the appearance was deceptive. Most of the overpriced units were owned by occasional Mainland shoppers from north of the border, converting their bribe money into real estate. The thought made me smile. Hong Kong's glistening façade had always disguised a disreputable underbelly.

I got to my feet and jogged back to my apartment and as I did, thoughts of Auyeung and Rufus Lam and Napoleon Wong crept in at the edges of my mind. By the time I was under the shower, my brain was rocking again with different permutations of what I should do next.

I had the radio on while getting dressed. The newscaster was trying to hype some alleged controversial news about election and how this would impact Jeremy Lau's chances. I listened only peripherally, then turned the damn thing off, preferring instead to go over the notes I had made the previous night following my meeting with Mrs Auyeung. My mind had been tired when I had gotten home yesterday, but still I had forced myself to brain-dump everything I could recall about the conversation on paper.

The first scan of the notes got me focused on the last part of our talk. David Auyeung, their son, the boy Mrs Auyeung said they hadn't spoken to in two years. She had only mentioned him when I had probed, happily volunteering everything about Chloe their daughter, but nothing about David.

So David was their family's black sheep. Why was I surprised? Every family had one. In my family, that was my role.

But the part about the parents not having seen their son for two years didn't sit right with me. Not in Hong Kong, where family was the bond of both society and business. Not that there was a difference between the two, but that was why it bugged me, I guess. I had no evidence of any connection between the estranged son and his father's disappearance, but it was something I needed to look into.

Twice more, I went through the notes hoping something would spark. Nothing did. Not until the third time. That's the thing with investigations, it's not like a puzzle where you get the pieces and all you have to do is work out how to fit them together. With an investigation, you have to find the pieces first. That's the hardest part. Most of the time they are right there under your nose, but so deeply embedded you only discover them by chance and when you do, you have to tease them loose and hope they don't withdraw back into nothing.

That third time I went over the notes, my mind caught on something, like the tip of a fine thread hooking the edge of a jagged finger nail.

Marriage not perfect, I had written down. It was a reference to Gladys Auyeung's protestations that the state of her relations with her husband had nothing to do with his disappearance.

Nothing is perfect, Mr Lee. Nothing at all. But make no mistake, Mr Lee. We are a strong couple, a strong partnership. That is all you need to know.

Those were her exact words. I replayed them over and over in my head, teasing out the thread, biting my lip with the effort of reaching for the thought, for the connection that was just out of my grasp.

Then the collision of the various moving crumbs finally pinged and lit a spark.

Nothing is perfect, Mr Lee. Nothing at all.

She was right, nothing is.

Except the state of Auyeung's pristine expense claims which I had found the day before in his office. Not a receipt missing, no item on any of the forms missed out.

When I was a young trainee, I used to handle household insurance claims. It didn't take me long to get a nose for fraud. And perfection always brought with it the strongest waft. I mean, who the hell kept receipts for everything?

It was that same waft I was getting now with Auyeung's expense claims. Something was out of kilter, something off balance. Something too perfect.

Something I needed to find.

My watch told me it was 6.30am. I needed to get to Auyeung's office before anyone saw me.

I straightened my tie.

It was time to start my day.

One of the skills I had acquired in my sabbatical was to teach myself how to pick a lock. I don't know why, it was just something that appealed to that puzzle-solving side of my brain, when I got fed up with Sudoku. Plus, having seen it done in countless movies, part of me wondered just how realistic those depictions were. Strange, the way your mind works when you give it enough space to think

Anyhow, the theory was easy enough. If you Google 'lock-picking', you get a mine of information on the subject, complete with several instructional videos on YouTube. I know because I've watched most of them.

The practical is the difficulty. First, I tried the locks on my bedroom door. Complete failure. Then I tried on my suitcases. Nada. So I gave up for a few weeks, until I was shopping for some light bulbs one day and saw some padlocks which seemed to rekindle the challenge I had set myself. I bought one, spent a few weeks playing about with it, like it was a Rubix cube, and finally one day whilst I was lazing on the sofa, working the tension-wrench and raking the pick along the tumblers, the thing clicked open on me.

After that, nothing seemed to stop me. No lock in my home was safe, not the bedroom doors, not my suitcase. One day I even went out, deliberately leaving my key behind, just to make sure I could use my newly acquired skill in a real (well sort of) situation. My doorman clicked his teeth and called me Soh-soh-dei when he found me delighted and punching the air, just because I had proved how easy it was to burgle myself. You could see both points of view, I guess.

Apart from that time, however, I had never had the chance to use my new skill in anger. Until now.

The lock on Auyeung's door was a simple pin and tumbler model, the cheapest and most common you could find on the market (which fit with Napoleon Wong's cost-conscious management style). Crouching down, I got the pick and tension wrench going, pushing the five tumblers up and raking away with the pin. After four minutes, I was still at it, cursing the security-conscious way Tabitha Yan had kept the key in her handbag, so I couldn't get it. But patience is a virtue, they say, especially with lock picking I've learned, and eventually, I managed to find the right position for the tumblers with the pin. Satisfaction blossomed in my chest, at the sound of the subtle 'click' as the lock gave way.

I was in.

The office was just as I had left it the previous day, files on the shelf behind Auyeung's desk, in-tray burgeoning with paper, yet still that horrible aura of disuse.

This was no time for sentimentality. I figured I had about half an hour before the office early-birds arrived, so I got to work quickly.

I started with Auyeung's expense claim file which had set me on this path. A quick once through confirmed what I had already seen. Pure perfection. Auyeung, the Boy Scout. Not a hint of impropriety. The lunch appointments were with suppliers and vendors of Gadgetech. There were short descriptions of their purpose, like "discuss new terms", "pricing scale" and "tax efficiencies". The receipts told me nothing more, only that Auyeung wasn't a big tipper, which went with the territory as a CFO I guessed; nor were the lunches that regular, so no hint that he was taking advantage of company coffers to have much fun.

I stood up from the desk and paced around, the ticking of my watch through the silence reminding me that time was limited.

Nothing was this perfect. That was the conclusion I kept coming back to, which meant what I was seeing wasn't the truth, or at least not the full truth.

Slowly the cogs started to whir in my head. It wasn't what was in the file that held the answer. It was what was missing.

I sat down again and went through the claim vouchers one more time, writing down the names of each of the suppliers and vendors on a piece of paper. Then turning back to the shelf, I ran my hand across the spines of the rest of the files crammed on there, mouthing the titles silently just in case I missed one.

My hand came to a stop. This time I said the name out loud, I don't know why, maybe just to see how the words tasted.

"Vendor and Supplier payments."

Pulling the file down, I opened it on the desk and winced as the sweet waft of old paper and dust hit hard. The file was divided into sections, each section representing a different month. There were a full ten months in the file, each month showing the payments which Gadgetech had made to all its outside suppliers, complete with copies of the cheques and completed authorization sign-off forms.

I listed out the names of all the suppliers and vendors mentioned. Then I compared it to the first list of companies I had made, the companies which Auyeung had entertained based on his own expense claims.

Auyeung's entertainment list was shorter, which stood to reason, given that if you are the CFO you are not going to go to lunch with all your business partners, only the ones most important to Gadgetech. But it was the ones not mentioned on Auyeung's entertainment list, but which were on my second list because they had received payments from Gadgetech, that I wanted to look at. Comparing the two lists, I circled the culprits. There were five in total.

For two of them, it was obvious from their names what they did. One was Xerox; rental for the photocopiers and fax machines, I guessed. Then there was a security alarm company.

The other three, however, the names didn't mean much.

Good Fortune Limited, Collex Limited and Seemax Limited.

I went straight for the invoices and added up the figures paid to these companies in the last twelve months. Good Fortune Limited, I was able to dismiss quickly. It had organized the firm's annual dinner, the month after Chinese New Year, when prices were rock bottom. Collex Limited turned out to be a courier company which Gadgetech had on retainer, again nothing unusual there.

Seemax Limited, however, was just referred to as a "consultancy". And when I added up the amounts Gadgetech had paid to it in the last three months, I knew I had struck gold.

Not a bad start to do the day, I was thinking to myself when a sharp voice severed the thought off half way.

"What are you doing in here?"

Napoleon Wong was standing in the door-way. He didn't look best pleased with what he was seeing.

The trouble was, what he was seeing was me, in Terence Auyeung's office, which I had just broken into.

CHAPTER ELEVEN

In situations like this, there's only one way to go and that's with the Tom Becker principle.

My mum and dad met out in Hong Kong in the 1960s, when my dad was posted here to set up a business outpost. Back then, Hong Kong was a tinder box ready to explode, its Wanchai bars flooded with US servicemen on R&R from Vietnam and its population terrorised by Maoist riots egged on by the Cultural Revolution raging north of the border. Britain still ruled this pimple on China's backside, but the whole place was on borrowed time, counting down to the inevitable day when it went back to China. Cold War politics made that an unpalatable prospect for many, who voted with their feet and got the hell out. My parents were no exception. They said good-bye to Hong Kong for good, and moved to the United Kingdom, to three-day weeks, strikes, power cuts, delays on trains, bad weather, apart from the hot summer of seventy-six, when I was born, two years after my big brother John.

Following John became a template for my early life. Trouble was, John was better than me at most things. I was content living in his shadow and not measuring up, but when I arrived on my first day at Hamlington Grove, the private school on the Sussex coast we were both dispatched to, that contentment quickly changed.

Hamlington Grove was the kind of school that sought to make boys into gentlemen, so they could fill vacancies in the army, civil service or City of London. John was made for the place. By the time I arrived, he was captain of several teams and destined for the Head of School position which would light up any CV. That I wasn't as good at sports as John, was something I already knew. But Hamlington Grove taught me that a bigger and gaping chasm existed between my brother and me, one I had never appreciated until then.

John took after my dad in looks. He was strong and tall and, well, white. Me, I was Mum's boy, slighter in build and with a complexion that wasn't Chinese enough for people to tell where I was from, but different enough for them to realize I was, well, different. Because

John and I looked different, people expected us to be different. I didn't disappoint. While John was fast on his way to becoming the school's best chance of getting somebody into Oxford from his year, I fell in with Tom Becker.

Every school like Hamlington Grove has a Tom Becker, a kid whose parents have too much money and too busy lives to care, so they leave their son to his own devices and he takes full advantage. Becker had a knack of searching out the boundaries of what society allowed and then going straight past them. He wore his tie low, his hair long and his shirt out. He smoked, treated lessons as optional, caroused with older girls from the nearby town and pushed every teacher with whom he came into contact to apoplexy, just because he could. That was the thing with Becker. He was smart, but he seemed hell bent on using his smartness for the things he wanted, rather than what his teachers wanted.

Becker didn't do friends, he was too 'out there' for that, but in me at least he saw an acquaintance. Why, I never really knew. Perhaps, he saw something of a kindred rebellious soul in me, someone who was different from the rest of those Anglo-Saxon born-to-rulers we were surrounded by. Whatever the case, he let me hang out with him. Many was the time when after dark, we would head up to the disused amphitheatre, Becker to smoke, me to listen to his anti-establishment philosophy.

It was on one of those evenings, that I remember asking him, "Becker, what do you do when you get caught?"

Becker dragged on his cigarette. As smoke gushed from his aquiline nose, he looked at me and said, "Guess."

I thought long and hard. "Deny it? Run?"

"Wrong." He pointed at me with the two fingers holding his smoke. "You deny something, you're admitting there's something to deny. You run, you're admitting there's something to run from."

Typical Becker.

"So what do you do?"

"You act like you're happy that they've found you doing exactly what you're doing. Like it's the most natural thing in the world. Get what I mean?"

"Uh, not really."

Becker took out his Malboros, lit another and looked at me. "Okay, so imagine, if Jonesy came walking round the corner right now. No good running 'cos he's already seen us. I could stub out my fag, hope he won't notice, but I already stink of the stuff. Plus those are reactions he'd be expecting, that he'd be ready to deal with." Becker bit his lip a moment. "But what if say to him, 'Thank God you're here, Mr Jones!' What then?"

"He'd think you were crazy!"

"Right! But would he know how to react? 'Course not. So then we've bought ourselves some time to explain and because we've gone straight on the attack, whatever explanation we give looks credible. I mean, think about it." Becker turned to where Jones might hypothetically have been standing. "'Thank God you're here Mr Jones. Me and Lee were out for a walk, talking about the origins of the second world war for our timed-essay tomorrow. Then we came across some kids from town, using this place to smoke. When they saw us, they scarpered, but look, they left one lit up. I was just putting it out. Fire hazard, you see. We should look for any more lit butts just in case. These things are a health hazard!'"

He said it with so much balls, even I believed him.

So there it was: Becker's principle of getting caught. One of the most interesting things I ever learned at that school.

And as I sat there with Napoleon Wong's beedy eyes burning holes in me, almost a quarter of a century later I found myself putting it into practice.

"Napoleon, you beat me to it," I said.

The comment caught Napoleon Wong like an unexpected kick in the gut. His shoulders dipped, his ire doused by a soupçon of confusion.

"I was about to call and ask you to come down here. Thought I'd go through some of the financials, get a feel for the types of warranties Rufus Lam will want us to provide in the sale and purchase agreement for the buy-out. Those things can be pretty tough to negotiate. Anyway, it all looks pretty standard, so it shouldn't be a problem. But I tell you what I did find. Take a look at this." While I was speaking my fingers were working the files, to one of the invoices I had looked at. Napoleon took it and stared at it bemused, the soupcon of confusion, now turning into an avalanche.

"Good Fortune Limited? What is this?" he asked.

"Good Fortune was the outfit you hired to organize the company's annual dinner earlier this year."

"So?"

"You realize they charged you time and a half for the MC? That's an extra HK$25,000. I've seen this kind of thing before from entertainment companies. They get their people to slow the evening down so it runs over by half an hour and then they hit you with a double-charge shown in the small print. You should let me call them, try and get some of that money back. Clauses like that are completely unenforceable..."

"We don't have time to talk about this now!" he said irritably. "I need your opinion on how the news today will affect my buy-out. I have a couple of calls to make first, but come to my office in fifteen minutes please to discuss!"

He disappeared before I had time to say anything else.

But just as I was breathing a sigh of relief and wondering what news he was talking about, his head reappeared round the door frame.

"Oh, and Scott."

"Yes?"

"Don't ever go in this office without my permission again."

CHAPTER TWELVE

I headed back to my hutch of an office and booted up the computer.

Tabitha wasn't in yet, but there were signs of life on other parts of the floor. None of it interested me, however. With what I had found in Auyeung's office, the pieces of the puzzle surrounding the mystery of his disappearance were slowly starting to fit together into a recognizable picture. My mind was buzzing with the implications and it was all I could do to tear myself away from the urge to log onto the Companies Registry website and download as much as I could on Seemax Limited. But tear myself away I had to, because I had fifteen minutes to find out what the hell Wong had been referencing by the "news" affecting his buy out.

It was only day two of working for Napoleon Wong. Already, I was getting used to his little God-complex, how he seemed to assume the whole business-universe spun around him and Gadgetech. At the end of the day, Gadgetech was just a middle-sized, private company. There was no way the buy-out was going to attract any press attention, even if the seller was Rufus Lam.

So it was with somewhat of a heavy heart that I found myself giving in to Napoleon's little whim by logging onto the Hong Kong Standard Newspaper's website to look for stories which could possibly be linked to the situation we had. Once I found it I would pop upstairs, massage Napoleon's ego, tell him what he'd want to hear and then I could get on with my day. After all, whatever it was, I was sure it wouldn't register between zero and zero point one on the Richter scale.

That was the thought process flowing through my mind as the Standard's home page uploaded. I shut my eyes a moment to try and reach a place of calm.

When I opened them, the headline on the screen hit me like freight train.

"Oh shit," I heard myself say.

The Richter scale hadn't just blipped. It had shuddered things to a whole new universe.

***

"You have seen this, I presume?" Napoleon Wong barked at me as soon as I walked into his office, punching the headline of the *South China Morning Post spread* out on his desk with a pudgy forefinger.

"RUFUS LAM DEMANDS OPPOSITION CANDIDATE IN RACE FOR CHIEF EXECUTIVE AND VOWS NOT TO PAY TAX," the front page screamed. Compared to the *Standard*'s "Lam weighs in to change history," the *South China* editor had favoured facts over sensationalism. Underneath the headline, there was Rufus Lam's picture. He was standing at a podium in mid-speech, a confident smile on his handsome face, the trade-mark silver cane tucked under one arm.

I picked up the paper and quickly scanned the story:

> *Tycoon Rufus Lam has taken the unprecedented move of promising to back an opposition candidate to run against Jeremy Lau in the race for the Chief Executive election.*
>
> *Lam, founder and head of the billion dollar Culture Media Empire, is known to have voiced his democratic sympathies in private, but this is the first time he has openly demanded full democracy in Hong Kong.*
>
> *In an editorial in* Dragon Daily, *Lam's flagship Chinese news publication, written by Lam himself, he is quoted as saying: "As a citizen of Hong Kong, I am free to make economic choices for myself and my family. I can choose where to have my children educated, or which doctor to go to when I am sick, or what I want to read. But still, I am not trusted with the responsibility to exercise a free choice on who should be the Chief Executive of Hong Kong.*
>
> *The government should always stand in service to the Hong Kong people, not act as a master, and Hong Kong people should have the power to have a full and completely unfettered say as to whom they wish to pay to perform this service. This process of pre-vetting candidates by an opaque nominating committee controlled by Beijing, denies us this choice. It has left us with a façade of an election process, in which we have a single candidate. That is not democratic. That is not universal suffrage. That is just a sham which does Hong Kong a disservice and makes us a laughing-stock in the eyes of the world.*

So I have decided to have my say. I will find and back a suitable opposition candidate, to run against Jeremy Lau in next month's election. Whoever the candidate I find is, he or she will run on the platform of giving HongKongers what they deserve: the principle of one-man one-vote in choosing their next Chief Executive; and candidates who have not been pre-vetted by a nominating committee controlled by the Central People's Government. If my candidate wins, he or she will immediately introduce legislation to do away with the nominating committee, so that finally all of us can have the election process we deserve.

You may ask how I plan to get this candidate through the current nominating committee process. The answer is this. We have tried civil disobedience before by taking to the streets. It didn't work. So now, I will try it again, but in a different way. Like all HongKongers, I pay my taxes every year (in my case, that is not a small amount). In return for these taxes, I get nothing. Not even the right to elect those whom I pay. So now, I am demanding that right. I hereby challenge the nominating committee to let my opposition candidate stand in the election. If it refuses, then I shall refuse to pay even one-dollar of tax this year or the next, or until Hong Kong gets true democracy. I do not encourage other Hong Kong people to join me in this new era of civil disobedience. But I will not dissuade them, if they are so inclined."

There has been no reaction to Lam's threats from Jeremy Lau himself, but a spokesman from his camp was quoted as calling Lam's move "nothing but a cheap publicity stunt". One thing can be said for certain, however. Lam's intervention will bring some much needed interest to what so far has been a dull – and one-man – race.

I put the paper down on the table and puffed my cheeks. Napoleon looked at me for a reaction.

"Interesting," I said, non-committally.

"We have to move ahead with the buy-out", Napoloen blasted. "And we have to do it fast before we get engulfed with this nonsense." He made a shooing motion with his hand at the newspaper. "I don't know what Lam thinks he is doing. It's crazy! But if he is using this as some sort of ploy to weasel out selling Gadgetech to me, I won't stand for it. We are going to ramp things up. Light a fire under him. Make it clear that I am not going to put up with this nonsense. I want the sale and purchase agreement and whatever other documentation we need to get this done, ready to go down to him tonight. You understand?"

Only when he was finished did I realize my mouth was hanging open. The very idea that Lam's intervention in the Hong Kong election was all part of some elaborate plan to avoid selling his stake in Gadgetech to Napoleon Wong was laughable. But who was I to point this out to my idiot of a boss?

Instead, I said, "Shouldn't be a problem. I can e-mail the documents to you later today and you can send them over to Lam by close of business."

Napoleon gave an approving grunt.

In the silence that followed I watched him staring maniacally at the newspaper, lost in his own little universe where he ruled all and what he said was the only thing that counted.

There was something about that moment which made me feel uneasy. Napoleon Wong was playing a nasty little game for his own benefit. The thought that I was being dragged further and further into it made me want to retch. I had left my legal career to try and get away from having to feel this way, like life was just one big compromise, a line that blurred a little bit more every time I crossed it, until one day it disappeared altogether.

But here I was, only a couple of days after my return, being tested again.

I didn't like that. I didn't like it one bit and something deep inside of me made me want to push back, if only to prove to myself I was still prepared to fight hard for my own soul.

"How are you going to make sure Rufus Lam goes through with the buy-out now?" I heard the words come from my mouth without planning them. Quickly moving for cover, I added, "I can see him trying to get the whole thing postponed until after the election, don't you think?"

Napoleon Wong looked up and smiled like a crocodile ready for lunch.

"You needn't worry about that, Scott. The strategy is taken care of. Just make sure the legal documentation is ready, understand?"

That was my cue to leave and I took it gratefully. But Wong's comment about having a strategy all worked out gave me the confirmation I needed.

He was up to something. And I was part of his little game.

CHAPTER THIRTEEN

I spent the next couple of hours working up the sale and purchase agreement, contract notes and instruments of transfer for the buy-out up to a passable level.

Next I went through Gadgetech's articles of association which told me the transfer had to be approved by the directors, so I drew up the necessary resolution. Gadgetech only had three directors. Wong, Auyeung and a guy I had never heard of, who was listed in the e-mail address book as the head of procurement. A stooge of Wong's, I guessed, and since it only took two directors to form a quorum and decisions could be made by majority, the fact that Auyeung was missing could be dismissed as a minor inconvenience.

I shook my head. Hong Kong corporate governance was a pure oxymoron. Companies could use the rules to get away with all manner of sins under the guise of legality. The tycoon class had been doing it for years. There was a time when I used to judge. Now I just accepted it for what it was.

By 11am, I was done. It didn't take much to effect a change of ownership in a company like Gadgetech. I e-mailed the stuff over to Napoleon and wondered what it was that corporate lawyers and investment bankers did all day for their money. Talked the talk and sipped champagne was my guess.

Wong acknowledged with a quick "thanks", which I took to mean he would stay out of my way for the rest of the day. That suited me just fine.

Next I put a couple of phone calls through to Phil Yip. The way I figured it, with Lam's announcement that morning he had some explaining to do. I called both his mobile and his office number, both without luck. So I left a message on his voicemail and with his secretary for him to call me back, first chance he got.

Then, without pausing, I went straight to work on the matters which had snagged my attention in Auyeung's offices that morning.

Seemax Limited.

According to the invoices I had found in Auyeung's files, Seemax was a company which had apparently provided "consultancy" services to Gadgetech. Those services, according to the invoices, had been spread out over a period of nine months and eighteen separate invoices, which split the fees down into nice bite size chunks of around HK$150,000 each.

But when you added them all up, the fees totaled three million dollars. That was some consulting service Seemax was performing! More to the point, each invoice had been approved for payment by the same single individual: Terence Auyeung.

I spent a few minutes googling around what I could find on Seemax, but got a big fat zero. It didn't even have a website. In this day and age when every two-bit outfit had one, that didn't make any sense for a company which had billed three million dollars to just one of its clients over a nine month period.

Next, I logged onto the Companies Registry and ran a search against its ownership. That drew another blank, although this one provided more confirmation for the conclusions I was quickly beginning to draw. According to its latest annual return, Seemax Limited was owned one hundred percent by a company called CMax (pronounced the same as its curious subsidiary, I presumed). CMax, so the information in the registry informed, just so happened to be incorporated offshore in the British Virgin Islands.

It figured.

If you want to hide the ownership of a company from prying eyes, the BVI is the perfect place to do it, precisely because there is no access to a public registry of companies like there is in Hong Kong. From a previous case, I had learned that places like the BVI guaranteed three things: sun, sea and secrecy. Hence, it attracted specific types of clientele: rich people trying to limit the tax they paid, or criminals trying to hide their ill-gotten gains.

I wasn't one-hundred percent sure yet which category CMax fell into, but I had a sneaking suspicion this had nothing to do with tax.

The company secretary for the Hong Kong subsidiary, Seemax Limited, was one of those two-bit corporate service firms that probably performed the same function for a thousand other companies. There would be no point in making any enquiries down that road, so I didn't bother. Anyway, I already had a pretty good idea who was behind Seemax and its BVI parent. It was a simple enough structure but still it would have needed someone with the right knowledge to have set it up.

A lawyer would have been the usual suspect, but for once there were no lawyer's fingerprints even close to this.

There was, however, an accountant: a CFO to be precise.

All roads led back to Terence Auyeung.

As CFO he was approving the invoices for the consultancy company, which I guessed he had set up, masking his links by incorporating its sole shareholder in the BVI. A simple yet effective scheme to funnel three million dollars out of Gadgetech. There were still pieces missing, but that's what it looked like.

And now he was missing.

Coincidence wasn't something to which I gave much credence. Facts and evidence were, but there wasn't enough yet to confirm my suspicions. Plus my theory was pock-marked with more holes than a Swiss cheese. I had, after all, been to Auyeung's home to see his wife. Auyeung definitely wasn't short of cash. So why would he need to funnel cash out of Gadgetech, if indeed he had? And where the hell was he now?

I checked my mobile to see if Yip had returned my call yet or any of my messages. He hadn't, so I tried him again, every which way. The girl who answered this time wasn't his secretary and told me he was in a human resources meeting. She didn't know I had worked with Yip for a number of years and had known him for many more. Being in a human resources meeting was his euphemism for avoiding calls, something he had never done to me before.

Maybe it was because I was having a bad day, or maybe it was because he was the one who had got me into this mess in the first place, but the fact that Yip was avoiding me ticked me off badly.

So I decided to do something about it.

CHAPTER FOURTEEN

Yip & Siu's offices were in Central, on the seventh and eight floors of Central Building on the corner of Pedder Street and Queen's Road. The blue-chip address was a far cry from their original Kowloon side location and a sign of how far Philip Yip had moved up in the world.

When we were students at Durham University, our law lecturers would never have picked Phil as the one most likely to rise to the top of his profession, but Phil's success had never surprised me. Sure, Yip & Siu was the firm founded by his father who had carved out a nice niche on cargo disputes that rode the back of Hong Kong's growing container terminal industry. But to pigeon-hole Phil as a brat riding his old man's coat-tails was just plain wrong.

Phil had never been great at the academic side of the law. But he had the necessary attributes required to succeed in the Hong Kong legal game. He could spend a whole day in meetings with one purpose in mind: to get work through the door. Phil had something every law firm partner needs: a decent line of patter to make it look like he was an expert in every field of law. In the evenings, he worked the private club scene like a pro, shaking the right hands, paying deference to the right people, getting his and the firm's name known and out there. His English education gave him the right accent and he worked it to perfection, seizing instructions from foreign companies looking to use Hong Kong as a platform to launch into the Mainland. His fluency in Mandarin impressed the hell out of Mainland companies too, looking to use Hong Kong as their route to the outside world. Bottom line, Phil could mix with everyone that mattered. He was the archetype Hong Kong *compradore*, bringing East and West together and skimming a fat piece off the top for his law firm.

In deference to his father, Phil had always kept the litigation department at Yip & Siu going. But it was under Phil's steerage that Yip & Siu had risen in the ranks to become one of the most respected corporate law firms in Hong Kong, substituting its functional Kowloon office unit for its plush Hong Kong Central address.

When I had been at Yip & Siu, although Phil had been on the verge of breaking the firm through to its new status it hadn't quite yet happened. The whole place still had that gritty knock-about feel to it, and I felt at home there. I took on the cases that no-one else wanted because litigation wasn't considered sexy any more. It was the part of the profession that lurked in the gutter. Solving grubby disputes in court had never been the Hong Kong way. But I was built for litigation and there was no job too small, no case too dirty for me to handle.

Those days had been fun, but the more Yip & Siu changed and re-branded itself into what it was now, a corporate law power house, the more I felt the passion for what I was doing eek away to nothing.

And one day it had just hit me. Yip & Siu wasn't the place for me anymore.

Phil convinced me not to leave. Take some time-out sure, call it a sabbatical, take a whole God damn year to get your shit together, he had pleaded. But both of us knew it was over. Phil had moved on to fulfill his potential as the firm's senior partner and then become President of the Law Society, hob-nobbing with the great and the good in Hong Kong society.

I had moved on too.

The bonds of our friendship remained as strong as ever, however. Phil always knew, if it hadn't been for my tuition back in our Durham days, he would never have got his law degree, let alone the lower second that was just about passable for his father to give him a training contract.

Phil Yip had always made time for me.

Until today.

And that pissed me off.

Yip & Siu's reception was all beige marble, gold lettering and air-conditioned spaciousness. Plants stood either side of the front entrance, a touch added by the Feng Shui consultant to welcome business through the door. Two receptionists, who looked like they belonged in a Tatler advert, were there to do the same. They had sweet smiles, name badges and matching uniforms that showed off their alluring contours. Times certainly had changed at Yip & Siu. Neither of them recognized me and the one called Candy asked me for my name and company.

"Scott Lee. Legal Counsel of Gadgetech. Here to see Mr Yip," I said.

Three years I had worked at the firm and never before had I felt so on the outside looking in.

Candy asked me to take a seat. I preferred instead to wander over to a shelf off to the side which had various Yip & Siu brochures on it, all done in the corporate brand, an embossed red dragon plastered on a navy blue background. It looked impressive, but made me feel nostalgic for the days of old man Yip and his cost-conscious approach to doing business. Chastising trainees for not re-using envelopes was the way, back then.

I picked up one of the brochures and flicked through it. It told me that the firm where I had worked slip 'n trip cases, was now an expert in equity derivatives. I shook my head in disappointment.

"Do you have an appointment, Mr Lee?" Candy asked, niceness her default setting.

"No I don't, but I…."

"I'm afraid Mr Yip is unavailable. Perhaps I could make an appointment for you and you could come back later?"

The niceness had a bit of force behind it now.

I took a deep breath, hoping we could still do this the easy way. "I'd like to see him now, please."

"I don't think that would be possible."

"Listen, Candy…" I leaned my elbows onto the marble reception top. My smile was in place, but I wanted to make it clear I wasn't going anywhere. "Could you ask Maureen Chau to come out here, please? She'll know who I am. Could you do that for me?"

Reluctantly, Candy made the call.

I waited. Five minutes passed. Disappointment and anger flooded through me like water through a storm drain in an amber rain warning. Looking back at Candy, she tried that sweet smile again, but it just looked painted on and I couldn't help but feel betrayed by the firm for whom I had billed so many hours. It was stupid, I know. Business was business and, well, lawyers were lawyers so what else could I expect? Certainly not to be treated like this. My disappointment festered and cultivated.

Eventually off to the left, the automatic door separating reception from the working offices swished open. There she stood, Maureen Chau, all five foot of her, arms folded, fingers tapping her elbows, looking at me like a mother who has just found her kid watching TV when he's supposed to be doing his home-work.

Maureen and I went way back. She had helped me with my Cantonese during lunchtimes and any client who had been rude to her had me to deal with. The closest thing I had to a godmother out in this part of the world was Mo.

"He can't see you, Scott. Not today."

"How are doing, Mo?" I leaned down to peck her on both cheeks. Tip-toeing up, she obliged.

"Busy! It's like the whole world has….hey!"

As I was going in for the second cheek-peck, I snaked my hand behind her and in one swift movement, plucked the security card that was dangling round her neck, up and over her head.

"Sorry Mo, but this is for Phil's own good."

Before she had a chance to respond, I was round her and running for the access door. Tapping the card against the sensor swished the door open and I was through. Turning back, I tossed the card at Mo's feet. Her bending down to get it would buy me a few more seconds which was all the start I needed on a lady in her fifties in an office where I once used to work.

Hurrying through the cubicles, I kept my eyes firmly fixed forward making out like I belonged there, passing people who were lost in their own tasks and not interested in who I was or what I was there to do. Eventually I found Mo's desk abandoned in a kind of outer lobby to Phil's office.

Phil's door was closed, but that wasn't going to stop me.

Out of the corner of my eye, I saw a secretary on the phone, listening to hurried instructions. I guessed it was Mo on the other end, because the secretary looked up at me, dropped the receiver and hurried to head me off. She didn't stand a chance.

I didn't bother knocking on Phil's door. I just waltzed on in and slammed it behind me.

There he was, Phil Yip, senior partner. On the phone, talking and smiling. He was mentioning something about the firm's experience in handling SFC investigations, but the sight of me standing there stopped him dead in his tracks.

I held up my hand, waggled four fingers in greeting and shucked my eyebrows, Harpo Marx style.

"Hey Stuart, you mind if I call you back? Something urgent's just come up," Phil said silkily before putting the receiver down. Then to me: "What the hell do you think you're doing? You're supposed to be at Gadgetech…we're not supposed to be seen together…"

"And you're not supposed to ignore my calls. So I guess that makes two of us in the dog house."

Phil scowled. "How did you get in here anyway, I thought I told Mo…" he stopped what he was saying

"Told Mo what, Phil? To block me? To screen out my calls? Last time I checked, Phil, I was still on the employee list here. In fact it was you who insisted I stay on when I wanted to leave. That's why I'm on "sabbatical", my fingers added the quote marks. "So what gives? You send me in to do your dirty work and then abandon me? Is that what twenty years of friendship gets you these days?"

Okay so perhaps I was being a little dramatic, but I needed Phil hurting, I needed him feeling like the shit he was being. Guilt was a great motivator and he owed me something I had wanted from the very beginning. If guilt didn't work, I had a Plan B, but not one that was too respectable. So I went about milking the guilt trip for everything it was worth.

"I really don't have time for this today," he said wearily. "I'm up to my eye-balls. Bombs are going off all over the place. So please, just go away and I'll call you as soon as things have calmed down. I promise."

He turned his attention to some papers on his desk, hoping that his little display of exasperation had been enough to make me leave.

Good luck with that!

"Bombs are going off?" I said. "How about Rufus Lam's announcement this morning? How about the fact that the shit storm you dragged me into is about to go nuclear? You don't think we need to talk about this right now? You don't think…." Suddenly a thought stopped me. "Wait a second, did you know what Lam was up to? Did you know he was about to bring the spotlight on himself right at the moment you had asked me to do some off-the-radar investigations for him. You son of a…"

"I don't know what you're talking about, Scott! And like I said I don't have time for this right now. So get out or I'll have you thrown out!"

Phil was up on his feet. We stood glaring at each other a moment. Friends of twenty years, tempers high, stress levels rocketing, both of us ready to unload our frustrations on each other.

Maybe I should have been the bigger man, done what Phil had asked, walked away until the heat had dissipated and we were ready to talk like adults. But I wasn't in the mood.

Instead I just started taking my clothes off, right there in Phil's office.

First went the tie. I flung it to the floor like it had offended me. Then I tweaked open my shirt buttons, angrily, defiantly and unashamedly, in a sort of confrontational striptease.

"What the hell do you think you're doing?" Phil voice rasped with exasperation and confusion.

"Plan B!"

"What?"

"I'm getting naked."

Following a slack jaw moment, Phil asked, "Why?"

"Because I know it would piss you off."

"Don't be stupid, Scott!"

"Oh we've passed the point of my looking stupid, Phil. Now it's your turn. What do you think Mo's going to say when she walks through that door any second, to see me strutting round your office in the buff? What's the secretary network going to do when I start running round out there like this? Maybe I'll even make it to reception, or a meeting room, give one of your precious clients more than they paid for? Think you'll be able to hush up the gossip chain after that? By five o'clock, there won't be a person on your client list who hasn't heard about that crazy naked dude running around Yip & Siu. The crazy naked dude that you hired. What do you think Rufus Lam would say if he found out? Now how about a picture together for your FaceBook page? Law Society President reunites with naked lawyer he hired. One for the diversity pages, don't you think?"

By now my trousers were round my ankles and I was fumbling off my shoes.

The door opened a jar. I saw through my legs it was Mo.

"Out!" screamed Phil.

Mo did as she was told, but not before she saw my hands move to the top of my boxers. I gave him a 'you asked for it' look and....

"Stop!" he yelled, palm up, eyes squeezed shut in horror in a way which, in any other circumstances, I might have found offensive. "Just stop! You win, okay! Just tell me what you want!"

"I want you to make an appointment for me and you to see Rufus Lam tonight. There are things we have to talk about. Things I have to ask him."

"Okay!" Phil tentatively opened his eyes. "Okay, I'll do it. I promise. Now put your clothes back on."

"Not until you've made the call, Phil. You've been fobbing me off from the start, so I want to make sure you do it."

"Now wait a minute," Phil started to protest, so my hands shot back to the top of my boxer shorts and started to move downwards. "Okay!"

I stayed where I was, partially starkers, threatening to do the Full Monty while my best friend called and made an appointment for us to meet with one of the most powerful tycoons in Hong Kong. Probably the bizarrest, most surreal moment in my legal career.

I guessed it was for Phil too.

But, hey, if it works, who cares?

CHAPTER FIFTEEN

I listened as Phil arranged a meet with Rufus Lam at 10pm that evening, then I got dressed and left him to go back to his day from hell. Mo was on the phone when I passed by her desk, so I mouthed her an apology for my behaviour. In response, she flipped her eyebrows, winked and softly bit the end of her pencil. It was either a bad joke or a dangerous compliment, I wasn't sure which but I took it as a good sign and felt my mood quickly improving to strangely euphoric proportions.

Most of the time, being a lawyer is pure drudge work, an endless round of word-smithing documentation and posturing negotiations. But then there are moments like these, glimmers of the spectacular, when you've outplayed the other guy and eeked out some fun in the process. Moments that somehow make it seem all worthwhile. When that happens, you feel on top of the clouds, that there is nothing that you can't achieve, that nothing can pop your bubble.

Walking out from Yip & Siu, I was in the middle of one of those moments. Life was good, I was on a roll.

Testing my luck, I put a call through Tabitha back at Gadgetech's offices to see if there was anything that needed my attention. She welcomed me with the words: "Mr Wong has been trying to get hold of you. He wants to talk to you urgently!"

Pop the bubble went. Just like that. Gone.

I found a quiet corner in a nearby Starbucks and called Napoleon.

"Where are you?" was the opening he threw at me.

"Central. I was consulting a lawyer I know on one of the aspects of the legal documentation for the transfer," I bluffed. "Purely on a no names basis of course. And for free. He's confirmed the wording used is correct, so you can proceed with sending the draft agreement to the counterparty."

"Counterparty?"

I cupped my hand over the phone. "Rufus Lam."

"Oh," he said.

With that one word, I sensed his distraction, a nervousness not usually present in his arrogant utterances.

"Napoleon, is anything wrong?"

Pause.

"I received a call…..from a journalist. She asked me about Rufus Lam."

I moved the phone to my other ear. "What did she want to know?"

Shallow breaths were all I could hear for a moment.

"Napoleon?

"She asked me if there was any link between Lam's intervention in the CE election and his decision to exit Gadgetech."

I shut my eyes. "What did you say to her?"

"I…..I told her she was talking complete nonsense. That it had nothing to do with anything at Gadgetech. This was purely a business matter and she could speak to my lawyer. Then I put down the phone. Bloody woman, who does she think she is and how did she know about…"

"Did she give you her name?" I cut him off.

"She said her name was….." I heard pages on a note pad being flipped. "Amy Tang. She writes for the *Economic Weekly*, apparently. Anyway, I bet it was Lam who leaked the information. Probably trying to get out of it. I told you we need to proceed quickly!"

"Then send him the draft agreement." Not in the mood for another lecture, I cut him short. "Put the ball in his court."

Pause.

"What about this journalist?" he asked.

I thought for a moment. "You didn't give her my number, so she has no way of contacting me. Which means she will either phone you again, or try and reach out to the legal department through the switchboard. I'll ring Tabitha and prime her with what to say. In the mean time, if she rings you again, the only words you say to her are 'No comment'. Got it?"

"'No comment.'"

"Exactly. I'll be back in the office in about half an hour. We can touch base again then if need be."

***

Hurrying back to the MTR station, I stopped off at a kiosk and asked for a copy of the *Economic Weekly*. It took a while for the vendor to locate it under the piles of the gossip and lifestyle magazines, so I guessed circulation was low.

Economic Weekly turned out to be one of the few bi-lingual publications on the market, with more in-depth analysis than you usually got from the dailies. The content was factual. There were few pictures other than graphs and charts. At fifty bucks a pop, I could tell why it wasn't perhaps the most popular read in the world.

The edition I picked up contained an article from Amy Tang, who was named on the inside page as a "contributing editor", a euphemism for freelance. The article was on the property market. Property was an obsession for the Hong Kong population. Home ownership was everyone's ambition, but with prices what they were, for a lot of people, an ambition was all it would remain. That seemed to be the slant of the article, which took an irreverent line against the lack of any government activity in solving the housing affordability issue.

The train had just left Fortress Hill as I finished the article and as I did, I felt my phone buzzing my attention in my pocket.

"Scott Lee."

"Lawyer Lee, they are trying to take my Combo again!" The words came out at me like strafe fire in a warzone, the voice unmistakably Mrs Lo's, the tough-as-nails owner of the basset hound whose right to reside I had been tasked with saving. Right now, this was not what I needed.

"They can't do this! They can't!"

"Slow down, Mrs Lo," I counseled, leaning my elbows onto my knees and massaging my tired eyes. "Tell me what happened."

"Remember, we agreed the managing agent would come in every day and check whether Combo bark? Well managing agent came in. He sit down. I go to kitchen to make tea. He tread on Combo's tail. Combo bark. He record on tape. He leave. Say he now has evidence. Say decision to get rid of Combo now reasonable. Nonsense, I shout at him. Tell him Combo only bark because he tread on Combo's tail. I bark too, if he tread on me!"

Probably bite him too, I figured.

"Did you actually see him tread on Combo's tail?"

Silence.

"I was in kitchen, I told you. But when I come back in, Combo licking tail. Only do that when someone tread on it by accident. But this no accident. I know my dog, Lawyer Lee. Now I have letter from managing agent, telling me their 'reasonable' opinion is Combo is nuisance. Nuisance, your head ah. Combo is not nuisance. They are nuisance. Policeman is nuisance!"

"Where was Combo when this happened, Mrs Lo?"

"He on his bed."

"You're sure?"

"Yes, I sure. He on his bed."

That made me smile. "Okay, tell me exactly what the letter from the managing agent says."

She did so. This time they had been careful, quoting all the right sections of the Deed of Mutual Covenant and citing the tape they had taken of Combo's barking (backed up by a witness statement from the managing agent himself, no less). On paper it seemed they had solid grounds for their reasonable belief that Combo had barked and caused a nuisance. They even cited the measurement of the volume. The fact that the letter had come direct from the agent and not a solicitor was also telling, as it meant they had avoided going through the process of appointing one, which would have caused significant delay through the tender process.

And all Mrs Lo had to support her defence was an unwitnessed accusation that the managing agent had trodden on Combo's tail when she wasn't in the room.

But all the while, Combo had been on his bed.

That was the key to it all.

The train was rolling into North Point now and passengers were leaving their seats to position themselves for a swift exit. I got up to do the same.

"Okay, Mrs Lo. Here's what I want you to do."

"You have an idea, Lawyer Lee?"

"Yes, I have an idea."

That was true at least. I was just glad she didn't ask me whether it was a good one.

***

The fifteen minute walk back to Gadgetech's office was pure discomfort, the air heavy with humidity which had enveloped the city like a damp blanket. Sweat trickled down my back and I knew that if I didn't get into some air-conditioning fast, I'd be soaked through. The pressure in the atmosphere was building and I could sense a rainstorm on the horizon. In the past, in weather like this, I would have cursed myself for forgetting my umbrella, but a decade here had taught me that a brolley offered little defence to a Hong Kong rain storm so there was no sense in beating myself up any more. If it rained, I was going to get wet, umbrella or no umbrella. It was a fact of life here.

Anticipating the relief that would come from getting back into air-con, I quickened my pace round the last few corners. Suddenly a shadow moved across my path, blocking me.

"Scott Lee?"

It wasn't a shadow.

It was a woman.

The sweat and heat were reaching unbearable measures and it was because of that I was caught off guard and confirmed that, yes, I was indeed Scott Lee.

"My name is Amy Tang, I'm with the *Economic Weekly*, please can you comment on…."

"No I can't." I went to go round her but she side-stepped into my path.

"I only want to know…." she persisted.

"I know what you want to know, Ms Tang. And I don't mean to be rude, but if I don't get into some air-conditioning fast, I'm going to melt. So if you don't mind…."

"I don't mind at all. That is, if you don't mind me joining you."

Damn this heat, I thought.

CHAPTER SIXTEEN

The relief of walking into a frosty wall of air-conditioned from the sweltering closeness of pre-thunderstorm humidity has to be experienced to be believed. It's like finally scratching a persistent itch which has been just out of reach all day, whilst quenching a desert-like thirst with the first glugs of iced water.

With my temperature dropping back to normal levels, I was able to get a grip, which was just as well because Amy Tang was shadowing me, like a mosquito in need of a meal. She was standing opposite me, arms folded in a pose that said she could do this all day if she had to. I gave her my hundred-yard stare and liked what I saw.

Her black hair was tied back in a functional pony tail. A few strands had escaped and were framing her face, which was pretty and completely unblemished, apart from a dusting of freckles across her nose. Jeans and a white blouse with the sleeves rolled up to the elbows completed the ensemble.

Amy Tang definitely had that dangerously cute look you see in a lot of Hong Kong women. A kind of innocence, coupled with an underlying driven determination. Like they could cuddle their Hello Kitty toys one minute and squash your dreams with a stiletto heel the next.

But it was her eyes that struck me most. They were brown, deep and alluring and almond-shaped. With weapons like that, she could either shatter a heart or weld metal, depending on her mood. That she was a journalist wasn't the only reason I felt I had to be on my guard.

"So what do you want, Ms Tang?" I ventured.

"I want to ask you some questions about Rufus Lam and Gadgetech."

I had led her over to a corner of the ground floor which meant we were out of range of the doors. No-one would walk past us or hear what we were saying.

"What makes you think I know anything?"

"Because you're Gadgetech's legal department."

"I am?"

"I've travelled a long way, Mr Lee. I'm not in the mood to play games." Her accent definitely smacked of an overseas education somewhere down the line, English or Australian, I wasn't sure which. Her attitude too, it was Hong Kong-pushy but with an edge to it that told me she wasn't afraid of confrontation. Probably even relished it.

"I don't know what you're talking about. And I don't know why you think I'm the head of the legal department of this Gadgetech place you keep talking about."

"Your secretary already told me. So can we stop messing around please?"

I narrowed my eyes in irritation. What the hell was Tabitha doing letting slip that information?

"Okay, the truth? It wasn't her fault," Amy Tang said, as if reading my thoughts. "I may have tricked her."

"May have?"

"Look, I am guessing you already know that I called your boss Napoleon Wong. He told me if I wanted any comment I could speak to his lawyer. So naturally, I phoned Gadgetech's main-line and asked to be put through to the legal department."

"Naturally," I said.

"They put me through to your secretary who answered saying 'Scott Lee's phone'," quote-marking my name. "I asked if I could speak to you. She said you had gone out, but would be back later. So I just waited outside for someone who looked like they might be called 'Scott Lee' to turn up here. With a Gweilo name like that, when I saw you approaching the building, I took a chance. Remember what I said when I walked up to you?"

"You said 'Scott Lee?'"

"And you answered 'yes'. So I know your name, I know you're the head of the Legal Department at Gadgetech and I know your boss has referred me to you to talk about Rufus Lam."

"I don't think I care for your methods, Ms Tang," I said. But that was a lie. Truth was, I was blown away by them.

"It's not breaking the law to make a few phone calls. So let's talk."

"No comment," I said.

"Oh come on," she bit her lower lip provocatively and swayed side to side. "We don't want to play that game do we?"

"And what game would that be?"

She shrugged a 'fair-enough' shrug.

"I'm going to write this story anyway and it's not looking like there will be a favourable slant on Gadgetech, if you know what I mean. So why not talk to me and convince me otherwise? Tell me Gadgetech's side of things."

I stuffed my handkerchief back in my pocket. It was no longer the air-conditioning that was sending a chill down my spine.

"I know a bluff when I see one, Amy," I said, since we had gravitated to first name terms. "You're fishing for facts you don't have yet. No facts, no story."

"You think I don't have facts?" she laughed. "Well let me see. I know that Rufus Lam is an investor in Gadgetech. I know that Terence Auyeung, one of Rufus Lam's closest business executives was put in place as Gadgetech's CFO. And I know he hasn't been seen in the last few weeks."

I said nothing.

Amy Tang smiled like a cat that got the cream. "They cancelled his speaking appointment for him at the Accountant's Chamber of Commerce. That's how I know. And I also know that Rufus Lam is now trying to sell his stake in Gadgetech, at the same time he has intervened in the election."

I held her stare a moment.

"Lam's selling his stake in Gadgetech? That's news to me." I said, I hoped convincingly enough, but her sigh indicated I was well wide of the mark.

"Your CEO confirmed it, Scott."

"I don't think he did...." I began, but then I recalled what Napoleon had told me. "Oh I get it. You asked Napoleon if Rufus Lam's decision to exit the ownership of Gadgetech had anything to do with Lam entering the election race. Napoleon told you it had nothing whatsoever to do with politics. And that answer, you think, gives you confirmation about the sale, right? A question that assumes facts, which the answer confirms. My, my, and I thought lawyers where unscrupulous."

"I prefer 'enterprising'", she said. "Anyway, where were we? Oh yes, I was telling you I have enough for a story. Which by the way, I am going write anyway and kill the deal unless..."

"Unless I give you something more."

She clicked her fingers and pointed. "Now you're getting it!"

My five am start had made this a long enough day already, but there was still a lot of it ahead of me. I made a show of checking my watch, playing for time, figuring out the best way out of this mess.

"Don't you journalists need a note-pad, a tape-recorder or something like that if I'm going on the record?"

She reached into her pocket and pulled out her phone, smoothed her fingers across its screen in a practiced technique getting to the right function.

"Hey, I didn't say I was going to go on the record. I was just asking about your recording methods."

Amy seemed to ignore my last comment and held the phone out to me like a microphone. I ducked backwards like it was going to bite me. We stood like that for about a minute, like two prize fighters working out each other's next move, although the way she had played me so far, I already had the sense that Amy Tang was five moves ahead. The speed at which she had manipulated me into this position was admirably frightening.

Time to come out of the corner punching, I decided.

"What do you want to ask?" I said.

"What's the connection between Rufus Lam's decision to exit the ownership of Gadgetech, Terence Auyeung's seeming disappearance and Lam entering into the CE election race?"

"Firstly, I am not sure what you're talking about when you mention Auyeung's disappearance or Rufus Lam's decision to exit the ownership of Gadgetech. But if Lam has decided to sell up, then the only person who would know the reason for it is Rufus Lam. You should be asking him. Not me."

She pulled away her hand and switched off the phone.

"That's not very helpful, Scott. I'm disappointed." She shrugged her shoulders in a way that pushed cutesiness off the scale. "Well, I guess I'll have to write the story without you."

She took a step back, making to leave.

"You could do that. Or…" I drew the word out. It hooked her like I knew it would.

"Or what?"

I shoved my hands deep into my pockets and gave her my best penitent school boy look. "Like I said, the best person to know what goes on in Rufus Lam's head is Rufus Lam. But I'm guessing getting an appointment with him is not that easy right now, especially for a pushy journalist like yourself."

"What's your point?"

I took a step forward and dropped my voice. "Maybe I'm seeing Rufus Lam tonight. And maybe, if you hold back on your story for now, I'll ask him your question and tell you what he says."

She shook her head. "Nice try, but no-one gets an appointment with Rufus Lam."

I shrugged. "You think I'm bluffing, suit yourself. Doesn't matter. Go ahead. Write your story. But every second you're typing, think how much better it would be if you had a quote from Lam."

She folded her arms and pondered, weighing up pros and cons.

"What's your meeting with him about?"

"You can't work that out for yourself?" Now it was my turn to toy with her. "You're the one who mentioned something about him selling his stake in Gadgetech. I am the lawyer who works for Gadgetech, so…."

It was enough to get her over the line.

"Okay," she said. "But I want your phone number, your home address and your promise we meet tomorrow morning and you tell me what he said. And you better make it worth my while."

I gave her my contact details, just like she asked.

As she walked away, I wondered how long it would take before I began to regret that move.

CHAPTER SEVENTEEN

I made it back to my flat by seven, showered off the sweat and stress which the day had so far brought me, then readied for the evening's bout.

Phil had told me to dress casual. I chose some khaki chinos and a black polo shirt lurking at the back of my cupboard. The chinos had pleats and the shirt smelt of moth balls. Damned if I could remember when I had bought them. Probably back in the eighties, when they were last in fashion, judging by the sewn-in turn-ups.

Slumping down on the couch, I turned off the lights and let the city's glow wash over me through the windows. That's the thing about Hong Kong. When they say it's twenty-four hours, they aren't kidding. The swish of traffic drifting up from the street below was a constant hum, punctuated only by the burst of a Maserati's V8 engine, giving its driver a few seconds' thrill between red lights. The neon skyline bathed my apartment, dancing shadows flittering across the walls.

Not for the first time, I wondered what I was still doing in this city. It surrounded me with noise and light and the kind of flaunted wealth and privilege that I had never seemed to mind on someone else, but could never accept for myself. I was out of place in Hong Kong, somehow I had always known that. My Seiko watch was adequate enough for me to tell the time, it didn't need to be a status symbol. I wore clothes for comfort not fashion, ate when I was hungry, cooked mostly at home and on the odd occasion when I did go out, I read menus right side across, prices first. It wasn't that I resented wealth. I just didn't understand it and since showing off seemed like harder work than living within one's means, I was content to let the city just pass on by me as I spectated from the sidelines.

What kept me here? I had often wondered. Maybe it was because I was stuck in a kind of apathy that made it impossible for me to move any place else. Or maybe it was because there was no place for me to move on to. Whatever the case, until I found a suitable alternative, Hong Kong was as close to home as I was ever going to get.

The sound of my phone lifted from my musings.

A message from Phil. *On my way. Get your ass downstairs.*
Charming.

I texted an acknowledgement and headed out into the night.

I waited by the curb on Wong Nai Chung Road, watching out for Phil's Mercedes. Since every other car that passed by was a Mercedes, it was no easy task.

A taxi pulled up at the curb.

"Don't just stand there. Get in!" Phil yelled at me from the back seat.

I jogged over, did as I was told and we sped off at a speed that made you wonder why anybody spent money on sports cars, when a Hong Kong taxi ride got you the same thrill at a fraction of the cost.

After a few minutes, it dawned that Phil was ignoring me in a petulant frump. He had this look on his face which said he wanted me to know it too.

"Let me guess." I eventually broke the ice. "You're still annoyed with me."

Phil's jaw muscles tensed.

"Would it help if I apologized?"

"It would help if you guaranteed never to pull a stunt like that again. It's all round the office that I had a naked man in my room."

I looked at him. "I'm kind of surprised you think a guarantee from me is worth anything. I thought you knew me better than that."

"You're unbelievable!"

"Thanks! But don't say it too loud, those office gossips might read more into it."

He looked like he was about to explode, so I took it down a level.

"Okay, okay," I held up three fingers like a good boy scout, "I hereby promise never to take my clothes off in your office again....unless you give me permission, of course. Now are we friends again?"

He didn't answer, but I knew the moment had passed. Face had been restored. He was senior partner again. The big Kahuna. In charge.

Sheesh!

"So what's with the taxi?" I asked.

"Rufus Lam likes to keep things low profile."

Fair enough, I thought. But Phil had a Mercedes and in Hong Kong Benzes were as low profile as you could get. The car of choice if you wanted to blend into a crowd and...but then I got it.

"Guess that personalized number plate's not looking such a good idea now, huh!"

Again, with the silent treatment.

After looping the wide arc round Happy Valley racecourse, the taxi took the flyover north before jolting down into the Cross Harbour tunnel.

"What is it with this Rufus Lam guy anyway?" I asked after a while. "You're acting like he walks on water. Has he promised you business if I help him out? Is that how this works?"

"Screw you, Scott!"

"Hey, I was only asking."

The taxi driver stopped to pay the toll on the other side of the tunnel on Kowloon side. I saw Phil's face in the glow from the light in the booth, locked in a deep frown, his features strained. My old Uni-buddy was showing signs of age. That made me feel old too.

"Hong Kong needs people like Rufus Lam to take a stand," he said after the taxi started moving again.

"You mean in the CE election?"

He nodded.

"Why?"

He looked at me like I was an idiot. "You know what most of my time as Law Society President is taken up with? Fighting with the Secretary of Justice every time he wants Beijing to override a Court of Final Appeal decision by clarifying the Basic Law."

"What? Ringo Pang? I thought he was one of the few people in government who had his head screwed on right?"

"Ringo's an A-One bastard," Phil said. "He sees which way the wind is blowing, the way in which Hong Kong is being slowly emasculated and blended into becoming just like any other part of China. Day by day, One Country-Two Systems is being eroded. We keep going like this, in ten years time the two systems piece will be history and before you know it, we're just the southern-chinese city of Hong Kong. Ringo Pang, he thinks it's inevitable, so why fight it? Why not just go with the flow, help it along by overruling the Court of Final Appeal wherever possible so he can ingratiate himself with the Central People's Government."

I sighed. "That's a pretty depressing picture you're painting, buddy!"

"It's the truth. Look around you, Scott. Look at Causeway Bay. There used to be a Tsa-tsan Teng on every corner. Dai Gal Lok used to be in Time Square for chrissakes. Normal people could go in and buy a meal. Now what have you got? Hand-bag shops, watches, designer labels, all catering for the Mainland tourists who are flooding into the place. Hong Kong's culture is being eroded just through force of numbers. And what does our government do about it? Nothing. Someone's got to make a stand before it's too late."

"And you think that someone is Rufus Lam?"

"Why not? He's got money, influence. Beijing hates his newspapers and he's worried that before long they're going to stretch the Basic Law to censor him. So he's got reason to fight this, too."

"Tell me something, Phil," I said. "Did you know he was going to intervene in the CE election, before you got me involved in this thing with Gadgetech?"

Phil sighed. "Look I may have known he was thinking of backing a candidate. But this civil disobedience thing! Threatening not to pay his taxes! I had no idea."

"Think it'll work?" I asked.

"I think it's a brave move, but he's playing with fire. Actually, it's worse than that. He's toying with Beijing."

We lapsed into silence.

Ten minutes later we were heading towards Sai Kung. The further we drove, the lighter the traffic got. Eventually, the taxi pulled into an underground bus depot. Phil paid the driver and got out.

"Come on, we're changing."

"Changing?"

"What are you, a tourist? This is the New Territories. We need a green one."

He pointed to a taxi on the other side of the depot and I got his meaning. The New Territories was the exclusive jurisdiction of green cabs according to the Government's taxi licensing system. Red for urban, green for New Territories, blue for Lantau. Living on the island it was easy to forget there was a Hong Kong beyond the urban sprawl, a Hong Kong that was as rural and free from congestion as any part of the world. A place that offered quiet, solitude, room to breathe and, yes, green taxis.

"One – three – one." Phil told the taxi driver in Cantonese.

I had no idea what he was talking about. Some sort of code, only understood by the locals, perhaps?

"Where are we heading?"

"You'll see soon enough," Phil said trying to be enigmatic, as if he was ushering me through a series of secret rituals into a world that only tycoons inhabited, where even the air was more rarified than the stuff I breathed day in, day out.

'Whatever', I thought, but I confess part of me was curious, especially when the cab turned off the main road and down a dust track, crunching gravel underneath us and bobbling through pot-holes. The streetlights disappeared. In the darkness, I began to wonder if this was sensible. If I got stranded would anybody find me? If I died here how long would it take for my remains to be discovered? The imagination can conjure up the strangest scenarios at the most inopportune of moments. Yet try as I might, I couldn't veer it off course.

It had been a long day, but somehow I felt it still hadn't yet begun.

Eventually, the cab pulled to a halt. We got out and I quickly took stock of my bearings. Yup, just as I thought. The middle of goddam nowhere.

My attention focused on a whitewashed wall over to my left. As the taxi's lights arced across it, moths the size of bats (or they may even have been bats) flitted into view. Geckos scampered like salamanders across its bobbly surface.

The taxi disappeared leaving us to the darkness.

Silence. No, not quite. The steady chirruping of those geckos and the lapping of water provided the soundtrack. But it was still a hundred decibels quieter than the city; a hard, awkward, tense quiet.

"Where are we Phil?"

"This way," he said.

I followed the sound of his Italian leather shoes crunching the gravel. We rounded a corner. It led to a gate. Through the gate I saw some windows with lights on.

Thank God for that.

"What is this place?"

"One-Thirty-One. One of Sai Kung's best kept secrets." Phil said with a sense of satisfaction that was lost on me. "Keep your underwear dry, Scott. It's a French restaurant, one of the best in Asia.

The chef used to be at the Mandarin Hotel. It's got Michelin star status written all over it. We're in for a rare treat tonight."

My foreboding disappeared.

"This is what Rufus Lam calls low profile?" I couldn't hide my disappointment. Dining at a Michelin star restaurant may have been a life long ambition for some people, but it was my idea of torture. Large plates with tiny bits of food dressed up as art.

Phil fawned over that sort of thing and was in his element. He swung open an iron-gate set in a high-brick wall and nodded me to go first.

I stepped through the gate. A trellis of vines reached down and tickled my head in the darkness. Another step took me out onto a moonlit pathway which trailed round an open expanse of lawn. The path led up to what must have been the restaurant's front door.

The night air tasted pure, its texture delicate and ethereal. I took a moment to enjoy the peace.

It didn't last.

The touch on my shoulder was light at first. I thought it was Phil trying to get my attention, but as I turned, the sharp dig of meaty fingers stabbed deep into the muscle to the right of my neck.

Pure, eye-watering pain seared through me. The type of pain that paralyzes everything, even the ability to scream. Instead, my mouth emitted a pathetic low rasp.

It must have taken only a few seconds for my survival instinct to kick in, but it seemed like an age. In almost disembodied fashion, I felt my hands move to my shoulder, desperately trying to prise the hand off me. For whatever reason my mind noted the smooth hairlessness of my attacker's fingers as my hopeless attempt led to the grip closing even tighter, turning up the pain to unbearable notches.

Gritting my teeth, I forced myself to bear it and through an aperture of clarity, I realised fighting wasn't going to work.

Instead, I went with the force, allowing myself to drop down on one knee. My downward trajectory was enough to loosen the grasp for the split second I needed. Pushing with my feet, I dove forward, tearing myself away from my attacker. I hit the grass in a disjointed roll. It wasn't elegant, but it was effective enough.

I knew I had to get to my feet quickly, so I scrambled around and upwards readying myself for the next wave.

But I wasn't fast enough.

The cold click of steel froze me in mid-crouch.

My eyes focused in terror on the barrel of the gun, now pointed half a metre from my forehead.

I tried to calm my shallow breathing, take in what was happening, but it was moving too fast for me to get a grip on anything.

"Stop, he's with me!" Phil's voice filtered through the buzzing in my head.

My attacker, up until that moment, had been just a large statue-like shadow, looming over me, as my concentration fixed firmly on the revolver. It took every effort in the world to see beyond that instrument of death and get a good look at its owner.

"You're a woman!" I heard myself saying

Call it deep-seated misogyny or just a damaged ego, but those were the first words out of my mouth at the realization that I had just been bettered by a member of the fairer sex. She was a mighty specimen too. Six-three at least, broad crocodile shoulders, dressed head to foot in black, her dark sheen hair bunned-up tight. Her face was full of sharp edges, prominent cheek bones, pointed chin and dead, unfeeling eyes focused on the centre of my forehead, where her gun was still aimed.

I raised my hands slowly, showing her empty palms.

"Someone told me the food here was to die for. Never thought they meant it literally."

Humour, my one defence in times of stress. No-one laughed, not even me.

"Cherry Blossom, he's with me!" Phil said again, this time with more force.

Cherry Blossom?

I just stayed quiet.

Cherry Blossom took one hand off the gun and clicked her fingers. That was the signal for two goons to emerge through the gate I had just walked through. Both were stocky with buzz-cut hair and oversized bull necks and deltoids which owed more to steroids than nature. They weight-lifter waddled over to me. The first picked me up by the collar, like I was a feather. He pulled my arms up and used his meaty calf to lever my feet apart, so I was in a star stance. The other one patted me down from behind. Arms, shoulders, belt, down to my feet then up the legs, paying particularly close attention to the groin.

"I'm usually not this easy, but I've always been a sucker for muscle-bound morons."

"Shut up, Scott!" Phil told me.

I didn't argue.

The goon behind me grunted something affirmative after he'd finished the pat-down. He and his partner waddled off at Cherry Blossom's silent command. Only then did she take the gun off me and slip it into her waistband. Turning to Phil, she gave what was either a grimace or a smile, I wasn't sure which and signaled for us to continue to the restaurant.

"Thank you," Phil said.

"No chance of a second date, then?" I called after her as she disappeared through the gate.

"Will you shut up!"

"No I won't shut up. In case you hadn't noticed, some giant from the island of Lesbos just came this close to putting a bullet through my skull. So if you don't mind, I'll take a moment to enjoy the fact that I still have the ability to speak by asking you what the hell was all that about?"

"That was Cherry Blossom. She heads up Rufus Lam's bodyguard detail. She's ex-Taiwanese Military Police."

"Rufus Lam has a bodyguard detail?"

"With his wealth? Of course!"

"You knew that and you didn't warn…?" I stopped. "Oh wait, I get it."

"Get what?" Phil started on up the path.

"That's why you let me go through the gate first. You knew they'd jump me. Your way of paying me back for taking my clothes off in your office, right?"

"Can we just go and eat?"

I stood there shaking my head.

Phil Yip. I never knew he had that kind of evil streak in him

Probably came from hanging around with me too long.

CHAPTER EIGHTEEN

One-Thirty-One was empty.

Whoever the proprietor was, though, had done a real number with the ambience. The place was full of continental charm, all terracotta-honey walls and soft lighting. A pair of patio doors off to the left looked out onto a gorgeous star-lit garden sloping down to a picturesque bay where the water shimmered in the night. It took my breath away, which was saying something after what I'd just been put through. Here was a side to Hong Kong I had never known before. A searing, calming, beautiful escape.

"Three Fathoms Cove," Phil said. "Impressive, isn't it?"

I rubbed my shoulder. It felt as bruised and mangled as my ego. Looking out onto Three Fathoms Cove, though, it seemed surreal that only a few minutes ago I had been staring down the barrel of a gun. The roller-coaster ride of Hong Kong life: it just never knew when to let up.

I went to wash my hands and splash some water on my face. The adrenalin dump was ebbing and fatigue was setting in. But I was here for a reason, so I told myself to get my head straight. After doing what I could to brush the grass stains out of my eighties Chinos, I put on my game face and rejoined Phil.

"How do you know about this place?" I asked him.

"Not me. This was Rufus's pick. You wanted to meet him, so we go wherever he says. He's booked out the whole place just for this meeting, so I hope whatever you've got to ask is worth it."

"Where is he, then?"

"Right here, Mr Lee."

I turned to where the voice had come from.

There he stood. The tall, thin figure of Rufus Lam, leaning nonchalantly against the door frame, taking me in, weighing me up for size. His shock of blonde hair shimmered under the soft lighting, his face was serious but good-humoured with it, as if bridging the gap between hard-nosed business man and fun-loving philanthropist that seemed to go with his image. A character was what you might call him on first impressions, especially the way he was dressed. He was wearing a mango shirt, topped with a paisley cravat and a silver-buttoned navy blazer, so perfectly tailored it looked like it had been made by an ethereal force. His creased white slacks and black shoes sparkled. The silver-topped black cane he was carrying completed the picture of the eccentric, handsome billionaire at rest after a brutal day in the boardroom.

"I see you met Cherry Blossom," Lam motioned with his eyes to the grass stains on my trousers. "She can be a bit rough, I know. But a man in my position can't be too careful."

"And what position might that be?" I asked.

It was a fair enough question in the circumstances, I felt, but still I could sense Phil tense up beside me, telepathically pleading with me not to embarrass him, not here, not now, not with Rufus Lam.

Lam flicked his eyebrows. His handsome face took a moment to weigh my comment.

"You think my obsession with personal security to be over the top, Mr Lee? Perhaps it is. But five years ago, my nephew was kidnapped. He was eighteen years old then, and they snatched him during his first year at university. We heard nothing for a week, other than an order not to call the police. I wanted to, but his mother, my elder sister, pleaded with me not to. Seven days later we received the ransom demand. The longest seven days of my family's life. I paid it, of course, half a billion dollars. Money means nothing at a time like that, not when it's your family."

The silent pause which followed was like a lead weight in the atmosphere.

"It changed my family's life." Lam leaned on his cane and shook his head at the memory. "Every time I see my nephew now, it reminds me that wealth comes at a cost. And that cost includes having to surround myself by a wall of security that makes people like you, Mr Lee, think I am a dilettante."

I wished the ground would open up and swallow me. "I apologise," I said. "I had no idea."

"Not many people do. I managed to keep the matter private and out of the press, because….well, the truth is I practically control much of it, so that part was easy. Some people may say that kind of self-censorship is arrogant and goes against the principle of freedom of speech. But I owe my nephew that much. He had gone through enough. It was important he be left alone to put the experience behind him."

Rufus Lam stepped forward. "You weren't to know, of course, Mr Lee, and given Cherry Blossom's rough handling of you, I don't blame you for being somewhat terse. But I hope you understand why I have to be careful."

He gave me a handshake replete with gravitas and in that moment, I was star-struck, meeting a man who bore such huge responsibilities on his shoulders. I had known him a few minutes and Rufus Lam had put me at ease.

"I guess it goes without saying, I've heard a lot about you," I said. It must have sounded weak and lame and I sensed Phil breathing a sigh of relief.

"Please sit," Lam said.

We went over to a table by the window. As soon as we had settled, a waiter emerged. Lam handed him the silver-topped cane. It was odd to see someone using such an item in this day and age. But it was Lam's trademark, one of his eccentricities which marked him out from everyone else. HongKongers recognized him as 'the man with the cane'. Most of the photos I had dug up during my research pictured him with it, as if it was an extension of him.

Without a word, the waiter poured us some wine. A Petrus, no less. And at the sight of the golden liquid sweating temptingly in the glass, the familiar salty taste of temptation tingled across my tongue. Years of practice meant I was able to control it, but its untimely resurrection served as a reminder of my weakness.

"Could we have some sparkling water, please?" Phil asked. I saw Rufus Lam's eyebrow flicker in surprise.

"Not joining me in a drink tonight, Philip? I'm sure Scott could do with one after his encounter with Cherry Blossom."

"Yes of course, I will Rufus," Phil said. "It's just that…"

"Mr Lam," I jumped in. "What you're witnessing here is how good a friend Phil is. The fact is it's me who doesn't drink. I used to and I liked it. In fact I liked it a lot and that was a problem. So now, just sparkling water for me. I guess, since you shared that story about your nephew, it's only fair that I put my deepest darkest secret out there too."

"I see," Lam said earnestly. "Friendship like that is important. And so is honesty. So let me also be honest with you," he looked at me with serious eyes and I wondered what the hell I had done now. "I hate being called Mr Lam. Rufus is fine."

Rufus Lam started laughing. It started as a high pitched chuckle before lowering into a deep and hefty laugh that spread the room in the warmth of his personality. As he slapped me amicably on the arm, I felt his charisma envelope me and for a moment, I was a believer, just like Phil. A believer that, yes, here was the man that Hong Kong needed. A man whose time had come.

The starters came: Gravalax with a dill and lemon sauce. Rufus and Phil gossiped about the great and the good of Hong Kong, people whom I had only read about. I stayed quiet, listened and savoured the smoked salmon which was really quite something. It was only when the main course of lamb arrived – pink to perfection and a melting, superlative texture – that Rufus Lam turned his attention back to me.

"So Scott, you are the man Philip has hired to do some detective work for me. You wished to ask me some questions?"

The lamb chops tasted like they had been cooked by the gods. The trouble was I had finished them in two bites. Michelin star restaurants, who needed them?

I turned to Rufus Lam and asked, "What do you think of Napoleon Wong?"

"What do I think of him? May I ask why that is important?"

I noted the avoidance.

"Mr Lam...I mean, Rufus...you have asked me to find out what happened to your friend, Terence Auyeung. He disappeared while protecting your investment in Gadgetech, the company that Napoleon Wong runs. Now you're selling your shares in Gadgetech to Wong. The state of your personal relations between you and Wong could shed some light on the reasons for Terence Auyeung's disappearance."

Lam sipped his wine. "Very well. As a businessman, I think Napoleon Wong has certain skills that keep Gadgetech running well."

"And as a person?"

"As a person?" Lam considered my question. "I do not know Napoleon Wong as a person. We do not meet socially."

I gave a low chuckle.

"You find it funny that I don't socialize with Napoleon Wong?"

"I find it funny that you feel the need to lie to me."

"Scott!" Phil almost choked on his lamb chop.

Rufus Lam, by contrast, appeared completely non-plussed by my accusation, so I bulldozed away.

"Forgive my directness, but I'd have a better chance of finding out what happened to Terence Auyeung if I knew the whole truth."

Lam seemed amused. "In what way do you believe I am being untruthful?"

"I think you know exactly the sort of person Napoleon Wong is. I think before you invested in Gadgetech, you did a full due diligence on him. And now you're desperate to get out of Gadgetech, so soon after Mr Auyeung's disappearance. That says a lot."

"It's because Terence has disappeared that Rufus is selling, I told you that," Phil said. "He was there to protect Rufus's investment in Gadgetech. Now he's gone, Rufus is doing the sensible thing and getting his money out." Phil looked imploringly at me, pleading with me to stop this line of questioning.

"Sorry, Phil, but that isn't the full picture. That's why I wanted to meet you this evening, Rufus. To fill in the gaps because I like to know what I'm getting myself into."

"You are stepping out of line, Scott!" Phil snapped.

"Maybe, I am," I said, then turned to address Rufus Lam. "But you have hired me to find out what happened to Mr Auyeung, by going into Gadgetech on the quiet. And that doesn't make any sense. You see, you're still an owner in Gadgetech, Rufus. You own your shares right up until the moment you sell them. So right now, you have access to all the information you need. And if you were such a good friend to Auyeung, you'd be using your right to gain access to that information. But you're not. You're selling your stake to Wong. And you're selling in a hurry. I want to know why."

Silence hit the room like the aftermath of an earthquake. Here I was sitting next the most powerful man in Hong Kong and I had just accused him of lying.

But that was the thing about not having a career any more. There was nothing holding me back from putting noses out of joint, no matter how powerful they were. It was something I was fast discovering I had a knack for.

Rufus Lam cast a long gaze through the window. Eventually, a wry smile spread across his lips.

"Your friend here is very perceptive, Philip. If a little direct."

"That's putting it mildly," Phil did little to hide his irritation. "Scott's way of doing things has always been a bit unorthodox. If I told you what he did to convince me to set up this meeting, you wouldn't believe me. But here we are. That's the thing, Rufus. Scott's the best at what he does because he pushes limits no-one else is prepared to push. It's not pretty."

"Well, let's see just how effective, shall we?" Rufus Lam looked at me. "I will answer your question, Scott. But as the client, I think I'm entitled to ask you something first. You obviously believe there is more to this than what you've been told. Why? What have you found out?"

I shifted in my seat. I never liked showing my hand before getting what I wanted, but Rufus Lam, like the wily business veteran he was, had turned the tables, taking Phil's damn compliment and using it to open me up like a can of beans.

What the hell.

"Terence Auyeung was stealing from you," I said.

I let the statement sit there a moment before pushing on.

"You put your friend into Gadgetech to look after your investment and he fiddled the books for his own advantage. It was a good scam, don't get me wrong, but it didn't take me long to crack it. Auyeung set up a company called Seemax Limited and hid his ownership through a BVI holding company. Probably more than one, but I haven't been able to get past the first layer. Then he used his CFO position to get Seemax a consultancy gig with Gadgetech and paid out on a number of invoices which he, as CFO approved. Each invoice was small enough not to be noticed in isolation, but when you add them all up it comes to three million bucks. Since his disappearance, no more Seemax invoices have been submitted. So that's what I've found out Rufus. After two days. But you want to know something else?"

He signaled for me to continue.

"I think you already know all of this. And I think it's got something to do with why you're having to sell out of Gadgetech on the cheap."

"Scott I think you should...." Phil wanted me to slow down.

"No, no," Rufus stopped him. "I need to hear this."

I took a deep breath and then asked the question I was there to ask. The one that went right to the heart of this whole set-up.

"Is Napoleon Wong blackmailing you into selling your shares in Gadgetech to him at a knock-down price?"

Rufus Lam stood up, took two steps over to the patio doors, thrust his hands deep into his pockets and rocked back and forth on his heels.

"This is a beautiful spot don't you think?" The question seemed directed at no-one in particular, less a question than a juncture in his thought process, spinning, cogitating, wondering, weighing up whether to respond with the truth or continue to play diversion. He was in no hurry whatsoever. After all, who the hell was I push him on this.

"Such a shame that most people in Hong Kong don't know about this place. But then again, its seclusion is part of its charm."

I looked over at Phil wondering what we should do next. Phil shrugged his shoulders.

Eventually Rufus Lam turned, sat back down and sipped his wine.

"It's not something I am proud of." His words came out in a low whisper. For a moment I wasn't sure if I had heard them, as if they had been said in some sort of dream. But, yes, Rufus Lam had given his answer.

"It was Terence's wife who told me she hadn't seen him in days," Lam said. "When I rang Napoleon to ask what had happened, he demanded to meet. I should have known from the tone in his voice that something like this was coming. Napoleon always did have a supercilious tone about him, but this was something different. There was a vindictiveness there. So I met him and you are right, Scott, he told me what Terence had done. He knew all about the 'theft of company assets', as he put it. He blamed me for it because I was the one who had insisted Terence work there." By now Rufus Lam was shaking his head, self-disappointment etched on his experienced face.

"Then came the request to buy me out," he continued. "Only it wasn't a request. It was a demand. It's a long time since someone has spoken to me like that. But Napoleon felt he had all the cards in his hand. I was to blame because Terence was my friend, he said, and as such I should pay the price. Or else."

"Or else what?" Phil asked.

"Or else he would go to the newspapers with it. Not my newspapers of course, but my competitors. And they wouldn't think twice about printing it and running the story for weeks on end. Not that I was too worried about that. But it was Terence's family I had to think of. I didn't want to put them through that. They didn't deserve it."

"That's outrageous," Phil said and he wasn't wrong. But I was sure there was more to Rufus Lam's motives than looking out for his best friend's family.

"I guess your forthcoming intervention in the Chief Executive's election had something to do with your decision, right?" I said. "I mean a scandal like this would hardly help your cause. Better to settle it quietly, do what Wong wants and let Gadgetech go."

My words looked like they stung like vinegar. No man likes to be brought face to face with the selfish ambition that drives him. But I knew that whilst selfishness was not always the sole driver for the decisions we make, it was certainly close to the heart of things.

Rufus Lam looked like he was about to argue, his eyes flashing with a dark anger that made me think I had crossed a line which should have stayed uncrossed. Something stirred inside me; a sickness at the pit of my stomach. But just as quickly as the anger in Rufus Lam had ignited, so it simmered away leaving me wondering whether it had been there at all.

"You have a very direct style, Scott," Lam said to me, "and you are right. The election was part of my considerations. It has been for some time now. Do you know when I first contemplated this step?"

I shook my head.

"October 2014."

I thought for a moment then nodded. "You're talking about the Umbrella Protests," I said. "You were a supporter?"

"Not openly," Lam said. "But privately, I was. It was an utterly exhilarating moment in Hong Kong's history, don't you think? Tens of thousands of students and teenagers, standing up for what they believed in, occupying the streets in a show of civil disobedience. Despite the government's provocation, they stayed peaceful, warding off the pepper spray and tear gas and rain and sun with nothing but umbrellas. Such a potent, but simple symbol. Hong Kong gained the attention of the world."

"Shame it failed to achieve its objectives," Phil said.

"Did it really fail, Philip? Is that what you think?" Rufus asked.

"Well, the government didn't budge an inch on election candidates having to be vetted by the nominating committee, did they?"

Rufus Lam sighed deeply and smiled to himself. "You know, during that time I would spend some evenings walking among the protestors. I dressed differently, so no-one knew who I was. What I witnessed left a deep impression on me. I have been in business for over twenty-five years, but I have never seen passion, strategy, teamwork and creativity like those youngsters displayed. Do you know what I did when it was over?"

"What?" Phil asked.

"I sent my recruitment manager into the universities and guaranteed jobs to some of the key behind-the-scenes participants when they graduated. Trust me, Philip, the demand for true democracy didn't die in 2014. The Umbrella Movement didn't fail. It just went into hibernation and matured and gained strength. Until now. What those students started, I am going to finish."

"By threatening not to pay tax?" Phil said. "You know that's a crime, Rufus! You could get arrested."

"It is also the ultimate and original form of civil disobedience, Philip."

"Original?"

"You're talking about Henry Thoreau," I said. "The American writer, who lived in the woods. He refused to pay his taxes because he didn't recognize a government that permitted slavery. Spent a night in jail for his trouble."

"I see you like reading, Scott." Lam said.

"I've had a lot of time on my hands."

"Well, you are right. I am prepared to do what Henry David Thoreau did. And I believe many will follow in my footsteps. Many of the Umbrella Generation are themselves tax-payers now, after all."

"Things could get ugly," I said. "You've thought of that?"

Rufus Lam nodded slowly. "Rest assured, I know what I am doing is a huge gamble. Not just for me, but for the people of Hong Kong. But we want and deserve a powerful voice. That is what I intend to give them."

"So that's it then. You're just giving up on Terence Auyeung," I said.

Rufus Lam's eyes shot me a dagger-like look. But again it quickly dissipated. "Don't misunderstand me, Scott. Just because I am selling out of Gadgetech, doesn't mean I'm selling out Terence. That is why I asked Philip for help and that is why he has found you, Scott. From what I have seen so far, I believe you are the right man for the task."

Phil seemed horrified. "Rufus, you can't let Napoleon Wong just blackmail you like this! You can't. It's just....well it's just not right."

Lam chuckled. "You, being a lawyer, will know that the difference between right and wrong is not always clear. But don't worry. I have dealt with many like Napoleon Wong before. Men with short-term ambition, who think they can get the better of others with pushy ways and unreasonable demands. So yes, I am giving into his short-term ambition. But that is all it is and that is something I can afford to do. Gadgetech was a good investment for me, but there will be others. And as far as Wong is concerned, he will in time discover that I am not a man to be trifled with. For now however, selling to him is the right thing to do." Lam turned back to me. "So where do we go from here?"

"I have one more question."

Lam nodded for me to proceed.

"Why did Auyeung steal from you?"

Lam let out a long sigh. "Like I said, the line between right and wrong is never easy for any of us to decipher. Terence was a good friend, but he had issues in his private life which I never asked about. And that was the catalyst for his actions here. A private family matter. Exactly what that matter was, I don't know. You have been to see his wife, I know. Gladys phoned to tell me. What she told you is all I know."

He fiddled with the stem of his wine glass. "I only wish Terence had come to me. Three million dollars is nothing. I know how that sounds, but it's true. I paid half a billion for my nephew. Terence is one of the few people who know about that. I would have given him the money in a second. I had no idea he was in so deep. But Terence is a proud man. He probably thought he would pay the money back before anyone even noticed. That pride, that determination, was what made him such a good businessman."

I sensed sincerity in his words and I decided not to push it further. I had many more questions, but the confirmation that Napoleon Wong was blackmailing Lam, at a time when Lam needed a lid kept on things because of his venture into the Hong Kong election, was enough to tell me that I was in the middle of something I should never have stepped into.

Realizations like this always come at the wrong time.
When it's too late to back out.

CHAPTER NINETEEN

5.30am.

The phone hammered me out of a convoluted dream, like a pile driver prising through my skull.

"I'm downstairs, I have coffee and I am ready for you to tell me how it went with Rufus Lam last night," a woman's voice said.

"Who the hell is this?" I heard myself croak.

"You mean you've already forgotten the friendly journalist you made a promise to yesterday? That's not very nice, Scott. Now buzz open the door. I'll just annoy your doorman until you do."

The pieces quickly fell into place. Amy Tang was on the war-path.

I buzzed her up and threw on some clothes. Leaving the front door ajar, I went to the bathroom and was in the middle of washing the sleep out of my eyes and massaging my tender shoulder, when she called out to me from the living-room.

"I hope you're decent."

"And I hoped I was going to get a few more hours sleep. Why do we have to do this so damn early? I was planning to call you later." I wandered out into the living-room, toweling my face and trying to ram my brain into gear.

She gave me a sly look. "Catching people off guard is how you get the truth. What happened last night with Rufus Lam?" She handed me a coffee and sat down on the sofa without being asked.

The first sip of coffee in the morning is pure perfection, like an explosion of bluebells in summer time. I let the caffeine go to work and slowly my thoughts came together. Amy looked pristine in a figure-hugging pencil suit, that alerted me to her alluring figure, which was saying something for that time of morning.

"Where the hell do you find a Starbucks open at five-thirty?" I asked taking another slug of latte.

"I don't reveal my sources," she shrugged, all cute-like, in a way that seemed to lace the allure with aggression. "What did you find out from Rufus Lam last night? Why's he selling Gadgetech? Where's Terence Auyeung?"

"Will you let me wake up first?"

"No! What happened?"

It was still dark outside. I shook my head to try and get some blood flow going. I had gotten in after midnight so I wasn't at my best, but the taxi ride home had given me time to order some thoughts, figure out where to go next.

And Amy Tang was part of it.

Yesterday she had caught me off guard, but despite her dawn raid I was ready with my play. The first of many in what was going to be another long day.

"You were right about Auyeung," I said. "He's gone. Disappeared."

"That's great Scott, but tell me something I didn't know. Like, where he is and why he's disappeared?"

I pretended to struggle with my conscience for a moment before answering, letting her think the journalistic third degree was breaking me down bit by bit.

"The 'where', I have no idea. No-one at Gadgetech does and nor does Rufus Lam, before you ask. Why he disappeared, I might be able to help with."

She pulled out a notebook and made a show of clicking the lid on her biro. "Go on."

I took a deep dramatic breath, pretending I was struggling with crossing the line, becoming a journalist's source.

"Auyeung was stealing from Gadgetech. Since Rufus Lam owns Gadgetech, Auyeung might as well have been stealing from Lam direct. So now you know."

Amy tried to poker-face me, but I caught her eyes widening with excitement. Christmas was coming early for her this year.

"Auyeung was stealing? Is that why Lam is selling his stake in Gadgetech to Napoleon Wong?" she asked after a beat.

"He didn't tell me."

"Come on…."

"Amy, he didn't tell me."

I looked her dead on, allowing her to search my face for tells. I gave her nothing. She wiggled the biro, tappity-tapping it on her note pad, putting it all together. "So, three years ago Lam invests in Gadgetech. He puts Auyeung in to keep an eye on the investment. Auyeung repays the trust by stealing from him. Now Lam is looking to dispose of his shares to Napoleon Wong. Why?" Again with the tappity-tap. Then it stopped. "Oh I get it. So the embarrassment of having one of his closest business allies stealing from him won't disrupt his election campaign."

She started to scribble, her hand moving fluidly across the paper and ending the summary with a stabbed full-stop. "You did good, Scott. This is something I can run with."

I made a face. "If you say so."

"There's more?"

"You're the journalist, you tell me."

She narrowed her eyes.

"What are you holding back?"

I did that 'wrestling with my conscience' thing again.

"I don't know this for sure, but I think...." I stopped myself.

"What?"

Casting a long gaze out of the window, I let Amy's eagerness build until it was brittle enough to snap with the lightest of touches.

"You're right. I did ask Rufus Lam why Auyeung was stealing from him."

"And what did he say."

"Nothing. Well, nothing concrete. But he did say that it was a private family matter."

"What does that mean?"

I shrugged.

Amy got up and started to pace, the hunger clear to see. The hook had been baited.

"I have to go and write this story!" she said after a moment.

"And what story might that be?" I asked, injecting a harsh edge to my tone. "Way I see it, Amy, you've got no story without evidence backing up your sources. I could give you that evidence. But I'm going to need you to do something for me first."

Amy Tang folded her arms, tapped her elbows and glared. "Scott Lee, are you blackmailing a journalist?"

"Who said anything about blackmail? I'm asking for your help because I figured we could help each other. I'm Gadgetech's lawyer. I need to find out what happened to Auyeung, just as much as you do. So why don't we work together?"

She took a step towards me and examined my face. I stared back into her eyes and felt her trying to play me with her stare, in the way that women do. It was a good try, but I was up to it, even at this time of morning.

"What do you want, Scott?"

"I want you to find someone for me."

"For us, you mean."

I shrugged an "if-you-say-so" and told her who I wanted her to locate.

"And what do I get in return?"

"Documentation which proves Auyeung was stealing from Gadgetech."

Amy sat back down on my sofa, threw an arm across its back and crossed her legs, making herself right at home.

"Okay, I'll do it. But if I give you what you want and you don't give me what I want...."

"Not going to happen, Amy. You can trust me on that."

She laughed. "You're a lawyer, Scott. It's not a profession with a great record of trust."

"This, from a journalist?"

"Touché," she said.

I was enjoying our little sparring match. It had been a while since a woman had flicked my interest buttons, but there was something about Amy Tang. A feistiness, that seemed to stem from a need to challenge everything in her path. Where that need came from, I had no idea, but there was part of me that wanted to find out.

"So what's he like?" Amy asked me, after a while.

"Who?"

She rolled her eyes. "Rufus Lam, of course. Hong Kong's self-appointed saviour!" The comment was dipped in sarcasm and spat out with a soupçon of cynicism.

"Not a fan, I take it?"

"Hey! I asked first. What's he like?" Ever the journalist.

I took another slug of coffee. "Impressive," I said. "A bit paranoid, but that's understandable for a man in his position, I guess. I'll say this for him. He has that 'sense of destiny' thing going on, that seems to be in the DNA of all successful business leaders and politicians. You know what I mean? That hubris which says: 'I am supposed to be doing this, because I am superhuman.'"

Amy giggled like a school girl.

"What?"

"So Scott Lee has fallen for the famous Rufus Lam charm. And I thought you had integrity. Well, it just goes to show how weak men can be."

I brushed the barb aside. "I'm right then. You're not a fan."

She shook her head.

"That must put you in a minority of one in the journalist community in Hong Kong, judging by what I've read."

"What can I say? My readers demand more insight."

This time it was my turn to stifle a laugh. "So you don't think the fact that he accounts for a large number of jobs in Hong Kong and is the epitome of a rags-to-riches story earns him some respect? You don't think the sacrifice he's making for democracy is a good thing?"

"Sacrifice?" Amy spat the word out like I'd insulted her. Her eyes blazed a sudden intense anger.

She took a deep calming breath and cast a long gaze round the walls of my flat.

"You like living here?" she asked.

"It's okay?" I replied, wondering where she was going with this.

"It's small."

"It's what I can afford."

She made a gun with her fingers and pretended to shoot me with it. "Bingo!" She said it like I had just uttered the key to life. I had no idea what cockamamy nonsense she was about to spill, so I just let her run with it.

"You're no different from anyone else in Hong Kong. Forced to be content paying an enormous portion of your salary to live in a cramped apartment, because tycoon land developers limit the supply to keep prices high."

It took a moment before the light-bulb went ding. "Oh I get it. And because Rufus Lam is a tycoon, you blame him for my....and Hong Kong's predicament. But he makes money selling papers, not real estate. And anyway, haven't you noticed that Hong Kong's not the most spacious place in the world. Land supply's limited. It's simple economics that drives the land price, not some tycoon conspiracy."

Amy made an 'eeeeh' sound in her throat and pretended to press a button on the sofa arm.

"Did you just quiz show buzz me?"

"I did, because, Scott Lee, you are completely wrong on both counts. Rufus Lam, not in real estate? Are you kidding me? That's just naïve. Sure he makes money selling papers. But what do you think he does with that cash-flow? He sticks it in hard assets. Real estate. Because that's where the real returns are. Only you don't know it because Lam's clever. He keeps his property investments out of the public eye. He teams up in joint-ventures with other tycoon buddies. And they are private ventures, so he avoids having to make any disclosures. Transparency's an enemy for a man like Lam. But you can bet that Lam's got a piece of most major developments that go on in Hong Kong, if only as a silent partner. And his tycoon developer friends are more than happy to team up with him. You know why?"

"No idea." I said.

"Because it's his papers that keep peddling the kind of rubbish that you've fallen for, Scott?"

"Okay, now I'm completely lost."

"Hong Kong's got no land supply, that's what we're all told, aren't we? We're just that same barren rock the British stole to sell opium to the Chinese with no space to speak of, that's the story we're fed! So we all have to live in high priced, fifty-storey blocks. But use your eyes, Scott! Hong Kong isn't just the island and Kowloon. North of Boundary Street, we have plenty of space. It's called the New Territories. Only we don't use it. Why? Because the government only tenders out new land for development when it wants to. They deliberately limit the supply."

"Okay, so what's the link with Rufus Lam?"

Amy rolled her eyes. "Put it together, Scott! The government limits the supply. But when they do tender a piece of land, it's in a portion that's so big only the ten biggest tycoon land developers in Hong Kong can afford it. And if you think it's a real tender process, you're wrong. Those guys share it out amongst themselves. You bid on this one, I'll get the next one."

"You've got evidence of that?"

She shook her head. "It's all done by phone calls, meetings in backrooms and handshakes. But it happens. The élite in this city pick up the land cheap, screw the taxpayer out of revenue, then add insult to injury by building pokey little flats and selling them at exorbitant prices. And you know why we put up with it?"

I shrugged for her to continue.

"Because of what Rufus Lam tells us in his newspapers. That land's in short supply. That it's just the way it is and we've got to make the best of it. While in the background he's right there taking his piece of the land development action. The rich get richer. The poor get poorer. And we all close our eyes to it."

Amy pushed her hair behind her ear and looked at me to come back.

I waited, taking in the intensity etched on her features and in the way in which she had put her argument. There was something she wasn't telling me.

"What about the stand Lam's making for democracy? You don't think he's trying to finish what the students tried to do when they occupied Central three years ago?"

She gave a derisive snort. "I think if you believe that, you don't understand what we were doing back then."

That made me take a step back.

"We?"

Amy leaned forward, flipped her jacket off one shoulder, stretched her collar open and twisted to show me something.

A small yellow Umbrella tattoo sat on the top of her shoulder, just below the neck.

"You were there?" I said. "A real-life Umbrella Movement veteran. I feel honoured."

"It was the last year of my PhD at Hong Kong University. Spent weeks in a tent at the protest site in Admiralty. I felt the sting of pepper spray in my eyes and the choke of tear-gas in my lungs. And you know why we all stood firm, even when sympathy for our cause was waning? Because we have a government that's controlled by the rich few at the expense of the rest of us. Hong Kong's the unfairest place in the world, don't you see that, Scott! The gap between rich and poor is sickening. Old ladies have to collect cardboard to make a living. The middle class live in tiny flats which cost the earth because the tycoons limit the land supply. We get to shop in a limited choice of supermarkets with extortionate food prices just to line tycoon pockets, because the whole thing's a cartel. We hustle along congested roads with no open space because every time a piece of land becomes free, they stick up another luxury block instead of a playground or a park or somewhere where we can have some open space. Sure we were protesting for democracy back then. But we were doing it because we thought if we could choose our government, it might make

Hong Kong a fairer and better place to live. We were doing it because of what people like Rufus Lam have done to our home!"

Amy leaned back on the sofa, her little outburst bringing instant relief to the uptight intensity that was her default setting. It was an outburst that told me a lot about her, about the dashed hopes and dreams of the Umbrella Generation she was part of. About its frustration; a frustration that had left Hong Kong so wound tight the place sometimes sizzled with tension.

But still, it wasn't the full story about Amy Tang. She was holding something back. I could sense it

"Is that why you're so interested in Rufus Lam?" I asked after a while.

Amy looked away from me, and I knew right then I was about to be fed something other than the truth.

"I think the people of Hong Kong have a right to know the truth about how the place they live in is really run. For the benefit of the few like Lam, at the expense of the many. Now he's trying to cast himself in the role of Hong Kong's champion of democracy. What a joke!"

I waited for her to continue, but she had said her piece, serving up statements of high principle that masked some hidden reality. This was personal for her, I could tell. Her passion went far deeper that just journalistic intrigue and political ideology.

Another item I added to my list of things to find out.

Right now, though, it was time to start my day.

CHAPTER TWENTY

Tabitha popped her head round my office door, just after 9am.

"Mr Wong isn't coming in today. Apparently he's ill."

"Apparently?" I asked. My attempts at thawing the ice-wall of professionalism which Tabitha had erected between us had so far not proven entirely successful. But her total lack of respect for Napoleon Wong was one thing on which we were fast finding common ground. As Terence Auyeung's former secretary, she came straight out of Rufus Lam's stable. The value of hard work was inculcated through to her core and as far as she was concerned, Napoleon Wong wasn't fit to shine Lam's shoes.

"Mr Wong has an Upper Respiratory Tract Infection," she said. "Or in plain English, a cold."

Tabitha was evidently an afficianado in the dark art of sarcasm. I always appreciated a fellow user.

"Thanks for letting me know."

Wong's day-long absence was music to my ears. After getting back home late the night before and Amy's early morning grilling, I needed to hit the pause button and think through the implications of the information I had so far learned.

My mobile rang.

It was as if the gods were conspiring against me.

"Hello!"

"Lawyer Lee. You not forget meeting seven o'clock tonight!" The staccato gun-fire of Mrs Lo's voice. "Combo need you. I need you."

"Don't worry, Mrs Lo, I'll be there. Your son's going to be there too, right?"

"Tak Ming coming. Don't know why. He useless. You a lawyer. I need you, not him."

We went through the routine of her offering me dinner, me declining and her ignoring me before the call ended. Its aftermath left me mulling over Combo's predicament. Hong Kong wasn't a great place for basset hounds. It was too humid, too built up, too damned uncomfortable. But it wasn't Combo's fault he was here. It was the fault of the breeder who had decided to make a quick buck selling cute little puppies. It was the fault of the Hong Kong fashionista who had fallen for Combo's soulful eyes because the furry little darling fit into her Prada handbag. Trouble was, puppies grew. In Combo's case, they grew big and round. Whoever had bought him had done the indecent thing and abandoned him to the government kennels. Combo had come within twenty-four hours of being put down, before Mrs Lo had turned up.

In return for being rescued, Combo provided Mrs Lo company in her old age, minding his own business and doing his best not to be noticed. Only some neighbour had now taken a dislike to Combo, not because of what he had done, but because of what he was; a dog.

I was in philosophical mood. Something about Combo's story chimed with my own. Neither of us really belonged in Hong Kong, but here we both were trying to make the best of it, without much luck.

To the outside world, Hong Kong was this great cosmopolitan city, accepting of foreigners and differences. But if you had lived here long enough, you soon recognized the prejudices that lurked below the surface. Prejudices against dogs in apartments. Prejudices against Mainland visitors. It added to the tension that already existed in this fast-paced, high-octane town. In recent months, I had begun to question why I liked this place. I mean, where else in the world would a neighbour – a policeman for chrissakes – go to such lengths to get rid of a dog belonging to an old lady?

When responding to a call for donations for earthquake and Tsunami victims, this city poured out its heart like no other. Other times, it could be callous and unfeeling and not even blink with shame. Hong Kong: it was still a riddle to me.

After a while my thoughts moved on and I began digesting what Amy Tang had told me about Rufus Lam that morning. How Hong Kong's saviour was, in her mind at least, the most pernicious force running through society, manipulating the news in his papers for the benefit of his own real estate investments which he kept hidden from the public. Was it true? I wondered. Did it really matter, if it was?

Probably not.

But I'll say this for Amy. She had piqued my interest. I went on-line and searched for articles she had written. Soon I was overwhelmed with material. Not only were there features in the *Economic Weekly*, but she ran a blog too, entitled "The Real Hong

Kong", which pledged to tell people how their unfair city really operated. I read post after post, drawn in by the tightness of her prose, the immaculate nature of her research and the outrageousness of her opinions.

Amy Tang was a crusader.

The premise running through her blog was that Hong Kong was built on a myth. It was not the perfection of free-trade and capitalism that everyone made it out to be. It was a city run by the tycoon élite for their own enrichment at the expense of the population. The big business families in Hong Kong controlled the government through high-level favours, like the odd trip on a private jet, use of a holiday home in the Bahamas or below-market-rent in a luxury tycoon-built development. In return, the government limited the land supply for development, turned a blind eye to the tycoon oligopolies that dominated the domestic market – supermarkets, electrical goods, utilities, cable television – and allowed them free rein to ignore corporate governance standards in a way that anywhere else in the world would have had minority shareholders racing to court. The result was this: Hong Kong was one of the unfairest places in the world with a chasm between the disgustingly rich at the top end and the down-trodden population at the other end, forced to line tycoon pockets every time they spent a single dollar.

I looked at the number of hits on Amy's blog. It wasn't impressive. But that hadn't stopped her venting her spleen at the rest of the press and at Rufus Lam in particular. Lam, according to Amy, was responsible for perpetuating the myth of Hong Kong's free market, because tycoons as a breed protected their own. In return for diverting stories away from fellow tycoon shenanigans, he shared in their wealth, taking minority stakes in many of his buddies' businesses.

To Amy Tang, Rufus Lam was public enemy number one. In her latest blog-post she derided his decision to intervene in the election as sheer self-interest. Rufus Lam was jumping on the legacy left by those who had made true sacrifices for democracy. Sure, Lam may give them hope again in the short term. But ultimately he would crush those hopes. Because Lam was thinking three steps ahead, trying to ensure, whatever the result of the election, that he and his tycoon cronies would still be in control at the end of it.

Phew!

It was a lot to digest. A week ago, I had been carefree. Now I was working for a tycoon, trying to find out what had happened to his closest business lieutenant, without it disrupting his audacious attempt to forge Hong Kong's path towards democracy. In doing so, I had unwittingly enlisted the help of the one journalist in Hong Kong who viewed the same said tycoon as Genghis Khan.

The one saving grace was, that so far, neither of them knew what I was doing for the other. But it was a delicate tightrope I was walking.

One slip and it was a long way down.

***

Taking a break, I went downstairs for some fresh air, my mind awhirl with Amy Tang and her iconoclastic views. It had been a while since I had met a woman so enamoured with the mental joust of debate. Good-looking too; not in a French Connection model type of way, but prim, cute and sassy with it.

I pushed the thought aside for later, went back to my office, picked up the phone and made a call.

"Don't tell me. You had a dream about being beaten up by a six-foot woman called Cherry Blossom. Let me reassure you, Scott. It wasn't a dream. I only wish I'd filmed it. Think of the number of YouTube hits, I'd get."

"Hey Phil," I said. "Did anyone ever teach you the first rule of comedy?"

"What's that….timing?"

"No. Be funny."

"Ha, bloody, ha."

"Listen up, I've got a question."

"Shoot!" Phil said.

"How much money does Rufus Lam make from real estate?"

Silence.

"Phil?"

"I got two answers for you Scott. What the hell has that got to do with anything? And how the hell do you think I would know?"

"You always answer questions with questions?"

"You always this annoying?" he shot back, then I heard a loud sigh on the line. "Seriously, Scott, why is this relevant to you finding Auyeung?"

"Does that mean you know the answer, but you're not telling me? Am I going to have to come down there and get naked again?"

Another loud sigh. "Okay. Look, yes, Rufus is a client of the firm. Nothing major, and no real repeat instructions yet. But we have done some work for him on the corporate side and it did relate to real estate. You know the Fragrant Harbour hotel chain?"

"Fragrant Harbour Hotels? Lam has a piece of that? I thought that was…"

"The Khong family's. Right. But Lam has a shareholding. Nothing much, just ten percent. We had to look over the joint-venture agreement for him. Look, Scott, as far as I know Lam does have some other property – as well as other – investments. What business man in his position doesn't? It's called diversification. But his main business is still media. That's what he knows, that's his bread 'n butter. That enough, or do you need more?"

I made a note, then decided to stir the pot, by throwing in a little of what I had learned reading Amy's blog. "So the Khongs sell Rufus Lam a minority stake. In return Lam gives them good press and avoids looking too closely at their corporate governance abuses. Is that how it works?"

"What? No, of course not."

"There's an obvious conflict, surely? Lam's in a position to quash adverse stories about the people he does business with. I bet he keeps his dealings with people like the Khongs secret. The corporate structure of the joint venture which the firm worked on. Let me guess; three layers of companies with the parent incorporated in the Cayman Islands?"

Pause.

"Labuan, actually, smart ass! Anyway, who died and made you Mother Theresa?" Phil said.

"So much for freedom of the press."

"The press is free under Lam!" Phil snapped at me. "Look at the way he's going after Beijing's anointed contender for Chief Executive. The guy's fearless. And do you remember when the Head of Planning Department had to resign because he hadn't declared that his wife's family owned those commercial properties he had just re-zoned so they could be redeveloped and sold as luxury flats? It was Lam's papers who broke the story. If this had been Singapore, he'd have been sued for libel. In Hong Kong, no way. Rufus Lam's newspapers hold people accountable."

"Yeah, everyone apart from Rufus Lam himself," I said.

Phil sucked his teeth. "What's all this about Scott? I thought after you met him last night, you were okay with Rufus?"

"Just looking at all the angles, Phil. That's what I'm paid to do."

"You're being paid to find Terence Auyeung. Not criticize the person who is paying you to do it. A man whose businesses provide employment for hundreds of thousands of people in Hong Kong and Asia, by the way. The same people who Rufus is standing up for in the election. If you want to cover all the angles, maybe you should ask them what they think of Rufus Lam."

Touché.

"Don't worry, Phil. I'm not looking to stir things up. I was just wondering whether there was any chance that the key to Auyeung's disappearance lay with Lam, that's all."

"Of course it does," Phil said. "You heard Rufus. He's being blackmailed by Napoleon Wong to sell up his shares in Gadgetech because of what Terence Auyeung did. Seems to me that Napoleon Wong's the one with everything to gain from Auyeung's disappearance. That's who you should be looking at, if you ask me."

I told Phil that I'd call him later if anything else came up, then hung up.

Phil was right in one sense. Napoleon Wong *was* the big winner in all of this. But then again it was Lam's public intervention in the CE election that had created the opportunity for Wong to exert pressure. There was no way he could have known Lam's intentions there, so I didn't buy that Wong was behind Auyeung's disappearance. At best, Napoleon Wong was an opportunist, taking full advantage of the situation which had fallen in his lap, with Auyeung's theft and vanishing act and Lam playing politics.

As for Rufus Lam, now I had two very different viewpoints. To Amy Tang, Lam represented everything that was wrong with Hong Kong, the icon of tycoon abuse. To Phil Yip, he was Hong Kong's talisman, the only one with the courage and status to stand up for Hong Kong's future in the face of the city being squashed by Beijing.

My mobile rang again.

It was Amy.

"The person you asked me to find," she said without any introduction. "I've found him."

That made me sit up.

"Already?" I said. I had been hoping it would take her more time, keep her out of my way for a while, whilst I figured out my next move.

"What can I say? I'm good at what I do."

"If you mean 'annoying the hell out of people', I wouldn't argue with that."

She ignored me. "We need to be at a bar called *Escape* in Wanchai. He usually hangs out there after ten o'clock."

"*We* need to be there?" I asked.

"Don't think you're doing this on your own, Scott Lee. You owe me the evidence on Auyeung. Quid Pro Quo, remember? Make sure you bring it with you. So where do you want to meet?"

Ten o'clock. Tonight. I already had a seven o'clock scheduled with Mrs Lo.

"Amy, let me ask you something. Do you like dogs, by any chance?"

CHAPTER TWENTY-ONE

"Oh, he's gorgeous," Amy said, as Combo rolled onto his side, raised a paw so she could tickle his tummy.

Turned out the answer was "yes", she did like dogs.

Combo groaned with pleasure as Amy scratched his midriff.

"He like you. Lawyer Lee you never said you had girlfriend. When you gonna get married?"

"Actually, she's not my girlfriend, Mrs Lo. Amy and I are just...."Amy looked up from where she was crouched next to Combo. I had to choose my next words with care, "... business colleagues."

Did she look away with satisfaction or a sense of disappointment? Hard to tell. We had a busy schedule ahead of us so there was no point in dwelling on it. First, we had a dog to save, then we were off to Wanchai, Hong Kong's very own boulevard of pleasure, in search of our next missing piece in the Auyeung puzzle.

Amy had certainly dressed the part. She was wearing a tight denim skirt that ended just above the knee and a black top with a low enough neckline to draw my attention. I again noted the yellow umbrella tattoo on her left shoulder and the matching Chinese characters for water and fire etched above each ankle. The only thing that didn't say 'seduction' were the flat-heeled baseball pumps on her feet. I guessed she had chosen them, just in case she needed to run. From what, I had no idea, but the sassy attitude and lack of fear made me think that she was no stranger to going into a situation and throwing down a handful of firecrackers.

"Mrs Lo, what time are we expecting your neighbour and the management office representative to arrive?" I asked.

"Fifteen minutes." She looked at her watch.

"And Tak Ming is on his way?"

"He coming. But I tell him not to say anything." Then turning to Amy: "It's his fault this happen to Combo. Neighbour who complain is policeman who once arrest my son, Tak Ming...."

I left Mrs Lo to explain her take on events to Amy and allowed my eyes to drift to Combo's bed, a kidney shape basket smothered in blankets and dog hair sitting opposite the front door. It was in the exact same position as last time I'd been here.

That was the key. That and Tak Ming turning up. Where the hell was he?

As if on cue, the door bell chimed. Combo emitted what was a cross between a bark and a grunt. Amy stood up and smoothed her skirt. Mrs Lo went to answer it.

I was about to breathe a sigh of relief when I heard the dulcet bureaucratic tones of the managing agent's representative formally greeting Mrs Lo on behalf of himself and PC Chong.

Damn ! Where the hell was Tak Ming!

The managing agent's representative was the same one we had encountered at the Incorporated Owners' meeting. Over thirty degrees outside, and he was still wearing that jacket with the elbow patches. His face looked cherubic and somehow apologetic, but behind it I sensed tension. He didn't like what he was there to do, but he was part of a machine-like bureaucracy which, now it had made a decision in line with black and white rules, could only move inexorably in one direction. And that direction meant the end of Combo.

By contrast, PC Chong's face was completely lacking in emotion. He stood ramrod straight in the corner, locked in a sour lemon grimace that suggested he wanted Combo's eviction dealt with as coldly and as efficiently as possible. Mrs Lo offered them both a seat. The managing agent's representative chose a dining-room chair. PC Chong stayed where he was. This wasn't a negotiation any more, as far as he was concerned.

"You remember Mr Lee. My *lawyer*." Mrs Lo stated my job with a mixture of pride and threat, the way most people who tend not to deal with lawyers that much do, providing my profession with a kind of reverence which it hardly deserved. I shook hands with them both and noted PC Chong's attempt to crush my knuckles. He was still sore at the way I had taken him for a ride last time our paths had crossed. I figured the knuckle-crush was his way of letting me know that this was payback time. Which it would be, if Tak Ming didn't show his sorry face soon.

"I suppose we should get down to business," the management agent's rep began. "I am sure you have read the letters we have sent, Mrs Lo and that Lawyer Lee has explained the position to you. I am sorry, but Combo, your dog, has to go. The noise he makes exceeds

130

the minimum allowable standards. We have proof of that now. Proof collected according to the method agreed by Mr Lee here. Three days ago, during a routine visit from my office, Combo's barking was excessive according to the sound measurement system installed."

"Nonsense! He only bark because you tread on his tail!" '

The managing agent's representative gave Mrs Lo an understanding look, his cheeks relaxed, his eyes full of sympathy, but his mouth set with determination.

"Mrs Lo I can understand it is not easy to lose your dog. But there is no need for wild accusation. Rules are rules, after all, and PC Chong is within his rights to exercise the terms of the Deed of Mutual Covenant which state that a dog should be removed if it is causing a nuisance."

"Nuisance, your head!" Mrs Lo wasn't giving in. "Lawyer Lee, tell him he is wrong. Tell him he cannot take Combo from me!"

All eyes turned on me. Mrs Lo's pleading reached down into my chest and tightened round my heart. Even Combo looked at me, his sad eyes waiting for me to perform my miracle, as Amy, still crouched down next him, kept scratching his ears.

Come on Tak Ming! Where are you?

I went over and crouched down giving Combo a pat next to Amy. Combo nuzzled her and groaned, loud enough to mask my whispering to Amy.

"Help me play for time," I said to her.

"Can we get on with this please?" PC Chong said. "I need to leave for my shift in fifteen minutes."

Amy got up, leaving me with Combo. In a flash, she was a different person. Gone was the hard-bitten journalist and in her place was a coquettish, wide-eyed female who was a sucker for a man in uniform.

"You're a policeman? Wow!"

I could swear I saw her flutter her eye-lashes. PC Chong's ramrod spine seemed to straighten further with pride. "I am."

"But……wait a second. You're not the one who wants to get rid of Combo are you? Not after all the courageous acts you perform in the line of duty. You cannot possibly be afraid of that dog."

Combo yawned, his breath almost melting my insides.

PC Chong blushed at Amy's questioning of his manhood.

"I'm not afraid of that….that animal," he said pointedly. "This isn't about him terrorizing people. This is about him not letting me sleep at night, so I cannot perform my duty to the Hong Kong people to the best of my abilities."

Oh this guy was good.

"Rubbish!" Mrs Lo. was on her feet. "This only because you screw up when arresting my son! Now you take it out on Combo. Poor Combo! Lawyer Lee, tell him!"

Although my back was turned, through her hysteria, I could hear Mrs Lo's tears. *Damn that son of hers!* Without him, I had nothing. But I had to do something. So I did what any lawyer completely devoid of a defence would do my position.

I made a confident assertion without any basis whatsoever.

"You're not taking this dog. Not today."

"I'm sorry, Mr Lee, but PC Chong is well within his rights…." The managing agent's representative started to blather, but it was clear PC Chong, recognizing my challenge, had had enough

"Oh give me the lead! I'll do it myself."

Right then Mrs Lo's apartment dissolved in activity. PC Chong grabbed the dog-lead from the managing agent's representative, ignoring his pleas not to do anything rash. Mrs Lo screamed what could have been a "no" but may have been just a cry of anguish. PC Chong leaned down to Combo with the lead. Combo growled and showed the policeman his teeth.

My hand shot out and grabbed PC Chong's wrist and pulled his arm away from Combo.

Then everything froze.

Four people and a dog witnessed me assaulting a police officer.

"Get your hand off me!" PC Chong growled.

"Leave the dog alone!" I shot back.

For a second, his ice-cold grimace melted to reveal satisfaction at the way I had over-stepped the mark, hinting at the consequences that were going to follow, consequences that he was going to take every delight in meting out to me.

"What's going on? Mum, are you okay?"

In the drama, none of us had noticed Tak Ming come through the front door. Which was saying something, given the great hulk's size.

Finally!

I released my grip on PC Chong.

"You're not taking the dog," I said. "What Mrs Lo said was completely true. The only reason why Combo barked is because you," I pointed to the managing agent's representative, "trod on his tail."

"What? There is no need for your nonsense accusations here," the representative started to protest, but the tremble in his voice was unmistakable.

"Where was Combo when you say you heard him bark, the day you came round?" I asked.

The representative was being coy with his answer, but we waited him out.

"Right there on his bed," he pointed to the collection of blankets on the kidney-shaped bed, in the centre of which was a very Combo-like dent.

I nodded. "Tak Ming, you want to show us?"

On the wall opposite to the bed was a set of shelves, on which stood the three figurines of Fuk, Luk, Sau, the three old men who symbolized wealth, fecundity and long life. Next to the third figure, Sau Sing Gung with his long ears, tall forehead and happy smile, sat an equally cheerful Buddha, laughing with contentment. Tak Ming stepped over to the shelf, as coyly as a six-foot brute could do and with his thick fingers plucked out a small black round object from the space between Sau Sing Gung and the Buddha. He tossed it over. It landed smack in my palm.

"Spy-cam!" I held it up between my forefinger and thumb. "After the incorporated owners' meeting, I recommended that Tak Ming install one and point it to where Combo spent most of his day. Two things you need to know about this spy-cam. Firstly, it only activates when it detects movement. Given that it's pointed at Combo's bed, it doesn't come on much. It's pretty regular, actually, I've seen the footage. Once every two hours, Combo gets up and turns to change position. Secondly, it feeds through via a web-link to Tak Ming's computer. And Tak Ming here has been recording everything."

We all turned to Tak Ming, who had the DVD ready. Without being asked, he loaded it into his mother's machine, reached for the remote and turned on the television.

Combo filled the screen, getting up, turning round, lying down, over and over again as Tak Ming fast-forwarded it until the display on the DVD hit the numbers he was looking for.

"Here," he said to the managing agent's rep. "From when you were here last."

"I don't have to listen to this. Come on we're leaving!" The managing agent's rep got up.

"Sit down!" Tak Ming unceremoniously shoved him back into his chair.

All eyes were on the screen now. There was Combo, asleep, minding his own business. Shadows moved across the wall above his bed, denoting there were other people in the room. Tak Ming turned up the volume so that we could all hear the recognisable voices of Mrs Lo and the managing agent's representative. It was all very amicable. Mrs Lo offered him tea. Then there was silence.

The shadow on the wall above Combo darkened as someone approached. Combo opened one eye and raised his head, just as a set of legs filled the screen, partially blocking out Combo. Trousers pressed with sharp creases and those shoes, the same shoes as the managing agent's representative was wearing now. None of us needed to say anything to make the connection.

"Stop it, please!" the representative said in a forlorn voice.

We all ignored him and watched in disgust as on screen his right leg moved forward and pressed gently down on poor old Combo's tail.

Combo's bark made us all jump, as Tak Ming had forgotten to turn down the volume. The tense silence which followed after he turned off the TV was so thick you could have sliced it piece by piece.

I could have told the managing agent's representative that if he didn't leave Mrs Lo alone, I'd have him arrested for perpetrating fraud. I could have told PC Chong that if he didn't stop this ridiculous vendetta, his superiors would be receiving a copy of the DVD as would every newspaper editor I could think of. Yes, we could have gloated.

But there was no need.

Instead, all I said was, "Combo stays."

And left it at that.

CHAPTER TWENTY-TWO

Tears of joy flowed like a river in springtime, after we got rid of the policeman and the bureaucrat. Mrs Lo hugged Combo, she hugged me, she hugged Amy, but the biggest hug of all was for her son, Tak Ming. The Prodigal had returned to the bossom of his family by saving one of its members. It was a touching moment and Amy seemed to enjoy it too, judging by the look on her face.

But we had other business to attend to that evening, so after another round of gratifying hugs, we made our apologies to Mrs Lo and Combo.

"I gotta go too, Mum," Tak Ming said, but Mrs Lo extracted a promise from him to go round there Sunday night for dinner so they could celebrate properly.

"I'll do my special Char Siu, you love that, I know."

All three of us took the lift downstairs.

"Thank you, Lawyer Lee," Tak Ming said to me. "You should have seen the look on that cop's face. Wait till I tell the boys about this, they ain't gonna believe it. Anything I can do for you, you just name it. Where you headed anyway?"

"Wanchai," I told him.

"Hey, me too. Got some business to attend to down there. Let me give you a lift."

We accepted.

Tak Ming had a four-wheel drive BMW. A nice set of wheels and a typical Hong Kong status symbol. I took the passenger seat while Amy rode in the back. In the side mirror, I could see the twisted looks of puzzlement on Amy's face as she tried to put together what Tak Ming did for a living. The muscles, the body ink, the scars on his thick fingers, the chunky rolex on one wrist, the silver chain round the other, the expensive car and the fact that he was heading out to Wanchai at night to 'take care of some business', didn't leave a lot to figure out.

Being a lawyer meant you got to know your clients' private lives, warts and all. Like being a priest in confession, only without the power of absolution. Through the years, I'd learned to accept how multi-faceted people were. Good and evil existed, sure enough, but different shades of both traits sat side by side in most of us. That's why I always cautioned myself before rushing to judgement about people. Tak Ming, here, was a case in point. A known gang enforcer who made his money through violent threats, but with a strong enough moral fibre to make sure his mum was always taken care of.

The train of thought got me thinking about Napoleon Wong.

First impressions were that he was a dreadful little man, a dictator on his own little bit of turf called Gadgetech. But there had to be more sides to him. That secret rendezvous with the woman in Hang Hau, for example. Who was she and what aspect of Wong's character did her existence reveal? A man capable of love and affection? A man capable of betraying his family, the pictures of which adorned the shelves behind his desk alongside the 'bought and paid for' industry awards?

My sense was that Napoleon Wong's obnoxious image masked a deep sense of fragility somewhere, maybe a trait borne out of desperation. But desperation for what? Recognition? Whatever the case, I had to get to the heart of it.

As we turned into Lockhart Road, I snapped off my thought process and came back into the moment.

Lockhart Road, Hong Kong's very own Sin Boulevard, was lit up by low-level seedy Neon advertising windowless clubs called "Bunny", "Paradise" and "Pleasure". Their entrances were masked by black curtains, but they left nothing to the imagination as to what went on inside. Especially with the leather skirted girls and their Mama-sans hanging around outside on bar stools, gossiping, flipping their hair and tugging on the arms of passers-by, trying to entice them through the curtains for a night of here-and-now washed down by a life-time of regret.

The Wanch was warming up for the evening. On the fringes were the expat bars, where regulars supped their San Miguels, ate bangers 'n mash and watched sport being televised on multiple screens. Closer to the action were those who had already moved on to a more advanced stage of their evening. Old Wanchai hands made small talk with the Mama-sans. Out-of-town businessmen walked around wide-eyed with disbelief, fear and growing temptation in equal measure.

Then there were those who had already surrendered. We passed a group of them, all white guys with protruding guts, receding hairlines and the stagger of too much alcohol, each of them arm in arm with a south-east-asian beauty, living out their own fantasy because they were thousands of miles away from home.

Back in the day, I'd had my own run in with Wanchai. A predilection for alcohol, which ran through my genes, had left me down here on a three-month binge. I'd met my fair share of girls, who had come over and hit me with their patter. But soon they realized I wasn't there for sex. I was there to tie one on and forget the ruination that had become my life. Soon they started leaving me alone.

Tak Ming asked us where we wanted to be dropped and was surprised when I deferred to Amy to give him directions. He let us out at the corner of Lockhart and Luard, outside the Wanchai institution that was *Mes Amies*. Inside *Mes* we could see the bar was full of expats, tightly grouped together so they could carry out a conversation in third degree heat above the blare of music. For them, this was fun. The locals didn't get it. But then again, they didn't really care so long as it made them money.

"This way," Amy said.

We took a left up Jaffe Road, a side street that ran parallel to Lockhart. In *Dusk 'Til Dawn*, a live band had just set up for the night and they were crooning through the timeless classic that was *Hotel California*. Somehow the song's reggae melancholic undertones summed up the Wanch in a way I couldn't explain.

"Mind telling me, what you're doing?" I said, as Amy slipped her arm through mine.

"Just getting into character," she said.

"What character might that be?"

She shot me a sideways glance. "Tonight, Scott Lee, we're a guy and a girl enjoying what Hong Kong's night life has to offer."

"Oh, I see. I thought you meant….." I stopped myself. Too late.

"You thought what?"

There's two ways to go in a situation like this. Either you change the subject, or you dig yourself further into the hole. Like an idiot, I grabbed myself a spade.

"Well, when you said getting into character….this is Wanchai and you're a girl, who some would say is not unattractive, so I thought…"

"You thought what?" Then she got it. "Wait! No way! That I'm a bar-girl." She pulled her arm away from me and wiped it like I was infectious.

I should have said what was going through my head right then and there. That there was no way someone like her looked like a bar-girl. That even in a denim skirt, black crop top and scuffed pumps, she was head-to-foot class and growing on me, in a way I didn't care to admit.

But instead I said nothing.

Eventually Amy stopped and signaled up ahead with her eyes. "That's the place," she nodded over to a bar. It was called *Escape*, its name announced in lightening bold neon lettering. It looked about as welcoming as a night in jail.

"You ready to do this?" Amy asked.

"Let's go," I said

A couple of pit-bull heavies were bouncing the door, not in the formal Western standing-to-attention kind of way, but by lounging on the stoop and making funnies with a couple of bar-girls who were on a smoke break. That passed for professionalism in Asia and they hardly gave us a second glance as we passed them and in through the door.

Escape was the kind of bar that hid its lack of décor by keeping the lights dim, the music high and the girls plentiful and easy. The thudding base of an Aerosmith rock anthem vibrated through my chest as I led the way down the short flight of stairs and into a dark underground cavern. The bar was central and oval-shaped and hugged tightly by suited businessmen with their ties half-mast. Cheap perfume assaulted me like mustard gas. Underfoot, it was wet; I didn't like to think with what.

Littered around the bar were standing tables, arranged in no particular order. Most of them were already occupied by either a couple in close tête-à-tête, or just a girl on the look-out for new business opportunities. I got my fair share of come-to-me smiles, until they saw I had Amy in tow. Amy's presence didn't put all of them off, though, and I felt violated by several sets of crocodile eyes. Off to the sides were dark booths, for the more private transactions to go down. We stayed well clear.

"Nice place!" I muttered, but Amy couldn't hear me over the din of the music which had moved onto Guns 'N Roses' *Sweet Child O' Mine*.

We found an unoccupied standing table and as soon as we had ensconced ourselves, a squat girl in black slacks and polo-necked shirt with a badge that identified her as a "waitress" asked what we wanted to drink.

"San Miguel," said Amy.

"Diet Coke," I said.

I caught the look on Amy's face. It was something I was used to. Time was, when I proffered an explanation without being asked. Now, I just didn't bother unless I was probed. Given that Amy was a journalist, it shouldn't have surprised me she was the probing sort.

"What's with you?" She leaned in.

"I don't drink." I caught a hint of Lily of the Valley springing from her neck. It was nice.

"Never?"

"I used to. Too much, that was the problem. So now.....just Coke. Sometimes I go for the full sugar variety, though."

That got a laugh.

"Least you won't end up like that." She pointed to the corner of the oval bar where a man sat alone on a stool. Every bar in Asia had at least one. He was middle- to late-aged, overweight, bulbous nosed, blood-shot eyed and nursing three-fingers of whisky. He wasn't with any particular girl, but they all seemed to know him and he didn't mind the odd arm draping across his shoulder to say Hello in a way that anywhere else in the world would have constituted a sexual assault.

Wanchai didn't make money from regulars, no-one hung around long enough in Hong Kong for that. It made its profit from transients who treated Hong Kong as a stop-off where they could push the boundaries and commit all manner of sins, without anyone finding out, because what went on in the Wanch, stayed in the Wanch. That was the Code. But then there were those guys like Bulbous-nose over by the bar there, who had never wanted the party to end. So he had stayed put, clinging on to his fantasy, locked in a time-capsule where he was constantly desirable to great-looking women, and with the help of a couple of Viagra pills, could always perform at the top of his game. He didn't see the sad, lost, broken individual whom everybody else saw. He never saw much, other than a blurring of reality, especially after the fourth Scotch.

Amy was joking when she suggested that that could have been me. But it wasn't so far from the truth. This was turning out to be an interesting night. A reminder of what might have been, if I hadn't cleaned up my act. A reinforcement of why sobriety had to be my default position now, no matter how low I sank towards temptation.

The music had moved onto *Smooth Operator*. Sade's mellow tones were enough to soften any sharp edges and the vibe in *Escape* seemed to chill, as did the volume, enough for us to carry on a conversation anyway.

"That was a nice thing you did for Mrs Lo," Amy said to me. "You work many pro-bono cases like that?"

"I do my fair share."

"I'm surprised Napoleon Wong lets you. I heard he wasn't the nicest guy to work for."

Ever the journalist, she was probing for information again, heading for turf I didn't want to stray into for fear of her finding out why I was really at Gadgetech.

"Pro-bono work is something I do in my spare time. Napoleon doesn't need to know what I do when I'm off the clock."

"The Law Society won't like it, though. Your handling cases without professional indemnity cover."

"Technically, I didn't represent Mrs Lo. She did all the work herself, in person. I was just there to offer moral support, ghost-write a few letters in her name and give her a few pointers in the right direction. Means, I don't cross the line and she gets what she wants, which is to keep a dog that she rescued and who doesn't do anyone any harm."

"Isn't that called breaking the rules?"

"I prefer 'bending'. Or making the rules work for you. That's the thing with the law, Amy. Too many lawyers out there think its black and white, but that's never been my experience. Law is like life. Constantly shaded grey. You just got to find the right shade to fit your purpose."

"Interesting philosophy. How'd that go down at Yip & Siu? Can't imagine Philip Yip endorsing your approach as President of the Law Society."

That had me shaking my head.

"Okay, I get it. You've done your homework on me. Point made. Can we move on now?"

Her eyes said 'no'.

"Okay, have it your way. You're right, in a way at least. I joined Yip & Siu when they weren't the corporate law heavy-hitters they've since turned into. We used to be a fringe firm, we didn't have our choice of work and just took whatever came through the door. Truth is, that was fun. It's what the law should be, making it work for people to solve their problems, rather than making them a slave to it. I had no problem in pushing things to the edge to get a result and putting the noses of the big boys out of joint whenever I needed to. Then one day Yip & Siu starts swimming with the big boys. The firm changed. Happens all the time. So I decided to move on."

"To Gadgetech?" Amy asked.

"Yeah. Why not? Napoleon Wong is…..well we're not friends, but who needs to socialize with their boss, right? And Gadgetech's a small company looking to punch above its weight. So it's got that same kind of upstart dynamism that Yip & Siu used to have. The pay's low and I'm only on contract. But it works for me. For now at least. Anything else you want to know, or are we finished with the interrogation?"

"Oh there's a lot more where that came from." She said it half in jest and half in threat and I wasn't sure how to take it. "Hey, check out who just slunk through the door. Right on time. Three tables behind your left shoulder."

A bar-girl wandered in the direction Amy had referenced, so instead of looking straight over, I let my eyes follow the girl's seductive saunter until she passed by the table, at which point I unhooked my gaze and locked onto the man who had just ensconced himself.

In the photograph I had seen, Terence Auyeung's son had looked like a young man with the whole world at his feet. His hair had been perfectly parted, his skin flawless and his eyes full of hunger and opportunity. But standing at that table in *Escape*, he looked completely different. He must still have been only in his twenties, but no-one could have described him as young any more. Gone was the hope and opportunity. The adventure had turned sour. Life was no longer something to be grabbed. It was to be endured under sufferance. The reality of the world had broken him and he had ended up here, in the Wanch, looking for relief or escape or to forget, you could take your pick of motivations and still arrive at the same depressing conclusion.

The waitress put a glass of whisky down in front of him without saying anything. He didn't sip. He slugged. And his face twisted in seven different kinds of pain before the alcohol worked its way through his body.

"Let's do this," Amy said and before I could stop her she was doing a fast saunter over towards our target's table, leaving me trailing.

I was still two-metres behind when she went up to him and said, "Are you David Auyeung?"

David Auyeung's face went through a series of fast changes. Shock, anger before slowly settling back under control. He shook his head.

"You have the wrong person."

"No," Amy pushed. "It's definitely you, David. We're not here to cause you any trouble. We just need to ask you some questions about your father. Like, do you know where he is?"

At the mention of his father's name, the anger was back. For a moment, David Auyeung looked at us with his haunted eyes which were sunk in deep purpling circles. It was a look of pure despair, a look of failure. A look which I'd been used to wearing when I had hit rock bottom just like David Auyeung had done. Which is why I knew what he was going to do next.

David Auyeung ran.

I reached out and grabbed his arm, but underestimated his strength. He ripped himself away from my grasp and in moment was gone, swallowed up in the dark bowels of the bar.

Amy was fast, though. She set off in pursuit. Her slight figure gave her an edge over me as she dodged and weaved her way through the humanity that got in her way, like a pinball pinging through ninety degree turns. I followed as swiftly as I could without drawing attention.

Up ahead, I caught sight of a door opening to the left of the stage. An instantaneous beam of light blared out and the silhouette of David Auyeung flashed through it, before the door closed again plunging the wall into blackness. Amy was next through the door, only three seconds behind and closing, her sylph-like movements hardly causing a ripple through the shadows. Then it was my turn. I hauled the handle and bulldozed on through, the light on the other side lazering my eyes.

Through a squint, I made out a corridor, strip-lighting overhead, white walls with paint peeling off the pipes hugging its edges like anacondas. It was only a short space and both David and Amy were

142

already through it. I raced down it, my footsteps and heavy breathing echoing off the walls, as I weaved my way through beer barrels and through a curtain where I hurdled a set of tipped-over cardboard boxes and found myself at another door.

Without pausing I went straight on through. It brought me outside, into a nullah which ran along the back of the bar and the other joints next to it.

Glancing right and left in the darkness, my next move wasn't immediately evident.

Then I caught sight of Amy. I froze with fear. She was in the process of being man-handled by one of the bald-headed meat-heads we had encountered out front bouncing the door.

Something happened inside me then. A fuse lit and fear died.

The next few seconds happened in slow motion. A strange sense of calmness descended on me. I was conscious of everything around me. The sweat sheening my brow, the taste of it on my lips, the stench of garbage assaulting my senses, steam coming from the second floor window up ahead, my heart smacking against the walls of my chest. I watched Amy flailing out kicks of desperation but hitting nothing in the darkness. The pit-bull was dragging her away. I knew I had to make a move.

But something stopped me.

A slight movement through the air on my right side. I sensed it rather than saw it. A nanosecond of energy which computed fast in my brain as something hard and heavy hurtled towards my head. Pure survival instinct made me duck to my left.

I was fast, but not so fast as to avoid the impact altogether which glanced off my shoulder. The adrenalin dump made me numb to pain right then. I just kept going with the momentum, swiveling round a full three-quarter turn towards my attacker, planting my feet, arms up protecting my head from wherever the next blow was going to come from.

I found myself face to face with the second meat-head bouncer. He was twice my size, all cosmetic gym muscles and tattoos, with a glint in his eyes that said he was enjoying his first taste of action in a long time. But he wasn't used to being at the sharp end; that was obvious. The second swing of the broom handle he wielded, was telegraphed and obvious, a backwards and downwards movement coming down towards the right hand side of my head.

143

I had more than enough time to fight down the flight instinct and instead step into him, so we were now at close quarters, removing any advantage the weapon had provided.

My left forearm shot skywards and slammed into his right wrist. The broom handle came loose and clattered on the floor behind me. Moving my weight onto my right foot, I went on the attack, landing a swift upper cut with my right fist in his midriff. The rush of wind through his fat lips told me I was spot on. Pushing home my advantage, I brought up my elbow into his chin with an unhealthy smack and he toppled like a redwood.

Amy was my next thought. Kicking and screaming, she was giving meathead number one a run for his money. He had his arms round her waist and she was off the ground as he tugged her back through the door we had just come through. Both her hands were on the door frame, her face a picture of desperate anger.

I had to think quickly. Positioned as she was, I couldn't get round behind her attacker which would have been the obvious route. So instead I went low and fast, shooting out a kick like a piston, the sole of my size nine sweeping under Amy and landing straight on Meat Head's knee cap. Not the greatest contact, but enough to make him lose both his balance and his grip on Amy.

As she went down I grabbed her arm, hauled her to her feet and we ran up the nullah, past the garbage, heading towards the entrance and to freedom.

But across the square entrance to the nullah stepped three more muscular figures dousing into nothing the sweet elixir of relief. Silhouetted against the light, two of the figures were wielding baseball bats. The other evidently didn't feel the need.

"Back!" I shouted, tugging Amy in the direction we had just come from. But we were out of luck.

Both the meat-heads I had put down were back on their feet. With egos sore, they were now out for some pay-back. Meat-head number one had retrieved his broom handle and had a look on his face which told me he wasn't going to underestimate me this time.

Amy and I stopped dead.

Instinct made me push her behind me as I desperately looked around the ground for a weapon, but there was nothing.

Then I heard Amy's voice scream: "Go! Go! Go!" I swiveled to see what she was doing. She had her mobile to her mouth and was shouting. "Get a car round here now, we've got five of them!"

What the.....

All five figures took a step back from us and turned to look, expecting the sound of sirens to cut through the night air. Then one of them broke and ran and that was the cue for the others to follow.

"Come on let's get out of here!" Amy said, pulling my hand.

We jogged up the nullah, took a left then a right back onto the main street. There was no sign of our attackers. No sign of David Auyeung either; but neither Amy nor I was too bothered about him at that moment.

She took my hand and we slowed to a walk keeping our gait as normal as a couple on a night out would do, so as not to attract any unwanted attention as we passed by the bar entrances. It wouldn't be long before the bluff Amy had pulled would be called. We didn't want to be around when it happened.

For once the sound of traffic brought relief. It meant humanity. We could lose ourselves in public anonymity once again as soon as we got to the next street....

"Wait!" a voice severed us into stillness, as we passed the last bar entrance on the street.

Amy and I exchanged glances, readying ourselves for an all-out sprint. But something inside made me turn and look. Maybe it was just to compute how many pursuers we'd be up against this time. Or maybe a familiarity with the voice had cut through my throbbing head.

"Lawyer Lee? Are you okay?"

Tak Ming Lo stood there.

I was as shocked to see him as he was to see me.

But I was no less relieved.

CHAPTER TWENTY-THREE

"You sure you don't need a drink? Or even a doctor? You're cut pretty bad, Lawyer Lee."

For a street enforcer, Tak Ming Lo sure had a sensitive side. After catching sight of us trying to get out of *Escape*, he had offered us succour in the club where he had just been finishing up his business, escorting me and Amy to an upstairs room, just above the dance floor. Throwing around orders like confetti, Tak Ming had elicited a towel and a pack of ice from a scantily-clad dancer. The towel was now pushed against my temple, staunching the blood flow from a nick left by the broom handle. The bruised knuckles on my right hand were firmly pressed into the ice pack.

"No doctor and definitely no drink," I said, even though the salt taste in my mouth left me craving three-fingers of Scotch to settle my nerves.

"Ms Tang?" Tak Ming asked, but Amy was giving the cracks in the wall the thousand-yard stare. Shock had well and truly settled in.

"She needs a brandy, a large one," I said.

Tak Ming barked an order to the girl at the door and she disappeared.

We were sitting around a Formica table, dance music from the club below throbbing through the floor in a muffled pulse. Tak Ming lit a cigarette and inhaled deeply. Smoke wound in circling twirls towards the ceiling before dispersing into clouded layers.

"What happened, Lawyer Lee? Looks like you got yourselves into some trouble." Tak Ming pointed the two fingers holding the cigarette towards the cut on my head.

"Hit my head dancing too energetically. At my age you'd think I'd know better, right?"

The bluff was about as believable as a politician's promise and the look on Tak Ming's face said he wasn't buying it.

"Dancing, huh? I thought it might have something to do with what went down at *Escape* this evening. Isn't that where you were?"

I didn't say anything. Amy continued with the blank stare. The bar girl came back and put a large tumbler of brandy down on the table and I made Amy take a few sips. She moistened her purpling lips and did as she was told in a way which was so very un-Amy-like.

"Tell me what went down, Lawyer Lee, I might be able to help," Tak Ming said after a while. "I owe you, remember. I've got some pull with the people who run *Escape*."

Tak Ming was completely different from the son I had seen being chastised by his mother for all the wrongs in her life. Gone was the meek and mild good-for-nothing oaf. Welcome Tak Ming, the street king, in control and in charge. Wanchai was his turf, a place where he collected cash for whomever he worked for.

And here he was offering me help.

"We were looking for someone. For another case I'm working on," I said. "Amy got a tip that he's a regular at *Escape*, that's why we were there. We saw him, went to ask some questions. He bolted for the back door. We went after him. Next thing we know, the bouncers turned nasty on us."

"You ran before settling your drinks tab," Tak Ming said. "And from what I hear, you gave as good as you got, Lawyer Lee. You know how to fight, right?"

"I've had to pick up a few tips along the way," I said.

"And the police?"

"What police?"

"One of the boys said you called them. That's why the whole thing got broken up."

Then I remembered Amy screaming 'Go, go, go' into her phone, as if initiating a police raid. A brilliant piece of quick thinking, one that had saved us.

"That was a bluff," I came clean. "There were no police."

Tak Ming gave me a dead stare. Then he started to laugh. It was a mighty laugh that emanated deep from within his belly.

"So first you save my Mum's dog from that scum of a policeman," he said. "Then you're causing chaos down at *Escape*. Some lawyer you are, Lawyer Lee!"

He shook his head, sucked down the rest of his cigarette, dropped it and trod it into the floor.

"Who is it you want to find?" he asked.

For a moment, I debated the merits of sharing that information. The fewer people who knew, the better. Plus, I couldn't see how Tak Ming would be able to help. But I needed a break and I needed one fast, so I figured it was worth the risk.

"His name's David Auyeung."

Tak Ming nodded. Then got up from his chair and went outside the room. Through the door I could hear him making a phone call. The words were muffled so I didn't know what he was saying, but the tone of his voice was unmistakable. It was that same take-charge tone in which he had barked round orders when we had first arrived here. Tak Ming was clearly a big man around these parts. One minute a mummy's boy, the next a street-smart player with respect. Again it made me ponder the complexities of life, the black and white stereotypes we look for in people, when the truth is we all live firmly in the grey, compartmentalizing, putting on different personas as the situation demands.

Looking over at Amy, I saw the brandy had done its work, eliciting some colour back into her cheeks. The haunting look was easing itself away with every sip and the confidence was on a slow drip back into her blood stream. She wasn't wearing any make up. Freckles spotted across her nose, but the rest of her complexion was fresh and unblemished. It gave her a natural kind of beauty.

"Bluffing a police raid?" I said after a moment. "That was inspired."

She looked at me.

"I liked the odds of my play better than relying on you taking all five of them down with your macho bullshit," she said. "What's our next move?"

Before I could answer, Tak Ming lumbered back into the room, sat down and slipped a piece of paper across the table to me. I unfolded it. It was the address of a company called Ross Mckintosh Shale.

"What's this?"

"Where David Auyeung works. He's an accountant, or something in finance like that."

"How…."

"Don't ask me any more questions please, Lawyer Lee. It's better you don't know. Maybe when you find him, you will understand how I have come by this information. Maybe you won't. It doesn't matter either way. But take it please and tell no-one where you got it from."

I nodded, realizing that Tak Ming had gone out on a limb for me, called in a favour to get the address because of what I had done for his mother. We were even now, his debt to me paid in full.

I looked over at Amy.

"Guess we've got our next move."

When Amy and I made it back to my flat, 2.30am had come and gone.

"Sit down!" Amy ordered, pointing to the sofa. I did as I was told. She disappeared to the bathroom, spent some time rooting round the medicine cabinet and came back with a glass of water and some tissue.

"Don't you keep anything on hand for emergencies? Antiseptic lotion, pain killers, bandages?"

"I don't make a habit of getting into bar fights."

Without asking for permission, she sat herself down next to me and began cleaning the gash on my head. Every dab stung like hell and the sensation of being taken care of was one I wasn't used to. I just went with it. So many emotions had played through me during the course of the day, one more wouldn't do any harm. It was nice. Amy's touch was firm, but precise, her eyes locked in concentration, her nose crinkling slightly, scrunching up the freckles on her cheeks.

Suddenly the dabbing stopped. Her eyes moved down to mine. There we sat next to each other in a moment of beautiful silence which seemed to draw us closer. I wasn't sure if I moved first or she did. Or whether it was just a mutual realization of what was going to happen next. But we kissed then, and it felt like that most natural thing in the world, our lips meeting first tenderly, but then slowly moving up the passion scale. I cupped her head in my hands, feeling her wild hair rake through my fingers, my heart beating like it was on fire.

Then she pulled back and with expert timing said, "I've got two things to say to you, Scott Lee."

"It can't wait?" I said, trying to move back in to where we had left off. She pressed her index finger to my lips, easing back my momentum.

"Thanks for saving me tonight. That was heroic. In a sexy kind of way."

"You should see what I do for an encore."

"Uh-uh," she silenced me. "That's the second thing I want to tell you. When I said your bathroom cabinet's devoid of emergency materials, I meant completely empty. If you get my meaning."

Oh shit!

"I don't believe this."

"Well believe it," she said. "Now go take a shower. I suggest you make it a cold one. You have to be at work in a few hours and so do I."

I did as I was told. The water did enough to ease the heat out of me, like a cooling radiator.

When I came back out, Amy was flopped onto her side, asleep on the sofa. I put her feet up and gently placed a light throw blanket over her. She snuggled into it without waking.

Then I just stared, wondering if what had happened had really happened.

My mind flash-backed thirty years to the days when I had been forced to join the Boy Scouts at Hamlington Grove. The conformity, the uniform, the sleeping in uncomfortable tents and eating burnt marshmallows had seemed completely pointless to me, and I had gotten out at the first opportunity. Perhaps if I had stayed in, tonight would have turned out differently. The chastising words of my scout-master came back to haunt me in full-blown stereo.

"Always be prepared, Lee! Always be prepared!"

CHAPTER TWENTY-FOUR

The next day the humidity hung in the air like warm syrup oozing through layers of pancakes. Summer was creeping up fast.

I got up feeling turgid, but as soon as my feet hit the floor, pain and dizziness knifed through my head, providing as effective a wake-up call as ever there was in this world. The degree of light trickling through the curtains told me the sun was already high in the sky. I was late, which probably meant I'd be in for an irritable lecture from Napoleon Wong, if he found out. Given what I had been through the night before, that was the least of my worries.

Then I remembered.

Amy.

The kiss.

I threw on a T-shirt and shorts and went out to the sitting-room. She was gone. The only traces that she had ever been there were a soft dent in the sofa where she had slept, a delicate freshly-showered scent that breezed round the room and a note under my alarm clock, planted firmly in the middle of the coffee table, its button flicked to the off position.

Thought you might need the extra sleep, the note said. *Will call later. Amy.*

Suddenly, I was fifteen years old again, trying to read meanings into words written by a girl I liked. *Will call you later.* So was I expected to wait by the phone, my heart fluttering every time it rang? And she had only signed her name. What was with that? Had she struggled, thinking 'love Amy' would send the wrong message, but 'all the best' would be too much of a let-down?

Give your head a shake! I told myself.

It had been a while since I had done the whole girl-boy thing. I was clearly out of practice. Instead of dealing with my feelings, I decided to lock them away in a compartment of my brain for later and went into the bathroom.

I wasn't a pretty sight, truth be told. My bed hair stuck out at all angles. My eyes were red raw. Purpling punch bags dripped down my cheeks. I could feel the beginnings of a zit forming under my chin. Then there was the head wound from last night's little contretemps. It had scabbed over nicely. I cleaned away the dried blood, bringing it down to the level of a bad scratch, but it would still take some explaining at work. Then I shaved, showered, dressed and was out of the door by eight-thirty.

Deciding to put all thoughts of the case aside for the duration of my MTR journey, I grabbed a *South China Morning Post* and a packet of mints from a 7-Eleven and waited for three trains to go through the platform before I found one with a free seat. Twenty minutes with the sports pages and fresh air was what I needed before facing the real world again.

But the front page headline was like a slap in the face.

> *Rufus Lam backs Elizabeth Leung to run in CE election. Mass Rally Planned in Support.*

I popped a mint, chewed it down and scanned the relevant articles.

Rufus Lam was kicking his election campaign into full stride. His chosen candidate, Elizabeth Leung, was a senior barrister and member of the Democratic Party. She had served three terms as a member in the Legislative Council. Backing her showed that Lam really meant business. Leung was a real heavyweight in Hong Kong politics; elegant, articulate and presentable. I recalled that Phil knew her well and had instructed her on a few cases. A real tigress in court, he had once told me.

Elizabeth Leung vs Jeremy Lau.

That was a debate I'd love to see. Me and the rest of Hong Kong.

The front page had two photos of Leung together with Lam. In the first, Leung and Lam were shaking hands and laughing. Like Lam, Leung was holding a cane, a symbolic gesture that they were a team.

In the second photo directly underneath, the canes Lam and Leung were both holding had been magically transformed into yellow umbrellas. Here was Rufus Lam resurrecting the symbol of the Umbrella Protests back in October 2014, the last time Hong Kong had stood up to Beijing en masse and demanded democratic change. It was a masterstroke of showmanship and a populist appeal to Hong Kong's soul.

Pages two and three were a double-page-spread, setting out Rufus Lam's strategy to get Leung's name onto the ballot sheet, even though the nominating committee deadline had long since passed. Together with his stated act of civil disobedience in refusing to pay any further tax unless Leung was allowed to run, he was employing a political technique that had become *de rigueur* in Hong Kong in the years following the Handover: a call for a mass demonstration. Again, Lam was pictured, this time on his own. He was seated, wearing a black shirt and black tie, leaning on that cane of his and staring straight into the camera. It reminded me of that famous old poster of General Kitchener saying 'your country needs you', calling on his fellow countrymen to enlist in World War I.

'I am going to march. I am going to let the world know that I am not going to pay any tax to a government that is not elected by true democracy. If you care about the future of Hong Kong, you will come out and march with me', Lam was quoted as saying. *'We need to double the turnout of 1st July 2003. We need to change the government's mind, just like we did on National Education. We need to shock the world, just like our students did with their umbrellas in October 2014. All our past acts have been leading to this moment. The moment when we complete the work of the Umbrella Generation.'*

1st July 2003: half a million HongKongers had taken to the streets to stop the government introducing anti-subversion security legislation, in a mass defence of freedom of speech.

September 2012: tens of thousands had swamped the government's headquarters, forcing the Chief Executive to call off his plans to implement 'brainwashing' National Education of Hong Kong's children.

October 2014: the Umbrella Protests; when in the face of tear-gas and pepper-spray and even Triad violence, the students and their thousands of supporters had stood firm by occupying Central, Causeway Bay and MongKok in a peaceful display of civil disobedience, to demand true democracy.

These three events lived large in Hong Kong's post-Handover history. These events had made Hong Kong's politicization one of the major stories in Asia.

And now here was Rufus Lam, reaching out to these three historic political benchmarks. Here he was telling Beijing that the past was never done. It was just in abeyance, rippling at the back of Hong

Kong's collective psyche, strengthening, maturing, waiting for someone to call HongKongers to storm forward once more.

That someone was Rufus Lam.

That time was now.

And I was right in the middle of it.

CHAPTER TWENTY-FIVE

When I entered his office, Napoleon Wong wasn't seated behind his ego-stroking desk, for once. He was in posing mode, standing magisterially by the window, hands clasped behind his back like a little emperor surveying his domain.

"Lam's people have called me about the draft sale and purchase agreement we sent over." He said it without turning to look at me, like I wasn't worthy of his attention. "They can agree most of the wording, apparently. Apart from Appendix One. You've done a good job, it seems, Scott."

He said it like it was a surprise. I didn't take offence. Given that this was my first management buy-out, I was as surprised as anyone. Nevertheless, I played the good corporate counsel, by stepping in to manage the client's expectations for a quick completion.

"That's good news, but I'm afraid we're not over the line yet, Napoleon. Appendix One contains the Representations and Warranties. They're going to take some negotiation. Don't expect it to be as easy."

Napoleon turned then and furrowed his brow in thought. I almost expected his tongue to come out at the effort.

"Representations and Warranties are the assurances you need from Rufus Lam as the Vendor with regard to the shares he's selling you," I explained. "Lam needs to warrant that he has disclosed everything that he knows about the business and the shares to you. That gives you legal protection, should any nasty surprises emerge after the purchase is completed. You don't want skeletons in the closet popping up after you've paid, do you?"

Napoleon gave me a dismissive wave of irritation. "I'm the CEO of this company. There's nothing Rufus Lam can hide from me! We don't need these….what did you call them?"

"Representations and Warranties," I said.

Any other in-house counsel would have felt deflated by his attitude. But Napoleon's petulant reaction provided me with an opportunity to do a little digging, so I grabbed a spade.

"What about Terence Auyeung?" I asked.

Napoleon's backbone stiffened at the mention of his name.

"What about him?"

I weighed my next words carefully. "Technically he's still CFO, even though he is not here anymore. And he was Rufus Lam's appointee. You may want Lam to warrant that Auyeung didn't tell him anything about Gadgetech that would affect the price you are paying for Lam's shares. I mean, what if Auyeung said something to Lam before he left that you don't know about?" Then I pushed it a little bit further. "What if that's the reason for Auyeung going and…"

"Enough!" Wong snapped, his voice high-pitched with anger.

I shut up and did my best to look contrite, moving my gaze to my shoes, then across to the bookshelf on which stood his industry awards and the few family photos he had.

Napoleon's son stared out from one of the photo-frames. He was wearing purple graduation robes and matching mortar-board, clutching a scroll and standing in front of the school building which was about to become his Alma Mater. I didn't recognize the school, but it was in Hong Kong according to the Chinese lettering on top of the building. I could see the family resemblance in his son. The round face and fulsome cheeks were the same as Napoleon's. But the eyes were so very different. They were the eyes of youth, full of expectation, full of hope at all that lay before him in a world of endless opportunity.

I wondered if Napoleon had ever looked on the world that way, before naked ambition had taken him in its grasp. Come to think of it, I wondered if I had ever had the optimism of youth flowing through my veins.

On both counts, I doubted it.

"We don't need Lam to warrant anything about Auyeung," Napoleon said after a while. His voice had eased down to matter-of-fact and the temper had gone from his face. "The value I get by taking back control of Gadgetech is far greater than the price I am paying Lam for it. Even if there is something that Lam hasn't told me, that's a risk I can live with, Scott. But I need this done quickly, understand? That's all that matters here."

I found myself nodding at Wong's reasoning which was hard to fault. "Then I suggest we simply go with a set of standard warranties. I can't see Lam's lawyers disagreeing with that."

"See to it," Napoleon ordered, and looked away.

I wasn't sure if that was my cue to leave, so instead I stayed and tried a little small talk. It was important to keep the boss on side, after all.

"Is that your son, Napoleon?" I signalled to the photo I had just been looking at.

Napoleon half turned.

"That's his last day at school," he said. Although his face wasn't turned fully towards me, I could hear the smile and warmth in his voice. "He went on to university and graduated five years ago."

I did the maths. That put Wong's son in his mid-to-late twenties now. A single man in Hong Kong, probably with a bit of money in his pocket, enjoying the high-life, no doubt.

Hearing Napoleon speak about his son in such warm tones made me wonder. Had I had misjudged this man? Maybe there was something likeable in him, after all. Human beings are multi-faceted characters. Dig below the surface, you never know what you might find.

"He wanted to be a lawyer at one point, you know," Napoleon said.

"Really?"

"But he decided to go into investment banking instead. More money, you see. And more status."

The needle Napoleon Wong put into those final three words had me smiling to myself. A nice little put-down.

What was it they said about the first impressions you had about someone?

Oh yeah! They were hardly ever wrong.

CHAPTER TWENTY-SIX

I went back to my desk, made the necessary changes to the agreement and e-mailed them to Napoleon to show willing. Then I told Tabitha I was popping out to get a coffee, rode the lift to ground and called Phil's mobile.

"What's up?" he answered after one ring, which surprised me.

"You're answering my calls. I guess I should feel privileged."

"What do you want, Scott?"

I told him about my conversation with Napoleon Wong, and Wong's reaction when I had suggested Lam sign a warranty about Auyeung.

"A warranty about Terrence Auyeung? You're playing with fire, my friend. Careful not to give yourself away."

"Don't worry, I know what I'm doing," I said, without really believing it. "Anyway, he chewed me out for even suggesting it."

"Hardly surprising. You heard what Rufus told us. Wong's using Auyeung's disappearance to blackmail him into selling the shares. He's rail-roading the deal through to get what he wants."

"Yeah, I know."

I hurried across the street, in a gap between a taxi and a minibus. If the minibus driver even noticed me, he didn't show it by reducing speed, or anything sensible like that.

"What are you thinking?" Phil asked after he realized I hadn't spoken for a while.

I decided to use him as a sounding-board. "Lam says that Wong's using Auyeung's disappearance to blackmail him. So did Auyeung just disappear and Wong jump on it as an opportunity? Or…."

"Or did Wong have something to do with Auyeung's disappearing in the first place," Phil finished my sentence. "I had the same thought. You ask me, if Wong's capable of blackmailing Rufus, he's capable of a lot more as well."

I reached the coffee shop and stopped outside. "There is that. But I'm not so sure. Napoleon Wong is a nasty piece of work, but it's hard to see him being capable of making his CFO disappear. There's also problems with the timing."

"The timing?" Phil asked.

"Think about it. Wong's blackmail is only hitting its mark because Lam's getting involved in politics right now. He needs to avoid bad publicity. But Auyeung did his vanishing act before Lam announced his involvement in the election. So how could Napoleon Wong have known about Lam's political intentions?"

"I don't think he needed to know," Phil said. "Rufus Lam is always in the public eye, and would be whether he got involved in the CE race or not. A person in his position is susceptible to blackmail any day of the week, if you ask me."

"Maybe," I said. "Maybe not. I'm going to need you to buy me some more time, Phil. That's why I'm calling. I need you to get a message through to Lam. He needs to slow things down on the sale."

"I'll see what I can do," Phil said. "Can I tell him what progress you've made?"

"Tell him I'm exploring a couple of things at the moment. Wait a second," my phone was beeping in my ear over the top of Phil's voice, signaling another incoming call. "I got someone on the other line, Phil. Better take this. I'll speak to you later."

I usually don't hang up on Phil like that, but the truth is I was hoping it was Amy. She had left so abruptly that morning after kissing me the night before, I kind of wanted to know where we stood. Suddenly, that whole adolescent thing had engulfed me again. Sweaty palms, shallow breath, my heart going bong-bongo....

"Hello?" I said in a voice that didn't even seem like me, as I tried to inject a rich, lower, chocolate baritone, which probably made me sound hung-over rather than confident and sexy.

"Lawyer Lee, is that you?"

It wasn't Amy.

I let go a slow breath.

"Lawyer Lee?" The familiar strains of the tattooed street-enforcer who had come to my rescue last night flowed down the phone.

"Tak Ming, what's up?"

"Just wanted to check if your head was okay. Oh and when I told my mum what had happened, she said she would make you some soup. I told her there was no need, but you know my mum. Stubborn."

I began to get this warm and fuzzy glow in my core. Why was it, when I had tried to make friendly conversation with Napoleon Wong, the CEO of the company I worked for, and my boss, it had left me feeling in need of a bath. But when it came to buddy-buddying with a guy who made his living throwing punches if people didn't pay up, I had no problem. My life sure had taken some strange turns.

I told Tak Ming to thank his mum for me and to save the soup for another time, when we could all sit down and have dinner together. I thanked him again for taking charge of things the night before, but he wouldn't hear of it after how I'd saved Combo.

I didn't hear myself signing off on the call. Instead my concentration became fixed on the line of cars parked on the other side of the road. In between a grey metallic Audi and an elegant Mercedes SLK sat a black Range Rover, its windows blacked out, its silver hub-caps glinting in the sun. Exactly the same make and model I had seen during my little jaunt up to Hang Hau, when I had decided to follow Napoleon Wong to his secret rendezvous with Ms Pink Towel Tracksuit.

My mind shot back to the face of the bald man who had photographed me. It was a face that held no emotion. Eyes dead to any feelings.

Was he in there? I wondered. Was he following me?

Suddenly the voice of sanity swept in, telling me my imagination was playing tricks, that seeing a black Range Rover in a line of cars in Hong Kong was about as common as seeing a Louis Vuiton handbag on a bus. But the sanity check didn't override the instinct in my gut and it was that which made me open the gallery of photographs on my phone, and scroll through until I had found the video I had shot in Hang Hau.

Re-living that moment when the window had whirred up and the car had sped off, I pressed 'pause' on a freeze frame of the Range Rover's number plate. Then I looked back at the line of parked cars, to see whether the parked up Range Rover was the same one. But it was so tightly squeezed in behind the Audi, I couldn't make out the plate.

I was just about to walk over and check it out, when a shadow fell on the ground next to me.

"Does your boss know you goof off on work time like this?"

It was Amy.

"Scott, are you okay? What is it?"

My eyes stayed fixed on the Range Rover for a few more seconds, but then her voice registered, dragging me back from the niggling distraction.

"Nothing. Sorry. Hi."

Oh yes, it's my smooth opening lines which make me such a hit with the ladies.

"Hi yourself. How's the head?" She reached up and brushed her fingers just above my eyebrow. A tingling current of electricity rippled down my spine.

"I'll live." Smooth and macho. How could she resist?

A few strands of hair had escaped from her pony-tail and were brushing her freckled, shining cheek like fronds from a palm tree. She was wearing a white shirt, black tight chinos cut off half way up her calves and the same pair of functional pumps from the night before. Not a single ounce of jewelry, no makeiup to speak of. Simple and fresh and no pretensions.

"What brings you out to Quarry Bay? Come to think of it, what brings anyone out to Quarry Bay?"

Again with the smooth lines. I was getting dangerous.

"Rufus Lam's all over the papers again," she said. "And I'm still sitting on my story because you promised me a better one. So I'm here to chase you up on it."

"'Promise' is putting it a bit too strong, don't you think? I merely suggested there might be the prospect of something more."

"You mean like last night?"

"You're still talking about the story?" I said hopefully.

Amy shot me a look to let me know she was letting the comment slide, which I wasn't quite sure how to read. "Let's go and see David Auyeung."

"What? Now?"

"Why not?" she shrugged. "Your friend Tak Ming gave us his work address. We're in working hours now, so it's a good guess that he'll be there. And it doesn't look like you're in any hurry to be at your desk."

"I don't know if that's such a good idea."

"This isn't me asking, Scott. This is me telling you that I'm going to see him. Just wanted to see if you want to tag along. How about it? Want to finish what we started?"

There was that flirtatious little smile again, but this time I couldn't read what was behind it. Last night we had kissed, the tension of being cornered in the back streets of Wanchai by a bunch of thugs leaving us vulnerable and in need of each other's comfort. Was that all it had been? A transient moment of comfort, brought on by a mix of adrenaline and fear and being thankful we had made it through without any bones being broken?

Now here Amy was, the professional journalist again, pushy and strident and playful in that machiavellian way all journalists have about them, watching and waiting to see what she could get out of me for her story.

Always the damn story.

As we began to walk, paranoia made me check back to see Black Range Rover again, see if I could get a glimpse of its number plate.

But it had already gone.

CHAPTER TWENTY-SEVEN

Central District, Hong Kong.

Here, business wasn't just business. It was life itself, the heart-beat which kept the money flowing through Hong Kong's arteries, untrammeled by a low colesterol diet of Mainland depositors looking to hide their assets, low fees and light-touch compliance. Here, the cash flowed fast and it flowed plentiful, but never in enough quantities to sate the appetite of the eager dealers fighting for space and clients in this square mile of vertical concrete. Central District was bursting with driven people constantly on the move and on the make, constantly looking to do more and be more, cut that corner, circumvent that law, searching for an edge to get rich quick, always working against the clock. They made the place hum with energy, an energy that was tangible from the speed people walked along its thronging streets, calling their brokers, phone in one hand, frantically hailing a taxi with the other, while swerving round the trolleys being pushed by old ladies collecting thrown-away card-board for ten dollars a load. Money and poverty shared these streets. Hong Kong didn't hide away its social problems, there wasn't the room.

Amy and I hadn't spoken much on the MTR ride down to this part of town. She preferred to do the one-fingered flick across her iPhone, scrolling through every bit of news there was on Rufus Lam and his CE pick, Elizabeth Leung. I called Tabitha, said something vague about having a meeting to go to.

"With who?" she asked. "What do I say if Napoleon calls?"

I had some pretty good suggestions, but thought it better to keep them to myself. Instead I told her I was meeting a lawyer, see if I could pat him down for some free legal precedents so I could start building a library for Gadgetech for when it starts expanding its business. That's what she could tell Napoleon, feed his ego, let him claim it was his idea later.

The train spat us out at Central Station, along with most of the other passengers. Amy and I took the long underground walkway across to the building called International Finance Centre 2.

The naming convention in Hong Kong always brought a smile to my face. It was a blind-spot in the city's otherwise entrepreneurial, idea-generating spirit. A district in the centre of Hong Kong called 'Central'. The district to its immediate west called 'Western'. To mark Hong Kong's achievement as an international finance centre, a developer had erected a building and named it 'International Finance Centre', which became shortened to IFC. A couple of years later, as if to reinforce the point, the same developer built a second, taller, building and called it IFC2. Hard work and getting ahead dominated the education system here. Nuance and creativity didn't get a look in. Literalism ruled all.

David Auyeung worked for Ross Mackintosh Shale, or RMS as it was now branded, which, through amalgamation, had become one of the largest accountancy firms in the region. It was headquartered on the forty-fifth floor of IFC2 and that's where Auyeung did his day time job as an auditor.

The ground floor of IFC2 had a visible security presence. Ghurkas in red berets and green khaki uniforms with epaulets strolled round ready to pounce on anything suspicious. One of them led round a Labrador sniffer dog, which had become famous for making gooey eyes at the tenants in return for snacks. Because of the security presence, they had a registration process for visitors. As we approached, I wondered how Amy was going to get us round that.

She didn't even head into the entrance, however. She strode right on by, with me in tow, through the shopping mall that connected IFC to IFC2.

"We're not going in?" I asked.

"He's coming to us."

"You've spoken to him already?"

She gave me a devious look. "I told him I was a headhunter representing an investment bank looking for new talent. I told him his name had come across my radar screen. Asked if he had time to talk about the opportunity. Turned out he did, so we're meeting in Starbucks in fifteen minutes."

"You lied, you mean."

"Don't you judge me, Mr Lawyer."

The Starbucks didn't have a separate shop, but was housed in a partitioned off area of IFC2's atrium. It was the developer's way of trying to squeeze extra rental out of a colossal waste of space. I went to the counter, ordered coffee. Straight coffee, black. In a paper cup. The barista looked disappointed at the lack of challenge. He soon cheered up, though, when Amy's order took five minutes to say. It involved double shots and skimmed milk and chocolate sprinkles and the exact parameters for the measure of foam for Little Miss Fussy.

"How do you want to play this?" I asked, whilst we waited for the Barista to work his magic.

Amy seemed to find the question amusing. "Are you thinking good-cop, bad-cop? This isn't the movies, Scott. All I want to do is ask David Auyeung some questions. I'm on a deadline, remember."

"Yeah? As I recall that's all we wanted to do last night and he ran like a wildebeest from a pride of lions. We need to make sure that doesn't happen this time. After all, it's gonna take him all of two seconds to work out that you lied to get him here."

We took a moment to hash something out. Amy went and sat down at a corner table. I hung round outside the partitioned entrance, pretending to show interest in a monstrous sculpture of twisted metal and fragmented edges that the developer had probably charged some gallery a small fortune to display. At least, I hoped it was a sculpture. Either that or I was showing an unnatural interest in the building's pipework.

Around me, life went on. It was amazing. Eleven o'clock in the morning on a weekday, and the IFC2 mall was buzzing with shoppers. The clips of Mandarin voices of the label-clad consumers, loaded up with oversized shopping bags emblazoned with Gucci and Louis Vuitton and the names of watch companies I had never heard of, told me the high-end good stores had hit their target demographic. Noveau-riche Mainland Chinese with more money than they knew what to do with, happy to blow it on status symbols, the pricier and shinier the better.

I sipped my coffee, shook my head and checked my Seiko. It told the time like watches are supposed to.

Auyeung was late. I began to wonder if Amy's faith in him showing up was misplaced, when, out of the corner of my eye, I saw him.

Outwardly he looked completely different from the broken figure we had seen trying to drown his sorrows last night. His face was clean-shaven. His skin was taut and unblemished, glistening with some sort of product that made him look younger than he probably was. His lank greasy hair was now clean and plastered down with gel into a brutally straight parting. The black suit fitted his thin frame perfectly with just the right amount of cuff showing. His green tie was soundly windsor-knotted.

It was the walk that gave him away, though. Edgy and rat-like. Every few steps his eyes darted left and right, wary with paranoia.

It was that wariness I was afraid of.

I knew what was coming. Our little encounter last night had given me a foretaste. He knew what Amy and I looked like, which meant what happened in the next few seconds was as predictable as a caribbean weather report at the height of summer.

David Auyeung turned into the Starbucks entrance, his face interview-ready and full of eagerness. He surveyed the scene looking for someone that resembled a recruiter. I saw Amy wave to him. I saw him lifting his arm to wave back, but then he stopped half way. Recognition hit home along with the realization that this whole thing was a set up.

David Auyeung's brain computed at lightening speed the message that he needed to get out of there fast. He bolted like a cockroach dodging bug spray.

This time, I was faster.

I sidled up behind him, so when he turned to run I was ready.

I reached out and grabbed his elbow clamping my hand shut as tightly as I could. His face filled with terror when he saw me. He tried to wrench away, but I squeezed and shoved him back through the entrance.

"I…please…I don't have it. Not yet. Give me some more time. Just a few more days and I'll get it to you," he stammered, his accent was high pitched and American, which surprised me for some reason. Gone was the cool interview-ready professional. Hello, whelping school-boy.

I had no idea what he was talking about. Since I didn't like being made to feel like a bully, I got straight to the point and asked him what Amy and I were there to ask.

"Where's your father, David? That's all we want to know."

Amy had seen what was happening and was quickly off her chair to join us.

A mix of confusion and fear worked across David Auyeung's face. My question seemed to have knocked his world apart.

166

"I…..I don't understand," he stammered.

"Your father, tell us where we can find him!" Amy said, lacing her words with a heavy dose of threat.

"Who are you?"

"We have an interest in helping you find your father," I said.

David Auyeung looked at me, then turned his face slowly back to Amy, eyes full of turmoil and confusion, wanting to trust us, but completely unsure about what that would mean for him.

Amy took hold of both his shoulders. "Where is he, David?"

Auyeung's mouth gaped like a goldfish then closed. He looked down at his feet, as if struggling to keep control on a deep sense of shame that was about to break through his fragile surface and overwhelm everything.

"He's dead," he said, his voice a pure tremor. "He's dead because of me."

CHAPTER TWENTY-EIGHT

We guided David Auyeung quickly away.

Uttering the words of his father's death seemed to make him crumple. I took hold of his arm. His legs looked like they were about to buckle, such was the grief and guilt working through his system. Amy was unsure what to do next.

But I knew.

I had seen that same look in David Auyeung's eyes before. It was a look of pure surrender, as the realization hit home that life was spiraling out of control. Right now, in the four corners of his mind, he was falling into a black abyss from which there was only one escape. I knew, because I had seen that same dark blank stare looking back at me in the mirror in the not too distant past. At the time I had thought there was no way out for me and no place to go except rock bottom. All I wanted to do in those days was make myself forget by drowning my mind into a state where the hard edges of the world were taken away and morphed into a parallel unreality where it all seemed okay. Until I woke up the next day and realized I had arrived. Rock bottom.

"Get some water," I barked at Amy. "Now!"

Taking Auyeung by the arm, I strode him over to a space below the escalator where we could have some privacy, hidden from prying eyes by that damn statue. Probably the first practical use to which that thing had ever been put. I shoved him up against the wall.

"Look at me, David!"

No response, so I gave him a quick slap on the cheek to snap him out of it.

"Look at me!"

Something registered through his vacant stare, a spark which momentarily brought him back.

"I know what this is. I know what it feels like. You're falling. Faster and faster, whirling, nothing makes sense, nothing is in control!" I checked his pulse. One-forty, like he was running a mile at full pelt. "That salt taste in your mouth, that bitterness? I need you to focus on it. Taste it. Be aware of it. It's adrenalin, that's all. Now breathe. Come on, you can do it with me, deep breaths. In through the nose, out through the mouth. In. Hold for a second. Now out."

We went through it together a few times. Amy returned with the water, but didn't interrupt the ritual we were playing out.

"Everything's slowing down now. Your feet. Concentrate on the sensation of your feet on the ground. You feel it? It's your base, your root. Nothing's moving now. It's like we're walking through warm treacle. Everything slow. Everything calm." I kept repeating the word 'calm' on every outward breath, as we continued the slow breathing ritual.

"Here, take a few sips." I signaled for Amy to hand him the cup.

David Auyeung drank it and kept on breathing. I felt his pulse. Back down to ninety. Good.

"Okay?" I asked him.

His eyes were fully engaged now. He nodded and said something breathless confirming it.

Another minute went by. I was sure the worst was past. The tenseness in his shoulders subsided. He took out a handkerchief and dabbed his brow and lips and blew out his cheeks.

"Next time it hits you like that, find a corner like this and breathe. Got it?" I told him. For a moment he looked like he was going to deny it. But then his face subsided and he nodded.

"How did you know?" he asked.

"Because I've been down this road myself. I recognize the signs. And I've learned the way back."

He smiled and in that moment, I knew we had found a bond. A bond born out of our own journeys to the same hell.

"You ready to talk to us about what happened to your father?"

"Who are you?"

Amy and I exchanged glances. Such an obvious question, but one we didn't have an answer for. If we told him Amy was a journalist, he'd shut the door on us faster than a civil servant at closing time. I could tell him I worked for Gadgetech, but I didn't know what reaction that would get. Associating myself too closely with Napoleon Wong was too much of a gamble.

"We're private investigators," I said.

"Yeah? Who do you work for?" There was something of a defiance now in his accent, a squeaky edge to his American twang. Chicago, I guessed, but I couldn't be sure.

"We've been hired by Rufus Lam to find out what happened to your father. He's concerned about him."

"Concerned?" Auyeung said it like he was testing out the word, trying to work out how it could possibly apply in these circumstances. He gave a derisory snort and shook his head. "Rufus Lam's concerned?"

The snort became a smile. The smile gave way to laughter, or more like a desperate cackle of disbelief and for a moment I thought I was losing him to the black abyss again. But I wasn't going to cut him off. I let him work through this little episode and get it out of his system.

"What's the word for it? When something happens that's completely the opposite of what you want....what you've been trying to avoid all along."

"Ironic?" Amy said.

"Ironic. Yeah that's it. Ironic. Rufus Lam wanting to help now. Damned ironic. Exactly what my father wanted to avoid in the first place, because he's such a damned trooper. Always trying to sweep things under the carpet. And look where it's got him. Dead, that's where!"

"He didn't want Rufus Lam's help?"

"No. I told him, begged him to speak to Lam. But he refused. Always so proud and stubborn." His eyes held a distant look.

"Let's take a walk," I said.

The three of us wandered through the mall, past the over-priced shops and out onto the steamy walkway which led to the ferry piers for the outlying islands. The midday sun was at its highest point, the humidity an unmerciful cloud. We slowed to a Hong Kong amble, walking at a speed which kept the beads of sweat from turning into trickling streams. The smog had taken a hike out of town for the day, somewhere there must have been a breeze blowing north, but I was damned if I could feel the benefit of it.

When we reached the piers, we took the stairs to ground and continued along the pavement. The roads were empty, but the ubiquitous traffic sounds spilled over from Connaught, Des Voeux and Queen's, the three main arteries connecting west to east. In the harbour, a horn from a cruise-liner made its presence known, as the ferries went to and fro across the busiest waterway in the world.

We stopped at a railing by Pier 6, formed a line and leaned on it, Amy and I flanking David Auyeung like a surrounding shadow. The walk seemed to have calmed him to the place we needed him to be. The view of the mesmorising harbour helped. A perfect spot to continue the Q&A. I shot Amy a look which said she should let me handle this one. She gave a quick nod back.

"What's it like working at RMS?" I asked after a while, breaking us back in gently.

"RMS?" A sardonic smile spread across Auyeung's thin lips. "It's like a slow death. I hate it. I'm an accountant, an auditor. Exactly what I've spent my whole life trying to avoid. Maybe some of us are just born to fail."

"Your father's an accountant. Did he encourage you to take the same career path?"

"'Course he did. Said I should get the qualification, which I did, like the dutiful son I am. Boy, was that a terrific waste of four years! But as soon as I qualified, I cut loose. I didn't want to number-crunch for the rest of my life, pulling down a salary, pay into a pension, like the rest of these drones you see in this place." He thumbed behind him to Central. "That may have been for Dad. But not for me. I wanted more. Start my own business, grow it, maybe one day IPO it. That was the plan anyway."

"How'd that work out?"

He looked at me, caught by the harshness of the question and for a moment I thought I'd pushed it too far.

"I tried. I failed. Twice." He let out a heavy sigh, as if the admission was hard to utter. "First time, I got into property. Bought two old flats on the cheap in sixty-year-old buildings, subdivided the rooms and rented them out on short-term leases. It worked for a while, that one did. Cash-flow wasn't too bad. Enough to finance the interest and some of the principal on the loan each month, cover expenses. Plus I had enough left over."

"What happened?" I asked.

Amy weighed in with the answer before Auyeung even said anything. "Illegal structures."

"Right," said Auyeung. "The lady knows her stuff. The rest of the owners in the building didn't like what I was doing, so they put the Buildings Department onto me. Said the partitions I had put up imposed too much weight on the structure, so they hit me with a buildings order. I tried to fight it, but copped a fine for my trouble. So I had to pull the partitions down. All my profit went on the modification costs, plus it killed the business so I had to sell them fast in a down market. Didn't make a damn penny, just because of a bunch of old men in string shirts who happened to be my neighbours and didn't have anything better to do with their time than make trouble."

"And the second time?"

He let go a rueful sigh.

"That's where this whole thing with Dad started."

The ferry to Disco Bay gunned its engine and spluttered off into the distance leaving a slow, dissipating white trail through the water.

"Do you smoke?" he asked.

"I don't, I'm afraid."

"Me neither," said Amy.

"I used to," Auyeung said. "But I gave up when the government banned smoking in public places. Remember that?"

"Yeah," I said. "No smoking in doors. That's why you can't go into a building now without fighting your way through a bunch of nicotine addicts in the doorway."

"Exactly. But the ban gave me the idea for my next business opportunity. All those bars and restaurants which you couldn't smoke in any more? People still want to go out and have fun, right, without having to go outside every fifteen minutes for a fix. So I started an on-line business, importing electronic cigarettes."

"Electronic cigarettes?" Amy asked.

"For sure. It's like the shi-shas you get in Middle-Eastern restaurants. You know, hubble-bubbles, hookahs. They work on water and batteries. Steam, not smoke. Now, think of a shi-sha the size of a pen. Enough to give you a nicotine hit, but without the tar: an e-cig."

Amy and I looked at him like he was nuts.

"Come on, this is Hong Kong. People spend money on stuff, just so they can say that they have it. I figured an e-cig was perfect. It's got that 'wow, this is unique' factor. I could distribute them through bars and restaurants to start, then do high end stuff too. You know, take it to someone with a Mont Blanc franchise or someone like that."

"What happened with it?

"I needed start-up capital to finance the imports, which meant taking out a loan. But no bank wanted to touch me, not after my property business had gone wrong. I asked my dad. He refused. Said I was the one who had chosen this life and had to make my own way."

His voice dropped a tone, as if laden with something. Anger? Regret? Guilt? It wasn't clear to me which.

"He was right, of course," Auyeung continued. "That's what every great businessman does, isn't it? Look at Rufus Lam. Wouldn't have got where he is today without taking a few risks. So that's what I did. I found a lender, who wasn't exactly official."

"A loan-shark?" Amy filled in the gap.

Auyeung nodded.

I could guess the rest, but Auyeung filled us in anyway.

"Figured if I could narrow the time gap between importing the merchandise and selling it through the retailers, I could pay the money back before I got stiffed with the twelve percent interest uplift."

"Your French suppliers let you down?" I asked.

"Who said anything about France? Those things are made in China, just like everything else." He shook his head again and looked down at his feet. "They demanded payment first before delivery. Should have seen it coming. You know the name of my supplier? Shing Seun Dihn Hei. It means 'Trusting Honest Electrics'. Trusting and Honest. Got to make you wonder, right? But in the heat of the moment, I just took their credibility for granted. I took the risk."

Trusting Honest Electrics. Maybe I was wrong. Maybe the Chinese had learned the dark art of irony in their naming conventions after all. "So you paid this Trusting Honest Electrics. And they didn't deliver," I said.

"That about sums it up. So now I'm stuck owing a loan compounding at twelve percent, with no way of paying it back. And these are not the kind of people you want to owe money to, if you know what I mean. They do business with baseball bats. They get their money back by extracting it, and not just from me. I knew they'd be knocking on my family's doors too. Which is when I came clean with dad. The full *mea culpa*."

Another ferry came into the landing bay. We watched it, working out our own version of the scene David Auyeung had described in our minds. I'd seen the likes of Auyeung before, cocky and confident with the ability to talk a good game, but light on substance. He thought of himself as a risk-taker, an entrepreneur. But at the end of the day, it boiled down to two traits: idleness and greed. Wanting to get ahead without putting in the hard graft. And as soon as one of his get-rich-quick schemes goes pear-shaped on him, he calls the one person whose advice he should have listened to in the first place. Good ol' Dad. A man who had spent his life grafting, slowly working his way up the ladder in Rufus Lam's organization through merit, serving as an unglamourous accountant, going to work every day to provide for his family. Only to have it all come apart, when one day his son presents him a bill for.....

We hadn't got to that part yet. I was getting tired of waiting.

"How much were you in the hole for, David?"

"Fifty."

"Thousand?"

He looked at me like I was the one who was crazy.

"Million?" I went up a level.

He nodded.

"And your dad was able to come up with the money?"

"He said he would. He was well off, but he didn't have that kind of cash lying around. I suggested that maybe he could speak to his boss.....but no way. He told me to leave Rufus out of it. No way Dad wanted Rufus Lam, the godfather of Hong Kong, knowing about his wayward son. Instead, he asked me to set up a meeting with my lender's representatives." Another rueful shake of the head. "That was my mistake. Listening to him. Because that's exactly what I did. And you know what he gets them to do? He gets them to agree to me assigning my debt over to him. Says he'll be personally responsible for it. Even had the paperwork all drawn up, like these people would have cared a damn what a contract said. But that was Dad, you see. I tried to stop him, but...."

His voice trailed off as he stared blankly at the water. His face was still cocky and confident, but the eyes were a blend of guilt and defeat.

"I told him I'd pay him back. Every penny. All I needed was a decent break, one deal to come off. But instead, he made me cut him a deal. Forget about business for a while and get a real job, one that pays a steady income, he said. So here I am at RMS auditing other companies' books. About the most boring job in the world you can find."

I let him stand there thinking for a moment before pushing things on.

"David, I need you to tell me what happened to your father after that. After he took on your fifty million loan. Did he pay it back?"

Auyeung's eyes turned into pools of glass. He took a few deep breaths, to stop himself from breaking down.

"He paid back a decent chunk, I know. About twenty million or so. But not all of it, he couldn't. Fifty million at twelve percent, soon became a very big number. Then I get a visit from the lender's representatives again. They broke two of my fingers and told me to talk to my father, get him to mortgage the house or something, they didn't care what. They just wanted their money. Told me if they didn't get it, they were going to kill him."

A taxi stopped on the road behind us, a family got off, the two small kids all gooey-eyed at the prospect of a ferry ride. Not so long ago the Auyeung family would have been doing the same, when David and his sister were young. A sad reminder of what might have been.

"I tried talking to Dad," AuYeung continued. "Tried to get him to consider the mortgage option, or just talk to Rufus, begged him, but he still refused. Said it was unfair on my mother and sister. So I laid it down straight, that these guys were serious, that they were going to kill him. I showed him my broken fingers, so he could see what they were capable of. But he refused to believe it. No way would they touch him because then there'd be no chance of them getting back their money. Once a CFO, always a CFO. Looking at life like it's just a balance sheet and not seeing the realities lying behind it." He shook his head slowly. "And so good old Dad – the man who had always told me to stop being such a risk-taker – rolled the dice with his life. A few weeks later, he's disappeared. No-one knows what's happened. But I know. I know 'cos those bastards rang me and told me. Said that I've inherited back the debt now…..That I still have to pay it back." He shrugged.

"You don't seem too concerned."

"Just wish they'd get it over with, that's all." He said matter-of-factly. "I'm sick of jumping at my own shadow. I'm sick of having to run. It's why I hang out round Wanchai every night. Part of me's there so I can just get blitzed. But I could do that at home with a bottle of vodka. I go to Wanchai, because I know they'll find me. Sure I'll run, like I did from you guys last night. No sense in making it easy. But sooner or later they'll get to me. Just like they got to Dad."

Auyeung's eyes drifted left and locked onto a jetfoil lifting itself up on its skis as it began its journey across to Macau. Perhaps he was thinking how nice it would be to be on board that thing right now, speeding away from the mess that his life had become? Perhaps he was regretting decisions he had made, and thinking about the other paths his life should have travelled? Or perhaps he was thinking nothing.

"So are we done here?" he asked, his face still seaward.

"One last question," I asked. "The lender you are into. Who is it? Give me a name."

Auyeung snorted derisively. "What are you going to do? Charge in there like the lone ranger and make a citizen's arrest. Way I heard it, you two were lucky to get out alive last night."

Amy and I looked at him. How the hell could he have known that?

"Yeah, I heard about your little run-in after I bolted. Think I went home? No way, I needed another drink. You don't hang around Wanchai as long as I have without getting to know people who hear things. Bar girl I was with told me about this couple who had run into some Five Dragon payroll thugs at the back of *Escape*. Don't know what you did to evade them, but you were lucky."

"Five Dragons?" I asked.

"The kind of people you don't want to owe money too," said Amy.

"Right." Auyeung didn't move to correct her. "Dangerous people. Women and drugs and protection, that's what they're into. And unofficial lenders to the people who the banks turn down. Most efficient enforcement department in the world. You pay, or you die. Simple as."

"Give me a name, David." I said.

"What do you mean?"

"The name of whoever it is that runs this Five Dragons thing."

"This Five Dragons thing?" Auyeung looked at me like I'd referred to Chairman Mao as some Chinese politician. "Looks like you got to teach your friend a thing or two," he added turning to Amy.

"I asked you for a name. Now are you going to help us out, or am I going to have to ring the senior partner at RMS to tell him one of his auditors is in deep to an illegal loan-shark."

David Auyeung's features suddenly flattened into nothing. "You know who you remind me of? My father. He always ordered me about, same way you're trying to do. Think I should obey you, Gweilo, just because I got Chinese blood running through my veins, like the good little Confucian I'm supposed to be? What, you think because you work for Rufus Lam, you own me like he owned Dad?"

He looked at me, his eyes hard with a misplaced anger at the world for dealing him such a rough deal. But I held his stare and showed no pity. Auyeung was just a brat who had been given everything by his parents and thrown it all away chasing the dream of the easy path to success. I had met Gladys, his mother, looked into her eyes and seen the sadness in her soul at losing her husband. All because of her son's stupidity and craving to get ahead without working for it.

A glacial silence passed between us. I let him work through his rage, as he thought about squaring up to me. But he never got that far. The ire dissipating fast like air hissing out of a tyre.

Amy decided to give him a prod anyway. "Don't worry, Scott. We can find whoever it is without young David's help here."

"Yeah?" he asked, trying to lace his words with scepticism.

"We found you easily enough, didn't we?"

More silence.

Then Auyeung told us in a low whisper: "Benson Chan."

"Benson Chan," I repeated the name.

I looked over at Amy to see if she wanted to ask anything else. She signaled a silent 'no'.

"Listen," Auyeung said then, "if you work for Rufus Lam, maybe you can pitch him my smokeless cigarette idea. I still got the business plan. We're talking a forty plus percent return on equity. It's a great opportunity for him to get in on the ground floor of something which could be massive....hey where are you going?"

I had already started to lead Amy away.

David Auyeung was a spoilt brat with no morals, out for himself and what life could bring to him so he could avoid having to put the effort in. Even with his father gone and a debt load he could never hope to pay back, he was still trying to get rich quick.

The search for money and wealth at the expense of depth and substance was a trait that ran through Hong Kong's veins.

Right then, I felt grubby even being there.

CHAPTER TWENTY-NINE

Terence Auyeung. Dead.

I had never known him and the news of his passing was hardly surprising, but I still felt the full sorrow of it. Someone had to tell Gladys, his wife, and his daughter. And his best friend, Rufus Lam.

But not until I had learned the full truth, I decided.

I had arranged to meet Amy after work, giving me time to pretend that I was still performing useful services as Gadgetech's lawyer, while she dug up what she could on Benson Chan, the loan-shark David Auyeung had told us was responsible for what had happened to his father. The afternoon proved a completely unproductive one, however. The look of devastation and pure guilt in David Auyeung's eyes when he had told us of his father's murder and the way he had so easily discarded it, by clinging to the desperate hope of the bad business proposition which had caused it, got me thinking about human nature again. How emotions made us complex beasts. Mix in a gambling and alcohol problem and you got a toxic cocktail too difficult to understand. That was David Auyeung. It had all been there in his edgy, unpredictable reactions that morning. He was younger than me. Somehow that made me sad about my own life, in a way I couldn't explain.

It got me thinking about my own father, too. We had grown distant after my mother's death. She had always been the glue that kept our family together; the soft cream filling in between the two stubborn bits of biscuit that were father and son. Dad and I had never got on. We were too alike, always believing we were right and with a weakness for alcohol that had almost destroyed us both at different times of our lives. For almost five years, we had gone without speaking. Thanks to my brother's efforts, in arranging big family-christmas get-togethers, now our paths crossed once every few years. It had got our relationship back on track, although we both knew we would never be close. Not without mum there and me choosing to make a life thirteen thousand miles away.

Sometimes the guilt at being so distant from my family would worm round my insides, winding me tight and making me wonder whether being out in Hong Kong was worth it. But I would always be able to work my way through and out the other side without too much damage. Did that make me any better than David Auyeung, I wondered. He had repulsed me, but I was beginning to wonder how different we actually were.

Amy rang me about five o'clock and told me she had a craving for Thai food. I suggested a place I knew on Caroline Hill Road. In keeping with Hong Kong's naming convention it was called *Thai Restaurant*, but it did a mean green curry and served salted lemon lime soda by the bucket, so suited me fine. Best of all, it had taken over part of the nullah running down its side with a smattering of Formica table tops and plastic chairs. Customers could sit outside and stare up at St Paul's convent in the evening light. A sight like that was rare in Causeway Bay these days. Who knew when progress and development would take it away and replace it with another bling-bling handbag shop for our Mainland brethren?

I made it to *Thai Restaurant* by seven. A Typhoon Signal Number One had been hoisted, the first of the season. The temperature was sweltering and stuffy, the pressure in the atmosphere so tangible you wanted to wring it out like a damp flannel. Sweat beads formed and dribbled down my back, but ten years in Hong Kong had told me not to fight it. There was no point.

Amy texted me and said she'd be fifteen minutes late. I ordered my salty lime soda and killed time by checking the CNN website on my iPhone. It had an Asia-Pacific section with a subsection on Hong Kong that told me it was all about the election in the city at the moment. Lam and his candidate Elizabeth Leung were making waves. Leung would have a clear lead in the popularity polls, the report said, but it was doubtful whether the tycoon's money could get her past the nominating committee. Lam's call for a mass rally to kick off his civil disobedience campaign, refusing to pay tax, would not be enough. The writer of the piece then wheeled out quotes from some high-profile rent-a-mouth political scientists, spouting high level principles about democracy and individual rights and how the election set-up in Hong Kong failed to meet those standards. But at least the piece was balanced enough to admit the governmental system which the British had used to run the territory since 1842 had hardly fostered the development of democratic rights.

The absence of democracy in Hong Kong no longer shocked me. I had felt things might change back in 2014 when the students had taken to the streets, put up their umbrellas and gained the world's attention. For a few weeks, there had been real hope. But I, like many, was proved wrong. The dream had been shattered by government intransigence. Maybe deep down it was my way of rationalizing the disappointment, but somehow I had come to accept the situation. Sure there was a contradiction in a pure capitalist system, focused on the individual's right to consume, refusing to combine it with the right to elect a government. But the trains ran on time, people made money and the Jockey Club charities filled the lack of a social welfare system. So why the fuss about punching a hole through a ballot paper?

Maybe I was being too simplistic, but that's where I had ended up on the issue. I had a strong sense of what was right and what was wrong and tried to apply those principles to the grey areas between the two. Beyond that, I no longer cared for politics or politicians.

Five minutes later, Amy turned up. She wasn't in the mood for small talk and got straight down to business.

"David Auyeung's story checks out." She slid into the opposite chair without as much as a hello.

"Which part?" I laid my phone face down on the table, giving her my full attention.

"Benson Chan," she said. "On the face of it, he's just a business man, a multiple entrepreneur."

"Multiple?"

"He runs restaurants, bars, clothing stores, even some flower shops."

"Since when did it become a crime to sell flowers?" I asked.

Amy looked at me like I was born yesterday. "Since it operates as a front for his other activities."

"Other activities?"

Leaning over the table, she lowered her voice. "Benson Chan used to be 14K."

She looked at me like it should mean something.

It did.

"14K. As in the triads?" I said.

She nodded. In the dim light of the nullah her eyes flashed with the eagerness of a journalist on a deadline. It was a look that told me to hold on if I was coming along for the ride, because she wasn't going to slow down for turbulence.

The waiter came over and asked if we were ready to order. Amy told him she needed another five minutes.

"Benson Chan earned his reputation when he was a 49er – a foot soldier – right at the bottom of the 14K hierarchy," she continued after brushing off the waiter. "He was tough. Handy with a chopper too, if you believe the rumours, and worked his way up the chain of command."

"Sounds like a delightful dinner companion."

She ignored my poor attempt at humour. "About fifteen years ago the 14K dissolved in factional in-fighting, it always did have a loosely connected membership. Anyway after things settled down, Benson Chan re-surfaced outside of the 14K, as a legitimate businessman, with shops all across the territory. I've been able to identify about thirty of them so far."

I thought about that for a second.

"What's the connection to David Auyeung?" I asked.

Amy leaned in again. "At first, the police thought Chan had retired. That the factional split had caused him to say 'enough was enough' and he'd gone straight."

"I sense there's a 'but'."

Amy nodded. "Chan used the factional in-fighting to grab a large piece of the 14K's loan-sharking business for himself. Not the lower end stuff, like the low-life who throw their lives away at the roulette tables in Macau. No, he takes the commercial loan segment, lending money to businesses that banks turn their noses up at. The operations he runs now – the restauraunts, the flower shops – they're fronts for his lending activities, which is where he makes the real money."

"And that's how Chan ended up lending money to David Auyeung for his smokeless cigarette idea," I said.

"Exactly," Amy said. "But Auyeung is small scale by Benson Chan's standards. Rumour has it, he has some listed companies on his client list."

"Seriously? What the hell do they say in their IPO prospectuses?"

Amy shrugged. "They just say they have re-financed their current loan structure to free up more liquidity. It's not a misstatement. It's just that they're not disclosing that Benson Chan is their lender. And anyway, Chan's not 14K anymore. Not until you fail to pay. Then guess who Chan has outsourced his collection services to?"

"His old 14K buddies?"

"Well, a breakaway section of them, anyway. They call themselves Five Dragons. Remember what Auyeung told us?"

"Five Dragons," I said, shaking my head in disbelief. The Securities and Futures Commission had put in place a set of listing rules to rival international standards on corporate governance. But you could have all the corporate governance rules in the world and Hong Kong businessmen, their lawyers and accountants, would find a way to snake round them. Being an international finance centre meant attracting the best talent. But who knew the uses to which that talent was put when it got here?

The waiter was hovering again. Our five minutes were up and that was all the latitude any restaurant in Hong Kong was prepared to allow. Amy wasn't interested in food, but I was famished so I ordered for both of us: mixed Sate and fish cakes, green curry, pineapple rice and a Thai salad on the side.

"You have any beer?" Amy asked the waiter in Cantonese. He told her they had Hoegarden on tap and Amy ordered a bucket of the stuff. I was okay with my lime soda.

"Benson Chan's a new breed of shadow banker," Amy continued after the waiter had left us. "He doesn't view what he does as illegitimate. He's providing a service to the lower corporate echelons which they can't get from the official banking system. He wears sharp business suits and works in an office, hires expensive accountants to audit his books and chairs board meetings. He even pays his tax. Not much, because he's registered a series of investment-holding companies in the Caymans which hold most of his assets, but it's enough to contribute to the government coffers. Like any other Hong Kong big-shot, he invests in rental properties, buys shares and joins every expensive club in town. Rags-to-riches, the real Hong Kong dream."

"I sense another 'but' coming," I said.

"But when it comes down to it, his interest rates are higher than the banks and if you don't pay…."

"He calls in his Five Dragons buddies to collect the debt."

"A shark's a shark, no matter how well it dresses. Another tycoon wannabe who preys on a population so used to being fleeced by them, they don't even know it's happening anymore."

The satay and fish cakes arrived along with Amy's comically-sized bucket of beer. She needed two hands to lift it to her lips. She took an indelicate slurp.

Maybe it was because alcohol was forbidden territory for me, but in the heat of that nullah, that action made her look so damned attractive. Amy's beauty was genuine and unforced, her hair mussed from being flicked out of her eyes all day. She glowed with a burning intensity that made me want to dig below the surface and explore the cause.

So I did.

"That last comment you made. About tycoons preying on the population," I said treading carefully. "You're suggesting Rufus Lam and Benson Chan are cut of the same cloth?"

"A shark's a shark, no matter how well he dresses," she repeated.

I let the statement hang in the hot night air a moment, dowsed a stick of satay in peanut sauce and devoured it, savouring the strong flavours so typical of Thai cooking. I'd never been blessed with European subtlety when it came to food. My taste-buds had been dulled by the cardboard meals they force-fed us at boarding school. Hints of this and shades of that or undertones of the other were lost on me. I needed spicy and strong and sweet and sour, to hit me in the face like a plank of wood.

"What's your story, Amy?" I asked her.

Her eyes flickered with a reflexive defensiveness "What's that supposed to mean?"

"I recognize a crusader when I see one. And I see one sitting in front of me. I've checked out your bio. You're a journalist, so it's not difficult to get hold of. You graduated in the top five percent of your class in Australia, you got a PhD from the University of Hong Kong. With your looks you should be on CNBC or Bloomberg. But instead you're working freelance for a paper that's read by fringe elements who make up less than a tenth of the population. I'm guessing that's because of your irreverent opinions and your history as an activist. No-one gets on in Hong Kong by taking on the establishment and I'm not talking about just the politicians. I'm talking about the super-rich who have their claws in every pie, who provide employment and homes and food and a life for millions. The people who make Hong Kong tick. People like Rufus Lam. You've got some sort of personal beef against him, right?"

I said it to intimidate her and by god with the black look she was giving me right then, I thought I had pushed it too far. But just as quickly as her face had darkened with anger, so it dissipated, back to objective, punchy pushy journo mode.

"So Scott Lee thinks he knows me? The lawyer who threw his career away. Twice. First at international law firm, Jackson Weiss MacDonald and now at Yip & Siu, just when the firm begins to get into the big-leagues. And to do what? Contract work for Napoleon Wong at Gadgetech? And you're accusing me of deliberately underselling myself. Well, at least I do it for a reason....you on the other hand…"

I cocked my head to one-side as if to say 'fair enough', but in her little outburst she had confirmed everything I had guessed about her to be correct.

"What reason, might that be?" I asked.

"What do you mean?"

"You said 'you do it for a reason'. So I'm asking 'what reason'?"

She knew I'd caught her with her guard down and for a moment she looked pissed off with herself. But then her features settled into resignation. She poked some Thai salad onto a fork and ate it.

"My father came to Hong Kong from the Mainland in 1965. Illegally, of course. He made the swim across Mirs Bay, along with many others. He got a job in a factory, worked his way up to the position of foreman. Then he set up a stationery store, which supplied small businesses with paper and pens and lai-see packets at Chinese New Year. It made him enough to put me through school and have some funds to study abroad, although I supplemented that waiting tables at the campus café. The rest, he invested for his pension in Pan Oriental Holdings Limited. Ever hear of it?"

"I've never pretended to know anything about the stock market," I admitted.

Amy almost smiled. "Pan Oriental was the listed company for the Ping family."

I thought for a second where I knew that name from.

"As in Horace Ping, the shipping magnate?" I said. "He died…when was it…..last year? His funeral was all over the papers."

"And like all obituaries, what the papers wrote was pure hagiography, leaving out some of the more unsavoury aspects of Horace's life. You know how Ping got rich? By smuggling petrol into the Mainland from Macau in breach of UN Sanctions. He was a criminal. Only now that China is a world superpower and everyone has to be nice to the communists, that interesting bit of his past seems to have been forgotten."

I snickered at her bluntness.

"Anyway," Amy continued, "Ping used his smuggling profits to buy a fleet of Japanese cargo containers. That turned him from millionaire to billionaire during the Suez crisis, when exporters paid five times the freight costs to any ship that could make it from the Far East to Europe. So everything was going well for Horace and Pan Oriental. Then he handed the reins over to his son, Maurice."

"Horace and Maurice?" The lack of originality of the Hong Kong naming convention had struck again.

"In China, they say the first generation makes money, the second generation enjoys it, and the third generation loses it. Well the Ping family skipped a generation. Where Horace was business genius, Maurice was a complete idiot. He decided to raise funds for Pan Oriental by listing it. That was when my father put his savings in. Not all, but most of it."

"What happened?" I asked.

"What happened was text-book tycoon behavior." Amy pressed her fork into the salad again, but this time she didn't eat. She just played with it, thinking. "You see, the Ping family kept overall control of Pan Oriental through majority share ownership. Not on paper of course, but through friends and family who Maurice financed to buy the stock. Which meant the true external shareholder base, people like my father, were in the minority, although they didn't know it. That meant, once Pan Oriental had received all funds in from its new minority shareholder base, Maurice Ping could do whatever he wanted with it. So he did."

I didn't like where this was going.

"What happened?"

"Under Maurice's direction," Amy explained, "Pan Oriental loaned the money out to almost two hundred other private companies which Maurice controlled. Those companies, again under Maurice's direction, squandered the money on what can only be described as horrifically bad investments. Like I said before, Maurice was an idiot. He overreached himself by planning massive property developments which went on the market just when the Asian Financial Crisis hit in ninety-eight."

"Ouch!" I said. "So the property market went into reverse, Maurice loses his shirt and can't pay back the loans to Pan Oriental."

"That about sums it up," Amy confirmed.

I pondered on the story a moment. It was a common one from around that time. Real estate prices were in an archetypal bubble, with everyone trying to eek as much as they could out of it, confident that they could time their exit right. But that's the thing with bubbles. They don't reduce like air hissing out of a tire. They pop. And when they pop, they leave pure carnage in their wake.

"How come Pan Oriental survives today?" I asked.

Amy smiled. "It shouldn't have. Pan Oriental was virtually bankrupt because of Maurice. All the loans Pan Oriental had made to support Maurice's bad business ventures were worthless. But instead of going insolvent, it was bailed out. By one of Maurice's tycoon buddies, who provided a bridging loan at market rates, but only in return for Pan Oriental agreeing to re-structure its loan base. So in return for the money, Maurice Ping agreed to write off HK$150 million in the intercompany loans which Pan Oriental had made. With the stroke of a pen, the money which shareholders like my father had worked all their lives for, disappeared. All because of a corporate restructuring agreed in a back room between two tycoons over Cognac and cigars."

Amy downed the rest of her Hoegarden, her eyes burning like phosphorous. "Within two years my father was dead. A stress-induced heart attack. The stress of not knowing what was going to happen to him and my mum in their old age, of having to admit to his friends that he had been so stupid as to bet on the fortunes of a single company. Of having to admit his stupidity to me, his only daughter."

She was lost in her own small world of memories which had been burned into her mind by tragedy and suddenly I saw her for who she was. Not a journalist any more, but a woman on a crusade, out for vengeance to right a wrong against her family. As Amy Tang sat opposite me wrestling with her Confucian sense of duty, I took in her features, which right at that moment made her look older, weighed down by the full burden of her family's tragedy.

"You know who bailed out Pan Oriental?" Her voice was like a whisper of smoke. But the way she had asked the question already conveyed the obvious answer.

"Rufus Lam," I said flatly, as the intensity with which she was chasing this story suddenly became clear.

"Rufus Lam," she confirmed.

CHAPTER THIRTY

Amy and I finished the Thai meal in a heavy and dark silence, neither of us hungry any more.

After splitting the bill, we took a stroll in the hot humid night, ambling up towards the empty behemoth that was Hong Kong Stadium. Half way up the pink steps that led to the entrance turnstyles, we sat down and took in the scene. Around us lay token stretches of grass implanted with decorative palm trees. Down below, driving instructors put learners through their juddering, nervous paces. Behind, we listened to the intermittent sound of clattering paws, as a yelping poodle skittered playfully after its master.

There was something so melancholic about Hong Kong Stadium. Maybe it was the fact that it was humbled by the dwarfing tower-blocks on three of its sides. Or maybe it was just the morose mood I was in that evening.

"Look at this waste of space," Amy said, apparently feeling like I did. "Three days a year, this stadium gets used for the Rugby Sevens. Just an excuse for you Gweilos to drink like fish and dress up in stupid costumes. The rugby's just a side-show, most of you can't even name the winning team. What's the point?"

"It's called, 'having fun'." I don't know why, but I felt the need to defend my white brethren.

"Fifty-year-old men staggering drunk through Causeway Bay, dressed as ballerinas and trying to hold onto their bladders? You call that fun?"

"It is to us," I said.

"And yet you're one *gweilo* who doesn't drink, Scott Lee."

This wasn't a path I wanted to go down, but what choice did I have?

"I gave it up," I said, "Alcohol that is. Fun I'm still partial too, where I can find it. And for the record, I'm not a *gweilo*. Not fully, anyway."

"You're not?" I felt Amy's eyes on me then, searching me for signs, the way that people always did when I told them.

"Guess your background check on me missed out that little tit-bit. My mother grew up on Patterson Street, about five hundred yards over that way." I pointed south east from where we were sitting. "Met and married my Dad when he was out here in the 1960s. They emigrated to the UK. Me and my brother were born and brought up there."

"And yet you decided to come to live and work in Hong Kong. Why?"

Now there was a question.

"Curiosity? Boredom? Money? Who knows?" I said. "I'm not sure there was much thought that went into the decision. It kind of just happened."

Although I had opened the lid on the subject it wasn't one I wanted to explore right now. We had spent too much time that evening going off on tangents. I wanted to get us back on track.

The night was quiet up by the Stadium. It was as if we had stepped out of the intensity of Causeway Bay for a bit and were looking back at it. Below us the members of the Correctional Services Club were playing football under floodlights, their calls of 'man-on' and 'offside' drifting up on the night air. Next to the pitch was the Indian Club, where a group of businessmen were enjoying a post-dinner drink on a sandstone coloured verandah that came straight out of the Raj. Beyond was a sea of neon signs advertising everything from insurance products to sporting goods, from watches to phone networks. To the left stood the South China Athletics Association, a huge inverted shaped spatula with the logo emblazoned down the side, a typical seventies structure that must have looked modern at the time, but now just looked kitsch and out of place.

That entire skyline was Hong Kong in microcosm. There was nothing subtle in this place, there simply wasn't time for it. Some people called it crass consumerism, others called it the result of the free-market. Too long ago I had stopped feeling anything towards it other than a kind of acceptance for what it was.

"Guess we'd better talk about where this Benson Chan thing leaves us," I said after a while.

Amy shrugged.

"So, Ms Journalist. What kind of story are you left with now?"

I saw her give a reluctant nod out of the corner of my eye. She took a deep, head-clearing sigh and made a start. "Terence Auyeung, business confidante of Rufus Lam is parachuted into Gadgetech to oversee Lam's investment in the company and the actions of its CEO, Napoleon Wong. It should be an easy job for someone of Auyeung's seniority. A nice little pre-retirement role, maybe. But Auyeung has a problem he has to deal with in his family life."

"His son, David." I prompted.

"Yes, David. A son who has inherited his father's business ambition, but without the skills. David embarks on a series of misguided business ventures, including the ridiculous idea of selling smokeless cigarettes. Only, he needs start-up capital to get it off the ground, but no bank is willing to lend unsecured. So David goes outside the banking system, to Benson Chan, and takes out a loan. For fifty million dollars."

Amy paused a moment. The size of the loan disgusted her as much as it did me.

"David's new business doesn't take-off," she continued.

"Surprise, surprise," I said, adding my own sardonic commentary.

"He can't pay back the loan. He asks Benson Chan to give him some time, but Benson isn't the patient type and calls in the debt-collection services of the Five Dragons. They do a great job in scaring David, threatening to kill him and leaving no doubt about how serious they are. David does the only thing he can do. He goes to his father."

"Sheer desperation," I said.

"Right," Amy agreed. "Terence Auyeung has done very well for himself, but he doesn't have fifty million up his sleeve. He pays twenty million or so to keep Benson Chan and his Five Dragons cronies at bay. But that only stems the bleeding for a while. Soon Benson Chan wants the full fifty back and the twelve percent interest. Terence doesn't have it. David pleads with Terence to talk to Rufus Lam. But Terence has his principles. There's no way he's going to drag Lam into David's mess. This is purely a private family matter. Nor is he going to let down his son. So Terence does the only thing he can do. He goes to see Benson Chan, maybe pays off another tranche in return for Chan accepting that the debt is Terence's now, not David's."

We sat in silence for a moment. A learner driver stalled in front of us, evidently panicking as the windscreen wipers did a quick tango. The lights flashed on and off. A taxi honked for a nice touch. Soon the learner got a grip, started the engine again and continued off into the night.

"Who knows what happened next", Amy said after a while. "Maybe Benson Chan was patient for a time but then his patience wore thin? Maybe when his Five Dragon buddies went to pay Terence a visit, Terence told them to get lost? But the end result, we know. Terence Auyeung disappeared. His son David says the Five Dragons killed him. The only proof we have of that is David himself. But the fact that the five Dragons are now after David again for the debt – we witnessed that ourselves in Wanchai – suggests that David's telling the truth."

I took it all in. Amy's utterances matched the very same conclusion I had reached. The only thing that was missing was Terence Auyeung's theft from Gadgetech, which he had probably used to pay back part of the debt to stave off Benson Chan for a while. He had created a false vendor's name and funneled money out through service payments which he signed off on. Napoleon Wong may have been a complete turd of a boss, but it seemed he had had nothing whatsoever to do with Terence Auyeung's disappearance. That was the only conclusion I could reach. In one sense Wong was a victim. But in victimhood Wong had seen an opportunity and was now using Auyeung's theft to blackmail Rufus Lam into selling his stake in Gadgetech at below the market rate.

I could have told Amy about those last pieces, but I didn't. It wouldn't have helped. She was on a mission to do harm to Rufus Lam. But all we had here was Rufus Lam as a victim, as a man who had, in many ways, been betrayed by his trusted confidante and was now paying the price by being the target of Napoleon Wong's blackmail. That could have made for a good story. But it wasn't one which Amy wanted to write. Not deep down.

"So, what now?" I asked.

"Good question." Her voice was heavy with deflation.

"Amy, it's still a story isn't it? David Auyeung, an X generation tragic figure who goes in search of a life on easy street and ruins his family in the process. A true-life parable, right here in Hong Kong."

There was almost a smile on those thin perfect lips of hers. "Maybe you should be the journalist."

"No thanks. I've got one gutter profession under my belt. Don't need another. Anyway you haven't answered my question."

"Which is?"

"What now?"

We held each other's gaze and there was something in that moment which I liked. Not sparks or fire-works, but a certain sense of well-being that comes with being with a member of the opposite sex and making a connection. A connection I wanted to take further.

But I guess some guys are blessed to have bad luck at moments like these. When you could most do with a dose of Mr Smooth and having everything fall your way, that's when the gods roll the dice and say 'uh-uh, not you fella'. Because just as I was about to make my move, something snagged at the corner of my vision.

A car had turned the corner, slowed down and come to a halt at the curb at the bottom of the steps where we were seated. Something glinted in the evening light and made me look.

It wasn't a learner driver this time.

Pristine sparkling hubcaps on a Black Range Rover glinted in the moonlight not ten feet away from where we were sitting. That's when I realized this wasn't over.

Not by a long shot.

CHAPTER THIRTY-ONE

There was a three-second silence. The kind of silence that comes before a storm unleashing its violent torrent.

Both doors on the Range Rover flipped open and two men got out.

One of them I immediately recognized. He was a skin-headed white guy. Last time I had seen him, he was on the other side of the camera which had been pointed at me up in Hang Hau, when I had been following Napoleon Wong. Out in the open like this, Skin-head looked so different. He was late-forties, I guessed, but he had this wiry frame that gave off an aura of pure, vicious power. As he walked up the stairs towards me, I felt the cold hand of fear close round my chest.

His companion was a good head taller, with a dark complexion – Filipino was my guess – and a rugby prop-forward's build. His walk was a weightlifter's waddle, his arm movements exaggerated by the size of his trapezius muscles.

I realized then, my suspicions had been correct, it wasn't just me being paranoid. That morning, it had indeed been their car I had seen. Which meant these two had been following me. Somehow being proved right provided little comfort.

"Scott, what's happening?" Amy asked. A jolt of panic had sent her voice up an octave.

"I don't know," I whispered as the Filipino weightlifter fanned away to Skin-head's left, blocking any chance of us making a run for it.

I stood up. Amy did the same.

Skin-head stopped three feet away and looked me up and down in a way that made me feel violated.

"Hello, Scott!"

Those were the first two words Skin-head spoke. They cut through the night like the swish of a Samurai's blade. Just two words, but his cigarette-hoarse English accent had managed to lace them with the purest bitter menace.

He knows my name. How the hell does he know my name?

"Who are you?" I asked, for lack of anything better to say.

Skin-head cocked his head to one side. Narrowing his eyes, he shot me a look which told me he was in charge and this was going to go down his way.

"Where is he?" he said.

"Where's who?"

He gave me a gap-toothed smile, devoid of humour and tinged by darkness and as it stretched to its fullest extent, a sliver of ice snaked down my back.

"Don't play games. Tell me where Terence Auyeung is. Otherwise, Tito will break the bones under your skin."

The bones under my skin? The turn of phrase surprised as much as terrified me.

Tito, the Filipino rugby player, grunted at me with pleasure, sending the nerves in my stomach into a tango. Then I did what I always do in times of trouble.

I started with the bad jokes.

"Hey, Tito, you know steroid abuse can lead to zits on your back and dwarfed genitalia. I'd lay off the pills if I were you."

Tito gave me flat eyes.

I lifted a hand and waggled a five finger hello, adding my best smile: Harrison Ford crossed with Liam Neeson.

"You stay where you are!" Skin-head pointed at Amy as she took a step to her right. Amy froze.

"How about you let her go?" I said. "That way Tito doesn't need to be embarrassed when we talk about how we fix his little problem." I held up my little finger and waggled it at Tito.

"Do that again and Tito will break it off!" Skin-head was clearly not in the mood for this.

"Bet that's what the girlfriend said to you last night, eh Tito? That is, if she could find it."

Skin-head didn't laugh. Tito's eyes blazed pure fury. I was sure I could make out steam coming from his bull-like nostrils.

"Tell me where Auyeung is, or Tito breaks the bone in your leg." Skin-head said it so matter of factly, like he was ordering a bowl of noodles.

That sure got my attention, but again 'the bone in your leg'? It was an odd way of putting it.

My next thought was that if it had just been me there, I could have made a run for it, I knew the area well enough. I'd move right, get the wall down to the ticket office between me and Skin-head, sprint to the car-park next door and up the stairs to Tai Hang Road. I reckoned I could outrun both these jokers. But there was Amy to think about too, so the calculations rushing through my head settled on a different play. One that involved telling the truth.

"Terence Auyeung is dead," I said

Skin-head squinted, his eyes forming slits. "Let's try that again shall we? Where is he?"

"Same question gets you the same answer," I said, trying to show no fear. "He's dead. Who are you guys anyway? Five Dragons? 14 K?"

Skin-head grinned again and the temperature in the air lost a few degrees. "Do I look like a Triad to you? The people we work for eat Triads for breakfast. They get what they want, when they want. And what they want now is to know where Terence Auyeung is!"

Skin-head stood stock still for a second. Then slowly he reached into his pocket and took something out.

A gun.

And when he pointed it at me, my world started spinning off its axis.

I raised both hands. "What happened to breaking my legs?"

"A bullet is just as effective. Now where is he?"

"Look," the time for humour was over. Welcome to panics-ville "I'm telling the truth here. Terence Auyeung is dead. His son owed money to a loan-shark. Auyeung acquired his son's debt. Didn't pay it back. You guess the rest."

Skin-head pointed the gun at my leg, but kept his eyes on my face. "He is not dead, Scott. I know he isn't dead. I think you know he isn't dead too. Where is he?"

"You think he's not dead, you find him!"

That was a mistake.

Skin-head's whole body turned into liquid, his feet moving smoothly into tripod stance, turning his torso sideways, his right arm straight as a snooker cue, the gun a comfortable extension of his right hand, his left moving to hold his right wrist as steady as a statue, eyes staring over the top of the barrel, taking aim, his finger starting the soft squeeze on the trigger. The whole move must have taken less than a second, but it was the confident choreography of a trained killer, moving to muscle-memory inculcated through years of practice under pressure.

The taste of bitter adrenalin flowered on my lips. I became conscious of everything and nothing: the shallowness of my breathing, the sweat blossoming on my upper lip, my heart rate pounding at one-thirty in my ears. My legs were pillars of lead, wanting to get me the hell out of there but unable to do anything other than wait for the gun to pop, the bullet to scythe through my thigh muscle and splinter the bone.

I waited for it to happen, braced myself for its inevitability: the pain, the dizziness, the blackness.

But then something changed. I wasn't sure what it was, but I sensed it in the air between us, a certain lightness in Skin-head's stance overriding his training. He started to relax the trigger pull. The tripod stance disappeared, the muscles in his jawline flickered intermittently with relaxation.

Then came that grin. A grin which defined evil. A grin which passed an unmistakable message. That he and whoever he worked for were letting me live. My life was in their gift, that's what this whole little charade had been about.

Who was I to argue?

As if to emphasize the point, Skin-head made a demonstration of showing me the gun. Holding it sideways towards me, signaling with his nose for me to look at it, to take in every detail of the black pistol which had come within the smallest element of pressure of ending my ability to walk.

I looked and drank in the sight, just like he wanted me to.

"Terence Auyeung *is* alive," he said. "Go and find him! Then you tell us where is. You understand?"

I didn't nod. I didn't need to.

"How will I know how to find you?" I heard myself say, although whether I was conscious of talking, I wasn't so sure.

"You don't!" Skin-head said. "We find you. You have forty-eight hours."

He pointed two fingers to his eyes, then at me and Amy.

I'm watching you both.

Tito grunted out a vicious growl.

Then Amy and I watched them amble back down the stairs, their movements as easy as tourists on a midnight stroll.

The Black Range Rover pulled away from the curb and disappeared round the corner.

CHAPTER THIRTY-TWO

We walked hand-in-hand, ignorant yet appreciative of the sounds and sights of another frenetic Causeway Bay night. This was what Amy and I both needed right then, her more than me. To lose ourselves in the wave of human energy seeking out their fix of consumerism. To absorb our minds in the simple act of avoiding the shoppers on their individual maniacal missions, because if we paused a second to think about what had just happened, the meltdown would be furiously efficient and brutally complete.

Leafleteers tried to shove advertisements at us; mothers with pram-like contraptions that resembled four-by-fours shoved us off the pavement; ubiquitous groups of Mainland tourists forced us to swerve our course. We were grateful for every single distraction.

Amy had the blank, thousand-yard stare of shock. The fire in those usually sharp crusader eyes had been doused to nothing. I knew what was going on inside her. I knew, because the same mix of adrenalin, disbelief and thoughts of what-might-have-been, had roiled my insides before. Being that close to death overloads the psyche and there's only one effective treatment I know for it. So for the first time in a long long time I found myself purchasing a bottle of whisky at a Seven Eleven.

We went back to my flat, kept the lights off and let the neon blare from the skyline filter through the windows, casting a soft glow around us. I sat Amy down on the sofa. She hunched forward, clutching her knees for comfort and slipped into a slow rock, reminiscent of a psychiatric ward. The blood had drained from her face, leaving only a gaunt alabaster.

And still she had that horrible lifeless stare into nothing.

I went to the kitchen, washed out the coffee suds from my West Ham mug and poured two fingers from the whisky bottle. The caustic scent of alcohol caught my nostrils like blossom on a summer's day. Oh God, how I missed it!

I made her drink it, slow sips at first, but then she got the hang of it and downed the rest, her face locked momentarily in a grimace, part

198

pain, part pleasure from the alcohol sting. She held the empty mug out to me, I did the necessary with another two fingers and handed it back. Boom! It was gone, just like that.

Slowly a warm pinkness appeared on her cheeks. Her eye-lids became heavy. I went through to the kitchen again to get some water for myself. When I returned, she was curled up in the fetal position, her chest gently rising and falling with deep sleep. I found a green Carlsberg blanket, a remnance from a collection I'd built up from yesteryear, and threw it over her. Then I went through to my bedroom and closed the door.

Lying on the bed, I sipped my water.

And that's when it started.

I should have guessed it would, but you convince yourself otherwise. You say to yourself that because you've been there before, the second time is easier. But when did having a gun pointed at you ever become easier? The delayed reaction I had successfully parried away all evening, was now smacking me in the shadows of the night, like a plank across the chops. I kept my eyes on the window, but all I could see was Skin-head and the gun. The mouth of the barrel had magnified into a cannon in my mind's eye. His finger smoothly pressing down on the trigger, only this time it didn't stop. There was no reprieve. I shuddered as the gun sparked and the bullet hard-throttled into my rib-cage leaving me bleeding out on the floor.

My life was as fragile as a piece of crêpe paper in a thunder storm and the rain clouds were gathering.

*What's the point, what's the point....*the rasps of hopelessness rattled around my brain.

And then I tasted it, that all too familiar saltiness drying my mouth, producing the harsh craving. The waft of that caustic scent of whisky came back to me. *Blossom on a summer's day.* The bottle was sitting just there in my kitchen, only a short walk across the living-room. Only a short walk and I could numb the pain.

My own personal black abyss was here again. I was heading over the edge and there was nothing I could do to stop it.

Before I knew it, I was up and walking, like an automaton, no intent other than to get some booze inside me, tie one on big-time, and let tomorrow take care of itself. On went the kitchen light and there it was, the whisky glowing like amber syrup in the bottle. I picked it up, held it in my hand, the coolness of the glass, that just-so heaviness.

Pure perfection. One sip, I told myself, but what the hell was I doing making a promise I couldn't keep. Long ago, I had accepted that this was part of my DNA. That one sip would become two, then the bottle, until I was out cold, which was all I wanted at that moment.

The swish of the screw cap was a Mozart symphony.

I guided the bottle towards my lips, expectant of that first taste, readying myself for what was to come....

"No!"

The voice shattered through my stream of unconsciousness and for a moment confusion reigned. Then I turned and saw her.

Amy.

Hair tousled and half hanging over her face. She wasn't wearing her jeans, just a shirt and although her eyes were still half closed, there was life back in them. My mind was still on the whisky and struggling to calculate what she was doing there, why she wasn't asleep, why she was trying to stop me from....

She walked over to me, took the bottle and poured it down the sink.

As the last vestiges of it gurgled away in the plughole, I felt a cold panic descend. It was like my insides had been scooped out. *Oh God, I need a drink, Oh God, I need....*

Amy stood in front me, stared into my eyes, reached round the back of my head, gripped a handful of my hair and pulled my face down towards hers.

The gentleness of her lips on mine lasted for seconds, before tongue met tongue and we stood locked in a deep sensual kiss, fireworks exploding behind my eyes and in my soul. I reached round and placed my hand on the small of her back. She responded, arching herself into me, twisting her grip on my hair as we began to move up the gears.

She gave a little moan of pleasure then pulled my face away from hers. We stood there in a half-embrace gazing hard at each other, breathing, letting our eyes do the talking, reaching the common understanding that, yes, we both wanted this. We both needed this. Right here, right now.

We went through to my bedroom and as soon as the door closed, we gave way to our mutual hunger for each other. There was desperation in the way we clawed off each other's clothes; in the kissing and pawing that ensued. From somewhere, she produced a condom, no doubt remembering my lack of preparedness from a few nights ago.

Then it happened. A sheer wave of physical pleasure spread through me, when she took me into her. The speed of our breathing meshed in sync as we quickened and slowed our pace, building and building the mutual passion that we wanted to lose ourselves within, until the final explosive crescendo, our timing perfect, as we cried out to thank our respective deities, touching our own version of sweet relieving heaven.

We lay there in the pale light streaming through the windows, Amy's head nestling snugly in the nook of my shoulder, the scent of alcohol a distant memory for me as I breathed in her smell. There were no words, no thoughts, just the calm that emerges from being completely physically sated, a calm that settled on us both, bedded down, and eventually carried us into a deep and dreamless sleep.

CHAPTER THIRTY-THREE

The fire-crack of a slamming front door bolted me out of an anxiety-laced dream.

Panic forced me to my feet. I padded out to the living-room, blinking out the drowsiness with every step.

Silence bloomed in the sweltering nothingness, except for the drawling of the air-conditioner in my bed room. Then the memory of the night before flooded back in, like a pregnant dam unleashing its flow. A night that had brought me face to face with the combustible nature of life. Gun-toting Skin-head and Tito threatening to cripple me, unless I did what they asked. The closeness I had got to falling back into the black abyss, one minute. The heights of ecstasy which Amy and I had scaled, the next.

I sauntered back into my bedroom, my heart rate pulsing in my temples.

The empty dent on the right hand side of my mattress, solved the slamming door mystery. Amy had made an early morning run for it.

So here I was alone.

Again.

I thought about feeling sorry for myself, but didn't have a country 'n western soundtrack to stimulate my wallowing. Instead, a strange mix of gratitude and disappointment moved through me. Gratitude that Amy's early exit had avoided that awkward post-coital morning-after exchange, where the talking came in unsubstantial niceties while we grabbed our clothes to get dressed under the sheets, like two penitent sinners trying to hide our naked embarrassment after happily grinding loins the night before. The disappointment came from the message which her early morning departure was sending me.

Don't think anything of it, Scott. We were doing each other a favour last night. We both needed what happened. Time to shake it off and move on.

I shrugged my shoulders and checked my watch. The sun was already up and I was running late for another fascinating day at

Napoleon Wong's emporium of fun. But that was the least of my worries.

Now two people wanted me to find Terence Auyeung. Rufus Lam, the guy who was paying me; and Skin-head who was forcing me to do it in return for letting me live They both wanted him found alive too, which was a problem, as so far, all roads led in the opposite direction.

How the hell was I going to prove that Auyeung's body was probably part of the concrete foundations for the new North Point by-pass, courtesy of Benson Chan and his Five Dragons buddies?

That was some problem to wake up to.

I stared out of the window. Hong Kong stared back at me accusingly, the pollution layering the air in several misted shades today, hinting at the decaying underbelly beneath the city's gleaming surface. I hadn't so much as scratched that underbelly last night, as given a firm stab in the ribs. Now the dragon was awake and ready to devour.

Skin-head's words came back to me, then. When I had tried to tell him Auyeung was no longer of this earth, what was it he had said? *He is not dead, Scott. I know he isn't dead. I think you know he isn't dead too.* The words were fired out with the kind of certainty that only came through knowledge.

Who were Skin-head and Tito, anyway? Or more to the point, who were they working for?

Benson Chan and Five Dragons would have made sense. Skin-head and Tito would have certainly made an effective debt collection tag-team. But Skin-head had laughed at the suggestion.

None of this was making sense any more.

So what now? I could call Phil, set up another meet with Rufus Lam. Come clean about my little encounter with Skin-head and Tito, see if he could provide some protection. Maybe he could lend me his bodyguard, Cherry Blossom, for a couple of days?

Stupid idea.

Then there was Amy. Lam didn't even know I had involved her in this. The one journalist in Hong Kong who hated his guts. I doubted he was the forgiving type, people who had acquired that kind of wealth never were.

This whole thing had turned into a mess of gigantic proportions and it was hard to see a way out. All I could do was take it one step at a time. Keep moving forward, until something showed itself. Which meant, right then and there, getting into my suit and continuing to play lawyer for Napoleon Wong.

I couldn't remember a time when I had focused so hard on the simple act of showering and getting dressed as I did that morning, absorbing my mind in every nuance of the task, noticing what notch my belt was tightened to, rooting through my drawer for the four-leaf clover cuff links my father had sent me last birthday and slotting them deliberately into place. I tied my tie three times to make sure the fat piece was exactly an inch longer than the thin piece and both laid straight on top of each other. For the first time, in what must have been a decade, I took a comb to my hair. This was nothing more than building a façade of calmness over the maelstrom of disaster going on inside.

But it worked. I persuaded myself to be calm and, for some strange reason, found myself looking forward to getting to work for a dose of normality.

As I opened my front door to leave, I looked back and cast a long last glance round the living-room, making sure I hadn't forgotten something. Some habits die hard and in that moment, I was glad they did because something snagged the edge of my vision, something that was out of kilter, something I hadn't noticed until then.

On the glass dining-room table, tucked over to the side, sat several sheets of paper with a post-it slapped on. My place was a constant mess, but I was sure the wad hadn't been there the night before. I let the door close, went over, picked them up and read the post-it.

Left early to get started. Got an idea. These are my notes on Lam and Auyeung. See if there's anything in there. Call you later. Amy X

I checked my watch. If I was any later, Napoleon might send out a search party. So I stuck the notes under my arm and headed out to the MTR station.

Strangely, the moroseness of my mood had suddenly improved. Maybe it was the result of the concentration I had put into getting changed. Maybe it was because I was still alive and able to walk. Or maybe it was the 'x' with which Amy had signed on the post-it.

Whichever it was, there was spring in my stride and a smile on my face.

The roller-coaster of Hong Kong life just rumbled on forward.

CHAPTER THIRTY-FOUR

I decided to ride the train through to Taikoo Shing rather than do my usual hop off at Quarry Bay. The extra five minutes would give me more time to review Amy's notes. There were no free seats, but a decade of riding the MTR meant I was sufficiently proficient in the 'Hong Kong surf' to read and balance at the same time. So, with knees slightly bent, standing side on to the windows, adjusting to the movement as the train juddered across the rails, I got stuck in.

Amy's notes were impressively detailed. They reminded me of a girl who used to be in my class at University, who used three different high-lighters and Tipex and was a real uptight perfectionist. I remembered how ready she always was with the conventional answer, but when we went off the subject matter in the textbook, she was completely unable to keep up. Last I heard, she was working on mega-deals at one of the big London corporate law firms. Probably suited her down to the ground. Each to their own, I guess.

Scanning through Amy's notes made me wonder if she had been like 'little Ms Conventional' in her formative years and if so, how she had ended up taking the road less travelled, becoming an investigative journalist. Probably had something to do with the story she had told me about her father losing all his money in a Rufus Lam bail-out, but that was a question for another day.

Amy's notes were typed and divided and sub-divided into neat little sections. The first section set out background details on Rufus Lam, Terence Auyeung, Napoleon Wong and Lam's investment in Gadgetech. The second section was a chronology of her investigation so far, taking her up to our interview with David Auyeung and the work she had done subsequently in digging the dirt on Benson Chan. There was nothing on Skin-head or Tito, of course, our encounter with them being less than twenty-four hours fresh. They were probably the people she was looking into right now.

Unfortunately, detailed though her notes were, there was nothing new in them for me. I had done my own deep dive on Rufus Lam and Napoleon Wong. Terence Auyeung, I'd already met his wife and son.

And as for Benson Chan, Amy had summarized what she had found out last night over dinner. Nevertheless, since Chan was the one I knew least about, I reviewed her notes on him a couple of times, to see if anything leapt out.

Benson Chan was, as Amy had told me, a 14K Triad turned legitimate businessman, who had draped himself in all the Hong Kong trappings that proved his conversion and new social standing. He had the impressive titles in each of his companies, the exclusive private club and charity committee memberships and a string of flats in fashionable chocolate-box-label developments.

He had a daughter. Her name was Precious. She was a paediatrician with her own up-market practice in Central.

I pondered that for a moment. A father, who had once been a vicious Triad enforcer, breaking bones and severing limbs to collect illegal debts, had produced a daughter whose job it was to treat children and make them well again.

Amy had noted down the names of the educational institutions Precious Chan had attended. A top international school in Hong Kong, Toronto University for her undergraduate degree and University College London for her medical degree. What did that say about Benson Chan and his decision to go legitimate, I wondered? So many times I had heard that having children changed people's worlds. Maybe that was what had happened here. Maybe bringing his daughter Precious into the world had made Benson Chan see the error of his ways. Maybe he was hoping the next generation would expunge his own sins. Or maybe Precious Chan was just another of her father's trinkets, a label to show he had made it, with the fancy educational establishments being equal to the private club memberships he collected.

Thoughts such as these were swirling round my mind as I disembarked at Taikoo Shing.

I rode the escalator up to the surface.

And straight into sheer mayhem.

***

The MTR exit was completely blocked. A crowd had formed, many of them journalists, I guessed, given the prevalence of cameras and microphones, but there were plenty of others too. Young people were holding up protest banners, some had opened yellow umbrellas. Old men in baseball caps were shouting at them, telling them to go to work and pay their taxes. All of them seemed to be swarming round a central figure whom I couldn't make out.

"Who is that?" I asked a nervous-looking station attendant, who was unsuccessfully trying to clear a path for commuters to leave the station.

"Jeremy Lau," he said. "No-one told me he was coming. You'd better find another exit. The police are coming. No way, you're getting out this way."

The answer surprised me. What the hell was Jeremy Lau, Beijing's anointed candidate in the CE election, doing here? Trying to get in touch with the grass-roots? Getting ready to give the soap-box a go? This was a rare sight indeed in Hong Kong. Political candidates walking among the masses. Rufus Lam's intervention had certainly shaken things up. Right before my eyes, Hong Kong was boiling with election fever.

"So troublesome, these politicians! Why don't they just leave us alone! I have to get to work!" A woman beside me, a matronly type with salon-curled hair and a sour-puss pout, evidently held a different view.

"You must find another exit," the harassed station attendant told her.

"No way!" she said and started to barge her way through the throng with a loud "*Mgoi!*"

"Please!" the station attendant called after her, but to no avail.

I decided to follow her trail, not wanting to waste fifteen minutes going the long way round.

It was the wrong decision. Soon we were well and truly stuck, moving through molasses, wedged in the midst of the crowd, which was thickening fast, as more and more people pushed into the station, learning that Jeremy Lau was here. Most were calling for him to resign. Others were shouting words of support. Above it all, journalists barked caustic questions.

"Get out of the way!" the woman I was following screamed; but everyone ignored her.

"Are you afraid of debating Elizabeth Leung?" one journalist shouted above the mêlée.

"What do you think of Rufus Lam refusing to pay his tax? If you're elected, will you have him arrested?" another cried.

"Get back please!" the station attendant called out over a megaphone, the growing panic in his voice unmistakable. As more people came up from the platform, the situation was fast getting out of control.

The sound of a siren cut through the air. I caught sight of a police van pull up to the pavement just outside the subway entrance. Blue uniforms jumped out. Orders were barked. Quickly, the police started to form a cordon round the station entrance, blocking the exit. It was entirely the wrong thing to do.

Around me, I felt bodies pressing in more tightly. I fought for space without any luck.

The police presence had made the whole atmosphere suddenly change. The situation was taking on a dangerous edge. Friendly banter was giving way to threatening cries. One section started to chant Rufus Lam's name. A plastic water bottle flew through the air, causing shrieks of panic from the people it landed on.

"I can't breathe!" the woman I had been following cried out, her sour-puss face now full of panic. The crowd was crushing her, swallowing her up.

More sirens blared and another phalanx of police offers arrived to reinforce their colleagues.

"Help me, please!" the woman screamed.

That's when I decided to act.

"Come on," I said, managing to thread my arm through the woman's elbow just before she fell. "Let's get out of here."

This wasn't the time for politeness. This was about survival and I barged my way through the bodies, dragging the woman with me.

"Hey!" someone shouted.

"Sorry!" I said, but continued to push on through.

"I…..I can't ….breathe," the woman gasped. "Please help!"

I tried to move as fast as I could, getting a sharp elbow in the ribs and a burst of swearing for my trouble.

Eventually, we made it to the edge of the throng, and were within touching distance of the exit.

I felt a hand on my chest.

"Use another exit! We are blocking this one off!"

It was a policeman. He was about a head taller than me, ten years younger and with a face that countenanced no argument.

"She needs air!" I shouted at him, trying to make myself heard, pointing at my companion, whose face had taken on a beetroot hue.

"You must find another exit!"

"I can't…breathe," the lady cried out again.

"Sorry, we're leaving!" I said to the policeman.

Suddenly the crowds shoved me from behind. Using this momentum, I led with my shoulder, barging into the policeman to create a gap. Big mistake! Before I knew it, the policeman had been joined by one of his colleagues and both were bearing down on me.

"Move back and find another exit!"

"Let us out!" I protested, angered by this officious nonsense.

"This is your last warning!"

"This lady is suffocating. You have to let us out!"

Neither of them listened. One of them put a hand on my chest and pushed me back.

And that was when I felt the red mist descend. Anger flushed through me. Anger at the world. Anger at Jeremy Lau for causing this. Anger at this over-officious idiot of a policeman.

I threw a punch.

It landed straight in the policeman's stomach, harder than I expected.

He doubled over, his eyes bulging, the wind knocked out of him.

His colleague gaped at me for a moment, unsure of what to do. But then his training took over and he was ready with his can of pepper-spray.

Right then, I felt something grab my collar from behind. Suddenly I was being hauled away, back into the crowds. I stumbled and lashed out, but nothing could stop the force at the back of my neck from dragging me backwards. All I could do was try to keep on my feet, totally bemused as to what was happening.

Whoever had hold of me forced me to travel in a semi-circle. We burst out of the crowd at the exit on the other side of the station. I felt myself shoved up against pillar and for the first time came face to face with my assailant.

Skin-head slapped me across the face, getting my attention.

"That was very stupid, Scott!" he said. "You don't hit police! They hit back. But not as hard as I do. Understand?"

"What the hell are you doing here?"

"I'm following you! And I am going to keep following you until you find Terence Auyeung for me. Forget this rubbish!" he signalled back at the crowd. "Just find Auyeung. That's your one task now! You have less than forty-eight hours. Get out of here and get on with it! Do you understand?"

He didn't wait for an answer and before there was a chance for the piercing words to register in my brain, he had turned on his heels and disappeared with a nonchalant waltz back into the crowd.

I stood there, my hands on my knees, sucking in deep breaths. Wondering what the hell had just happened and what I was supposed to do next.

CHAPTER THIRTY-FIVE

I quick-stepped it out of there and made it to the office in a daze of terror and confusion. I willed myself to focus, but it was no good. The cries from the crowds back at the subway station were still ringing in my ears. Rufus Lam had shaken the city out of its apathy and the streets were reaching boiling point. Things were going to get ugly. Case in point: I had assaulted a policeman and been rescued from an imminent burst of pepper-spray by a psychopath who was now dogging my every move. It wasn't even 9am!

Throughout my entire career there had never been a problem I couldn't think through, given enough time and space and latitude. Sometimes the solution came through working the law to the limits of what it allowed, bending it to breaking point if need be. Sometimes I had even crossed the line, when the means justified the end. But always, I had managed to find a way through the myriads.

Time and space: that's what I needed right now, to shut myself off for a while to think and get my head in the right place. But as soon as I got into my office, Tabitha was hovering, like the efficient work-horse she was and from the look on her face, it couldn't wait.

"Morning," I said, trying to mask the turmoil inside.

"Mr Wong was down here looking for you. He was asking where you were."

"When was this?" I said.

"About half an hour ago. Are you okay?"

I nodded although I wasn't really sure if that was true.

"What did you say to him?" I asked.

"I said you had an early morning meeting in Central."

"Thanks," I said. Secretarial loyalty was as precious a commodity as existed in the corporate world and it looked like I had finally found my way round to Tabitha's good side. "Did he say what he wanted?"

"No, but he left something on your desk for you to look at. He seemed...he seemed..." She was searching for the word.

"What?"

"Kind of happy?"

That made one of us, I thought.

"Okay. Listen Tabitha, I need a moment. If there are any phone calls, could you just take a message?"

She said she would.

I went into my office and closed the door.

Sure enough, on my chair was a hard-copy print-out of the latest draft share sale and purchase agreement. Napoleon had scribbled a message on the front of it: *"URGENT. See my hand-written comments. When you get in, please incorporate the changes first thing and e-mail it back to me, so I can get it off to the Purchaser asap."*

I spent a few minutes flipping through the comments and found myself impressed by the detail with which Napoleon had gone into it. Evidently he had no problem keeping up the pretence that this was a proper transaction and not one he was eliciting by lurid blackmail.

But wasn't that always the way with fraudsters and thieves? Their mistake wasn't in the fact that they missed something, but in the fact that they hadn't. Perfection wasn't normal. It was a red flag, though I doubted it mattered as both parties to the transaction needed it to go through. Napoleon Wong, to regain control of Gadgetech; Rufus Lam, to get shot of it so he could concentrate on the election.

It was clear Napoleon had read all the warranties and checked with the necessary people to ensure he had the requisite "knowledge and belief" to sign off on them. Under the warranties in relation to the collectability of book debts, he had written in the details of two outstanding invoices Gadgetech was disputing. Under the section on stock, he had indicated that he had received confirmation from his procurement people that the information was correct.

The urgency of Napoleon's message bothered me, though. He was looking to close this deal fast, which meant, once the transaction was done, I would have outlived my usefulness and would be on my way out. The window I had for finding Auyeung was closing fast.

I rubbed my temples. The walls were pressing in on me, boxing me in and there was nothing I could do about it. I shut my eyes, breathed in, and counted to ten. Told myself to keep a cool head. Then I booted up my computer, made the necessary changes to the disclosure provisions of the document and e-mailed off a marked up and clean copy to Napoleon.

While I was at it, I checked the other e-mails in my in-box. The operations department wanted me to review the renewal contract for a photocopier and a lady in marketing had a question about whether there was any issue using Gadgetech's logo on a business partner's websites. They were mundane tasks, but mundane was good right now, mundane was what I needed. So for the next hour I absorbed myself in those tasks and felt better about myself for it.

That's the thing. I have never been the type of lawyer to coast my way through, basing my advice on gut-feel rather than solid research. Legal practice for me has always been a constant struggle, trying to bend the law's malleable parts to fit a client's needs. That takes work and patience, strong concentration and a disciplined flexibility. It's hard graft, most of the time, but that's the part of legal practice I have always loved and if I could only have ignored the parts I hated – the politics, the egos, the pathetic posturing and false bonhomie, the manipulation of billable hours and the slavery to form rather than substance in a litigation process that venerates the former and lip-serves the latter – then maybe Phil Yip and I would be trading jokes at partnership meetings right now. But that has never been me. I am a purist. Often I hate myself for it, but a person can't change the way he's hard-wired.

Okay, get to your next move, Scott! Come on, the voice in my head told me then.

I took stock of where I was. It wasn't pretty. Thought upon thought rattled through my mind, each more frustrating than the last as I hit a series of brick walls and closing doors.

Terence Auyeung, Rufus Lam, Napoleon Wong, Benson Chan, Skin-head, Tito, all of them individuals I hadn't even known a week ago and now they had come to dominate my life. None of this was making sense. None of it at all. I felt the agitation clawing at my insides, making me want to get off my chair and do....who knew what. I looked around me, to the boxes of paper next to my desk, the post-it notes with phone numbers scribbled down, my legal note-pad with jottings from several phone calls, the usual paraphernalia that came with legal work, all the way to the draft sale and purchase document Napoleon had left me to work on.

And then it hit me.

What do you do if one door closes, Scott?

You find another door.

I picked up the draft sale and purchase agreement and stared at it.

And slowly an idea started to percolate through the mist.

CHAPTER THIRTY-SIX

"Hi there! It's Angela isn't it?"

I knew it was.

"Is Napoleon in?"

I knew he wasn't and wouldn't be back for at least an hour, Tabitha had that information at her fingertips.

"Do you mind if I just leave these documents in his office? He wanted me to comment on them as a matter of some urgency? If I could just leave them on his chair with a short note, so they're the first thing he sees when he returns, that would be great."

Silence.

Angela Tan was Napoleon Wong's executive assistant. As terrifying as Napoleon was to the people who worked here, Angela Tan outdid him on that score and then some, according to the reputation rumour mill. And based on the permafrost in the atmosphere between us at that moment, the rumours were spot on.

She wore pointed, black-rimmed glasses, a permanent grimace and if looks could kill, then hers would have been the prototype over which arms dealers would be salivating. She was, in short, Napoleon Wong's guard dog; a Rottweiler with typing skills (allegedly), so the only way I was getting into his office was with her consent.

"I'll give them to him." Without even looking up from her screen, Angela held out her hand. Her fingers were tipped with challenging scarlet nails. She expected me just to hand over the documents, but if I did that, I would lose my opening.

That's when I turned on the ol' Scott Lee charm, shooting her my best Matt Damon smile. I thought about complimenting her on her sense of style, when I realized that time was limited and as irresistible as I was, I needed something more. So I combined the charm offensive with a skill that all good lawyers have to deploy at one time or another in their careers.

I lied.

"Did you sign the confidentiality agreement, Angela?"

Her eyes moved off the screen and blazed onto me. How dare I question her, that look said.

"What are you talking about?" Her words dripped condescension like maple syrup from a bear's paw.

"I'm Scott Lee, the new lawyer here…."

"I know who you are, Mr Lee. Mr Wong has hired you to assist him with Project Waterloo. On a contract basis, I understand." She said the word 'contract' as if it tasted bitter in her mouth.

Okay then, was my first thought.

Project Waterloo? was my next.

Oh my God, is that what Napoleon's calling it? Really?

I breathed deep and put some extra wattage into the smile, until my cheeks started to cramp. "That's exactly right, Angela; and one of the first assignments Napoleon asked me to do when I arrived was ensure that all those involved with, uh, Waterloo, sign a confidentiality agreement. We drew up the list of people who needed to sign. Has he asked you to sign yet?"

Her blazing eyes softened at the edges with pensiveness, as she tried to think her way out of this blatant challenge to her authority.

That was the stick I'd served up – the big loss of face into the depths of which none other than Angela Tan was staring. Now came the carrot, the way out I was about to offer.

I lost the smile and tapped my lips with my forefinger as if reaching for a memory that would explain the meaning of life.

"You know what? I recall Napoleon saying that he wanted to sit down with his most crucial employees, on a one-on-one a basis and explain why he was asking them to sign. I know he's been busy. Perhaps he hasn't got round to you yet? I'm sure you were one of the crucial people he had in mind, given the level of information you're trusted with. Everyone knows how important you are to Gadgetech, Angela."

She let my words permeate a moment, then nodded her head. "You're probably right, Scott."

It was 'Scott' now, I noted.

"But that's the thing," I said. "Until you sign a confidentiality agreement, I can't hand this over to you." I held up the copy of the sale and purchase agreement for her to see. "I'm sure you of all people must understand the importance of following the rules."

Yes, Angela Tan certainly did. I was talking her language now. Time for the coup de grâce.

"I'll tell you what. I'm pretty nervous about leaving documents on Napoleon's chair like this. Maybe you could make sure no-one else goes into his office until he returns? And I'll remind Napoleon to sit down with you first thing and get you to sign the confidentiality agreement. He really needs you in the inner circle on this one, Angela. We all do."

I held her stare for five seconds while she let the compliments seep in. Then Angela Tan signaled with her head. "Leave them on his desk, not his chair, he doesn't like that. I'll make sure no-one else sees them."

"You're a star. May I borrow a pen and some paper, just to write him a note?" I added, setting up my excuse for hanging around in there a little longer than necessary. She gave me what I wanted and I laid it on thick with the thanks as she unlocked Napoleon's office door and ushered me in.

***

I let Napoleon's office door fall shut behind me, then immediately switched it up a gear. Three minutes was the most I had before Angela began to get curious, so I had to move fast.

First was the note. I scribbled it out with whip-like speed. Then it was out with my iPhone and on with the video.

I had no idea what I was looking for, but I knew that, to a man like Napoleon Wong, his office was the headquarters of his strategic operation, the place where plans were made and plots hatched. This was his sanctuary, so if there was proof of what Napoleon really knew about Terence Auyeung, then it had to be in here somewhere. That was the logic I was working to.

I started with his desk, going over everything that was on there, which wasn't much apart from a fancy pen-holder, a leather blotting-pad and some of those useless silver toy gadgets that people who spend too much time at work find amusement in.

I tried the desk drawers. They were locked. It didn't surprise me and there was no time to pick them.

When I made it to his in-tray, I switched from video to camera mode and carefully snapped every document that was in there. Nothing I recognized, or that seemed relevant. Just industry magazines, a couple of invitations, some copies of spreadsheets which meant nothing to me, but I zoomed in anyway and made sure I got good shots. I quickly went through his bin and photographed whatever was in there too.

Then it was back to video mode, as I ran the phone over the shelves behind his desk, smoothing my away horizontally across the spines of files and books, the industry awards, and the family photos.

Just as I was finishing the last shelf, I heard a click from the door. Whirling round I saw the handle moving downward.

Panic seized me, but I bit it down and used it for what I had to do. In one fluid movement, the phone went back into my pocket, I sprinted two steps to the other side of the desk and picked up the sale and purchase agreement.

"Is everything okay?" Angela Tan asked, her Rottweiler instincts twitching, suspicion lacing her voice.

I had taken a big risk coming here, snooping around in the middle of the day. But taking a risk gave me an edge, heightened my awareness, sharpened my antennae to hold whatever bluff I needed to play.

So in the face of her suspicion, I locked my brow in deep thought and steadied my juddering heart rate. "Oh, hi Angela," I said, as if her coming through the door right at that moment was exactly what I'd expected. "I was just thinking whether I needed to mention to Napoleon...no...no...I'll call him later." I laid the agreement down on his chair.

"Not there," Angela said.

"Oh right. Forgot, he doesn't like it." I carefully put it front and centre on the desk and smiled. "Thanks for your help. You've been great."

She looked like she was about to ask me something, but my mobile started ringing in my pocket. *Thank God.*

I pulled it out and looked at the screen.

It was Amy.

"Sorry, Angela, I should take this," I said, and strode past her out of the door. "Hey," I said into the phone. "Am I glad to hear you!"

"We need to talk," Amy said without any introduction. "Now!"

CHAPTER THIRTY-SEVEN

McDonalds was wall-to-wall with fatigued school-kids, all of them around sixteen years old, dressed in white uniforms and black shoes that seemed to dare them into non-conformity. They looked like they belonged to some strange cult which had beaten all the free thought out of them. Since the Hong Kong education system focused on welding the next generation into diligent worker drones, who paid their taxes on time and were content with the aspiration of property ownership, I wondered how far from the truth that actually was.

I found a free plastic seat next to a boy with adolescent fuzz on his top lip, buds blaring music into his ears and a glazed look in his eyes, absorbed in something on his lap-top. If he was still of this world, the only sign of it was the occasional suck he took on his supersized Coke which had already been inhaled down to a bottom-of-the-cup throttle.

Amy turned up after five minutes. The sight of her was pure antidote to the sterile atmosphere. She was wearing a dog-rescue-home T-shirt and tight-fitting jeans and looked good enough to eat which was more than I could say for the Big-Mac, turning cold in front of me.

We need to talk. Now! That was all she had said on the phone. Given the way we had left things this morning, without a word, I was reconsidering my choice of the golden arches as the venue to have this conversation. But right then, as she sauntered across to me, my mind cast back to how last night I'd explored every part of her womanly contours. For a moment I was lost in that blissful memory.

"You couldn't have found somewhere more quiet?" Amy said, bringing me back to the here and now as she sidled her way in opposite me, doing her best not to lay a hand on the table-top for fear of picking up bacteria.

"Here's good," I said. "We need noise."

"Why?"

I didn't answer, wanting her to get to the point. "What's so important that you needed to drag me out of work in the middle of the day?"

218

"Not here, Scott. It's too loud."

"Yes, here, Amy!"

"Scott this place is…"

"It's what we need!" My sharp tone made her sit back, so I came clean. "The two men from last night. They're still following us."

Her face dropped three degrees.

"How do you know?"

"I had another encounter this morning."

Her mouth dropped open. "Are you all right?"

I nodded. "Their way of letting us know that they're watching us, until we do what they want us to do. Whoever 'they' are."

Amy's eyes filled with fear and started to dart around.

"They're not here," I said. "It's too public, which is why I chose it. But they know we're in here, Amy. They're watching, I know they are."

I could see she wanted to get up and run, to make this all go away, so I held my hand out across the table. She looked at it blankly for a moment, before she reached out and squeezed it, the bond from last night reforming instantly, as if the stress of the situation was forcing us to draw emotional strength from each other.

Something in my chest went warm and gooey at her touch.

"You okay?" I asked

She took her time, but eventually she nodded. I asked if she wanted anything to eat or drink.

"I guess McDonalds hasn't started serving liquor yet."

That got me smiling. "You said we needed to talk about something?"

My question came out reluctantly because deep inside I didn't want to have *that* conversation. Past history says those types of conversation never end well for me. Most men like the idea of one-night stands. But I'd drifted enough in my transient life to see the point. Deep down, though I hated to admit it, I wanted more. I wanted to stop drifting and lay anchor somewhere, for a while at least if only to test out what it felt like.

Right then, I readied myself for another bout of disappointment, trying to predict how Amy would phrase it. *Last night was fun, but …It's not you it's me.…Let's get to the end of this, then we'll see what happens…*None of these thoughts should have even been entering my head given the predicament we were in. But the mind is a strange thing. It can't help where it goes, or where it lands, so I just went with it and readied myself for let-down.

"Why didn't you tell me about Napoleon Wong and Daisy Lai, Scott? I thought we trusted each other?"

Okay, so I wasn't expecting that.

"Daisy Lai? Who the hell is Daisy Lai?" I said.

"Don't play me, Scott. If we're going to find out what happened to Terence Auyeung, you need to be honest with me."

"I have been!" I said, my voice lathered with hurt and shock. "I have no idea what you're talking about. Who's Daisy Lai?"

Amy stared at me, searching my face for signs of the truth. I had done the same in witness interviews before, letting the awkward silence build and do its work for me. A damned effective tactic, I realized now that I was on the receiving end.

"Amy, what's going on? Who's Daisy Lai?"

Her hard stare stayed on me another ten seconds. It seemed like an age. Then she seemed to come to a conclusion. What conclusion, I couldn't tell, but she pulled out her phone and after touching and swishing her fingers across the screen, she slid it across the table.

On the screen was a photograph.

I stared at it. At first it confused me. It was a photo I had seen before, for sure. I agonized to latch onto the whispering familiarity for which my memory was reaching. The synapses in my brain started to buzz, as the building blocks slotted into place and led me to the answer.

Sure, I knew this photograph. In fact, I had taken it, which meant…suddenly I felt a deep emotional chasm opening in my chest.

"You went through the photos on my phone when I was asleep?" I said.

Amy shrugged off the accusation. "Why did you keep it from me? We had a deal. I hold the story about Rufus Lam. You tell me everything."

"Your story? Are you joking? Amy, we're being tailed by some pretty vicious men, and you still think you're chasing a story? We'll be lucky if we come out of this alive! And what was last night, then? Just your way of pumping information out of me?"

"This isn't about last night."

"The hell it isn't!"

"This is about you not telling me everything! Why didn't you tell me about this photograph?"

The hurt and anger frothing through me had risen to a tidal wave. How could I have been so wrong about this woman? Right then, it was me who wanted to get out of there and run until I could forget about it all. Amy, Rufus Lam, Napoleon Wong, to hell with them!

"Okay, I get it." She held up her palms as if trying to hold back my venom. "You're angry at me for checking out your phone…"

"You think?"

"But I still want my story on Rufus Lam, okay. That's what I do, Scott, I'm a journalist. The story may have changed, but don't think for a moment I've dropped it."

"What's it changed to? How to violate someone's trust by going through their phone records after you've screwed them?"

The kid with the ear buds next to us, broke free from his trance and glanced over at me, then at Amy, before realizing this was none of his business and going back to his lap-top.

"That's not fair. Last night was…"

"Was what?"

She looked around and leaned over towards me. "Do we have to do this here?"

"I told you," I said. "We're being followed."

"I get that," Amy said, "By two thugs who want us to find out what happened to Terence Auyeung. Auyeung was Rufus Lam's right hand man. Don't you see, Scott? To me, that's a story. And the Rufus Lam slant means people will want to read it. So I'm going to do everything I need to do to find answers, whether you like it or not!" Amy sighed and took it down a level. "This morning, I didn't want to wake you up. After last night, I figured some sleep would do you good. Clear your head for the task ahead, that kind of thing. I also figured after last night…well…maybe we had reached a level of intimacy where it would be okay for me to check out your phone. If I was wrong about that, I'm sorry. But listen to me. This photograph," she reached across and tapped the screen. "This could be the key to finding out what happened to Auyeung. So can we talk about it, please?"

I took three deep breaths, trying to slow down my thoughts and get a grip. There was too much going on inside my head, not least of all the question of whether I had made a bad misjudgment about Amy

Tang. I had put myself out there, left my vulnerabilities open. In return she had taken a baseball bat to them, damn her.

But now wasn't the time for self-pity. I forced myself to push the entire maelstrom to one side, compartmentalized my feelings for later and found the sweet spot of objectivity which had long been my default position.

I picked up her phone and examined the photograph.

It had only been five days since I had followed Napoleon Wong after our lunch at his Channing's Club, but it seemed like an age away, so much had happened since. I let the memory play out of the long taxi ride out to Hang Hau in the New Territories, where the pace of life was slower, all the way wondering what Wong was doing there. Until a woman had turned up to meet him. The same woman sitting across the table from Napoleon in the photograph I had snapped.

Her back was to me, in that little restaurant called *Lardo's*. She was wearing a black base-ball cap, large sun glasses and a fashionable pink-towelling track-suit. I remembered her being dropped off by a silver Mercedes, just minutes before I had taken that photo. I remembered that pink tracksuit being emblazoned with "Juicy" across her pert, gym-fit backside. I remembered Napoleon being so delighted to see her. And I remembered thinking 'wow', when she took off those sun-glasses.

I told Amy.

She thought about it for a moment.

"Why were you following Napoleon Wong?" she asked.

Now there was a question. I hadn't come clean about why I was working in Gadgetech. My working for Rufus Lam wouldn't go down too well with her. She still thought I was just Gadgetech's legal counsel.

I thought about telling her. But given the way she had come into possession of this photograph, I decided to keep a few cards back.

"When Lam announced he was getting involved in the CE election," I said, "Napoleon got worried it would de-rail his buy-out of Gadgetech unless the deal got done fast. He wanted to make sure there wasn't anything else out there that could de-rail it. We already had Auyeung's disappearance to deal with, and with all the publicity surrounding Rufus Lam, things were already pretty shaky. Last thing he wanted was anything else to crawl out of the woodwork, know what I mean? So he asked me to do a full inventory on everything going on, make sure nothing else would show up in the due-diligence to ruin the buy-out's smooth passage. Napoleon gave me full carte-blanche, so I took it to mean nothing was off limits."

"Even him?" Amy asked.

"In my judgement that's what was needed," I shrugged. "It's a management buy-out, Amy. The reputation of the management is the be all and end all. In Gadgetech's case, Napoleon Wong is the management. He's also my boss. So to protect his reputation, I needed to find out everything about his reputation that could harm it and keep it from prying journalists, like you. This," I slid her phone back across the table, "was what I found."

"What did he say when you asked him about it?"

"Never got the chance. This photograph was taken only five days ago. You know everything I've been involved in since then. There hasn't been much time for cozy little chats with the boss. In fact, until you showed me this, I'd forgotten I'd even taken it. That's the truth. That's why I didn't tell you."

Again she gave me that prying stare, prising me open, testing the veracity of my explanation.

"Wait a second," I said. "Did you see the photos which followed this?"

"Scroll along," she said. "I sent more than just this one to my phone."

"'Course you did, because that's what journalists do." I couldn't help it, but I picked up her phone again anyway and scrolled away.

There it was.

The Black Range Rover with the silver hub-caps. Skin-head with the long-lensed camera pointed directly at me at the start of the video I had made. It was up in Hang Hau we had encountered each other for the first time.

I had assumed Skin-head had been following Napoleon. But after last night's encounter, maybe I was wrong. Maybe they had been following me right from the beginning.

But why?

I stored the question for later and scrolled back to the photo of Napoleon and his pink track-suited lady friend.

I looked at Amy. "You going to tell me who this Daisy Lai is? Or are you just going to keep accusing me of keeping stuff from you?"

Amy got up from her seat. "Follow me!" she said.

CHAPTER THIRTY-EIGHT

We jumped into a taxi and hurtled off to Central, to a building name Amy had barked at the driver which I had never heard of.

On the way, we sat in silence, the tension ratcheted up to a level you could curdle. A sideways glance told me she was bottling up her anger as much as I was. My comment about her violating my trust after screwing me had crossed a line I had never wanted to cross. But in the heat of anger my mouth had engaged before my brain and resulted in a car-crash. For me, that wasn't unusual.

There was a part of me that felt entirely justified in my petulance. But when I saw the pure ire in Amy's tense features, something stirred deep within my core. Suddenly, I was torn between wanting to scream at her and wanting to grab her and hold her tight and tell her everything would be okay. It was an internal conflict I couldn't understand, let alone control.

The taxi darted its way through traffic like a pin-ball, leaving my stomach somewhere south of where it should have been. Eventually we screeched up at the pavement outside the building. We were somewhere in Sheung Wan, on the opposite side of the road from the waterfront.

Amy shoved the driver a one-hundred note, got out without saying anything and just assumed I would follow, which I did, like a Hong Kong school-kid freshly beaten, but fully compliant, my brimming rebellion screwed down tight for now.

I craned my neck and looked up at the building. It was tall and flashy and nondescript, like most commercial buildings round this area. The type of building I had passed a hundred times before without it even registering, because it blended in so easily. Even its name – The Mid-Point – was as functional as it was unmemorable. Real estate did not come more prime than this in this area, but somehow it blended into the background, a typical Hong Kong rent-churner for some lucky landlord.

Amy had already opened up a lead, so I jogged to stay in step as she stalked across the reception area, her shoulders high and determined, her head straight ahead, her gait the walk of a person on a mission. If she acknowledged my presence at all, she was doing a great job of hiding it.

It was a cavernous reception area, with escalators going up to an atrium on one side. People criss-crossed its grey marble flooring, hurrying to ever more important destinations. A couple of geriatric, blazered security-guards milled around. A cleaner worked a mop over one quarter, the yellow sign telling people to watch out because the floor was slippery, proving nothing more than an additional obstacle to pedestrians.

Amy stopped at a wall on the far side of the reception area and stared upwards. Posted on the wall was a list of company names, all of them businesses which had offices here in the Mid-Point, I figured. The list was ordered in two neat columns in alphabetical order, each business occupant with its own metallic magnetic strip.

"What's so special about this place?" I asked, the first words which had passed between us across the four waterfront districts.

Amy pointed towards the bottom of the right-hand-side list, at the companies beginning with "S".

I read them off. "Starlight Assets, Starlight Aviation, Starlight Group, Starlight Logistics, Starlight Risk Consultancy, Starlight Transport, Starlight Shipping."

Amy still refused to meet my eye.

"So it looks like the Starlight group has its offices here," I said. "What's that have to do with anything?"

"Have you even heard of Starlight Transport?" she asked.

"These days I skip the business section on my way to the sports pages."

"Starlight Transport used to own this building."

I considered the answer a moment, then shrugged my tired shoulders. "A company that makes money owning property in Hong Kong. What are the odds?"

She rolled her eyes. "Starlight Transport has an interesting background. And an interesting ownership structure."

"Yeah?"

"Ever hear of Rolo Lai?"

"He likely to be in the aforementioned Sports pages?"

"He's head of the family which founded and runs Starlight Transport."

"So?"

"What kind of business do you think a business called Starlight Transport is in?" Amy asked.

"You just told me. Property. Transport too by the sound of it?" I played along.

"It used to be one of the biggest players in the transport sector. Shipping, aviation, logistics, they all used to be Starlight's focus when Rolo Lai's father, Raymond was in charge. But then in the early nineties, when Rolo took over, shipping-freight rates went through the roof and Starlight's profit margins went the other way. So Rolo tried to diversify."

"Into property?"

"Into property," Amy confirmed. "In the early nineties. This place, the Mid-Point, was Starlight's first property venture. It was completed in May 1997, one month before the British handed Hong Kong back to the Chinese in June. Two months before the Asian Financial Crisis."

"So?"

"So, Rolo Lai bought at the top, just before the market crashed. He bet all of Starlight Transport's assets on red, spins the property roulette wheel. It comes up black. Starlight Transport was insolvent. It should have gone into liquidation."

"I'm guessing it didn't, otherwise there would be no point to this fascinating story of yours." Sometimes my sarcasm can be corrosive, and the look Amy was giving me now said she was finding it hard not to slap me.

But that wasn't Amy's style, it turned out. She just turned the other cheek and stared up at the list of names. Her arms were folded. A strand of hair had escaped the tight pony-tail and was brushing her chin. Tiredness etched her features. But still the crusader. Still so damn beautiful.

"What happened?" I asked.

"Daisy Lai, the woman with Napoleon Wong in the picture on your phone. She's Rolo Lai's daughter. A socialite, by all accounts. Likes to be seen at the right clubs and the newest restaurants on the arm of the right kind of man. Actors, pop stars, tycoon bachelors with big trust funds. She doesn't hang around with the likes of Napoleon Wong. Trust me."

There it was: the link.

"They looked pretty cosy when I saw them. And I didn't get the impression she wanted people seeing them together. I mean, Hang Hau? Come on."

"I did some research," Amy said. "There's more to Daisy Lai than just being a social butterfly. She has an MBA from Brown university in the US. She plays a big part in Starlight's business. Rolo's right hand by all accounts."

I took a moment to process that. Napoleon Wong and Daisy Lai. Gadgetech and Starlight Transport. I couldn't see the fit.

"Come on then, Amy. Spill it. You've got me curious. Why didn't Starlight Transport go bust when it got into the property game?"

"Because Rolo Lai is connected to the right people," Amy said.

"What people might these be? The tycoon network? The Triads?"

Amy shook her head. "Starlight sold this building and leased back the top five floors. The official price was low, but there was a side agreement whereby the purchaser paid the full pre-1997 price. That was five times the market price at that time. A purchase at overvalue, a classic bail-out mechanism in Asia. Of course, this is all rumour and the rumour has never really been confirmed. But Starlight was bust, I know that for sure. Yet here we are looking at all of its group companies on that list," she pointed up to the wall. "Somehow, Starlight survived."

"You think the rumour was true, then?"

"I do. I think the purchase of this building at overvalue back in '98 bailed out the Lai family by giving them enough liquid assets to see them through the crisis and out the other side."

"Who was the purchaser? Who was Raymond Lai connected to," I asked again.

"The Landlord of this premises is called Lee Wan Investment Holdings," Amy said.

"That supposed to mean something to me?"

"It's not supposed to mean anything to anybody. It's a private equity front for the real owner, which owns Lee Wan Investment Holdings through a Cayman registered company."

"Amy, get to the point! Who bailed out Starlight, who's this Rolo Lai connected to, and why is his daughter, Daisy, knocking around with Napoleon Wong?"

Amy didn't say anything. She turned her eyes away from the list on the wall and looked at me for a moment. Then she looked back at the list and pointed to the first column. I followed her finger to the name of the company she was signaling.

And when I saw it, the whole world started to spin off its axis.

CHAPTER THIRTY-NINE

When Amy and I left the Mid-Point Building, we saw it straight away.

There on the other side of the street: the silver-hub-capped Range Rover parked on double yellow lines, its tinted windows wound up tight, but we knew who was sitting behind them, watching us, layering on the pressure.

"See those bastards?" I said.

"Yes," Amy replied. "What should we do?"

"Let them follow us. We're doing what they want."

"Want to catch a taxi back to Quarry Bay?"

"No," I said. "Let's take a tram. It won't shake them off, but no-one said we had to make it easy."

So that's what we did, waiting at the tram-stop in the middle of the road and then climbing up to the top level when one arrived. We took the seats at the front. They were wooden and jarred your spine with every bump across every interchanging rail, but the knowledge that our stop-start progress would piss off the pursuing Skin-head and Tito offered some crumb of comfort.

We stared out of the open windows. The heat and pollution were trapped at street level, leaving a bitter scent on the tongue as the tram jerked and dinged its way slowly eastwards across. We didn't speak, both of us lost in our own thoughts, trying to figure out how the discovery we had just made at the Mid-Point Building impacted our position.

For some reason the discovery made me think back to my childhood, so I just went with the stream of consciousness and let it play out.

I had grown up in a simple world, a world divided into black and white, good versus evil, east versus west. A world where capitalism and communism had stared each other down across the hostile front line of the Berlin Wall, disgusted at the other's society. The capitalist West was symbolised by Ronald Reagan's United States, a shining white New Jerusalem, built on the principle that the individual should have freedom to make his own economic and political decisions, to pursue profit and the American Dream, because greed was good and the driver of all progress. The Soviet Eastern bloc, the evil empire, offered the complete contrast, where no-one was permitted to own anything or do anything because the means of production and distribution were in state hands, freedom was suppressed and athletes were able to win sprint competitions because they were drugged up to their eye-balls by sinister men in white coats.

It was a safer, more predictable world back then. Sure, each side had a nuclear arsenal enough to blow the world up four times over. But the US President and Soviet General Secretary both had their own red buttons. One push from either was Armageddon. It made for a dangerous, despicable, but perfect symmetry and a complete stalemate. Neither party could dare make the fateful decision, because it would end it all for everyone. We were safe in a nuclear world, we thought, because of 'Mutual Assured Destruction'. We were safe because the world had gone MAD.

It was in this Eurocentric world I grew up, where James Bond killed Soviet hard men and bedded their blond girlfriends every couple of years, where Rambo reinvented the American experience in Vietnam because history was written by the winners, and where Rocky symbolized the American rags to riches story. It was, as I said, oh so very simple.

Then came Perestroika and Glasnost. Then came Reagan's edict for Gorbachev to 'tear down this wall'. And in '89 down it came, unifying Germany and splintering the Eastern Bloc into nation-states with funny-sounding names which no-one had ever heard of. The Cold War…and history…were over. The West had won and democratic capitalism was the victor, the principle on which society was to be structured, going forward.

Or so the world thought.

But then came China, and history re-started with a vengeance.

***

As the tram rattled on, I became increasingly agitated.

The silence that lay between Amy and me was doing us no good. We needed to banter through the implications of what we had found, test out scenarios, throw around ideas, argue them through and tease out the truth. The public tram was no place to do this, so at my instigation, we jumped out at North Point and snuck down to the harbour, to the dog park which skirted the water's edge. It would eventually lead me back to my office, but not before we had talked things through.

'Dog park' was a strange name for the strip of white concrete and brown decking by the open water that blazed under the midday sun. But in a city so short of space, this was all there was to spare for man's four-legged friends. Even then, they had to share it with lunch-time joggers who sweltered up and down at a slow pace, sweating out their morning's stress.

Hong Kong Harbour was calm today. There was hardly a breath of breeze. Out on the dark blue water, a yacht looked like it was about to confront a container ship. The ship blasted its fog-horn and sent the yacht on its way.

As Amy and I started our saunter, a little poodle, braving the heat, skittered past us chasing a red ball. The ball was far too big for its mouth, but it still managed to clasp it between its jaws, its tongue hanging out the side panting up a storm. From behind us, the owner called for the poodle to bring the ball back. I hoped there was a drink in it for the poodle.

We walked for around three minutes until we found ourselves on our own, exposed to the sun. Sweat beads and heat prickled under my collar. Amy had her hand up to her forehead. I wondered how I was going to kick things off, but she beat me to it.

"What do you think?" she asked.

"I think we've bitten off more than we can chew. A bit like that poodle with the ball back there."

Amy wasn't in the mood for joking around, so I took a deep sigh and got to it. "The China Overseas Investment Corporation. The COIC. Okay, so I've heard the name before. I just can't think where. But I'm guessing, with a name like that it's owned by the state, right? The Central People's Government up in Beijing?"

Amy gave a slow nod. "COIC was established in the early nineties. Nobody knows exactly how much capitalization it has. And its ownership structure is pretty unclear too. But put it this way. The people who run it once worked for Chinese state banks, so yes, COIC is more than likely a state-owned enterprise. No-one knows exactly what it does, but there are a lot of rumours."

"Like what?" I asked.

"Like COIC was one of a number of vehicles set up by the Chinese government in the nineties to invest in assets abroad which might one day serve Chinese interests."

I thought about that for a moment. "So what are we saying here? COIC bought the Mid-Point building from Starlight Transport to serve Chinese interests?"

Amy smiled sweetly, as if pleased I had asked the question because it gave her a chance to test out a theory.

"Back in 1998," she began, "after the property market had plummeted and Starlight Transport was desperate to find a buyer, COIC stepped in and made the purchase through corporate trusts established in the Caymans, making it difficult to draw a link back to it."

"But you seem to have done so," I said.

Amy shrugged. "I did some research about five years ago for a piece I wrote about Chinese state-owned enterprises venturing into foreign markets."

"Sounds interesting."

"You know much about modern Chinese history, Scott?"

"How modern are we talking? Doctor Sun Yat Sen declaring the republic in 1912 and attempting to unify the country?" I asked, pleased that it gave me a chance to show some knowledge. "He failed, of course, but Sun was your classic heroic failure. Now he holds the mantle of godfather of the Chinese nation, which isn't a bad mantle to hold. After Doctor Sun, things go from bad to worse, however. Warlords splinter China into territories of factionalized in-fighting. Then the Japanese invade and occupy Manchuria. Instead of fighting them, Chiang Kai Shek turns on Mao and the country descends into civil war. Mao goes on his Long March, regroups, comes back and defeats Chiang. He declares the People's Republic in '49. The communists win, Chiang's nationalists flee to Taiwan."

"Not bad," Amy said. "But it's what comes after that, I'm talking about."

I gathered my thoughts and continued. "Some say Mao achieved what Sun set out to do, unifying the nation. He was also a Marxist and redistributed land to the poor. But then he decided to try and force China to industrialise with his Great Leap Forward in the fifties. Thirty million people died of starvation as a result. Then came the Cultural Revolution, Mao's attempt to reinvigorate the communist doctrine by unleashing his red guards to purify China of bourgeois influences. It was chaos. People were desperate to get out. Including your dad, right? He swam to Hong Kong, you told me."

"You have a good memory. And a good knowledge of history," Amy conceded.

"To study the past is to divine the future," I said. "Isn't that what Confucius said?"

"Now you're just showing off," Amy smiled. "But keep going. Let's see how up-to-date you are."

I stopped, leaned on the rail and looked out into the harbour. East Kowloon on the other side was a mishmash of silver new-builds and construction projects. Just like the rest of Hong Kong, always reinventing itself.

"Mao dies in '76. In come the Gang of Four who try to continue the legacy of retribution against Mao's enemies. But they don't bank on Deng Xiao Peng, the chain-smoking, football-loving Long Marcher with the baby face and the iron will to survive his continual purges. Deng finally comes in from the cold, taking power; and in '78, he sets China on a new path. He adopts capitalism from the West. Rumour has it he said, 'to get rich is glorious'. True or not, it was Deng who unleashed the Dragon and boy, did it start to grow. Then in '89 the Berlin Wall comes down and the Cold War ends. Communism is dead, supposedly anyway. The Soviet Union is no more and everyone thinks it's only a matter of time before the Chinese follow suit. Suddenly everyone is clamouring to get into China's market of 1.3 billion consumers, all it needs is for the bulging damn to reach breaking point."

We pushed off the rails and continued walking.

"June 4th 1989," I continued. "That was supposed to be it: the turning-point, the storming of the barricades in Tiananman Square, China's very own Berlin Wall collapsing under the weight of popular protest. But Deng sent in the tanks and regained control. That's where the misunderstanding came, you see. Deng's plan was never to copy the western model of capitalism, not wholeheartedly anyway. His plan was to take capitalism and Chinesify it. Individual economic freedom was a powerful force, but couple it with the full backing of authoritarian power, and one day, China would shake the world. And guess what? The world's shaking. That about bring us up to date?"

"Almost," Amy said. "But didn't you just quote Confucius at me. Something about studying the past to divine the future? Why don't you divine?"

"Never been one for predictions, Amy," I said. "Anyway, aren't you the journalist? Why don't you tell me how this ends? Or at least how this is all connected to the China Overseas Investment Corporation."

The concrete path forked in front of us. Without thinking about it, we veered right, steering away from the harbour and into the shade of the tree-lined walkway. On the left was an exercise area for the over-sixties with Tai-Chi wheels and stretch beams. On the right was a bench. We took the bench.

Amy leaned her elbows onto her knees, let her dark hair dangle seductively over her cheeks.

"Have you ever heard of the Self-Strengtheners?" she asked.

"Some sort of gym franchise?"

She made a face. "It was a movement in nineteenth-century China. Its proponents said the way to modernize was effectively to copy-cat western techniques. Why re-invent the wheel, when you can get the inventors to give you the design? Especially, if you have something the inventors desperately want. It never worked out for the Self-Strengtheners back then. But that's exactly what China is doing now. 'You want to sell your goods and services to our 1.3 billion population; you give us your technology first'. That's how all these joint-ventures on the Mainland work. Only the market-access piece is still tightly controlled. It's the same with foreign policy. Every move China makes abroad is with one aim in mind: to secure raw materials or advanced technology to assist with its domestic development. China doesn't care who it deals with, provided its domestic interests are fulfilled. And you know how the Chinese government does it? Through Chinese companies that are either directly owned by the state or closely tied to it. Under Chairman Mao, state-owned companies were totally inefficient iron rice bowls. Under the new régime, Chinese companies have been transformed into competitive world beaters and serve as key instruments of foreign policy. If China wants something, it uses one of its companies to go and get it. Like you said, Scott, China has Chinesified capitalism."

"So let me ask again," I said. "What's this all got to do with the China Overseas Investment Corporation buying the Mid-Point building from Starlight Transport? Unless there's an undiscovered oil field in Sheung Wan, none of us know about, what was the point?"

Amy swiveled round. "There's one thing you missed in your historical overview, mister Smart-Arse. The one that all of you Gweilos miss, because you look at things through Western-tinted glasses."

"And what might that be?"

"The Chinese government doesn't think short-term, like Western politics. It takes the long-term view. It thinks in terms of generations. You can do that when you don't have elections to worry about every few years. When you change your leaders only once every generation."

She pushed herself up and started to walk again. She didn't beckon me to follow, but I took my cue anyway. "Buying access to raw materials and technology is just one phase of what China's been doing, don't you see?" she said. "Phase two is more subtle and goes on well below the radar screen. Phase two is about securing influence for the future, by doing favours now while you have the money. You scratch someone's back when they desperately need it scratched, that debt's good for a long time. Ten, twenty, thirty years down the road when you need to call in the debt, you call it in. Phase two is what the China Overseas Investment Corporation does. Phase two is about soft-power."

I mulled on that for a moment. "Looks more to me like a vulture fund. Starlight Transport was in trouble because the property market had crashed. COIC moved in to pick up the Mid-Point, Starlight's prized asset, at a distressed price."

Amy shook her head. "There you go again with your western way of thinking. Always looking at the bottom line."

"What are you talking about?"

"Remember I said COIC bought the Mid-Point at an overvalue. The deal was done in 1998, after the Asian Financial Crisis had hit, but they fixed the price as at year-end 1996, six months before prices plummeted. It wasn't a distressed sale, Scott. It was a bail-out. COIC saved Starlight Transport and Rolo Lai."

A jogger headed past us in the opposite direction. He was heavy-set and his feet slapped down hard on the concrete. From the look on his face, he was hurting. Jogging in the mid-day sun seemed like the last thing he wanted to be doing.

"How do you know about all this?" I asked.

"I'm a journalist. It's my job to know."

That made me chuckle. "Fine. Then let me circle back. What the hell does this all have to do with Gadgetech?"

"The picture on your phone, of course," Amy said, as if it was the most obvious thing in the world. "Daisy Lai is Rolo Lai's daughter. She's part of Starlight Transport's management. The company that benefited from the munificence of a Chinese bail-out in '98. The company through which the Chinese Overseas Investment Corporation can now directly execute the influence of the Chinese government. And there's Daisy Lai on your phone, having a cosy little chat with Napoleon Wong."

"What?" I said. "Amy, there could be a hundred different reasons for Daisy Lai meeting with Napoleon."

"Like?"

"Let's start with the most obvious," I said. "Napoleon Wong is sleeping with her."

"Scott!"

"What? It happens. It did last night for us, remember?"

She shot me a sideways smile. "Napoleon Wong? Yuck!" She screwed up her face in part disgust, part disbelief.

"Lord Byron was a hunchback. Toulouse-Lautrec was a dwarf. They were two of the greatest lovers in history."

"Yes, but still…"

"Napoleon Wong is the chief executive officer of a sizeable Hong Kong retailer which is rapidly becoming a household name. He's a powerful man in his own little world. You've heard about power being an aphrodisiac, right?"

"Starlight Transport dwarfs Gadgetech in size, Scott," Amy said wearily. "So I don't think Daisy Lai has been swept of her feet by Napoleon Wong because of the sense of power he exudes."

"Okay, but it's a scenario. I'm just saying we should try to list out all the possibilities before jumping to any conclusions, okay?"

"Fine. Have it your way. Napoleon Wong and Daisy Lai are having an affair. I'll accept that it's a possibility, albeit a remote one. What else have you got?"

I thought for a moment. "Napoleon is just about to buy-out Rufus Lam's share of Gadgetech. Maybe he's looking for another investor to fund Gadgetech's expansion after he completes the buy-out? Starlight

Transport is a potential investor. That meeting with Daisy Lai could have been to talk about fund-raising. He was pitching Gadgetech to her."

Amy stopped, crossed her arms and tapped her fingers on her elbow.

"You want to fund-raise, you do it in a board room in Central," she said. "You don't do it in an out of the way restaurant in Hang Hau."

"Fair enough," I admitted. "But again, it's a possible explanation to add to our list. After all, maybe he or she likes that particular restaurant. Maybe they don't want people to know they're talking?"

"What else?" Amy said.

We kept walking and thinking, reaching the end of the trees and out into the blazing sun again. I ran a finger under my collar, squinting through brightness.

Eventually we reached a patch a grass, an oasis of greenery in this concrete desert we lived in. There was something refreshing about seeing such a rarity. Apparently, I wasn't the only one who thought so. A couple had chosen it as the venue for their wedding photographs. There was the bride, dolled up to the nines in her veil and make-up, leaning on her husband who was decked out in his white tuxedo. They seemed to sparkle together in the sunlight.

Anywhere else in the world, it would have been an incongruous sight. But this was Hong Kong. Wedding photographs were vital to any newly-married couple, provided they didn't cost the earth and fit in with their holiday allowance, which was why it wasn't unusual to see them being shot in a place like this on any given weekday lunch hour.

"Maybe they're in love?" I said. "Napoleon and Daisy Lai, I mean."

"We already did that one," Amy said.

"Love isn't about what you look like or how much power you exude, you know. It's about two people finding an unexpected connection which no-one else can explain."

"And you believe that?"

I stopped and looked at the couple. The bride cradled her head on her husband's shoulder, her false eyelashes fluttering, her smile lighting up her whole face. The husband kissed her forehead and she shrugged her shoulders and snuggled up to him. It looked like true love I was witnessing. Whatever trials they faced going forward they would always have this moment in time immortalized in these pictures, here in this Dog Park on this weekday, and appreciate what they had.

I realized then what I had to do. I realized I had to come clean with Amy about who I really was.

"I don't know what to believe," I said. "But before we go on, there's something I need to tell you, Amy. I haven't exactly been honest with you. I want to say sorry for that and I hope you understand. But whatever we've got ourselves into, we're in this together. So you deserve to know the truth."

Amy turned and stared at me.

"What are you talking about?" she asked.

"I am a lawyer, that part of it's true. But I'm working for Rufus Lam. That's the reason I got the job in Gadgetech," I confessed. "Rufus Lam is my client."

CHAPTER FORTY

Eight-thirty at night and I was still in the office, the single beam of light from the desk lamp my only illumination and sole companion, the darkness beyond it a perfect summation of the way I was feeling.

I didn't know why I was still here. The rest of the Gadgetech staff on the floor had cleared out by six-thirty, apart from Tabitha who had stayed behind out of a misplaced sense of loyalty. I had chased her out at seven. Since then, I'd been on my own, wallowing in a deep, dark ocean of a mood. A mood which surfaced all the mistakes I had made in my life. A mood which seeped right into the marrow of my bones and brought me down into the gutter of depression and puddle of self-pity. Right then, it was no longer about me finding a way out of this mess. It was about whether I really wanted to, whether there was a point to it any more.

Amy had reacted badly to my admission about working for Rufus Lam, the man she blamed for ruining her father's life. I should have expected it, really, but there was a part of me that was ever the naïve optimist. Right up until the moment she had slapped my cheek and launched into a full tantrum of hurt and disbelief. Insults and swear-words had spilled from her beautiful lips like machine-gun fire, every one of them finding their mark in my soul, or what was left of it at least (which wasn't much according to her).

"What kind of person are you? All this time I thought we were working together, but you're nothing but Rufus Lam's whore? What did he want you to do? Stop me from writing about him? Fuck you, Scott! Fuck you!"

I had tried to grab hold of her, but she had stormed off, the steam rising off her. The commotion had caused the newly-wed couple to pause their photo shoot and look over. They probably hoped this wasn't some sort of an omen they were witnessing, a vision of themselves in five years time.

I had nodded an apology at the interruption, turned and kept on walking until I had made it back to Gadgetech, shutting myself up in my office, letting the air-conditioning bring me down to the melancholic state in which I now found myself.

If I smoked, now would have been the right time to light up. If I drank, now would have been the time to get wasted big time, and it certainly crossed my mind. But instead, those past mistakes I was thinking about came back to kick me in the gut.

There hadn't been a string of other women in my life to reminisce about, but there had been enough to create a solid track-record of regret. A girl called Sarah I had been out with a few times back in my London days. She was a homely sort, perfect marriage material and that had scared the hell out of me. We had broken up in the worst way possible. Not with a clean ending, but with our relationship stuttering to a halt as I made excuse after excuse for why I couldn't meet her, hoping that we could somehow take a subtle step backwards to the easy road of friendship. Of course, it never works that way. I had hurt her. We didn't speak now. She was married, to an investment banker no less, living happily in Kent with her kids and her coffee-mornings and, I hoped, no memory of the disaster that was Scott Lee.

Then there was Kimmie Yang. The only mistake we had made was putting our respective careers ahead of a relationship that could have been so special. Kimmie was dead now, but I was still here. I had thought Kimmie was the one. I had thought I would never again feel that same electric current that rippled between us every time we were together.

Until I met Amy.

Amy was something else, a real crusader, a person of substance in a world of surface appearance. Together, we crackled like kindling, sparking ideas, matching each other intellectually punch for punch. She was special and, I had to admit, there was part of me which had hoped that we could have become special to each other one day. But that afternoon she had stormed off because I had lied to her, straight into Scott Lee's book of failed relationships.

Sometimes, life sucked!

Placing my elbows on the desk, I let my forehead fall onto the heel of my palms and let go a heavy sigh. I told myself I had done the right thing by coming clean. It was the least Amy deserved, given the dilemma we were in, a dilemma she had faced by looking for a way out, teasing out a lead from the photographs on my phone which I had kept from her, and presenting us with another possible path to go down. A woman of pure action; that was who Amy was. And if she was prepared to face adversity with that kind of attitude, she deserved the truth. Even if the truth was likely to shatter the brittle bond built between us.

It was the right thing to do.

All I could do now was hope that when her jets cooled, she would come back and let me explain. The chances were slim, though.

I stayed on that train of thought for a while longer, letting the full vengeance of my mood crescendo and work its way out on the other side, until all that was left were the lees of a melancholic solitude which had become my default position.

Then it was my turn to get to work on the strands which Amy had teased out for me that afternoon.

I rubbed the rawness out of my eyes and got started.

***

Midnight. Three hours of hard research later and I needed a break.

I got up, stretched my back, rolled out my shoulders and blinked myself awake. I popped a can of Red Bull. It had been a long night and was going to be longer still. My melancholic mood was gone. Once again I was the determined lawyer looking for answers in the only way I knew how. By total immersion in the facts, by building evidence and letting it take me wherever it led. By exploring every dead-end to a brick wall or break-through. By treating everything as relevant, until there was something hard and fast to say it should be discarded.

Tonight, I was coming out of the other side of this thing with some idea about what was going on, I promised myself.

Ten minutes later, I settled back down and went over everything I had dug into in the past three hours, revisiting every step I had made to make sure nothing got missed.

It was a painful process.

But it was worth it.

My research had started out with a guy called Hank Rasmusson.

Hank was the Wisconsin-based author of a blog called HFF, short for 'Hank For Freedom'. A long-whiskered self-styled Joe Shmo who billed himself as a leading conservative commentator. Hank was pro-guns, pro-life, pro-liberty and pro-you believing in a God who was all-American. He trash-talked big-government, demonized Franklin Delano Roosevelt, hated Obama and riled against any Democratic

Party policy that involved the use of public money. His long-on-rhetoric, short-on-statistics style, was like a firebrand preacher's and about as illogical.

I disagreed with just about everything Hank wrote, but I had found his blog because a Google search had led me there, to a piece which Hank had posted last November.

In it, Hank railed against the rise of China, or the 'new yellow peril' as he termed it. China was, according to Hank's misguided knowledge of history, 'Pearl Harbour all over again'. 'Those Chinese are using our knowledge against us!' his words screamed.

> *Look at this company called ZTE. Supposed to be one of the biggest Chinese tech players and you know how it does business? By buying up US technology and selling it to Iran! We'v caught them doing it! Selling surveillance technology of all things, can you believe that! China's getting hold of our technology and selling it to our enemies. That makes China the enemy, as far as I'm concerned. They're out to get us, people. They're pissing down our backs and saying it's raining. Thank the Good Lord those bozos in Washington have had the sense to do something. But how long are those rubber-backboned liberals gonna hold out? And you think ZTE's the only China corporate up to these shenanigans? Think again! So my fellow Americans, grab your Glocks and Berettas. Grab your hunting knives. 'Cos you're gonna need 'em.*

Hank then proceeded to list his top-twenty Chinese companies that were looking to hoover up American inventions and intellectual property. Most of the names on the list only went to prove that Hank was a top-drawer idiot. ZTE was there. But at number two on his list, he had put Samsung because it was Apple's biggest rival. Samsung was Korean, of course, but according to Hank the Chinese were using the 'bonds of eastern brotherhood' to enlist Samsung's help in accessing US technology. Same with Hyundai, the Korean car-maker, Hank's number five....like I said, Hank was a top-drawer idiot.

On and on the list went, filled with Hank's nonsensical, prejudiced commentary.

But it was the company Hank had listed at number twenty which my Google search had snagged and the reason I was forcing myself to read his drivel.

The China Overseas Investment Corporation. COIC.

This one had no commentary from Hank and I guessed it was only on his list because he needed a number twenty. There was a footnote, however, which referenced as his source, an article called *"China's growing corporate influence"* in a publication called *"The Eastern Economic and Foreign Policy Report"*.

Earlier that evening, I had clicked the link to the reference which Hank had left, but it was broken. So I had gone back to Google and plugged in the name of the publication and article. This had brought me to a website which served as an article database. You could have access to any article you wanted, for ten dollars a pop. I paid my ten bucks and the article was e-mailed to my Yahoo account fifteen minutes later.

Before revisiting the article, I looked further down the list of results on my original Google search for the Chinese Overseas Investment Corporation to see if I was missing anything. Nothing snapped out. COIC had no website and no Wikipedia page, which was unusual in this day and age. That meant Hank For Freedom's blog – and the article he had led me to – were the only pieces of information I could find.

I went back to my Yahoo. The e-mail with the article was still top of my in-box. I hit download again and for the second time that evening, the article's title page hit me like a punch to my solar plexus.

"China's growing corporate influence –
The role of state-owned entities in China's foreign policy
By Amy ML Tang"

Amy! Of all the journalists in all the world…

No wonder COIC had sounded familiar. I had seen this article before, I realized, when first checking into Amy's background. Her writing and research had impressed me then. It impressed me even more now.

Earlier I had read the article on screen, but this time I printed it out. I leaned back in my chair and over the next hour and a half I read it again, twice. The second time, I had a yellow highlighter and biro in hand to make notes of the pertinent excerpts.

It sure was fascinating; as completely absorbing as Hank-For-Freedom's blog had been vacuous nonsense. Although, I'll say this for Hank. He, like me, had read Amy's article. The facts Hank had used that were not blatant falsifications had simply been plagiarized straight from Amy's research.

The article set out the thesis Amy had put to me that afternoon as we had swapped ideas in the Dog Park. That China's foreign policy was based on one simple aim: using the outside world to achieve its domestic development.

Amy laid out how this was being achieved through private Chinese companies, whose opaque ownership structures and means of appointing senior officers tried to mask their true role as instruments of the Chinese state. Through these companies' investments, China had already secured an ever-ready supply of raw materials to fuel its domestic economy, showing absolutely no qualms about dealing with pariah régimes. Chinese money was, apparently, developing oil refineries in Iran, securing natural gas supplies from Burma, leasing copper mines in Afghanistan, acquiring land in the Democratic Republic of Congo and clinching mineral deals in Zimbabwe.

Amy then set out how the Chinese were going after advanced technologies too, fulfilling the vision which the Self-Strengtheners had developed in the nineteenth century. Why should Chinese companies waste time in starting at the beginning when they could just buy themselves up to date? But here, Amy pointed out, Chinese ambitions had been curtailed by Western government's suspicion. A prime example was a US government probe into Chinese tech-giant ZTE in 2012, for purportedly selling technology to the Telecommunication Company of Iran in purported breach of US sanctions. (No doubt this was where Hank For Freedom had got the idea for his blog.)

ZTE, Amy wrote, had done its best to allay concerns by announcing that it was curtailing its Iranian business. But this was just one example of the concern and suspicion that the activity of Chinese companies was creating among foreign governments. In 2006, Huawei, another Chinese tech-giant, had abandoned its bid to buy British defence company Marconi when Conservative politicians raised national security concerns. Huawei had to do the same in 2011 with its proposed bid for US-based 3Leaf systems when the Committee on Foreign Investment in the United States raised objections.

Similar barriers had been placed on the expansion plans of other Chinese corporate juggernauts like Lenovo, Haier and particularly the Chinese National Oil Offshore Corporation, which had given up its bid for Unocal after being portrayed in the media as a tool of the Chinese government.

But it was the next part of Amy's article which was of most interest.

According to her, going after raw materials and advanced technology was just the first phase of these concerted Chinese corporate actions. There was a second phase of expansion being planned, a phase which had so far floated under the radar screen of Western commentators, but which Amy predicted would have far-reaching consequences for the balance of economic power in the world.

Phase Two was not about the Chinese securing hard assets. It was about the Chinese securing influence. Not for the here and now, but for the future when China would most need it. Through specifically targeted investments, Amy suggested, China was building a web of favours or IOUs around the globe, which it could call in at any time when it needed to. And one of the main vehicles it was using to exercise this soft power was the little-known Chinese Overseas Investment Corporation.

No-one was really sure when COIC had first been set up, but Amy surmised in was in the mid-1990s. Its ownership structure was hidden through a series of trusts registered in the Cayman Islands, but according to Amy, its largest current shareholders were the China Investment Corporation and the China Development Bank, the two bodies responsible for wielding China's investment power abroad. Under their purview, COIC had been groomed.

But it was in Hong Kong, that COIC's strategies had first been tested.

Why Hong Kong? Because it was the perfect place for COIC to cut its teeth.

Hong Kong may have returned to Chinese sovereignty in 1997, but the one-country two-systems compromise guaranteed the city a high degree of political autonomy and the eyes of the world were constantly watching to ensure that autonomy was maintained. So for the Chinese government to make its establishment of control over Hong Kong complete, it needed to build more subtle levers of influence; the type of influence which was devastatingly effective, but could only be established over time.

And so Hong Kong offered the perfect place for COIC's first deployment.

Amy ended her article, less with a conclusion and more with a challenge to her readers.

> *As HongKongers, we would do well to keep a close eye on every investment which COIC makes in Hong Kong, for therein lies the template for the way in which China will seek to build influence in the world. Each time COIC spends money, we must ask ourselves: What lever of influence does it buy China? And when will China seek to pull the lever?*

When indeed, I wondered, as I set the article down on my desk.

CHAPTER FORTY-ONE

3.30am.

The taxi home cost me two hundred dollars, but it didn't matter. I was putting it on Phil's tab, let him be the one to claim it back from Rufus Lam. As we sped out of the Cross-Harbour Tunnel, I asked the driver to drop me. The walk home would do me good; help me come down from my Red Bull high.

Causeway Bay, one of the most populous areas in the world in the day-time, was a ghost town at night, the silence so out of place it cried out to be filled. Around me, the neon bedecked buildings seemed to sag, as if letting out the stress and heat of the day. A ten-car taxi queue sat at the rank outside the deserted Sogo department store. I could almost feel the hope given off by the lead driver when I came into sight; that I was that juiciest of fares: a drunk expat in need of a ride out to Stanley. Hope quickly turned to disappointment, however, as I hurried over the interchange, where only hours ago, hordes had met in the middle, like two armies clashing when the lights changed.

On Hysan Road, I laid out twenty bucks for a 'sausage-bread' to calm my roiling stomach at a 7-Eleven. The too-cheerful attendant was glad of the company and offered me a pack of chocolate wafers to go with it, but more sugar was the last thing I needed. She gave me a dollar off the previous day's paper and I tucked it under my sweaty arm-pit as I left the shop.

I felt his presence before seeing him.

Cold fingers of fear tickled down my backbone.

"You have been working late, I see."

The voice froze me to the spot. It was an effort to turn round, but a horror-movie-like fascination drew me.

There he was: Skin-head. Leaning up against a piece of bamboo scaffolding, hands in his pockets, as if hanging round outside a 7-Eleven at three-thirty in the morning was the most natural thing in the world. His rat-like eyes worked me up and down, his humourless smile as terrifying as anything that existed on this earth.

"Have you yet something for me on Terence Auyeung?" he asked.

May be it was the gravel in his voice which irked me. Or may be it was the way he asked, 'Have you yet something for me', an awkward turn of phrase. Or may be the fatigue was finally pushing me to breaking-point. Whatever it was, suddenly there was fire in my belly.

"Why don't you stay out of the way and let me get on with it?" I said through clenched teeth.

Skin-head pushed himself off the scaffolding, chuckled and stepped into my personal space. Our gazes locked.

"Tick-tock," he said, adding extra spit to the words.

He sauntered away, his smooth efficient gait unmistakably that of someone trained to inflict harm. But not without letting his evil eyes linger a moment longer, before he disappeared round the corner and into the darkness, like a demon of the night.

***

Ten minutes later I was back home, shallow breaths catching in my throat. Shutting and bolting the door behind me took on extra significance that night.

I drew the curtains tight, checked that the windows were locked down and hit the air-conditioner, allowing its helicopter drawl to drown out the sense that Skin-head was still out there somewhere. Watching me, tormenting me.

I told myself it was safe here, but the mind believes what it wants to believe. There was no way I was getting any sleep, but I needed something to absorb my racing thoughts, so once again, I re-immersed myself in the task at hand. I let facts of Gadgetech and Terence Auyeung and Rufus Lam fill my head, until my brain was burgeoning with a maelstrom of jumbled ideas and loose connections.

It was working. My breathing slowed.

I was getting close now, I could feel it. But still so agonizingly out of reach. Like looking at a photograph through misted glass. The colours all there, but the image a messy blur.

Time to see if I could wipe away the condensation.

I found a yellow legal pad, ripped the top sheet off, tucked my feet under me on the sofa, and began scribbling it all down. No rhyme or reason. No order to it. Just a complete brain-dump of everything I had learned and retained. It was oddly cathartic, relieving my mind of its burden. When I was done I had filled three pages.

I got up, walked around. Sat down and reviewed, trying to draw lines between the bullet points, seeking out connections, but every connection I came up with just gave rise to a slew of extra questions which rubbished it.

Four-thirty came and went. Still no sign of the elusive mistress they called fatigue.

Terence Auyeung.

He was where this whole thing had started.

Rufus Lam had parachuted his close compadre into the CFO position at Gadgetech to safeguard his investment against the naked ambition of CEO, Napoleon Wong. But Terence had ended up stealing some of that money for himself, in a well-worked false-vendor scam. Why? Because his son had overreached on a shadow-bank loan and was into Benson Chan for a monstrous amount.

Why hadn't Auyeung just gone to Lam for help? Pride was the obvious answer. But where was his pride when he was stealing from Gadgetech? And why not steal more? Why not clear the debt completely, pay Benson Chan back in full. If he had, then maybe he would still be alive.

But according to Skin-head, Auyeung was still alive, instead of propping up the concrete foundations of the North Point by-pass, which according to his son, David, was where he had ended up.

And who the hell were Skin-head and Tito working for anyway? Benson Chan was the most obvious suspect. Just a couple of hands-on debt-collectors working for a loan-shark. But how could I be sure? I drew a line from Skin-head to Benson Chan and put a question mark.

Like ripples in a lake, Auyeung's fraud on Gadgetech had knock-on effects. Napoleon Wong had uncovered it and, instead of going to the police, was using it to blackmail Rufus Lam into selling his share in Gadgetech to Napoleon at an undervalue. Rufus Lam could have fought back, sure, but he had decided against it. Gadgetech and Wong were just a minor distraction, as far as he was concerned. It was the bigger picture that mattered to Lam: the election for Hong Kong's Chief Executive and bringing democracy to the territory. The hitherto apolitical tycoon had gone all in, thrown the full weight of his finances, influence and reputation behind Elizabeth Leung, who was taking on Beijing's hand-picked mouth-piece, Jeremy Lau. Rufus Lam was taking a principled stand, refusing to pay his taxes, calling for a mass rally and asking other HongKongers to join him to get Elizabeth Leung's candidacy past the nominating committee.

Lam's reputation was now well and truly on the line.

And what about Napoleon and his girlfriend Daisy Lai, daughter of Rolo Lai and part of the family which ran the Starlight Transport Group?

Starlight Transport: according to Amy the corporation had been bailed out back in 1998 by the China Overseas Investment Corporation, the vehicle which China was using to build a network of soft favours, to underpin its foreign policy. Favours which could be called in at any time, whenever and wherever needed. Hong Kong had been COIC's testing ground for its 'favour building' diplomacy, Starlight Transport one of its first major plays at the height of the Asian Financial Crisis. Decades later, here were Napoleon Wong and Daisy Lai, the Starlight Transport heiress, getting all nice and cosy in an out-of-the-way restaurant in Hang Hau. Connection or just coincidence?

I flipped through my notes.

Here it was, everything I had learned, put down on paper, arrows and lines and crossings-out all over the place.

But still it was one big ol' jumbled mess.

***

5.00am now. Caffeine dehydration, lack of sleep and air-conditioning had dried my throat into a prune. Every time I swallowed, my saliva tasted Red-Bull. I put the pad down, went to brush my teeth, drank two glasses of water and splashed some on my face.

I picked up the pad and settled back down on the sofa. This time the notes just looked like a big question-mark.

I flipped to a fresh sheet and started again. Forget the facts, I told myself. Figure out what makes the best story and see if the facts tie in.

They don't teach this in law school; you pick it up along the way, in thinking on your feet in negotiations, in explaining away good points raised by your opponent in court. It's a process which treats the truth as a wet piece of clay, capable of being moulded into a beautiful voluptuous statue for a judge to fall in love with.

Okay, take it from the top, I told myself.

On the first line of my blank page I wrote the name of the China Overseas Investment Corporation. Five lines beneath it I wrote Starlight Transport. Then I joined the two names up with a downward-pointing arrow, representing COIC's bail-out acquisition of the Mid-Point building in '98, the IOU which COIC fully intended calling in one day, when the opportunity came for Starlight to act.

But what opportunity?

Five lines below Starlight Transport, I wrote the name Gadgetech and connected the two with another downward arrow. This was the little head-to-head between Daisy Lai and Napoleon Wong I had caught on camera in Hang Hau. Maybe that was the influence flowing down, the play which COIC was making? But again came the question: Why? Something important to which Gadgetech was connected, perhaps? Or even someone.

A further five lines down I wrote Rufus Lam's name and pointed to it with another arrow flowing down from Gadgetech. Rufus Lam was succumbing to Napoleon Wong's blackmail. Lam was being forced to sell his stake in Gadgetech to Wong at a knock-down price, buying Wong's silence on Terence Auyeung, the trusted business associate whom Lam had put in Gadgetech, but who had ended his days ripping off the company.

So far so good. Each link in the chain of arrows fitted the facts I had found.

But it was the final link I was coming to, where the trouble lay. The pieces of the jigsaw didn't fit and even contradicted the leap I was about to make. But I made it anyway.

Five lines below Rufus Lam's name I wrote the words "Hong Kong Chief Executive Election". This time the arrow between the two names was dotted, in deference to the contradictions which immediately began rumbling through my mind. It's a knee-jerk reaction every lawyer has, immediately seeing the negative details that destroy the big picture. The most effective cross-examinations work on that dynamic.

Wong's blackmail was based on Auyeung's theft. But Terence Auyeung had stolen from Gadgetech to pay off his son's debt to Benson Chan. It was a desperate action taken by a desperate father seeking to solve a personal family problem. A problem caused by the bad decisions made by his wayward son. Bad business decisions involving smokeless cigarettes, a stupid idea so totally unrelated to anything else I was looking at, it didn't make sense.

Could it really be that Auyeung's son's screw-ups had architected the opportunity to trigger the chain reaction of influence down from COIC? I doubted it. It was just sheer coincidence, it had to be. Bad coincidence as far as Terence Auyeung and Rufus Lam were concerned. Good for Napoleon Wong.

But still just coincidence, and not the only coincidence either. The same could be said about Rufus Lam's decision to enter into the election. I had been there when Napoleon had found out about that. I had seen his little tantrum. It was a genuine reaction. He had no idea that Lam was going into politics. And, crucially, Lam's move had happened after Wong had made his move with his blackmail stunt to force Lam into the buy-out. Hard, then, to build a case that Wong was somehow being used by COIC to engineer the buy-out to influence the CE election.

And what influence could COIC be looking to have anyway?

Coincidences built on coincidences. Fundamental questions unanswered.

But as I looked down at my diagram, something inside me said I was getting close. Instincts like this develop over time and with experience. There comes a point in a lawyer's career, when you stop ignoring them in favour of objective analysis and learn to trust them.

According to the clock, it was ten past six in the morning now. Blue shades of dawn were creeping through the curtains. And irony of all ironies, the fatigue was now closing me in its grasp, my eyes sore and heavy, my head filling fast with cotton-wool clouds.

I went through to the bedroom, stripped and got under the covers.

One hour, I told myself. One hour to crash out and recover.

Whirling thoughts crescendoed into a typhoon of black nothingness in my mind, as I hurtled towards sleep.

CHAPTER FORTY-TWO

I was out for the count, shut down in a dreamless, recharging sleep. The phone must have been ringing some time before it lifted me back to the land of the living.

"Yeah!" my voice was pure sandpaper and had lost three octaves.

"Scott, is that you? Are you asleep?"

Damn stupid question, but not a million miles from the truth. Took a good fifteen seconds for the room to stop spinning; another three for me to remember who and where I was. Through one eye, I saw the time. 7.48am. I had been asleep for all of ninety minutes. It felt like longer, but no way near long enough.

"What's going on, Phil?" I croaked.

"I was about to ask you the same question. Haven't heard from you in a couple of days. Thought I'd just check in, see how things are going with our friend, Napoleon Wong. Any progress for me to report back to Rufus?"

I bolted up, swung my feet off the bed and tried to concentrate on the coolness of the wooden flooring under my toes, the taste of leather in my mouth, the tenseness around my eyes as I tried to squint out the harshness of the morning light; anything to force me awake.

"Yeah, sorry about that." I cleared my throat, like a ninety year-old. "I've been immersed in something, hoping it might lead somewhere," I said, keeping it light and circumspect. "Haven't quite got a full handle on things yet."

"Anything I should know about?"

I pinched the bridge of my nose, in an attempt to stem the giddinesss that comes from sitting up too quick.

"You okay?" Phil asked.

"Yeah, yeah, I'm good. Long night, that's all; working through a few things. Give me the day to try and figure it out. I'll call you this evening with an update. How's that sound?" I said, stalling.

"Make sure you do. Need to keep the client happy, you know how it is. You sure you're okay?"

"Everything's good," I said, trying to sound convincing. "Just feeling a bit groggy that's all. Like I said, it was a long night. How's the family?" I moved to change the subject.

"That's the other reason I'm calling. Alison wanted to see if you can join us for dinner this Saturday. It's your godson's birthday?"

"Its Peter's birthday? Oh damn, I completely…"

"Don't worry about it. He's getting to the age when he thinks spending time with his parents is totally uncool anyway. Can you believe that? Me, uncool."

"What are the odds?" I dead-panned.

"Listen, it'd be great if you could make it. Be doing me a favour actually. My Dad took Peter to school the other day and found out one of his classmates is the son of the new head of marketing at Hong Kong Electric. You know what Dad does? He invites the parents over for Peter's birthday party! Tells me to bag him as a client, can you believe that? Dad's been ambulance-chasing at his own grandson's school."

I chuckled at that. Old Man Yip still had a keen eye for the opportunity.

"And you Law Society president and all," I said.

"I'm telling you, if I get a complaint out of this, I'm changing the family name. Listen, I've got to go. Let me know about Peter's birthday. If you can't make it this weekend, how about we hook up next Sunday?"

"What?" I asked.

"The Pro-democracy rally Rufus is pushing. In Victoria Park. To try and force the nominating committee to put Elizabeth Leung on the ballot sheet for the election," Phil said.

"Oh that!" I suddenly remembered what I had read in the paper a couple of days ago. Rufus Lam was organizing a march to serve as a clear demonstration of popular support for Elizabeth Leung.

"Word is, it's going to be bigger than the July 2003 march," Phil said with pride in his voice. "Rufus has his newspapers all over it. He's telling people it's their civic duty as Hong Kong residents to turn out. They're expecting a million to turn up. Can you believe that? One million people. Be incredible if they reach that kind of number. Alison and I are taking the kids, no matter what Dad says. Could be a historic moment for Hong Kong. You should walk with us."

I agreed to think about it, then rang off.

Rufus Lam's mass democracy rally was ten days away.

My head felt like it was still full of cotton-wool. And here I was, back where I had left off. With Rufus Lam and the damn CE election.

I put the kettle on and showered, did some stretching and made some toast. I felt a lot better for it and more awake. While I was eating the toast, I skimmed the paper I had bought from the 7-Eleven earlier that morning and wondered how I could have missed it. It was cover-to-cover Rufus Lam and the big march.

"Come join us, Rufus Lam challenges HongKongers", the headline screamed. "And bring your umbrellas!" the sub-heading quoted Lam as saying, in a media-savvy attempt to link what he was doing back in October 2014, when last Hong Kong had reached boiling-point in its call for democracy. I skimmed the front page, the follow-ups on the inner pages and the op-ed. The demonstration was being billed as 'a make or break moment for Hong Kong's future', the pinnacle of the city's political maturity. – The time when the Umbrella Generation's democratic aspirations would finally come to fruition. There were plenty of warnings about security as well and the police's expected reaction to the rally. Would the riot shields come out this time? The pepper-spray? The tear-gas? Would rubber bullets be on hand?

A deep sense of unease took me in its grasp.

I had already received a glimpse of the high emotions flooding through the city's hot veins, with the crowds flowing into Taikoo Shing subway station the previous day. Hong Kong was fast becoming a tinder-box. One spark and it would blow.

The rally would dominate the news for the next ten days until it got underway. Lam would make sure of it.

Finishing my toast, I sat back down on the sofa. My legal pad was still there on the coffee table.

I looked again at the diagram I had sketched out and picked up right where I had left off.

I had been awake all of fifteen minutes.

The solid arrows I had drawn represented established links in a chain of evidence connecting the China Overseas Investment Corporation all the way down to Rufus Lam, through Starlight Transport and Gadgetech. But the final dotted line, the link to the CE election, was still proving elusive. Ninety minutes of sleep hadn't changed that. Morning had not brought any parting of the clouds or crystal clarity.

For a moment, I felt no better than those conspiracy theorists fascinated by JFK's assassination, Lord Lucan's disappearance and Princess Diana's death. Sad individuals who liked to fit life into a series of compact explanations.

But life didn't work like that. It was random and fragile, unpredictable and out of control, that was the reality. It was about the day-to-day, about the mundane, about people and relationships and families. People like Phil who worked hard for his kids even though they thought he was as cool as a Noddy Holder haircut, not that they would even have a clue who Noddy Holder was (thank heaven for small mercies). It was about grandparents like Old Man Yip meaning well, but being seen to interfere. Generation after generation who thought they were better than the last. It never changed, the cycle just kept on repeating itself down through the ages.

I needed to get to work by nine o'clock, no point in drawing attention by being late in again. I headed out of the door, took the lift to ground and exited the building.

The sky was grey with bulging, pregnant clouds, the air sticky with humidity. Hong Kong was in one of its darker moods today and it seemed to be reflected by the unamused faces of the commuters heading with me, drone-like, down to the MTR.

I couldn't help thinking about what Phil had told me about his dad and started to chuckle. It helped lift my inner gloom. Old Man Yip had been a real go-getter in his day. When he was building up Yip & Siu, the colony's economy was in developing mode, skyrocketing along to dizzying heights with the other Asian Tigers. Old Man Yip had never let an opportunity to seek out a new case pass him by. He was sledge-hammer blatant in his approach. Some lawyers had that knack, that thick skin, that complete and utter shameless devotion to making money. They were the ones that made it in the profession, and who could blame them? It was hard work convincing people to spend their cash on expensive lawyers to solve problems they never wanted in the first place. The best rainmakers in the business never passed up an opportunity to flaunt themselves and Phil's dad was top drawer. If that meant meeting clients at networking lunches or cocktail parties or industry conventions, or just picking them up randomly amongst the parents of your grandchild's school, he was prepared to do it in the blink of an eye …

The thought stopped me hard and fast, right in the middle of the street.

His grandchild's school...

A woman clicked her teeth as she swerved to avoid me. I didn't bother to apologise, so lost was I in the thought.

The adrenalin began to pump, my skin prickling at the prospect that I was about to take a giant leap forward. The information I needed was in my office at Gadgetech. I hurried onwards, sensing I might have finally found the key that would slot the missing pieces of the jig-saw into place.

CHAPTER FORTY-THREE

Hi, this Amy, leave a message after the tone.

Whoah, that was too short, too abrupt, too…well too Amy-like. No: 'I'm afraid I'm not available to take your call at the moment'. No: 'I'll call you back as soon as I can.'

I hung up mid-beep, thrust my mobile down on the desk like it was radioactive. Last time I had spoken to her, she had slapped me and stormed off, cursing my very existence.

Now I needed her help.

It was going to be hard enough talking to her in person, but doing it by voicemail? Oh man! I pondered it a moment, assessed all other options, realized they were zilch.

Voicemail it had to be.

Okay, breath in, hold it, then out again.

I re-gathered, prepared, picked up the phone, dialled, wetting my dry lips with my dryer tongue as Amy once again uttered her instruction.

"Amy, it's Scott. Don't hang up. We need to talk. Yes, you deserve an explanation and yes, you have every right to be upset. But listen, I'm on to something. There's just one additional piece of information I need to fit things together. And I need your help to find it. I've tried myself, but…look you're the investigative journalist." I told her what I needed. "I know it might seem pretty random, but trust me on this one. I'll explain when you call me. Look, this is the story you're looking for, trust me. So please just…just pick up the phone and call. And…and I'm sorry, okay. For everything. So…just call me. Please."

***

Forty-five minutes before I placed that call, here's what had happened.

I had just stepped into the office picking up on that wisp of an idea which had hit me as I'd been walking down to the MTR.

It's strange how the brain works.

One minute you find yourself mulling on a particular subject, then suddenly, pow, you dredge up an innocuous and totally unrelated piece of information, buried somewhere in the dark recesses of your subconscious. The grey matter gets to work and, bingo, you draw a connection between the two. A connection which snaps your attention. A connection so seemingly random, but when you see the link, you chastise yourself for not having seen it until now.

Tabitha wasn't in yet. I closed my office door to signal no distractions, and sat down.

Amy's notes – the copy she had given me – were locked away in the bottom drawer of my desk for safe-keeping from the night before. I reached down and fished them out, frantically flipped through the pages, until I found it. There it was: the profile she had put together on Benson Chan, Mr Loans-Are-Us himself.

Terence Auyeung had stolen from Gadgetech to pay off his son's debt to Benson Chan. That had been the trigger for what had followed: Terence's disappearance, Napoleon Wong's discovery of the theft and his use of it to blackmail Rufus Lam into the management buy-out.

Or so I had assumed.

But that's where I had it all wrong, you see. Terence Auyeung was just a segueway between what had gone before and what had followed, a single domino being toppled by another. Yes, he had stolen from Gadgetech and, yes the reason for that was because his son, David, had borrowed the money from Benson Chan.

But why from Benson Chan? That was the key. Why not one of the other hundreds of legitimate loan companies in Hong Kong? There were enough of them around, targeting the unsuspecting with their incessantly annoying telemarketing, luring people in with their interest-free rate periods, then tightening the screws as soon they were hooked.

I had never even thought to ask the question.

Not until I had been chuckling to myself about what Phil had told me about his father, Old Man Yip. See what I mean about how strange the workings of the brain can be?

I shut my eyes and recreated my thought process to see how I had made the leap.

I thought back on what Phil had told me and pictured Old Man Yip on grandfather duty, waiting to pick up Peter from his school. Standing there outside the school gates, probably grumpy as hell at having to wait; he had always been a stickler for punctuality and time-keeping. So he passes the time by making small talk with the other parents, turning it into the net-working opportunity that all senior law firm partners see round every corner they turn. "So what business are you in", he asks one parent, a shark-like glint in his eye. The parent answers. Old Man Yip doesn't hesitate and goes in for the kill. Name cards are swapped, invitations made to Peter's birthday party and Yip & Siu has another strong lead to getting a juicy new case on its books. Right there, at the school gates, a new business relationship is born.

And that's when the synapses in my brain had gotten to work.

School...

Opening my eyes, I looked down at the profile on Benson Chan which Amy had sketched out. Once a 14K Triad enforcer, Benson Chan had reinvented himself with the full veneer of legitimate business man. He was on the right committees, had memberships of the right clubs, attended Hong Kong Chamber of Commerce get-togethers, and had given his daughter, Precious Chan, the exclusive education of every parent's dreams.

That was the leap my brain had made.

Straight to a piece of information which had fish-hooked my attention in Amy's notes without me knowing it at the time I had first read it.

Precious Chan, Benson Chan's daughter, the paediatrician with the clinic in Central. Amy's notes informed me that Precious had attended medical school in London, university in Toronto and international school in Hong Kong.

School...

I logged onto my computer, pulled up Google and searched against Precious Chan's name. There it was on the list of registered doctors on the Medical Council's website. The list told me she had an MSc from London University and the date she had obtained it.

How many years did it take to do a medical degree? My annoyingly perfect elder brother John was a surgeon at the John Radcliffe hospital in Oxford. I thought back. It seemed like his medical studies had lasted forever. At least six years, I recalled.

Before her medical degree Precious Chan had done her undergrad in Toronto. I added on another four years for that. That meant it had been around ten years since she had left school. Ball-park, it was the right sort of timeframe, but I was still going on pure guesswork.

Navigating back to the Google search, I scrolled further down the list of hits. There was a Precious Chan with her own website: a herbal specialist in the United States. Not the same person. My Precious

Chan was listed on a website called FindDoc.com, but that just listed out her medical qualifications again, her clinic address and how to make an appointment. Nothing I needed or didn't already know.

On page two of the search, I found a link to a conference run by the *Professional Forum on Child Health* at the Queen Elizabeth hospital two years ago. I clicked on it. Up came the poster, a flyer for the conference, a half-day event. Dr Precious Chan had spoken at a forty-five-minute time-slot on the subject of 'Treating Adolescents'. Below the poster there was another link that told me to 'Click Here for Handout'. I did.

The handout was a five page pdf file, the last two pages setting out biographies and headshots of all the speakers. My fingers tingled on the mouse as I scrolled through to the piece on Dr Precious Chan. It was a classic portrait shot, her hair hanging down to frame her face, touching the collar of her white coat and the stethoscope draped round her neck to signal that, yes, she was a doctor. She had a pretty face, a warm smile and a professional glint in her eye. In the bio below the photo, once again the medical qualifications took precedence, along with a list of articles she had written.

But when I read the last sentence of her bio, the air in my office disappeared, leaving an audible, harsh vacuum of nothingness in its place.

> *In her spare time, Dr Chan likes to do yoga and scuba dive. She was born in Hong Kong and went to school in Tai Po before travelling abroad for her medical studies.*

There it was again, the reference to school, setting my brainwaves tingling.

I pressed 'print'. The machine whirred into life behind, but I was too zoned in on the trail to collect it. Navigating back to Google, this time I searched for schools in Tai Po, found what I was looking for and pulled up the website of Tai Po International School. Different photographs of smiling kids filled the screen, playing sports, studying in the state of the art library, pulling funny faces on field trips.

I could imagine Precious Chan being one of those kids of yesteryear. Maybe she was the popular good-looking girl in class, or maybe she wore glasses and braces and hated school, studying the hell out of everything. Who knew?

But it was the banner at the top of the page that drew my attention: 'Tai Po International School' written in calligraphic gold lettering. Under the menu tabs running below the banner, to the right hand side was the button that would transform the website from English into its Chinese version.

I clicked it.

The banner changed.

It was still the same design. The Chinese lettering was in gold on a purple background and equally prominent as the English version. I couldn't read Chinese, but something about those characters sent a whisper of familiarity trembling in my frontal lobe.

Out came my iPhone, my fingers trembling with anticipation.

I pulled up the photographs I had taken with it.

The last one was the blurred end shot of a video I had filmed. I touched the play button on screen.

It took a moment for the picture to steady but when it did, Napoleon Wong's office filled the screen. It had been taken during the little visit I had engineered, deploying the ol' Scott Lee guile to get past Angela Tan, Napoleon's guard dog of a secretary.

The video smoothed across Napoleon's snooker table desk, nothing on there but executive toys to keep him amused. Then it moved behind the desk and on to the shelves. I could see myself back there, filming, doing my best to keep my hands steady and moving slowly enough. A hell of a risk I had taken, any minute Angela Tan could have come in. No way I could have come up with any sort of cogent explanation for what I'd been doing if she'd caught me in the act.

The spines of lever arch files moved from right to left across the screen. This was where I had thought something might ping, so I had taken my time. But looking at them now, the names on the spines were of little relevance to anything I knew about and I doubted whether Napoleon was even familiar with the file contents. He didn't seem the type of boss to waste his time too much on pieces of paper.

Next came the shelves, filled, not with books, but with the industry awards and family photos.

Truth be told, I had filmed these as an afterthought, but those shelves had caught my attention every time I had been in Napoleon's office. I remembered my interview with him, when I had talked Napoleon into hiring me on contract. Those industry awards had told me what kind of person he was. All show and no substance, or so I had believed. Bought and paid for trophies; pieces of glass and plastic that allowed Gadgetech to boast at the bottom of its letterhead that it was the number one in the Kitchen White Goods (Blender and Mixer category). Talk about living the dream!

The video scanned across every award on the top shelf, then moved on to the second shelf.

"Come on, come on, where is it?" I muttered under my breath.

'Top electronics retailer in the New Territories East Region', 'Employer of Choice Award: category 3', 'Innovation and Thought Leadership', on and on it went and I was beginning to wonder whether he had moved it, since...

Then it came into shot.

I tapped 'pause' and stared at the screen, at the photograph of Napoleon Wong's son, one of the few personal items on show. The image on my phone was on the grainy side, but I could make out the picture clearly enough. There he was, in his mortar-board and purple graduation robes, ribboned scroll in hand, staring into the camera, his face replete with his father's features, the chubby cheeks, the high placed nose, but eyes filled with pride and the hope of youth, not the cynicism of the earlier generation. Underneath the photo was a strip of white with black lettering which read: Class of 2002.

2002. I made a mental note.

But there was something else in the picture which interested me more. With forefinger and thumb I expanded the picture and zoomed in on the signboard at the top of the building in front of which Napoleon's son was standing. The name for the school that was about to become his alma mater, spelt out in Chinese lettering. In gold on a purple background.

The same Chinese lettering on the website on my computer.

Tai Po International School.

Could it be that Precious Chan and Napoleon Wong's son had been at the same school?

My mind jumped back to the first step in my thought process, to Old Man Yip making small talk with other parents outside the school gates, a business relationship forming just like that. Parents of schoolchildren, meeting each other, forming bonds, finding connections. It happened every day.

Benson Chan and Napoleon Wong. Did their children go to the same school?

Did Benson and Napoleon know each other? Had their paths crossed outside the school gates, at parent-teacher evenings, at end of term award ceremonies, at graduation?

I couldn't be sure of the link, not just yet. Even if their kids had gone to Tai Po, how could I be sure they had been there at the same time? It was still tenuous.

2002 was when Napoleon's son had graduated according to the photograph, but what about Precious Chan? I searched and searched, but in these days of data privacy protection, that kind of information isn't readily available.

Dead end. Close, but not close enough.

That's when I had called Amy and left the world's most awkward voicemail message.

***

She kept me waiting a full hour and a half.

I tried to distract myself with Gadgetech work, but it was a slow day for legal requests. Tabitha had phoned in sick at ten o'clock. She didn't sound too sick and had done little to pretend, so I figured she had an interview. With Auyeung gone and me only on contract, I couldn't blame her, so I had told her to feel better soon and that I'd see her tomorrow.

The diagram I had drawn last night on my legal pad stared up at me from the desk. The solid arrows pointing down from the China Overseas Investment Corporation to Starlight Transport to Gadgetech to Rufus Lam, solid enough connections. But this new piece of information, gave the whole thing a different slant.

All along I had assumed that Napoleon Wong was just taking advantage of events. The ruination of Terence Auyeung had presented itself as a fortuitous opportunity on which Napoleon had stumbled and he was milking it, like manna from heaven, to force Rufus Lam out of Gadgetech.

But what if there was more to it?

Terence Auyeung had stolen from Gadgetech to pay off his son David's debt to Benson Chan. Maybe Benson Chan and Napoleon Wong knew each other? Fathers bumping into each other at their children's school one day, they get talking and… My phone grumbled in my pocket, breaking the thought in half. I fast-fumbled it up to my ear.

"Precious Chan graduated from Tai Po international school in 2002," Amy Tang's sweet voice uttered before I even had a chance to say anything.

2002. The same year as Napoleon's son had graduated. They weren't just there at the same time. They were classmates. Another link in the chain solidified.

"I'm glad you called," I said. "We need to talk."

CHAPTER FORTY-FOUR

Amy looked fabulous.

Black T-shirt underneath a light-weight grey hoodie, cuffs rolled up to the elbows and a pair of snug jeans that fit exactly like they should. Her hair was still tied back in a pony-tail. It was the first time I had seen her wearing glasses. She was the complete package. Simple. Sensual. Combustible.

"So where's my story?" Her first words.

"Story?"

"You promised me a story on your voicemail. I'm not here for anything else."

"I'm sorry about…"

She held up her palm and cut me dead.

"At least let me try to explain," I protested.

"I don't want to hear it. From now on, it's all about the story. Which, by the way, you're going to give me. Right now!"

I tensed up at the distance she was putting between us. "You think Tito and Skin-head are just going to let you write it? They're out there, Amy, looking at us right now. You can't do this on your own."

"Do you really think this would be the first time someone has tried to stop me publishing something they don't want people to read? I get it all the time, Scott. It means I'm doing something right."

"Have any of the others put a gun to your head? Because that's what we've got at the moment, Amy!" I snapped.

She stood there, arms folded, her eyes blazing at me through her lenses as anger worked its way through the muscles on her face, her jaw clenching, her chin fixed with defiance.

"Are you going to stop wasting my time, or am I going to have to turn round and walk away?"

I opened my mouth, about to argue. Stopped. Closed it.

"Okay, you win," I conceded. "Let's take a walk."

She had agreed to meet me back at Citiplaza Mall in Taikoo Shing. Its cavernous inside provided air-conditioning for comfort and a large open public space, with shoppers milling between the different levels, for security. Our shadows, wherever they were could still see us, I was sure of that. But they would have been hard pressed to try anything in here.

The south end of the mall housed an ice-rink. We wandered in that direction, the silence stretching between us like a taut wire. We rode the escalator to the upper level and leaned on the railing to watch. Below on the ice, wannabe starlets pirouetted through their paces alongside Bambi-legged beginners taking their first tentative slides. Tiger mums barked instructions from the side-lines, whilst their maids looked bored at their side.

"I read your article about the Chinese Overseas Investment Corporation," I made a tentative start. "An impressive piece of research. You really think it's being used as a vehicle for Chinese foreign policy? I mean all that stuff about building a 'web of favours' by buying influence. Is it really true?"

She shrugged. "You read the article. Tell me I'm wrong. Oh wait, don't bother, because I don't care. The story. Now!"

"Fine," I said. "But you're not going to like it."

She turned her face towards me. She wasn't smiling. "Okay, Scott. I'll bite. Why won't I like it?"

"Because Rufus Lam isn't the bad guy. He's the victim. He's being set up."

She gave a sarcastic snicker. "This from someone he's paying. Why am I not surprised? Just another person he's bought off to believe in his propaganda, aren't you, Scott? Rufus Lam, the rags-to-riches saviour of Hong Kong, isn't that what everyone thinks?"

"Okay," I said. "I guess I deserve that. But he's paying me to find out what happened to Terence Auyeung. That's my job and that's the story, so do you want me to go on, or are you just going to throw rocks?"

She looked back down at the ice, pouted and shrugged.

I took a moment to figure out the best place to start.

"Terence Auyeung," I said. "He was a good man, a solid husband and a good father. It's common knowledge that he worked for Rufus Lam for years. He's one of Lam's most trusted advisers and closest allies. If it's made public, then news of Terence Auyeung's downfall will hurt Rufus Lam, that's pretty much a given, especially given Lam's involvement in the Chief Executive election. It raises significant questions about the integrity of Lam's friends and the choices Lam himself has made. Suddenly Lam isn't the type of man you want to trust with Hong Kong's future. You see what I mean?"

Amy's brow creased. "I'm not sure that I do."

"Look, I'm saying that if you're someone who wants to hurt Rufus Lam, then hurting Terence Auyeung, ruining his reputation, is an effective way of doing it. And Auyeung makes for an easier target than Lam himself, because he has a weakness, remember?"

"His son, David," Amy said, catching on.

"That's right. David. The black sheep of the family. A lazy risk-taker with a trail of failed get-rich-quick schemes in his recent past. An easy patsy to be tempted into overreaching on a loan for his latest business venture. And the likes of David Auyeung always have a next business venture in the pipeline. So he'll bite when someone offering easy money comes knocking on his door. Doesn't take long for the venture to turn sour, though. As night follows day, David Auyeung's in trouble. He owes some very dangerous people a lot of money and they want it back. So David goes to daddy for help. Only this time the debt is too large for even Terence to cover. But this is his son we're talking about, his flesh and blood. A matter of life and death which forces Terence to take the desperate measure he did, stealing money from Gadgetech. The temptation was right there, he was CFO after all. He had complete access to Gadgetech's money and the skill to cover his tracks. But as soon as Auyeung dips into company funds, the set-up is complete, don't you see? Now, he's nothing but a dishonest thief, using a position he was appointed to by Rufus Lam, no less, to commit his crime. Makes Lam guilty by association, at least that's how any decent member of the journalist community could spin it. The perfect set-up."

Amy's eyes stayed on the ice-rink below, but I could tell she was absorbing every word, weighing it for authenticity. "That's some hypothesis. It gives rise to two questions, though. Who and why?"

I smiled at having drawn her interest. "Who and why," I said. You're right, Amy, that's where this whole thing starts and ends. So ask yourself, who stands directly to gain here?"

"From Auyeung disappearing?" she asked.

"From Aueyeung disappearing having stolen Gadgetech funds."

Amy frowned. "Your boss Napoleon Wong, for one. He's getting control of Gadgetech at a discount."

"Bingo! Napoleon Wong, our first contender. A two-bit CEO of a medium-sized retailer which hit big only because Rufus Lam chose to invest in it as a vehicle through which to launch his e-news platform. To start with, I bet Napoleon welcomed Lam's investment. I mean, this is Rufus Lam we're talking about. His name alone was enough to shoot Gadgetech to the big leagues. But sooner or later Napoleon realizes that, with Lam's investment, he's no longer in control of his company, especially with Terence Auyeung ensconced as CFO watching his every move. Worse, he's seen as riding someone else's coat-tails. Resentment grows. Image means a lot to an arrogant man like Napoleon Wong, it's what drives him. I saw it the first day I met him."

"So you're saying Napoleon Wong set up Terence Auyeung to force Lam out of Gadgetech?" From the way she asked, Amy wasn't buying it.

She was right not to.

"Napoleon Wong has been using Auyeung's theft to blackmail Lam into selling him his shares at a discount. That's why Lam hired me to do some digging into what happened to Auyeung on the quiet. That's the only reason why I work there, for the moment at least."

"You're in there under cover?"

"Something like that. That's what I wanted to tell you yesterday, but you didn't give me the chance."

Indignation locked on Amy's face, followed by a flash of admiration. Both disappeared as quickly as they had arrived.

I continued. "I always assumed Napoleon's blackmailing of Lam was purely opportunistic. The way I figured it, when Auyeung disappeared, Napoleon did his own digging. He finds Auyeung's fraud and thinks all his Christmases have come at once. But I was wrong. Turns out, I haven't given Napoleon the credit he deserves. He set Auyeung up to take the money in the first place."

Amy gave a little gasp. "You mean he made Auyeung take the money?"

"As good as," I said. "Napoleon's son graduated from Tai Po International School in 2002. According to you, so did Precious Chan, daughter of Benson Chan; Mr Loans-Are-Us himself, ex-triad member and all-round nasty piece of work. There's the connection that turns this whole thing on its head, Amy. Benson Chan, the man who lends money to David Auyeung and gets his hooks into his father, Terence. He knew Napoleon Wong from the start. Their kids were classmates."

As I spoke, Amy fished around in her bag and pulled out a book. It was a purple hard cover, A4 size, fading at the edges with age. She flipped to a page she had marked with a post-it.

"What've you got there?" I asked.

"Tai Po International School Year Book. Graduating Class of 2002. When you asked me to find out what year Precious Chan had graduated, I rang the school and said I was doing an article on career advice for teenagers on how to get into the medical profession. Dr Precious Chan was my case study. I told them some year book pictures would give the article authenticity. In return, I promised the school a free full-page advert in the publication which had commissioned me. They were ecstatic."

"And they just gave the year book to you?"

Amy gave a half-smile. "Promise someone something for nothing and it's difficult for them to say no. Anyway, look!" She pointed to a picture. It was a head and shoulders shot of Precious Chan. She had a toothy grin and looked way short of the professional image she would later cultivate, but the beginnings were there. "It says here she was grade eight violin, in the school orchestra and something called the Spring String Quartet. Now, look here!" Amy turned the page. "Hannibal Wong, Napoleon's son. A 'cello player, no less, also in the orchestra and…"

"The Spring String Quartet," I nodded. "Rehearsals, recitals, just the type of things proud fathers like Benson Chan and Napoleon Wong would go to. Their paths cross. A business relationship forms."

"And one day Napoleon wants to get Rufus Lam and Terence Auyeung out of Gadgetech," Amy picked up the strand of thought. "He works out that David Auyeung is Terence's weak link. Then asks his good friend, Benson Chan to target David for a loan he can never pay back, so his father has no choice but to dip into Gadgetech's funds. Is that how this plays out?" She bit her lower lip in thought. "Seems a bit…I don't know…machiavellian for a man like Wong. And to do something like that just to buy out Rufus Lam from Gadgetech? That's a huge risk. You really think Napoleon Wong is capable of that?"

"No," I said. "Not without help and not without the right incentive."

270

She looked at me, confused by my answer. "Incentive?"

"This doesn't start with Napoleon Wong," I said. "He's just a tool being used by someone else. Sure he stands to gain by getting Rufus Lam out of Gadgetech, but he isn't the only one, not by a long shot. That's where we come to your second question, Amy. Why?"

I fished out my mobile phone and scrolled through the photographs. When I found the right one, I held it up and showed it to her.

"That's the picture you took of Daisy Lai in her little head-to-head with Napoleon in Hang Hau," she said.

"Yeah, the one you stole from me. But I'm willing to forgive and forget, if you are."

She made a face.

"Daisy Lai, key family member in the Star Transport Group," I said. "When I first saw them together, I thought maybe Napoleon and Daisy had a little romance going on the side. But that's not two lovers we're looking at. That's Napoleon reporting up the chain. Star Transport, the company which almost went belly up in '98, but lived to fight another day because of the bail-out engineered by..."

"The China Overseas Investment Corporation," Amy finished my sentence.

I let it hang there, percolating through her mind, giving her a moment to let the building blocks slot into place.

"And so I come to the well-researched article I mentioned. The one you wrote, Ms Amy Tang. The one which tells the world that COIC is a vehicle used to make investments that buy favours for the Chinese government. Favours that give China influence where it may need it one day. Favours which can subsist for years and years until the need and opportunity arise for them to be called in."

The muscles in Amy's face tensed and relaxed as she processed the pieces I was laying out for her. Slowly, she nodded, understanding. "They probably knew Rufus Lam was going to make trouble in the CE election," she said.

I felt myself agreeing. "Right now he's Mr Popular in Hong Kong. The only tycoon in the city who's fighting to bring democracy here. The rest of them kow-tow to the Central People's Government in case it harms their profits, but here's Rufus Lam poking Beijing in the eye and Hong Kong people love him for it. But you've seen the news. Lam's popularity is making the Central People's Government nervous. They're under pressure. They're thinking they may not get the man they want in the CE hot seat. That is, unless they force their candidate down our throats. But think of the fall-out when that happens. A massive campaign of civil disobedience, led by Rufus Lam, which makes the Umbrella Protests seem like a walk in the park. We're talking taxes not being paid, people taking to the streets again. Hong Kong would no longer be that little pimple on the southern tip of China which can be left to its own devices. It will become completely ungovernable and a problem that the rest of the world will use to beat Beijing with. The question is, what can they do to stop Lam? The answer? Engineer something that will make Lam's popularity take a nose-dive just before the nominating committee says 'no his candidate can't run'. I mean what would happen to public opinion if just before the nominating committee's announcement, it's made known that Rufus Lam tried to cover up the theft of one of his business associates. By paying off Napoleon Wong, no less, because that's exactly what Lam's doing. It may be he's doing it for the right reasons. But people won't see it that way. Just another dirty tycoon trying to cover his tracks. Suddenly, Jeremy Lau, the man Beijing wanted from the beginning, doesn't look so bad an option."

Amy shook her head slowly, working through the implications. "It could be just the excuse Beijing needs to close the door on the idea of a popular elected Chief Executive in Hong Kong forever. Finally they get the control they want here. And without a single shot fired."

"That's a hell of a return on that little investment COIC made back in '98," I said. "It also means you've been right all along, Amy. That article you wrote? It's coming true."

Any ignored the compliment, her face twisted deep in thought. "So they sent Daisy Lai to approach Napoleon Wong. To offer him something he couldn't refuse. Maybe an investment from Star Transport in Gadgetech with no strings attached? Maybe access to the Chinese market? Daisy Lai has the weight of the Chinese government backing her, so whatever it is, it's too tempting for Napoleon to turn down."

"All he has to do is this one thing," I said. "Use the opportunity that's right there, in his company. Set up Terence Auyeung. Of course, they give Napoleon some help; he's not the sharpest tool in the box. My guess is they point him in the direction of Terence's son. Maybe they even suggest the plan of hooking him in with a loan."

"But Napoleon's the executioner," Amy said. "He has to be, so as to give deniability up the chain. There's no way they can trace it back."

"But executing isn't a problem for Napoleon," I said. "He knows Benson Chan. The perfect man to do the dirty work. To lend money to David Auyeung and call in the debt from his father when the son can't pay. It's probably Benson Chan who tells Auyeung to use his CFO position to take the money from Gadgetech, when he can't pay…if he wants his son to stay unharmed, that is." I said, completing the last link.

On the ice below, a coach was using expansive, smooth gesticulations to show one of his students what he wanted her to do. Peels of laughter crept in from the other side of the ice, where one of the beginners was being helped up by his friends after falling flat on his backside. Beyond the rink, shoppers went about their business. Office workers hurried with intent, some listening to music as they went, some talking on the phone, some texting. Serial multi-tasking was the new Hong Kong disease. People didn't feel productive unless they were doing at least three things at once.

"You were wrong about one thing," Amy said. "Rufus Lam isn't the real victim in all of this." She turned and faced me, arms folded, her eyes locked with a look of intense determination. "Hong Kong is."

I couldn't argue with that.

CHAPTER FORTY-FIVE

I went back to work. Amy needed to time to think it through, just like I had done, and she was still pretty tetchy with me for not telling her about my deal with Rufus Lam. I told her to call me when she was ready. If she really wanted to.

That Friday afternoon the office reminded me of Combo, Mrs Lo's basset-hound, it was so fatigued and slow-moving. Early on I got copied in on a couple of e-mails from Napoleon Wong that didn't require any action, just his way of convincing himself he was working, I guessed. Then the e-mails stopped as Gadgetech's leader took off early for the weekend. News trickles down to the troops fast when that happens. The office breathed a big collective sigh of relief.

I tried to figure out my next steps, but my brain was treacle-thick and needed time out, so come five-thirty I said to hell with it and headed out. The MTR was jammed full of weary commuters on the ride home, so I compartmentalized myself away in my head and allowed thoughts of Lam and Auyeung, Skin-head and Tito, Napoleon Wong and Daisy Lai to spin through my mind without making any attempt to latch onto them. At the top of the first escalator in Causeway Bay subway station, my phone juddered in my pocket. It was a 'What's App' message from Phil, to go with a missed call. 'Any news?' he asked.

Damn, I had completely forgotten I was supposed to provide him with an update. I let go a heavy sigh. Tomorrow, I told myself.

I can't remember walking home. It's like that sometimes when you're dog-tired, sweaty and ping-ponging your way through heavy crowds. But a tram full of party-goers brought me to my senses half way up Wong Nai Chung Road. A bunch of twenty-something tourists on the top deck thought they were being original and hilarious with their bawdy caterwauling at pedestrians, toasting everybody with paper cups of cheap white wine as they went by. Oh to be young again. I debated whether to wave back. I didn't bother.

The sky had darkened. Shadows and street light beams washed over me as I ambled through them. I was ready for mindless TV, for sleep, for restoration, for renewal. Tomorrow was Saturday and Amy and I could start again. Tonight, however, I needed to shut down.

That's what I was thinking when it happened.

***

As I approached my building, I started to reach into my pocket for my front door keys. My hand never made it.

A sudden, vice-like grip took hold of my arm and dragged me into the nullah that ran down the side of my block. Darkness swallowed me whole. I was just about to let go a scream, when I got slammed into a wall, my head rebounding off it like a football. The pain was a jolt of electricity bringing me to my senses. My eyes focused. I could see him now, just in outline, but I knew it was him.

Skin-head.

A flash of anger and macho irresponsibility pushed me off the wall, my fist balling up and ready to lash out. I was working on pure instinct, fight-ready and about to dish it out.

I was too slow.

The punch connected with my rib cage, bone against bone. I didn't even see his arm move, it was so fast. Suddenly, I was doubling over, a shard of wincing pain piercing through my side, blowing out my wind, balling me up into a writhing mess of gasping and phlegmy coughing. He didn't let me go down. He slammed me back up against the wall, his arm shooting out to pin me up there by the throat.

It may have been only a tenth of a second he held me there like that, letting me choke, but it seemed like an age. He let the terror and sense of helplessness build. Those same, dead eyes, that little evil grin. This was what he was on this earth to do, that look told me. This was just administrative paperwork to him.

Eventually, he released the grip down a notch, but he kept his wiry steel talons wrapped around my throat. I was ableto hear my constricting breath ricocheting through his cold, bony fingers.

"Time's up, Scott!" He said it like he was enjoying it.

"If you wanted a date, I'm more of a sucker for chocolates and flowers."

There I went again, humour in the face of terror. My own personal Tourrette's. Even as the words came out, I knew I was going to regret them. I was right.

Skin-head snaked his free hand behind his back and came out with his gun. The same one he had pointed at me three nights ago. This

275

time he touched the barrel against my right cheek, paused, then traced the cold steel in a line across my nose and back again, until it was pressed in between my eyes.

"Bang," he whispered. "It's that easy. I told you to find Auyeung for me. Where is he?"

"You said, by the end of the week."

"What do you call this?"

"The week ends on Sunday. I've got two days."

"I said forty-eight hours. Anyway, you are not positioned well to argue."

"No," I said, grating against his awkward phraseology again. 'Not positioned well to argue'. What was all that about?

"Look, I'm getting close. I need till Sunday," I pleaded.

His jaw worked some chewing gum round his mouth, the only flickering movement in the darkness. The gun stayed on me. He made me look at it, drink it in, imagine what was going to happen the next time he saw me.

"Sunday," he said. "Till then, I'm watching every move you make. And remember this. I see one word from your girlfriend in a newspaper, she dies. You understand that?"

My eyes popped open as a new adventure in fear took me in its hold.

"We know what she does for a living, Scott. We know everything. We know about your little talk at Taikoo Shing this afternoon."

"We're working together on finding out what happened to Auyeung. We're getting close."

"If you say so. But make sure she doesn't do anything stupid. Now shut your eyes."

I did as I was told.

Even though I knew he was gone I kept them shut for a full five minutes, counting out every one of those three hundred seconds.

***

As soon as I was through the front door, I called Amy. She told me she was typing up a first draft based on our conversation. A thousand words, she had down, aiming to publish Monday.

It was not what I wanted to hear.

I told her what had happened and ordered her to get herself round to my place. She could bring her computer if she wanted, but I wanted her with me, so we could face this thing together.

Maybe she had forgiven me, or maybe from the tone of my voice, she could tell how deadly serious I was, but for once she didn't argue and I was thankful for that small mercy.

Somewhere between the time I hung up and the time she arrived, another conclusion hit me. Skin-head and Tito – whatever their real names were – worked for COIC. It was the only thing that made sense.

Napoleon Wong and Daisy Lai, COIC already had in their pocket. Benson Chan, they didn't care about; Chan was, after all, just a two-bit hoodlum made good who probably had no idea what Napoleon had got himself involved in. But COIC was China's manifestation of soft power, power which it exercised through influence and knowledge. It couldn't stomach not knowing what had happened to Terence Auyeung. If Auyeung was dead, they needed proof. But if he was still alive, he was a big problem to their agenda, the only link in the chain which COIC didn't control.

Auyeung surfacing at the wrong moment would blow apart COIC's plan to ruin Rufus Lam's reputation and send the CE election in Beijing's – and Jeremy Lau's – direction. That was why Skin-head and Tito were so desperate to find him.

How they knew to lean on me, I couldn't exactly figure out, but somehow they knew I was working in Gadgetech for the purpose of looking into Auyeung's disappearance and that Amy was a hungry journalist chasing down the same story. They also knew I was working for Rufus Lam. Skin-head had told me as much on our first encounter, which made the odds of me getting through this thing in one piece longer than West Ham's chances of winning the Premiership.

"Are you okay?" Those were Amy's first words to me, as she came through the front door, her voice trembling as she put a black hold-all down on the floor.

I lowered myself gingerly onto the sofa, pressing the ice-pack under my shirt against my torso. My ribcage felt like it had been penetrated by a pneumatic drill, but the discomfort of the conclusion I had just reached about my survival chances far outweighed the pain.

I removed the ice-pack to show Skin-head's handy-work to Amy. It had been one hell of a punch. The bruising had already turned an unhealthy purple hue, blending to jaundiced yellow at the edges. Skin-head knew what he was doing, he had targeted the punch with precision, not on the soft tissue and muscle of my stomach, but against the thin layer of skin covering my lower rib. If he had hit me any harder, my ribcage would have been crushed like a bird's nest under a hammer. Amy winced at the sight and folded her arms into a tight hold as if trying to ward out a biting ice wind, even though it was thirty degrees in my apartment.

I laid out for her what had happened again. It provided just as little comfort the second time round. Amy just stood there nodding, listening, absorbing, flipping her hair occasionally, but not committing or agreeing to anything

Then I told her what my plan was.

It was a plan borne out of pure desperation and arrived at after all other sensible options had been weighed and discarded. I said it was our only hope, because that was what I believed.

"Let's see what the morning brings," she said, her wan nervous smile doing little to hide the fear which had bedded down and taken hold. "You're in no state to make decisions now."

She walked over and sat down beside me, took hold of the cold compress and held it for me. Eventually her head rested down in the nook of my shoulder. Her hair smelled of lilacs. It was nice, and right then the most comforting thing there was in this world. I put my arm round her and closed my eyes. We stayed like that for a while, just holding each other close, whether out of affection or desperation, I couldn't work out and didn't much care.

Right then, it seemed it was all we had.

CHAPTER FORTY-SIX

It was still dark when I woke on Saturday morning. I had been dreaming that I was a fakir lying on a bed of nails, with one of the nails protruding out and poking me hard in the ribs.

Amy had beaten me out of bed. She was at my dining-table, her hair wrapped up in a towel. She still smelled of lilacs but this time it was shower fresh and pervaded the whole living-room in a refreshing effervescence I wasn't used to waking up to. Her fingers were dancing across the keyboard of her lap-top, as deftly as a Russian ballerina's tippee-toes. The look on her face told me she was ready for action.

I wished I felt the same way.

"Gordon MacKenzie and Antonio Martinez," she said without looking up from the screen.

"Who?" I said, hurrying through to the kitchen to fetch the first of the many coffees I would need to get me through the day.

"Skin-head and Tito. That's their real names."

That piece of news stopped me dead. I pushed a hand through my hair and coughed and immediately regretted it, as pain stabbed my lower abdomen, reminding me of the predicament we were in.

"You okay?" she asked.

"How the hell did you find that out?" I asked, getting into gear. No time for self-pity, not today.

"Your theory about our two followers being connected to COIC got me thinking. Two foreigners in Hong Kong? How did they get their ID cards?"

I wasn't sure if she was expecting me to answer, so I signaled for her to continue.

"Every foreigner working in Hong Kong needs a work visa, right?" she said.

"Right. So?"

"So I have a contact in the Immigration Department. Let's just say he owed me a big favour and I called it in. Luckily for me he was at work, he's been there since three this morning, pulling some information the police needed urgently for a search and seize warrant.

I asked him to pull up all the work-visa applications of all new employees of COIC in the past year. Guess what? There weren't any."

"So?" Monosyllabism was about all I could handle.

"So then I asked him to try the same for the Star Transport Group and guess what?

"What?"

"Gordon MacKenzie and Antonio Martinez recently joined Star Transport as Crisis Response Managers on two year contracts."

I let that one percolate. "How can you be sure they're Skin-head and Tito?"

"Take a look," she pressed some keys and swiveled the lap-top round so I could see the screen. "He sent through the passport photos submitted as part of the paperwork."

Sure enough, there they both were. Skin-head and Tito. Gordon MacKenzie and Antonio Martinez. My blood ran cold at the sight.

"That's some favour your immigration guy owed you."

"I found out he'd been accepting payments in return for information for a piece on unlicensed investigation agencies in Hong Kong I was writing. My editor pulled the article because I didn't have two sources to corroborate, so it never got published. Anyway I decided not to expose my contact to the authorities in return for him helping me out now and again."

Damn, I was glad she was on my side.

"That's not all," she continued. "Our friends Gordon and Antonio both listed NDT Consultants as a previous employer in their visa applications."

"Who are NDT Consultants?" I asked. But I was pretty sure I wasn't going to like the answer.

"A subsidiary of NDT Security? It's an outfit which provides protection and security personnel on contracts across the world. Oil companies in the Middle East, container ships travelling through areas known for piracy. No job too dangerous, provided the price is right."

"They're mercenaries?"

"That's what I reckon. And get this. Last year, NDT Security won a contract providing protection for a Chinese multinational mining bauxite in Sierra Leone. It all fits."

I sipped my coffee, worked this new information through the mill and came up blank. Amy went back to her lap-top and continued to type.

"So we know who they are now," I said after a while. "Nasty pieces of work paid to do a dirty job, no matter what the rights and wrongs. Means they're serious people. But we knew that already. My ribcage has got the marks to prove it. Gets us nowhere apart from deeper in the hole."

She looked up from the screen. "Apart from one thing, Scott. It means you're right."

I probably looked confused at her answer, because I was. "About what?"

"About everything. There, I said it. Satisfied?" She continued typing.

"Tell me you're not still thinking about going to print with this, after everything we've been through!"

"Don't you get it? The plan you have. I'm agreeing to it. It's our only option."

I gave her my complete dumb guy look. It wasn't a stretch. "So you're agreeing that we have to tell Rufus Lam about this?"

"Look, I can't pretend I'm happy about that. But I've been up since three thinking about it and I get it now. He's our only hope for getting out of this mess in one piece. Lam has the resources to provide us with protection."

"That about sums it up," I said.

"And he's my only hope for coming out of this with a story."

I shook my head. "Still thinking about your damn story."

"Scott, it's what I do. Listen, you know I can't stand Rufus Lam. He ruined my father, and if you ask me, he's bad news for Hong Kong. But what COIC is doing is even worse. They're trying to rubbish Rufus Lam's reputation, just to give the nominating committee an excuse for refusing to approve Elizabeth Leung's candidacy in the election. If she isn't able to run, who are we left with? Jeremy Lau, that's who: Beijing's yes-man. People have a right to know what's going on, don't you think? Especially with his rally going on next week, and the election only a few weeks off?"

I sipped my coffee and let it go to work. Throwing ourselves on Lam's mercy had been my idea because he had the resources to keep us safe. Hell, he surrounded himself with Cherry Blossom and her team of heavy-duty body guards and probably had a safe house somewhere we could hole up in until this thing was over. I hadn't factored in that Amy still wanted to publish her story, but I was beginning to see how that might work to our advantage. A story about how Beijing was deliberately trying to scupper Elizabeth Leung's candidacy in the election was high risk, but Amy was right. It was in Rufus Lam's interests for a story like that to be written.

"So the question is: how do we get to Lam without MacKenzie and Fernandez finding out?" Amy asked after a while. "You realize we can't do this over the phone, right? Lam's openly challenging the Central People's Government. Trust me, they're watching every move he makes, probably monitoring all communications too."

"There's no way we're doing this over the phone," I agreed.

"So how do we get access when Mackenzie and Fernandez are watching us?" she asked.

"That part I haven't quite figured out yet," I admitted.

Silence.

Amy put her head down and started typing again. I left her to it and went to wash and shave. The image staring back at me in the bathroom mirror was not a pretty sight. My skin was dry. Crows feet sprung like spiders webs from the purpling bulges under my eyes. I had aged ten years in less than two weeks.

Shaking off the thought, I washed and dressed, had a second cup of coffee and some food. I made the bed, collected up the dirty washing strewn in random places throughout the apartment and then went round and filled a rubbish bag with trash. It was a relief to be doing normal household chores, a metaphor for clearing out my cluttered mind. Amy left me to it, she was too absorbed in her writing even to notice me.

I took the rubbish bag out to the pick-up area in the stairwell and almost tripped over the maid from the downstairs flat who was sitting on the step talking on her mobile phone. Her name was Sonny. She was chubby in a homely kind of way, with thick forearms, developed from lugging groceries every day. Sonny always had this bright look of happy innocence on her face. I liked that.

Sonny and I knew each other from the day I had helped her lug an Ikea wardrobe up six flights of stairs, which for some reason the delivery guys had assembled on the ground floor. She was from Indonesia and that same night she had knocked on my door and given me a bowl of curry to say thank you. The spice in it had nearly taken my head off. But it was the best damn curry I've had in my life.

"Sorry sir, good morning!" Sonny said, quickly hanging up the phone and standing up like a kid who had just been caught with her hand in the biscuit tin.

"It's okay Sonny, didn't mean to interrupt. You carry on."

"No, finished now. Up so early this morning, sir? It's Saturday you know."

"I know. Busy day ahead. You're up early too."

"I want to call Jakarta early, before Jonathan wake up," she said. "My brother's birthday, see."

Jonathan was the kid Sonny looked after for the family downstairs. She had two children of her own back in Jakarta, but like thousands of other women in her position, Sonny had left them behind to take care of someone else's offspring in a foreign country. Having a live-in domestic helper was a purely Hong Kong phenomenon. It relied on an arbitrage that stemmed from a monthly salary of a maid here, being double that of a professional office worker back in Indonesia.

First-timers in Hong Kong had trouble with the morality of the whole set up. I know I did when I first arrived. Sure, a pittance of a salary in Hong Kong enabled Indonesian and Filipino women to support their families back home in a way they couldn't if they had stayed put. But when it meant separating a mother from her children, it left you wondering about the social cost. Years go by, though, and you stop questioning the society you eventually become part of and become accepting of it. Right or wrong, it just seems to happen that way. But one thing that still left me reeling was the social divide between the maids and everyone else here. It stuck in my craw, every time Sonny addressed me as 'sir'. I couldn't stop her though, but that didn't mean I'd ever talk down to her.

"How's your brother celebrating?" I asked.

"New girlfriend, but my parents don't like. She is no good."

"Forbidden love eh?"

"Sir?" She didn't get it.

"Never mind. Your kids okay?"

"Yes, my mum says they are doing well in school. My son likes football very much, he plays all the time with his friends outside."

"How about Jonathan?"

She shrugged. "He has Chinese class this morning. I have to wake him up to do his homework and eat breakfast."

That made me smile. For kids in Hong Kong, Saturdays were one endless round of extra tuition, homework and CV building. In Indonesia, kids still got to be kids.

"Sunday tomorrow, Sonny. Your day off. You got any plans?"

She shrugged and put out her lower lip. "Usual thing. Go out, sit down, chit-chat with friends. But so crowded, you know."

Truth is I had only been keeping the conversation going because inside I was craving normality and shooting the breeze with Sonny on everyday concerns seemed a perfect road to it. But like I've said before, the brain's a funny thing. The more you try to block and parry away from a problem, the more it brings you back to it. Sometimes through a constant slow tug. Or sometimes, like now, with a violent shove.

A shove that made an idea suddenly go ping inside my head.

"You mind if I ask you a favour, Sonny?"

As I told her what I needed, her smile widened, but somewhere along the way, the look of innocence in her eyes gave way to a devilish gleam.

CHAPTER FORTY-SEVEN

Victoria Park: an expanse of tree-lined pathways and concrete football pitches surrounding a precious grassy area. It sits on the edge of Causeway Bay, as inconspicuous as a crab in your morning bowl of cereal. Back in the day, its designers had probably thought they were creating an oasis of tranquility in the heart of Hong Kong's urban jungle. Boy, did they get that wrong! Victoria Park is as frenetic as any other part of the city it serves. Its tennis courts are constantly booked solid, its pool always full. Park wardens have to make sure people run the same way round the jogging track to avoid clashing. The basket-ball courts and bowling greens hum with competition. Old men argue politics on its benches, and if you could bottle the pent-up energy unleashed in the playgrounds, you could probably power Africa.

Yes indeed, Victoria Park is recreation Hong-Kong style: all-action, bursting at the seams and constantly on the move. At least it is Monday through Saturday.

But I was here on a Sunday.

And on a Sunday, Victoria Park belonged to Indonesia.

I stood in my T-shirt, knee-length shorts and sports shoes, on the sweltering walkway that crossed over King's Road, leaning on the railing and trying to focus on what was to come. Not an easy task, with the pandemonium of cackling, cooking, dancing, laughing and singing going on around me.

Sunday meant this part of town was transformed into one massive colourful campsite carnival. It began on walkways like this, stretched down to the pavement below and continued to every inch of open space in Victoria Park and beyond. The Indonesian domestic helper community on their one day off a week, claimed this part of the city for themselves. They laid out card-board boxes as picnic mats, set up their stoves, did each other's hair, dressed up in their finery, practiced dance routines for talent contests, swapped mobile phone tips, borrowed money from each other, prayed together, laughed together. It was an unbelievable sight.

Hong Kong had failed to build any sort of proper recreational areas for these thousands of helpers that made this city work. It was a complete disgrace. And yet, the Indonesian community had taken the lemon the city had dealt them and made lemonade, teaching HongKongers that you didn't need flashy premises to create a community. All you needed was heart. So, disgraceful though it was, there was something wonderful about it too. Just another of those inexplicable contradictions this city of contrasts served up on a daily basis.

I checked my sports watch.

Five minutes to go.

My heart started to pound. In this cloying heat, that wasn't good. Time to focus, I told myself. Closing my eyes, I filled my head with positive self-talk, pushing out all thoughts about what could go wrong, because the moment I let that happen, I knew it was over. This was the one chance Amy and I had. I had to delude myself it was going to work.

Another look at the watch told it was show-time.

Pushing off the railing, I weaved my way down the stairs to the pavement, keeping my head focused in the present. It took me a while to pick my way through the maids who had carpeted the whole area. A waft of Indonesian Rendang hit my nostrils like mustard gas. The sound of drums filled the air above the car horns and traffic. Somewhere in the distance a thousand mobile phones trilled.

Through the main entrance to the park stood the darkened copper statue of Queen Victoria, seated on the throne, sceptre in hand, as incongruous a sight as ever there was in this world. I continued to pick my way through the domestic-helper army, until I was at the base of the statue. Keeping my eyes fixed on the 19th century monarch's sour-puss face, I stopped and waited, my shirt clinging to my back in the soggy air, my muscles tingling and ready to go.

"I wonder what she would have thought of all this."

The voice came from over my right shoulder. Right on time.

"You're very punctual," I said, my eyes still front and centre. "But I guess, what else would you expect from a mercenary. – Gordon MacKenzie, right?"

The catch in his breathing lasted only a split second. But it was there. The only sign in our few encounters that something I had said had shaken him. I turned and faced him.

"And what about Antonio? Where's he hanging out?"

Skin-head aka Gordon Mackenzie was wearing a linen sports-jacket, jeans and plimsolls. There was no need to wear a jacket in this heat, not unless you were hiding a revolver and shoulder holster. A shard of fear pierced my thoughts. I pushed it out. No time for the negative today.

His hard eyes were on me now, as dead as a debt-collector's heart. "You have finally found out who we are. What took you so long?"

One step forward. I could feel his hot breath on my face, a waft of gum and nicotine.

"Now, impress me by telling me where Terence Auyeung is?"

"Where's Tito, or Antonio, or whatever his name is?"

"Never mind. Now, stop messing around!"

"Auyeung's dead," I said. "I told you before."

The dead stare he was giving me seemed to light with fire.

"So will you be, if you don't..."

I blasted my knee upwards hard, getting as much momentum behind it as my hip could generate. I was fast and had caught him off guard, but Gordon Mackenzie hadn't survived in some of the world's worst hell holes without sharpened reactions and instinctively he was rotating to throw my aim off. He dulled the blow some, but not enough to stop my knee connecting with his groin. Not as hard as I'd have liked, but satisfying enough. You hit a guy in the groin with any sort of force, he isn't getting up any time soon.

Gordon went down, his dead eyes bulging with water and anger in equal measure. I followed up with a two-palm shove. It was enough to send him to the floor.

I turned and sprinted.

The adrenalin dump had me in its grasp and I was fully in the moment. Space and time were suspended and I was acutely aware of everything. Bursting out onto the concrete football pitch open area, I ran, dodging pushchairs and groups of maids and palm trees, like a wing three-quarter on the rugby field heading for the touch-line.

Then I saw him.

A flicker, gnawing at the corner of my vision to start with, but soon transforming into a tangible moving force, heading straight in my direction.

Tito barreled in from my right. He was the size and speed of a ten-ton, fuel-injected truck. Yes, I had been expecting him, but he was moving fast. Faster than me.

I bit down the adrenalin, slanted right, pumped my arms, only one thought in my mind now. *Go! Go!*

Out of the football pitch area, I hurdled a wall and slammed straight into a jogger, sending him flying. With no time to apologise, I found my footing and kept going. Across an exercise area, an old woman smoothing through her Tai-Chi routine ignored me. I hurdled another wall and hit the massive grass field at Victoria Park's epicentre. Almost every inch of it was occupied by the Indonesian army of maids. It was like an outdoor rock concert. A quick glance over my shoulder told me Tito was still clinging close on my tail, shoving the unfortunately-placed jogger back to the ground, eyes on me, only one aim in mind.

Damn!

Time to deploy Plan A.

I saw them over to my left. A dance troupe of maids, dressed in Britney Spears outfits, shocks of blond hair and ribbons and bobby socks, shaking their stuff in perfect choreography to a fast beat blaring from a boom-box. I headed in their direction, pausing for a moment when I got there. Tapping the leader on the shoulder, I pointed at Tito, twenty yards behind me now.

"Are you Sonny's friend?"

"Yes."

"Him," I said, pointing back to Tito.

"Okay," she said. "Go, go."

I didn't need a second invitation and sprinted off. Two seconds later, girly screams spliced through the air behind me. By now, I was at the edge of the grass and under the trees. I risked a glance back to see Tito throwing my Britney Spears heroines off him, like a wild rhinoceros splaying a pack of wildebeest in his wake.

No time to rest, I kept on going, edging round the pond where old men raced their model motorboats. I was on the western edge of the park now, a maze of concrete, tree-lined paths where lovers could neck in peace, old men could take their afternoon constitution and maids could shelter from the sun.

Eventually, I reached the rendezvous at the white-tented bandstand.

"Sir! Here!" Sonny said.

I almost didn't recognize her. Gone were the cut-off jeans and T-shirts of her work-day routine. In its place, she wore a lilac jilbab, the traditional garment worn by Muslim women and a head-scarf of the same colour. She looked so different, so poised and respectable. Only her face was visible and somehow it made her look like the happiest person on earth.

My lungs were gasping for oxygen and I couldn't get the words out, to say how relieved I was to see her, to thank her again for arranging all this, the dance troupe diversion, letting me use her phone to make a couple of calls when we had met in the stairwell yesterday. And now the final piece of the escape plan we were about to implement.

She beckoned me to follow her down the pathway and round the corner where a group of her friends waited, all bantering and dressed in the same way as Sonny. As soon as they saw me, they surrounded me like hungry birds would a discarded loaf. One handed me a towel to wipe off the sweat. Then all I had to do was stand there as they buzzed around dressing me, until head to foot, I was wearing the same outfit they were. The full jilbab and headscarf.

"Want to see?" Sonny took a picture with her phone and showed me. Not a bad transformation, I thought, although I was glad that I'd shaved as closely as I had that morning. "Very pretty, sir."

They all dissolved in giggles and then we got down to business, moving as a group, me in the centre, now just another domestic helper on her day off catching up on the week's gossip with friends.

We hit the main path and headed west, one of them threading her arm through mine and jabbering Indonesian at me. I fixed on a grin and nodded, getting into the part, but all the while darting my eyes at each passer-by. I was nervous at the thought of discovery and ready to sprint again at any moment.

The path swerved left. We were only a hundred yards away from the exit I had chosen, the green iron gates just beyond a small play area at the northwestern tip of the park. A hundred yards from pulling this off. A hundred yards from freedom.

We passed under a flyover, a reflexology walkway appeared on our right.

But up ahead appeared the most vile apparition my mind could imagine at that moment.

My heart stopped.

Gordon MacKenzie and Tito. Walking towards us at a slow but deliberate pace, their eyes on everyone and everything, searching, searching.

How the hell did they know!

A split-second decision to choose. Turn and run, or try to sneak past.

I tapped my partner's arm and that was the signal for the group to close ranks around me. The talk and laughter went up a notch as we headed as one, straight on by them.

They didn't even notice. We were twenty yards past now. The gate to freedom in sight.

I should have kept my eyes front. I should have just looked ahead.

But I didn't. Pure instinct made me flip my head to see if they had noticed and as I did, Gordon Mackenzie's dead eyes looked straight at me. A split second, that was all it took.

One mistake.

"Hey!" he shouted.

I grabbed the fabric at my knees and was off. Breaking out of my group, I sprinted for the gate.

I could hear their footsteps, the screams from Sonny and her friends as they slowed them up, if only for a few crucial seconds.

Through the gate, I ripped off the jilbab and head scarf, my eyes searching.

Where was it? Come on!

The high-pitched blast of the Yamaha engine piercing the air was the most beautiful sound in the world right then. The bike screeched to a halt on the road in front me, throwing off smoke from its back wheel. The driver was dressed head to foot in black leather. In this heat, that took some doing. Up went the helmet visor.

Cherry Blossom's agate eyes looked at me. Those same eyes which had last stared down at me when I'd been taken out, heading into the restaurant to see Rufus Lam. She signaled for me to get on.

I straddled the bike, wrapped my arms round her waist.

MacKenzie was moving at warp speed towards us, only yards away now, his right arm stretching towards me. I leaned to avoid him.

He lunged at me, and just as he did my whole body thrust backwards from the jolt of the bike's acceleration. His hand missed me and grabbed air, but as he fell he caught the back of the bike. In that tenth of a second, he got dragged ten yards, it seemed, but then he seemed to let go.

The last thing I saw, before the air blast from the acceleration turned my eyes to water, was Gordon Mackenzie spinning and rolling across the tarmac like a broken rag doll and Tito still hauling ass after me, but disappearing into the distance.

CHAPTER FORTY-EIGHT

The bike careered west, ducking onto the backstreets.

We slalomed through traffic, missing bumpers by inches and pedestrians who crossed our path by even less. Cherry Blossom leaned us at impossible angles round corner after corner until I was lost and disoriented.

She pulled us up onto a pavement and into the shadows of a building with a jolt. Unstraddling the bike, she dragged me off with her. Before I had a chance to say anything, she was patting me down, her large hands finding every crevice, although hell knows what she thought I was hiding on me.

She located the mobile phone in my shorts pocket. Took it out, removed the battery in one practiced movement, threw it into a nearby bin and crunched the phone under her boot like a cockroach.

"Hey!" I protested, but she was having none of it.

"Get back on!" she ordered, her voice as clear as day through her helmet.

I did as I was told.

Next thing I knew, the spare helmet she'd had laced through her elbow was being shoved down on my head, the strap tugged tight under my chin. Suddenly, I was plunged into pitch blackness. The visor had masking tape plastered on the inside and was stuck down tight. I couldn't see a damn thing.

"Hold on!" she said. A domineering woman of few words was Cherry Blossom.

Off we thundered again and all I could do was obey.

I had ridden pillion once before while backpacking around in Greece after law school. But that was a moped I could have outpaced at a swift jog and at least on that occasion I'd had the advantage of vision. This time the differing screeches of the engine and the speed of the wind on my skin were the only clues to where we were going. It was a horrific sensation, being blind at speed. Every swerve sent me reeling with fear, every bump was magnified into bone crushing proportions. I tried to control my breathing, to move beyond the fear and disappear into a compartment of my brain where I could make believe this wasn't happening. But it was hard to concentrate on anything but the image of Gordon Mackenzie losing his grasp on the back of the bike and spinning across the road. If that wasn't the last time I saw him, the next time I was a dead man for sure.

In every sense, right now my life was in Cherry Blossom's hands.

Eventually, I had no real notion of how long, the bike's engine lost a few octaves. I could feel the road undulate and twist. The sound of crunching gravel billowed beneath us, bumping me to hell. We skidded to a stop. I pitched forward, my arms still locked tight on Cherry Blossom's muscular frame. The engine cut out, but there was no way I was getting off until she gave me my cue, which came in the form of her forcing my cramped arms open.

My legs were like jelly and I stumbled across the ground, the sense of ongoing motion jettisoning me all over place, like stepping off a treadmill after banging out ten kilometres at speed.

I struggled for dear life to get the helmet off, but someone grabbed my arms. Scratch that, two people. I felt myself lifted off the ground and dragged like a rag-doll. I just went with it because there was nothing else I could do.

The temperature suddenly turned air-conditioner cool and I sensed we had crossed a threshold to an indoor setting. My ears popped the remainder of the screeching engine into nothing and now I was conscious of Cherry Blossom's voice barking orders in Mandarin, and the grunting acknowledgements from my companions either side. I pushed out the disorientation and told myself to get a grip.

I felt myself being escorted down a spiral staircase. Voices in the distance, different and muffled, were coming closer and closer. A door opened. The voices peeled into silence. A palm in the small of my back pushed me through. The door shut. Hands fumbled with the straps under my chin and the helmet was hauled away.

The harsh brightness lazering my newfound vision turned the world into a watery blur. I shut my eyes, counted three and blinked until I could see.

It was a room. A white room. Really white. White walls and ceiling. White sofa and coffee table. Carpet, white. Ornament statuettes, white. You get the picture.

In this dazzling ambience, Phil Yip in his worsted navy-blue pinstripe looked as out of place as a fly in a Michelin-star restaurant's lobster bisque. He was standing ramrod straight, arms folded tight. That usual look of worry, responsibility and concern on his face was magnified up three notches.

Sitting on the edge of the sofa was Rufus Lam, his blonde hair almost transluscent against the whiteness around him. He was wearing a red open-necked shirt, blue waistcoat, white jeans, brown loafers and no socks. One arm was slung on the back of the sofa. His other hand rested on that silver-tipped cane of his. His handsome face was turned towards to me, his look serious, which seemed sort of odd given the flamboyancy of his outfit.

Cherry Blossom took up a position behind the sofa at Rufus Lam's shoulder. She squatted down and whispered something in his ear, catching him up on what had just gone down. Lam stayed concentrated, absorbing it all, processing it. When Cherry Blossom was done, she stood up to her full height and cast a long shadow across the white carpet.

All eyes were on me now. I took that as my cue.

"Hi," I said, digging deep into the full repertoire of my stunning opening-lines.

"You okay?" Phil asked.

"Nothing that a whisky wouldn't cure."

Phil gave me flat eyes. "This isn't the time for jokes, Scott."

"Sorry, Mother Theresa," I said. But he was right. I had reached for the safety-ground of humour again to steady my nerves which were roiling in the calmness of this room, in the complete and utter contrast to what had just gone before.

"It appears you have had quite an ordeal, Scott," Rufus Lam said. "Rest assured, you are safe here."

Those were the words which, right then, I needed to hear. They were delivered with an assurance that countenanced no question. I nodded a thanks and started to breathe slowly.

"Are you warm enough? Do you want a change of clothes?" Lam asked.

"I'm good," I said.

Just then the door opened and in walked a maid with a white tray and a white bone-china tea-set. She placed it down on the coffee table and started to pour, but Rufus told her he would take care of it.

He poured three cups, asked Phil and me if we took milk and sugar, then settled back down on the sofa. The taste of the Earl Grey on my lips was pure nectar. Not enough to get me to relax, but close enough in the circumstances.

"How's the election going?" I asked, just for something to say.

Lam weighed the question a moment and chose his words deliberately. "I'm happy enough with progress. The voice of the people of Hong Kong is being heard by the whole world. They are simply asking for the right to vote for a Chief Executive who hasn't been hand-picked for them by the Central People's Government. It is a reasonable enough request and something which has been guaranteed to us in the Basic Law. We are merely asking that the Central People's Government make good on that commitment, by letting the nominating committee allow Elizabeth Leung to stand as a candidate. You as a lawyer should appreciate that, Scott. Especially after the way the nominating committee was rammed down our throats, despite massive discontent."

It was a flawless statement, delivered with poise and grace and reasonable in its suggestion. But it was total bull and Lam must have known it. Hong Kong wasn't asking for anything any more. It was demanding it and it was Lam's intervention which had whipped up Hong Kong into frenzy once more. He was the one who was forcing the issue, pulling the strings, linking his campaign to mass protests of the past, making it clear that he was taking on the mantle of the Umbrella Generation. It was him standing on the front line, staring into the eyes of the Central People's Government, neither of them backing down, both daring each other to blink first.

Rufus Lam was a brave man. A crazy man, but a brave man all the same.

"And what happens if Beijing refuses again?" I asked.

"Then they shall bear the consequences of a hugely disgruntled population refusing to pay its taxes to a government they do not want," Lam said, his tone rock-steady.

"Is that where it ends?"

Lam raised his eyebrows at the question, contemplated some more, as if debating whether to reveal a secret.

"I actually believe the Central People's Government will take the reasonable approach this time. I believe they will, very soon and very publicly, allow the nominating committee to approve Elizabeth Leung's candidacy. And I believe she will win against Jeremy Lau in the election. Hong Kong will get the democratically elected candidate it wants."

"Scott, are you going to tell us what the hell is going on?" Phil asked, trying to get us back on topic.

"I'm sure Scott will tell us in his own time," Lam didn't seem to be in any rush.

"No," I said. "Phil's right. I'm here to tell you what I've found. I mean, what we've found."

"We?" Lam asked.

It was time to come clean.

"I've been working with a journalist," I said. "But please hear me out before you rush to any judgement."

Lam brooded in silence a moment. For a man in the media industry, I found it strange how the word 'journalist' could strike such concern in him.

"Very well," he said after a while, motioning for me to begin.

"Have you ever heard of the Chinese Overseas Investment Corporation?"

Lam thought long and hard about that one too, but eventually shook his head.

So I told him. Everything. About how COIC was a vehicle being used by China for soft power, buying influence to create a web of favours for when they were needed. About how one of those favours had been established right here in Hong Kong, just after the Handover with the bailout of Star Transport. How that favour was now being called in, all these years later, through Daisy Lai, the Star Transport heiress hooking up with Napoleon Wong with one specific aim in mind: to set up Terence Auyeung and go public with a story that would pose significant questions about Rufus Lam's integrity and judgment on the eve of an election which Lam was trying to make a turning-point in Hong Kong's history.

When I finished laying it out once, Lam asked me to take him through it again, only this time more slowly, so he and Phil could ask me questions. So I did. And they grilled me like a well-done steak, Phil pummeling me with question after question, Lam weighing in now and then with a follow-up here and there, both of them testing out every link in my story, working out for themselves how all the different pieces fitted together. I threw in additional information this time, about Gordon MacKenzie and Antonio Fernandez, two former employees of NDT Consultants, now here on work visas for Star Transport. About how we had tracked down Auyeung's son, David, to his place of work and found out the truth about the money he owed to Benson Chan. About how Benson Chan and Napoleon Wong knew each other from their children being in the same class at the Tai Po international school.

We went over it a third time. The questions kept coming and I kept batting them back as honestly and as fully as I could. As each new fact emerged, so the tone of scepticism in their voices eroded. Eventually, the questions seemed more like requests for confirmation. I let them ask and ask until they had punched themselves out.

After a while, the room lapsed into a heavy, exhausted – but tense – silence. Phil had his arms folded still, his brow knitted and his eyes narrowed straight on me. I wasn't sure what the look was trying to tell me and I didn't much care. He was the one who had got me into this mess and I had done the job.

"So Terence is dead," Lam said after a while.

It wasn't a question, but I nodded my confirmation anyway.

Rufus Lam stood up. Leaving his cane on the sofa, he paced over to the patio windows and stared through them without seeing. Lost in thought, he tugged gently at his bottom lip. He was the picture of coolness, not a flicker of tension on his face. I wondered what was going on in that head of his. Thoughts of his old pal Auyeung maybe? About Napoleon Wong's treachery? About the election? It was hard to tell.

Eventually he turned to me.

"I have lost a good friend," he said. "Gladys has lost her husband. Does she know yet?"

His voice was laden with sadness as he asked.

"No," I said.

Lam pondered my answer.

"Philip was right about you, Scott," he said. "Your methods are unorthodox, but they are effective. This is …" he paused, reaching for the right words. "This is not what I had been expecting."

"It is what it is," I said.

Rufus Lam nodded and rubbed his hand across his face. And with that motion, something changed in him. Gone was the sadness. Suddenly his eyes had turned to pieces of flint, hard and determined, ready to take up a challenge and strike out at the enemy. He was the businessman again, the man who had battled his way to riches and a place at the top echelon of Hong Kong society. A man who, despite the dilletante clothes and expressions of eccentricity, was not afraid of a bare-knuckle fight. Here he was once more, the tycoon, girding himself to charge headlong into the fray.

"It seems we have only one option," he said.

I knew what he was going to do.

I didn't even need to suggest it, although I was more than ready to do so.

"This journalist you have been working with," he said, his voice laden with steel. "Let her publish her story. She has earned the right, I believe. Let her publish these findings as widely as she can. Let the people of Hong Kong see how the Central People's Government operates to manipulate an election which they already control. And let Beijing live with the consequences of its actions."

It was the conclusion I had come here for. The one I had promised Amy, and hearing it coming from Rufus Lam's lips was what I needed.

"She's going to need your protection." I said. "We both are."

"Then you shall have it," Lam promised. "Where is she now? I will send my people immediately."

"She's at a secret location," I replied. "Let me go with them, I can show them where."

"Very well." He barked some orders at Cherry Blossom. All this time, she hadn't moved from her position behind the sofa.

She nodded at Lam, then walked over to me.

"Let's go," she said.

I didn't need a second invitation.

CHAPTER FORTY-NINE

We were outside in the courtyard in front of Rufus Lam's summer hide-away, a colonnaded house that was so white it reminded me of pictures of the US President's residence. The courtyard was a circular set-out, with white marble chipped gravel surrounding a fountain centrepiece which looked like it had been carved by Michelangelo.

A wet blanket of humid steam hung in the atmosphere making the whole world tire under its weight. The sky was gun-metal grey. It felt like the colour of impending doom, although I couldn't put my finger on why.

The day had been a long one so far, and even though everything had gone as planned, I was still on edge. Until I knew Amy was safe, I'd remain so.

"You don't need to go, you know." Phil was all concern, cool as you like even in this weather, in his worsted suit. "I'm sure Cherry Blossom can handle it."

I looked at him like he was being stupid, which he was. He raised defensive double palms to me.

"I'm only saying. And I'm sorry. For getting you into this in the first place. Okay?"

Phil Yip was my oldest friend. In my itinerant life, I hadn't collected many of those, which meant the ones who stuck around were solid as granite. We had been through a lot together.

"Don't worry about it," I said.

"After this is over maybe we should talk about you coming back to work?"

"Don't push it, Phil."

Again he gave me flat palms, then patted me on the shoulder.

"We'll talk later," he said, then went back inside the house to politic away with his new favourite billionaire client.

Cherry Blossom was on the other side of the fountain. One of her underlings was giving her directions, showing her on his iPad, brushing his thick fingers across the screen. Suddenly her mobile phone trilled out a piece of classical music, which surprised the hell out of me. As she answered and listened, I had visions of a seven-foot school girl playing 'cello with dreams of being the female Yo Yo Ma. How she had got from there to the Taiwanese military police, to protecting Rufus Lam, was a story which, another time, I would have liked to delve into. For now, however, I contented myself with the thought of how life had a habit of sending you down unexpected pathways from which there was no way back. All you could do was go with it, or wallow in regret.

Eventually, Cherry Blossom got what she needed. She signaled me over and handed me a helmet, one I could see through this time. She straddled back onto the Yamaha, fired up the engine, pointed it south, and off we went, me riding pillion again, but being able to see made a hell of a difference to the quality of the journey.

The Hong Kong landscape glided on by, as varied and strange a sight as existed on this earth. A background of rugged, inhospitable granite mountain peaks, covered in thick green shrubbery, made you think how anyone could live here. Huge modern tower blocks clinging to their side, answered the question with defiance, bearing testament to the achievements which human endeavour could make possible in the face of adversity. Hong Kong: it was an aberration. Neither the environment nor history had provided this place with any advantages. And yet here it was; a gleaming international finance centre which had taken its opium-trading past and turned itself into a bustling megalopolis. Life had sent the city down an unexpected pathway and the city had just kept on sprinting, no time for regret or reflection or anything other than how to make more money.

Cherry Blossom sped the bike up a ramp and out onto the four-lane highway, leaning us into the fast lane and cranking up the acceleration. I hung on tight and let my thoughts go.

I pondered how much of a gamble it had been, going up against Mackenzie and Tito in Victoria Park that morning. Sonny and her pals had helped me out every step of the way, but it could have gone oh so very wrong. If Phil hadn't got the message through to Rufus Lam, which I had given him to pass on using Sonny's phone the day before. If I hadn't been able to outrun those two goons. If Cherry Blossom had pulled up on her Yamaha a split second later, I wondered if I'd still be alive.

Again the image of MacKenzie's hard face spinning away from the back of the Yamaha, swam through my mind. The anger in his eyes, which said next time I was a dead man for sure.

There would be no next time, however. I tried to comfort myself with that fact. We were safe now. This was over.

Only it wasn't, not for me.

Not until I knew Amy had the protection she needed.

I didn't give a damn about Amy's story or Rufus Lam's election. But she was passionate about both, and somewhere along the way, I had become passionate about her. The whole Victoria Park plan had been my suggestion. There had been no magic to it. Pure distraction was all it had been. Just a spin on 'hey your shoe laces are undone' and then getting the hell out of there when their attention was turned. Keeping Mackenzie and Tito's attention occupied with my escape, so Amy could just slip away somewhere safe, finish writing her story and wait for me to show up with the cavalry.

Hardly rocket-science, but it had worked a treat. Sometimes the simplest and most obvious plans do.

So why did I still feel so on edge? Maybe it was because it had all happened so fast, that my sense of well-being still needed time to catch up. But my antennae were sensing something was out of kilter, like a seagull could sense a coming storm. It was playing at the edges of my mind, like a movie star's name that no matter how hard I reached for, it still wouldn't come.

The eastern harbour tunnel spat us out of its southern mouth and we cruised along the highway back into territory with which I was familiar. Overhead, the grey, pregnant clouds were taking on an ominous darkness. The heavens were about to open with a vengeful deluge. Lightening flickered in the distance over the peaks of Lantau Island and beyond. Being on the back of a bike was the last place we could expect any refuge. Cherry Blossom, as if reading my thoughts, gunned the engine to a high pitched screech and rocketed us onwards to our destination.

We screamed up Pak Tam Au Road, a one-in-six gradient that took us above the city, avoiding its main arteries. When we hit Tin-Hau Temple Road we started to weave our way back down.

Amy had told me the address. I had memorized it, given it to Cherry Blossom, and she had worked out the route. It was a sixty-year old tenement block in a back street area off Tai Hang Road. The place

301

on the first floor belonged to a professor Amy knew. He had inherited it and kept it empty, free for his own thinking time and out of the hands of the greedy developers.

Cherry Blossom drew the bike up to the pavement and cut the engine, locked the bike and indicated for me to lead the way. I took off my helmet and handed it to her.

Access to the block was limited to a stone staircase with uneven steps that no-one knew about, apart from the estate agents who trooped around a steady stream of expats looking for a place that matched their size needs and rent expectations. It took me a moment to find it. By now the sky had darkened to breaking-point. The wind was whipping up and rain started to spit from the heavens. When that starts to happen in Hong Kong, you run for cover. It's like a thirty-second warning.

I two-stepped it up the uneven staircase, Cherry Blossom close on my shoulder. Just as I hit the top step, the clouds opened up. Thick soaking raindrops pummelled down on us. We sprinted across the patch of concrete and open grass for the doorway, making it inside just as the first round lightning split through the heavens with its electric forks. Two seconds later, the thunder-clap came, so loud I could feel it in my chest.

The doorway led us into a darkened stairway. The block had been built in the days before lifts. The whole place belonged in a Hammer House Horror movie.

Cherry Blossom's jet black hair was plastered down by the wet. It lay across her broad shoulders and face in thick rope-like strands. In a practiced, fluid movement she bent her head down, letting it all fall lose, then flipped it back and tied it up. She was ready to go. Ready for business.

Letting your hair grow long was probably one of the perks of being a bodyguard in the private sector. I doubted they had let her wear it like that when she was serving in Taiwan's...

And that's when it hit me. The piece of information which had been playing at the corners of my mind, thundered front and centre.

I had this whole damn thing wrong.

CHAPTER FIFTY

The rain was coming down in sheets, rattling against the windows on the ground floor. Cherry Blossom looked down at me, her large figure casting a dark ominous shadow in the stairwell even in this dim light.

Our eyes met.

In that moment, she knew I'd worked it out.

The brain. We're not in control of our mind, no way. We're at the complete and utter mercy of its randomness. The way its hundred billion neurons interact, snapping electrochemical processes which draw links between information and lead to conclusions that were always there, but you would never in a million years have put together with conscious thought.

That's how it was again for me. The whole process took less than a tenth of second, but here's how it went.

Cherry Blossom flips her rain-wet hair and ties it up, leaving me marveling at the discipline of this Amazonian, at how it must have been a relief to her to be able to grow her hair like that, now that she's out of the army game and in the private sector.

The neurons bounce and Cherry Blossom's hair-flip moves me onto to Amy, the way she tucks away wayward strands behind her ear when she's thinking. Such a simple, yet such a seductive move from a woman so unaware of just how damn attractive she is. It's the simple things which were drawing me ever closer to her.

Amy. She's one in a million…

She…

The neurons collide into each other, electrochemical processes are produced, finally dragging that flickering which has been at the hinterland of my mind out of the grey and into the light.

Suddenly Rufus Lam's words to me earlier that afternoon crashed in like a tidal wave breaking on the seafront barrier.

This journalist you have been working with. Let her publish her story. She has earned the right, I believe. Let her publish these findings as widely as she can.

To preserve Amy's anonimity until I knew he was on board, I had been careful not to mention her by name. Only by profession. Throughout my entire recitation, she was only 'the journalist I have been working with.'

And yet, Rufus Lam knew the journalist I had been working with was a woman. No doubt about it in his voice. No room for error in the words he had used. *Let her publish her story. She has earned the right, I believe. Let her publish these findings as widely as she can.*

He knew who Amy Tang was. Of course he must have done, she was one of the few journalists in Hong Kong who had gone out of her way to cultivate an anti-Rufus Lam platform in her articles.

She was his enemy.

And here she was on the eve of an election, about to publish a story making out Rufus Lam to be the victim of a conspiracy. A story which would whip up public anger and bring the masses onto the streets in support of his campaign and his candidate. A story which would have all the more credibility because it came from the one journalist in Hong Kong who hated his guts.

Rufus Lam knew I was working with her.

He had known all along.

This whole thing was a set-up.

But now I knew who was really behind it.

And as Cherry Blossom's eyes met mine in that dank, dark stairwell, with the storm raging outside, she realized I knew it too.

This was just a job to her, one last big pay-off promised by Lam maybe, before she sailed off into a beach-side retirement. Shooting me would be like filling in an application form. An annoyance, but necessary to complete the task she was being paid to do.

Cherry Blossom already had her gun out and ready. She pointed it at my chest. A flash of lightening lit up her game-face. Not a flicker of emotion showed.

As for me, it was another day, another gun. I knew the drill by now, or least I should have done, my heart accelerating like a bongo, the vice of fear enclosing like steel bands round my ribcage. I had ridden my luck too many times. Today was luck's expiry date.

Right there, in that dank stairwell, I was out of plays. The exit was blocked by Cherry Blossom's massive frame. The way upstairs to where Amy waited, oblivious to her fate, was off limits too. There was no way I could get any sort of warning to her, not without Cherry Blossom putting me down.

Not only had I failed to keep Amy safe, I had brought death to both our doorsteps.

"Go up!" Cherry Blossom ordered.

"Go to hell!" was my retort.

The round-house kick came out of nowhere, her foot hitting my jaw like a sledge-hammer, spinning me into the cold concrete wall. I crumpled to the floor, panting hard, flashing comets going off behind my eye-lids, the bells of Big Ben chiming in my skull.

Before I came to rest, Cherry Blossom grabbed a hand full of my hair and was dragging me up the stone stairs. My feet scrambled beneath me. The edge of a stone step clunked into my back somewhere near the kidneys. She gave my hair another haul and another stone step glanced off my tail bone, shooting pain up, down and sideways through my body. Harder and harder Cherry Blossom yanked, panting like a rabid dog that hadn't been fed for a week.

The first floor landing offered me no respite when we got there. Even through my daze of pain, I hoped beyond hope I could slow things up. Cherry Blossom could beat me to hell, I swore to myself. Still I wouldn't tell her which flat Amy was in. But the block was a one-flat-per-floor construction, so bang went that plan along with the last vestige of my hope.

Like I said, today was luck's expiry date for me.

Through woozy vision, I saw Cherry Blossom aim the gun at the lock in the door and fire three times. Wood splintered, the stench of burnt powder filled the hot stairwell. Big Ben turned into an alarm clock ring in my head, but this time my brain engaged. I let the burning fire unleash a blood lust inside of me that finally stoked me into action.

Cherry Blossom made to kick the door, but as she did I reached out and grabbed a heel. Her connection with the door was full. She splintered it open, but my grasp on her other leg sent her toppling sideways into the wall with a clunk. It sounded decent enough.

"Amy, get out of there!" I screamed at the top of my voice above the ringing, but the same heel I had just tugged landed square in the meat of my stomach blowing out my wind.

Cherry Blossom was some athlete, I'll give her that. She was on her feet again as I crumpled into the fetal position, sucked in air, trying to clear my mind.

Looking up, I saw a high-ceilinged, cluttered, front room open up before me. Two sofas, bursting bookshelves, a heavy glass-cabinet, beige walls with cracks in them. And on the other side of the room was Amy, mouth open in a shocked 'o', frozen in time, seated at a dining-room table, lap-top open.

"Get out!" I screamed again at her.

Three things happened in the next split second.

Amy looked down at me. Cherry Blossom was swinging the gun in Amy's direction. I leapt from the floor, my hands like claws aiming for Cherry Blossom's neck which was about my face height. I missed her neck but managed a shoulder barge. It wasn't much of a contact, but it was enough.

The gun went off three inches from my ear drums, tossing me again into a ringing deafness. Cherry Blossom was off balance and I charged her again, my hands grabbing leather and holding on for dear life. We crashed into a book-case. Paperbacks rained down on us from the top shelf like bricks. She threw me over the back of the sofa.

Amy had her lap-top under her arm and was darting through to a back room somewhere.

Cherry Blossom had the gun up again. I hit the floor and kicked the sofa with everything I had. It slammed into Cherry Blossom's side. The gun went off and took a chunk of plaster out of the beige wall.

I was on my feet. Grabbing two books, I hurled them at Cherry Blossom. The first glanced off her shoulder, the second hit her square below the eye.

I used the second it had bought me to run after Amy.

Grabbing the side of the freestanding glass-cabinet I hauled it over with all my might. A brutal crash filled the universe as it toppled over, angling across the room, creating a barrier. I ducked as another gunshot sounded, the heart of its trajectory whistling by my ear.

I shouldered through the door into a bedroom.

Amy had the window open. She had climbed out onto the ledge and was about to try to lower herself down, but it was too far a drop.

Sprinting over, I grabbed her shoulder to gain her attention.

"I'll lower you down!"

Our eyes met and in that moment, a strange sort of detached calmness descended on me. It was as if neither life nor pain mattered any more. Time seemed to slow down. I was conscious of nothing then, other than righting my wrong and getting her to safety.

There was a desk by the wall. I shoved it against the door figuring it would buy valuable seconds. Not a second too soon, as the door handle rattled and Cherry Blossom started to shoulder it through.

No time to waste, I shoved a chair under the window and clambered on.

"My laptop," Amy screamed from the other side of the glass.

"There's no time!"

But the look in her eyes told me she wasn't going anywhere without it. So I grabbed it off the bed and handed it to her through the window.

We were only one floor up, but looking down it seemed like ten.

"I've got you," I told Amy, taking her elbow in both my hands.

She looked at me, nodded, then lowered herself down the outer wall as far as she could. Hand over hand, I moved my grasp from her elbow to her wrist, tiptoeing on the chair, stretching out of the window as far as I could.

The crashing at the door stopped. It was not a good sign.

Amy looked up at me and nodded.

We both let go together.

She hit the ground with a yelp and rolled and was in the process of getting to her feet, when I turned round to see how much time I had...

Cherry Blossom was already through the door and had a window on the other side of the room, open. Her arm was stretched through and she was taking aim at Amy.

"No!" I heard myself scream, picking up the chair and hurling it as an advance guard as I launched myself behind it. From the look on Cherry Blossom's face, I could tell the gun shot had whistled wide. I grabbed the lapels on her leather jacket and tugged her back from the window. She swatted my arms away like they were matchsticks. I saw the blur of her fist, just before it hit my nose square on. The sound of a crunching splat, ricocheted through my front lobe. It was the sound of an ice-cream cone meeting tarmac. I was wheeling backwards now, my legs elastic bands. I went down against the opposite wall. No way, I wasn't getting up from that.

Panting hard and woozy as hell, I was conscious only of a red warm stickiness oozing down my face and neck, breathing through my mouth because my nose wasn't functioning.

Looking up, I found Cherry Blossom aiming the gun at me.

They say that your whole life rushes before your eyes in situations like this, but that's bullshit. I was spent and somehow ready and resigned to what was about to go down. I let my eyes fall shut, concentrating on the sound of the rain pelting the windows.

A gunshot cracked the air.

And a micro-second later, I felt nothing.

CHAPTER FIFTY-ONE

There was only blackness.

At first the thought amused me. *How the hell can you feel a colour, you moron!* The brain, even on its way to death, plays tricks, it seems, it's spinning neurons pelting you with crazy thoughts. Maybe it was just the body's way of preparing you for the ultimate agony. The one that ends it all. Any minute, I expected it. The bullet scything through my ribcage, pain blooming in my chest, carrying me away to nothing.

But the only pain I felt was in my nose, which was throbbing like a base player with the amp cranked high. With every throb the pain became more acute and it made me wonder: was this what death was like? Your final end-state frozen in time forever? Just my bad luck, then, to have had my nose broken just before I bit the big one.

But that didn't make any sense and the fact that I was even capable of having that thought made me wonder whether in fact...

I dared to open my eyes.

Cherry Blossom stared back at me. She was slumped on the floor, side on, her face locked in that same perfect visage I had seen moments earlier when she had been standing, taking aim at my chest. Only this time her forehead had a blemish: a single perfect round hole, blood dripping from it like honey down the side of a jar, snaking down in a neat track to the wooden floor where a pool was slowly coagulating.

I heard a voice.

Speaking in Mandarin, or at least I thought it was.

Footsteps creaked on the floor around me, but I was too tired to move. All I could do was wait for the shadows to materialize into my field of vision.

The footsteps stopped next to me.

I could hear the sound of breathing come close and sensed someone crouching down beside me. The voice spoke, but not to me. Yes, it was definitely Mandarin. The sweet swish of the tones sliding off the tongue. Right then it was like music to my ears because it told me I was alive and well enough, at least, to recognize the differences between languages.

Whoever it was was speaking on the phone. It sounded like orders being given, but what the hell did I care. It was a beautiful language, one I needed to learn and I promised with the second chance at life I'd just been given, I'd give it a go some day soon.

The voice stopped. I was conscious of being looked at.

I forced myself to turn my head.

In that moment, everything made sense and then again nothing did.

Gordon Mackenzie stared down at me, working a toothpick round his mouth, gun in hand. There was a scratch down the right side of his face and I could hear his breath, like a huffing horse.

I don't know why I laughed, but I couldn't help myself. It welled to the surface from deep within my core. A relieving, hysterical cackle which left me spluttering on my own blood. Each cough sent my nose to a different stratosphere of pain. I eventually regained control and looked my ol' pal Skin-head in his searching, soulless eyes.

"Who are you?" I heard myself asking. Shock had taken me in its hold and I was glad of it, because if I had to process any of this without my mind parrying out the trauma, I might as well have curled up in a ball. Instead, I pushed myself up so my back was against the cold concrete wall.

The door opened. Tito steam-rollered into the room, crashing furniture out of his way as he manhandled Amy in after him, a giant hand clutched around her matchstick arm. Still she clutched her precious laptop to her chest with her free hand, like her life depended on it. Tito tossed her to the floor next to me. Her hair and clothes were soaked through, her chest heaving in gulp-fulls of oxygen.

Outside the rain pelted hard at the windows, the wind whistling eerily.

"Oh God!" Amy's voice came out in a hollow rasp. I followed her eyes to Cherry Blossom's dead body on the other side of the room. Cherry Blossom's flat eyes were still open and staring at us.

"You okay?" I asked.

I know. Stupid question.

Amy turned to me, and from the look on her face, I was none too pretty a sight.

Gordon MacKenzie was standing over us now, clicking his fingers to gain our attention. "We need to do this quickly, please. Tell us what you know. Now!"

"How do we know we can trust you?" I asked. It was a weak riposte, but something inside me felt obliged to offer it up anyway.

He crouched down. "I just saved your life by placing a bullet in between her eyes." His left arm pointed at Cherry Blossom.

Again I let go a hysterical laugh. *Placing a bullet in between her eyes.* Gordon Mackenzie, the trained killer with the awkward turns of phrase.

After it had subsided, I looked at Amy. She was in no state to talk and in any event she didn't know what I knew. So I decided to take the lead. I didn't have it all worked out, not by a long shot. For one thing, I hadn't a clue how Gordon Mackenzie or Tito fitted into this whole thing. Or how they had found us here. So instead I went with the one fact I was sure of now. The one fact which made me feel so damn stupid for ever becoming embroiled in this thing in the first place.

"It was Rufus Lam," I said. "He set this whole thing up."

"What?" Amy spluttered.

"Go on!" Mackenzie was as confused as Amy. I didn't blame either of them.

I looked at Amy. "I've been wrong all along. Had this whole thing ass-backwards. I figured Rufus Lam was the target. That this was the Chinese Government using its vehicle, the Chinese Overseas Investment Corporation to organize the set-up, just to discredit Lam right before the election. But that's what Lam has wanted us to think all along. Make it look like he's the victim of the big bad mainland bully, the same bully which has been denying Hong Kong democracy all these years. He wants to swing so much sympathy and outrage in his favour, there's no way the Central People's Government would stop the nominating committee from letting his candidate run for Chief Executive. And if his candidate Elizabeth Leung runs, she'll win. But Elizabeth Leung is Lam's candidate, not Hong Kong's. She's the candidate whom Rufus Lam controls. That's what this is all about. Power and control."

Amy's brow creased in thought and confusion. Gordon MacKenzie worked the toothpick, trying to figure things out. Tito stood like a rock, not seeming to give two hoots. He was just paid muscle doing his job.

I turned to Amy. "What better way to give this whole thing the air of authenticity, than to have the one journalist who hates his guts break the story."

"I'm part of the set-up?" Amy asked, not wanting to believe it. "Is that what you're saying?"

"He set us both up, Amy." I said. "Everything I found, I was supposed to find. Because every link in the chain is true. That's the thing with the best lies, they always start from the truth. Daisy Lai of Star Transport approaches Napoleon Wong. She gives Napoleon the idea of setting up Terence Auyeung. Napoleon sees it as his chance to grab Gadgetech from Rufus Lam at a discount, and enlists the help of his old friend Benson Chan. It's all true. But tracing it back to the Chinese Overseas Investment Corporation, that was all our doing, Amy. We put two and two together and made fifty, based on an article you published five years ago. You, the journalist who hates Rufus Lam. He must have known about your article, Amy. Hell, he probably knows every word in every article you've ever written. We didn't jump to any conclusions. He just led us there. We were supposed to find what we found."

"What?" Amy's question came out in a breathy whisper.

"Rufus Lam hired me to investigate Gadgetech," I said. "My involvement in this whole thing starts with him deliberately getting me involved. And how about you, Amy? How did you get involved in this? How did you know where to find me that day we first met? When you accosted me outside Gadgetech's offices, remember?"

She thought about it for a moment. "A tip-off." She said it like it was an admission of guilt.

"Let me guess. The caller didn't leave a name or a number. Anonymous, right?"

She nodded slowly, the true horror of the situation slowly dawning.

"It was Rufus Lam. Everything starts with him, the chief string-puller," I said. "He had one of his people tip you off because he wanted you to write that article you have on your lap-top right there, Amy. Everything starts with Lam. And today it was supposed to end with him too."

That confused Amy even more. "What are you saying?"

"He set you up, the journalist who hates him, to write a story exposing how Beijing has used the COIC to try to damage Rufus Lam's reputation. But Lam wants your story to have maximum impact.

What better way to ratchet up the public outrage than if the person who publishes the exposé dies in mysterious circumstances the day before it goes to print. That's what she came here to do." I pointed at Cherry Blossom. "Kill you. Kill me. Take your lap-top. Publish your story."

Amy's look of confusion segued into shock and then into pure unbridled anger.

"Bastard!" She spat out the word with a venom I wanted to bottle and make Rufus Lam drink.

"Get the nominating committee to confirm Elizabeth Leung can run. Win the election against Jeremy Lau. Put in place a Chief Executive he can control. Democracy Hong Kong style, with the biggest tycoon of them all controlling the press and the government. Not a bad outcome, if you ask me. That's what this was all about." I summed it up. "Power and control."

A gust of wind rattled rain drops against the windows like a bucket of gravel being tossed against the glass. The storm was whipping to its height outside.

"The only thing I can't figure out is you two," I said to Gordon MacKenzie, pointing at him and Tito, who was still leaning against the wall like a good soldier. "Two former employees of NDT Consultants, now here on work visas with the Star Transport Group? It makes you look like part of Lam's set up. After all, he seems to be behind Daisy Lai's move on Napoleon Wong. Only here you are saving our skins. It doesn't make any sense. So who are you?"

Gordon Mackenzie's eyes went into slits. The grinding toothpick slowed.

"Daisy Lai," he said, his eyes on Amy for a second, then moving back to me. "She's been a person of interest to our employers for some time. They made an investment in Star Transport, you two have that correct. They wanted their investment preserved. So when Daisy Lai started meeting with Rufus Lam, our employers sent us to find out what was going on. We found her meeting with Napoleon Wong. And guess who else we found following them? You, Scott. And when we followed you, we realized you were working with Ms Tang here."

I remembered the first time we had seen each other outside Lardo's restaurant up in Hang Hau. Gordon MacKenzie aka Skin-head, in his silver-hub-capped Range Rover pointing his telephoto lens at me. Another piece in the jig-saw was taking shape.

"We weren't sure whether you were part of what was being planned at first. But then we worked out you were investigating Terence Auyeung's disappearance for Rufus Lam," Gordon continued. "So you became our best, and our only means of finding out what we needed to know. That was why we placed you under a bit of pressure...to make sure you kept your investigation going."

"Pressure!" I put disdain behind the work.

"That's how we do things in my world, Scott. I'm not here to ask for your forgiveness. Rufus Lam may have thought you were working for him. But we had you working for us."

I almost laughed, but I was completely out of gas.

"So what? You don't work for Star Transport?" I asked.

"No," Mackenzie admitted. "That was just a cover created by our real employers, in case anyone started asking questions."

"But I saw your work visas!" Amy said.

"Fakes," Gordon replied, as if that explained everything.

"So who do you work for?" she asked. "Who can fake immigration documents like that?"

Gordon MacKenzie stared at her and said nothing.

"The Chinese Overseas Investment Corporation," I said. "That would be my guess."

Gordon MacKenzie crouched down on his haunches again. His face turned to the floor a moment and he lifted it back to me, revealing the kind of smile that comes with knowledge that's about to shock a person to hell.

He was right about that.

"Try higher up in the chain of responsibility!"

At first I didn't get what he was saying. But after a moment it dawned on me. The Mandarin voice speaking on the phone when he had first walked in to the room. That was him.

"Who the hell are you? People's Liberation Army? Chinese Intelligence?"

He stared hard at me. Neither a nod nor a shake of the head. But the look said I had either hit the mark, or was so damn close that I should stop asking questions.

"You don't look Chinese," I said. "I'm guessing Gordon MacKenzie isn't your real name either."

He snickered at that. "It's amazing what a good plastic surgeon can do."

I wasn't sure if he was joking or not. But then it hit me. His ability to speak Mandarin so perfectly. The occasional awkward phraseology in his English speech.

"And you still haven't answered the question I keep asking you," Gordon Mackenzie continued.

"What's that?"

He took the toothpick out of his mouth and pocketed it, running his tongue round his gums.

"The reason we started following Daisy Lai in the first place is because we were tipped off that she was meeting with Napoleon Wong. Someone knew Rufus Lam had got to her and told us we should pay close attention. Do you want to guess who the call came from?"

I processed the question a moment before the answer pinged.

"Terence Auyeung," I said

"That's right," Gordon Mackenzie confirmed. "The people I work for believe Auyeung has done his country a great service by putting us onto this whole thing, whatever it is. An act of patriotism, they're calling it. But then, soon after the tip-off, Terence Auyeung disappeared. Which is why Tito and I have been tasked with finding him. My people do not abandon someone who has served his country in such a manner. So for the last time of asking, Scott, where is Terence Auyeung?"

I shook my head slowly. "Sorry, Gordon. Answer's the same as before. Auyeung owed Benson Chan money. When Chan went to collect, Auyeung told him to go screw himself. Benson Chan isn't the sort of man you say that to and walk away in one piece. Auyeung's dead. He's been dead a while. His son, David, told us."

Mackenzie's eyes narrowed into slits of concentration as he tried to guess if I was telling the truth. "If he's been dead so long, tell me how he tipped us off about Daisy Lai, the day before we tailed her up to Hang Hau?"

That shook me. My Hang Hau trip was two days after I'd started working at Gadgetech. Long after Auyeung's disappearance.

"What?" I said.

"You heard. When we get a tip off like that, we act quickly. You want to know something else? Auyeung told us he was afraid. He didn't say of what or who. But he said he couldn't trust anybody."

"Meaning?"

"Meaning Rufus Lam," Amy said, a sudden urgency in her voice. Mackenzie, myself and even Tito turned to look at her. "Terence Auyeung is Lam's corroboration, don't you see? Otherwise it's only the evidence that Scott and I have found that gives him the story. He needs something else to turn up – something we haven't found. And it has to come from someone else, to reinforce the story's credibility."

"Like what?" I asked.

"Like....like I don't know....like Terence Auyeung turning up and corroborating everything we publish."

"There's no way Auyeung would do that, not if he tipped these guys off to Lam's scheme in the first place," I said. But as soon as the words had left my mouth, it hit me like a two-by-four. "Unless it's his body that turns up, along with a suicide note."

Outside, the storm was beginning to slow its course, heightening the quiet into which the room had suddenly lapsed. Cherry Blossom's blood pooled and congealed on the wooden floor. I dabbed at my nose with my T-Shirt. Gordon MacKenzie took out another toothpick and popped it in his mouth. Amy was a ghost next to me, Tito a block of stone standing over us.

"You think Rufus Lam is holding Auyeung somewhere?" Mackenzie said. "Just so he can fake Auyeung's suicide at the right moment to add authenticity to her story?" He pointed with his thumb at Amy.

"If Auyeung's still alive, that would be my best guess," I said. "Look around you, look what Lam's capable of."

It made sense.

"Then the question is: where would Lam be holding him?" Mackenzie asked.

"How the hell are we supposed to know that?" I said doing little to keep the incredulity out of my voice.

"I think I know," Amy said.

Again, the hard silence spilled through the room.

"You can show us?" MacKenzie asked after a moment.

Amy nodded.

"Let's go then."

CHAPTER FIFTY-TWO

Ten minutes later, the five of us were loaded into the silver-hub-capped Range Rover.

Tito was driving, taking us east on Amy's directions. A man of few words was Tito, a doer not a talker, pure execution his forte. On Mackenzie's instructions, he had rolled up Cherry Blossom's body in a carpet, slung it over his meaty shoulder, carried her down the stairs and dumped her in the back of the Range Rover. Hence, the five of us. All in a day's work for Tito, not a flicker of emotion as he completed the task. He could have been measuring up for curtains.

It was my first time witnessing a dead body being taken away like that. Then again, it was turning out to be a day of firsts for me. In the fullness of time, I was sure the experiences I'd been through would open up deep emotional chasms. For now though, I found myself just accepting the situation.

Amy was in the passenger-seat, her laptop open, surfing through all the files she had on Rufus Lam. Like me, she was beyond shock, lost in the zone of chasing down the story she had been waiting all her life to write. Rufus Lam, the man who had ruined her father, had turned out to be the total scumbag she always knew him to be. He had set Amy up to get her to write the story he wanted her to write, then he had sent Cherry Blossom to kill her. Quite the boy-scout.

I was in the back seat behind Tito, mulling on that. From my encounter with Cherry Blossom, my nose was broken, my lower back battered and bruised from being bounced up the stairs. Railroad-track scratches decorated my arms and legs. Apart from that, physically I was fine. Inside me, though, was where the real drama was taking place. I had led Cherry Blossom straight to Amy, all thanks to Rufus Lam. He had used me like a sacrificial pawn in his sick little chess game. Just collateral damage, that's all I was to him. That thought had ignited the slow burn of anger and the flames were now being fanned.

I was going to take down the bastard.

Gordon Mackenzie sat next to me.

"How did you find us back there?" I asked him, trying to fill in the missing pieces and keep my mind off the cadaver that lay just beyond my back-rest.

He shot me a side-ways glance, a look of power and superiority and totally lacking in soul. It was a look he had shown me so many times, it was losing its effect.

"The bike you were on. I attached a magnetic transmitter under the back seat. We tracked you all the way to Lam's place and back again."

"How did you..." I stopped, as the memory came back to me. Mackenzie reaching out and grabbing onto the back seat of the Yamaha as Cherry Blossom had sped away. Enough purchase to stick on a magnetic transmitter. An enterprising move, and an insight into the level of people with whom I was now dealing.

"So are you going to tell me who you are really working for?"

Again with the sideways emotionless glance.

I rolled my eyes.

"They won't tell us anything they don't want to," Amy said without looking up from her laptop in the front seat. "But I'm guessing it's the Ministry of State Security. Chinese intelligence."

The air went out of the car with that assessment.

"So all that stuff about plastic surgery was true?" I asked Mackenzie.

Mackenzie kept his eyes forward.

"If you ask me, Tito got the better end of the scalpel."

The rain had eased off to a slow spit. The sky was starting to clear. Tito flicked the wipers off so all we could hear was the wet tarmac hissing underneath us. He checked with Amy that he was still heading in the right direction.

Amy confirmed it. She was in charge now. A career's worth of work on Rufus Lam, the man who had ruined her father, was finally paying off. She knew everything there was to know about the man and his opaque business interests. She knew the ownership structure of his media group, how he had retained a majority stake in his listed vehicle which in turn owned minority stakes in several other listed companies enabling him to exercise a web of control throughout the group, whilst accepting other shareholders' money. She knew the insurer from whom he purchased his Directors and Officers insurance coverage. And she had a lock on his real estate dealings.

Ten months ago, one of Rufus Lam's private companies had purchased a residential property in Mei Foo. It was an eighty-year old dilapidated dump, which some slum landlord had been using to farm rents. Lam had picked up the building at auction for a song. An unusual move for Lam, re-development wasn't really his style which was why the purchase had stood out for Amy. Planning and other permissions had sailed through without the environmentalists, politicians or other crazies kicking up a stink. Residents had been cleared out and time-tables had been set. But work had yet to begin.

Right now, it was empty. A forgotten, skeletal relic, rotting away.

The perfect place to hide something. Or someone.

Twenty minutes later, we were there. Mackenzie told Tito to do a drive by, so we could scope out the place. Tito grunted his agreement.

The street was virtually empty, a picture of decay and neglect. Lam's latest purchase was one of the first buildings on the right. It looked as though it was rotting from the outside in. Its lower floor windows were tagged with graffiti and strewn with flyers and posters. Air-conditioners hung redundantly from the window units of the upper floors. Pieces of corregated iron, mesh and metal bars were attached at random places. Down one side there was bamboo scaffolding that looked like its only purpose was to hold the place up.

"Looks empty," was my revealing assessment.

"No," Mackenzie said. "Look at the cars."

A BMW, a Lexus and some kind of van were there, the only vehicles parked on the street. Mackenzie made a phone call to someone, spoke in Mandarin but I could tell he was reading off the three license-plate numbers.

A ten second pause.

"Do you know a company called Golden King?" he asked.

"That's one of Rufus Lam's," Amy said.

"It owns those three vehicles," Mackenzie said. "The building isn't empty."

He told Tito to pull up.

"What do we do now?" I asked.

"We're going in. You're staying here."

Mackenzie got out of the car. I made to do the same, but Tito hit the door locks.

"Wait here!" Tito ordered, a deep, bellowing grunt.

I watched Mackenzie walk over to the three vehicles. There was intent in his stride, as if his whole body was wired tight and ready to strike.

The door of the Lexus opened. I recognized the man who got out. He was one of the goons who had greeted me in the garden of One-Thirty-One by lifting me off my feet, on the occasion of my first meeting with Rufus Lam. Cherry Blossom's team member. He had no neck and was all steroid muscle. His tree-trunk arms swung out like helicopter blades when he walked. His face was all aggression, like he was going to break Mackenzie in half if he tried anything.

Without even breaking stride, Mackenzie walked over and snapped his fist into the goon's Adam's apple. Even through the car window I heard the tomato squish. The goon crashed to his knees, clutching his throat and turning purple. Mackenzie finished him off by slamming his head into the Lexus.

Seeing what was happening, the van driver jumped into action, out of his vehicle. He was built like his buddy and sped towards Mackenzie like a runaway truck. Mackenzie flexed his arms, stayed relaxed, made himself a target, side-stepping out of the van-driver's path at the last second, raising a knee, flipping him at the waist, the van-driver's own momentum cracking his head against the concrete.

Mackenzie felt the bonnet of all three cars, checked around inside the Lexus and the van. The BMW was locked. Then he strode back over to us. The whole episode had taken him less than thirty seconds.

"The engines are still warm. They haven't been here long."

Amy and I exchanged an anxious glance. "They're cleaning house." I said. "Cherry Blossom was sent to deal with Amy and me. These guys are doing the same with Auyeung. He is in there, he must be."

Mackenzie said something in Mandarin to Tito.

"You two stay here," he said as Tito got out of the car.

Again, I was about to argue, when the sound of glass breaking stopped us all in our tracks. Fragments rained down from above. We looked up and saw the torso of a man leaning out of the window on the top floor. He had white hair and from this distance looked so frail, a gust of wind would have taken him. He was shouting and screaming something, I couldn't make out what, but the terror in those cries was unmistakable.

Through the window behind him I could see a jumble of hands on him. Someone was trying to throw him out.

"It's Auyeung!" I heard myself shout.

Mackenzie and Tito glanced at me, then sprinted towards the entrance of the building.

The first gunshot pinged off the pavement in front of them. The second forced them back. I saw the rifle poking out of the first floor window, smoke filtering from its barrel. The third and fourth shots pinged off the van which Tito and Mackenzie had now taken refuge behind. Tito was on his belly. Mackenzie was crouched down behind the bonnet and 'sneak-a-peak' ready.

The silence which followed was so complete, I could hear the sound of my heart pummeling. It was a phony silence, a silence in which everything seemed to stop for a second and made you wonder if this was really happening.

The answer came, seconds later, when the whole world erupted around me.

A second and third shooter launched themselves out from the building's doorway and a first floor window, raining down gun-fire on the Lexus, pinning Mackenzie and Tito down tight. Tito was a brave soul. He got to his feet, his revolver like a toy in his meat-cleaver hand returning fire. But the first-floor marksman clipped him in the shoulder for his trouble. The ground shook as he went down like a wounded elephant.

Above us, Auyeung's assailant redoubled his efforts trying to force the accountant out of the window. Screams of terror cut in above the gun-fire.

I was half crouched down in the back seat, watching all of this, wondering why this strange sense of calm detachment had descended on me. My mind was working on warp speed. This whole scenario was playing into Rufus Lam's sick little hands. The story he had planted on Amy to make it look like he was being set up for a fall by Beijing; a suicide note from Auyeung backing the whole thing up. Two Chinese agents killed in a gun fight at the scene of Auyeung's death would only give the whole thing an air of added credibility and conspiracy.

No way!

Mackenzie was drawing fire, Tito was down but the big bull was doing his best to assist, firing with his good arm from the ground.

That left me and Amy.

Channeling my anger into the purest focus, I knew what I had to do.

I reached for Amy's hand through the gap in the front seats and gave it a squeeze.

"You see a chance, you run, okay?" I said.

"What are you going to do?"

I didn't answer. Just gave her hand another squeeze, then opened the door facing away from the building and stepped out.

Crouching low, I controlled my breathing and took an assessment of my next steps. Auyeung was still fighting the good fight, but there was no way he could hang on. I had to get up there.

The scaffolding. It was the only chance we had.

I looked over at Mackenzie, pointed out what I was going to do. He looked up at Auyeung. Fired a couple of shots up in that direction, making sure he was high and wide. It forced Auyeung's assailant back into the building, gave the old boy some relief and me some time to get up there and lend a hand.

Staying crouched low, I padded across the street and started to climb. The bamboo creaked and bent with every step, but it didn't give way. Four storeys was all I needed to ascend. It didn't look that high from the ground, but by the second floor the confidence was beginning to ease out of me.

I climbed and climbed, my movements fluid, my back no longer hurting, but the lactate in my arms made them burn. Still I climbed, concentrating on my breathing, ignoring the gun-fire, the bits of mortar chipping off the wall. Auyeung yelled, "No!" and I could see his assailant was on him again.

Another scream. This one from the marksman on the ground floor. Mackenzie had nailed him and was running across the street, Tito giving him cover fire, keeping the bastard on the first floor occupied.

A few more steps, I was level with Auyeung. The old man's face was etched with effort and fear and fight. He was three windows across from me. He saw me, his eyes momentarily brightening with hope, but it disappeared as his assailant's arms were on him again. They were thick and muscled and for the first time I saw his face. Another of Cherry Blossom's henchman, Tweedle Dum's Tweedle Dee from the night at One-Thirty-One.

I turned myself round on the scaffolding, so I had my back to the building. Then I planted my heel through the window closest to me, smashing it through. Turning round, I worked out a jagged piece from the frame. A quick inspection told me it was good enough for what I had in mind.

When I used to drink, I'd ended up in enough seedy Wanchai joints, to know the dark arts of pole dancing. Quite a time to be putting that experience to use, four floors up on a building's exterior. Thankfully, there wasn't much time to think about what I was going to do.

Auyeung screamed.

I had the piece of glass in one hand. Clutching onto the bamboo pole with my other hand, I locked my feet tightly together round the base of the pole. Then I straightened my legs and arms and swung myself outwards in a wide arc, extending my hand with the piece of glass in it to its fullest reach.

Missing Auyeung's ear by an inch, I plunged the glass into the meat of Tweedle Dum's bicep. He yelped and fell back.

I caught Auyeung by the shoulder and shoved him back through the window. Catching the ledge, I let go of the scaffolding and hauled myself in after him.

Tweedle Dum was down but not out. I punched him in the face. Twice, putting everything I had behind the second one. It hurt like hell, but it felt damn good.

Just then the gun-fire stopped.

The door opened.

It was Mackenzie, out of puff and sweating. Without pausing, he went into a tripod stance, his gun levelled at Tweedle Dum, still writhing on the floor. Tweedle Dum looked like he was about to say something.

Mackenzie fired.

I shut my eyes.

Silence.

"We've got to get out of here," Mackenzie said. "Now!"

CHAPTER FIFTY-THREE

Tito was bleeding, so Mackenzie drove us out of there. Fast.

But not before we had dumped Cherry Blossom's body in the decaying building with her dead entourage. I helped Mackenzie move her because of Tito's bad arm. She weighed a ton, but dumping her on a piece of Rufus Lam's real estate, seemed an appropriate tomb. After Mackenzie had unfurled the carpet, I frisked her and took her mobile phone. She had crushed mine, so I figured she owed me. Just shows how much the last twenty-four hours had twisted my ability for logical thought, that I could come to that conclusion while handling a dead body like it was a household chore.

Amy was gone.

She had done what I'd told her to do and got out of there when she could.

Next to me on the back seat, Terence Auyeung was a gibbering wreck, old and bruised and stinking of urine. He had pissed himself with terror. Who could blame him? The accountant had been milliseconds from being tossed through an open window, bullets hailing around him. But he was alive, at least. Tito gave me his blood-stained jacket and I wrapped it round the poor old man.

"You're safe now, Terence," I told him. "So is your family."

"Who are you?" his voice was a whisper of smoke.

"My name is Scott Lee. I know your wife Gladys and your son David."

I left it at that. The rest was too much to explain.

"These men will make sure you and your family are safe," I signaled to Gordon Mackenzie and Tito.

"That's right, Mr Auyeung, you are safe with us," Gordon Mackenzie said with more authority than I could ever muster on my best day.

Terence Auyeung: safe. I wondered if the same thing went for me.

I needn't have worried.

Gordon Mackenzie drove us to a place he knew, I wasn't sure where, I hadn't been paying attention to the route, so lost was I in contemplation of what had gone before. Thinking about Amy, where she was, hoping she was safe. Missing her, wanting to wrap my arms round her and lose myself in her smell.

It was a safe house, Mackenzie told me when we arrived. They would clean Auyeung up, make sure he got the right medical attention, then they would move him and his family, offer them the opportunity to set up a new life some place else, wherever they wanted.

"Rufus Lam's right-hand man," I said to ol' Gordon MacKenzie, as Tito helped Auyeung towards the door and out of ear-shot. "He's a useful asset for your bosses up north. Should help to clip Rufus Lam's wings a bit."

"We can do the same for you," Mackenzie said. "Set you up somewhere else, I mean."

The offer came as a surprise.

"I kicked you in the balls," I said. "I guess I should apologise for that."

"Why? I pointed a gun at you and I'm not going to apologize," Mackenzie retorted.

"You saved my life."

"You found him for us," he signaled at Auyeung. "Just like we asked you to."

"Asked?" I said, then shrugged my shoulders. "Gordon, if that's your name, it's been a blast. But I don't care if I ever see you again. No offence."

"None taken," he said, almost friendly. "Do you want me to drive you somewhere?"

Now there was a question. Where now?

I knew where. Same place I always go when my life's in crisis.

"Let's go," he said when I told him.

I turned to the Range Rover, but then a thought hit me.

"You mind if I do one thing first?"

I told him what I wanted and why.

That evil little grin spread across Gordon Mackenzie's face as he worked it through. "Tito could you wait a moment, please!" he said to his number two.

The man mountain stopped, Auyeung dangling off his shoulder.

"Go ahead," Mackenzie said to me.

So I did.

***

Sunday night, I don't know what time – somewhere along the way my watch had been crushed – Gordon Mackenzie dropped me off in Stanley on the south-side of the island.

"The girl," he said. "We can't protect her if we don't know where she is."

The girl, meaning Amy.

"I get that," I said.

Amy had the complete picture about Rufus Lam. She finally had her story, a story which could destroy him. That still made her a target for Lam. Now, more than ever, in fact. Mackenzie and Tito couldn't protect her, unless she accepted the same deal which was going to be offered to Auyeung. A new life some place else.

I knew Amy. I knew she wouldn't go for it. She had the story. So did I; which meant I would also continue to be in Rufus Lam's sights.

Protecting us both was now down to me.

When I got out of the car, there were no sweet nothing good-byes between Gordon Mackenzie and me. An appreciative nod to each other was all we could muster. It was a nod that said it all.

I wandered around till I found the right street and the right home. It was a home I had been to many times before. A home where I was welcome, although I didn't know how welcome I would be that evening.

Philip Yip answered the door. Same worsted suit trousers he'd been wearing when we'd met up at Lam's earlier in the day. The jacket and tie were off, the cuffs un-linked and rolled half-way up his forearms. His face tangoed through the emotions of shock at my appearance, relief that I had appeared at all and then professionalism as he flipped his business persona into place.

"What the hell happened? Rufus has been calling me non-stop. He can't get hold of Cherry Blossom."

"She's dead."

That put a cork in his mouth.

I gave him the potted version of what had happened. About how she had tried to kill Amy and kill me. How Mackenzie and Tito had turned up in the nick of time and how we'd found Auyeung.

"What?" he said, so much incredulity dripping off a single word. The fact that he couldn't bring himself to believe me, his best friend of twenty years, sent a shard of anger spiking through me. Phil was the reason I was embroiled in this mess. So I bottom-lined it for him.

"Rufus Lam is a dirty corrupt bastard, Phil. My advice to you is cut all ties with him before it rubs off."

He let me in then, but not before sending the kids to bed so they wouldn't see their Uncle Scott looking like a hobo. His wife Alison went into full doctor mode, treating my wounds. A busted nose, some bruised ribs, enough cuts to open a discount ware-house and more muscle strains than I had muscles. It would hurt more in the morning than it did now and I should get myself to a hospital, was her final verdict.

Apart from that I was just dandy.

I showered, dressed in one of Phil's tracksuits, then joined him out on the terrace. A cooling breeze was coming off the sea, carrying in a fragrance of salt and perfume from the trees.

"Can you take me through it again?" Phil asked.

So I did. Then a second time. He didn't interrupt with any questions, just listened taking it all in, letting it process and settle and spark anger behind his eyes. He paced around, his tension rising until it reached breaking point. Then he turned and started to stalk off in the opposite direction.

"Where are you going?" I asked.

He stopped. Swung round.

"To see Lam. Tell him I'm going to expose everything he's done and everything he is. And if he comes near you, or me, or my family, I'll…"

"Stop it, Phil!" I said it too wearily, but there was part of me that was pleased that the old Phil I knew had finally surfaced. Not the clean-cut, politically astute President of the Law Society. But the friend and father, who, when one of their own is wounded, doesn't take it lying down.

"I got you into this, Scott," he said.

"*He* got *us* into this, Phil. You, me and Amy. And we're going to get ourselves out of it."

Phil's hands were balled into fists at his side. "You know that bastard's organized a lunch tomorrow, with all these Hong Kong big-wigs? Most of them are his rich friends. He's trying to get them to join him in threatening not to pay tax. There will also be some members of the nominating committee. He's trying to charm them. Get their support for Elizabeth Leung running against Jeremy Lau. The election is only a few weeks away and he's got his bloody democracy rally next Sunday. It's all over the news. He's invited me to this damn lunch to help drum up support. As the President of the Law Society, I'm supposed to make him – and Elizabeth Leung – look legitimate. He's been using me all along!"

I turned and looked out to sea and thought about what Phil had just said. I thought about Amy and whether she was safe and it hurt me not knowing. But we needed to do this right. And that meant making Rufus Lam sweat the night.

"Where's this lunch tomorrow?" I asked.

Phil told me and when he did, for the first time that day, I almost felt like smiling.

"Perfect," I said.

CHAPTER FIFTY-FOUR

The restaurant was called One-Thirty-One.

It was where I had first met Rufus Lam. That this should also be the place for the end, provided such a perfect symmetry to this whole thing.

I turned up unannounced and late, deliberately, making my entrance once all his other guests had arrived. They were collected on the lawn overlooking Three Fathoms Cove, gossiping and chuckling about the raft of different topics that rich people found to gossip and chuckle about. The cost of the Champagne which the penguin-suited waiters bustled in and out of the patio doors from the restaurant, could have fed five Hong Kong families for a decade. It made me sick.

The day after the storm, the air was fresh, the sky blue and the clouds candy-floss white. A cool breeze rippled the water with a crêpe paper effect.

I grabbed a juice from a waiter's tray, surveyed the chattering circles of people, made my selection and then inserted myself. A lady in a sparkly cocktail dress was telling a funny story. She wore a velvet jacket with a fluffy edge and when she laughed the top half of her plastic face didn't go along with her mouth.

Rufus Lam was in a tie and a suit today, conservative for him, apart from the bright yellow handkerchief and tie combo.

When he saw me, his smile cracked like bone-china under a hammer's weight.

I raised my right hand, waggled five fingers at him and gave him my best grin.

He continued on with the chit-chat for another five minutes, before finding an excuse to leave and pull me aside.

We made our way down to the water's edge, out of ear-shot from the rest of his cronies. Not once did his politician's smile flicker, it was like it was painted on.

"What are you doing here?" he asked, still smiling, apart from in his eyes, which looked at me like he wanted to kill me. It was a look I was well and truly used to by now.

"Thought you might need some extra help. Your personal security seems to be a bit lighter on the ground than last time we met."

Not for the first time, my attempt at humour was wide of the mark.

"I asked you what you are doing here, Mr Lee."

It was Mr Lee, now, I noted.

"I'm standing in for Phil."

He didn't flinch, not a muscle. Not an ounce of fear in his appearance.

"Whatever you think you know, you're wrong. And you and that journalist friend of yours better be very careful what you say about me, or…"

"Or what?"

His smile widened. I wasn't sure why.

"Hong Kong needs democracy, Scott. It deserves democracy. That is the only end here. And for that end, the means which are justified are considerable. Democratic rights aren't presented to you on a plate. You have to fight for them. Sometimes the fight is dirty, but somebody has to take it on. I am doing that on behalf of the Hong Kong people. Ms Tang took part in the protests three years ago; she should understand what I'm doing. You and she need to think about the ramifications of publishing what you think you know. Half truths. Lies. Because it won't just cost you dearly. It will cost Hong Kong."

"Spare me the political crap, Rufus." I spat the words at him. "Hong Kong has always been just a plaything for people like you. People who make their money by keeping politicians in their pockets and screwing the rest of us. People who have a vested interest in keeping things as they are and retaining control if things have to change. Adapt and survive, that's what this is all about. You're a chameleon, Rufus. Sure you'll be seen as the one giving people democracy. So long as it's your candidate they vote for. That isn't democracy. That's painting a veneer of democracy on a bunch of tycoon-manipulated hand-puppets. You can put lipstick on a pig, but at the end of the day it's still a pig. Same old, same old."

The smile stayed fixed, but the glare he was shooting me was pure bile, his eyes offering a window to the twisted dark soul which lurked beneath.

"What do you want?" he asked.

"You threatened me, so I'm returning the favour," I said. "I don't know whether Amy's going to write her story. The truth is I hope she does. I hope she exposes your lies for the crap they are. But I will make you this promise, Rufus. If you ever come near me, Amy or Phil or his family again, it won't just be your political bullshit that'll be exposed. It will be the full, unredacted truth. That you're nothing but a murdering bastard."

The cool breeze wasn't enough to dowse the fire in Lam's eyes.

"What are you talking about?"

"I did the job you hired me to do," I said, retrieving what I needed from my jacket pocket. "I found Terence Auyeung. Alive."

I handed him Cherry Blossom's phone. I had used it to take a picture of Terence Auyeung and myself outside the safe house. The final favour Gordon MacKenzie had granted me.

"Twenty minutes before that was taken, your old business associate and friend was about to be thrown out of a window by one of your hired help. I don't think he was too happy about it. Attempted conspiracy to commit murder amounts to a lot of jail time, Rufus. And if you come near us again, Terence will tell the world what kind of monster you are. Have you got that?"

I let it lie there, sipping my juice, taking in the fresh air and the beautiful vista stretching out before me. It was tainted only by the fact that I couldn't yield to the urge to punch Rufus Lam, give a bit back of what he deserved.

But I comforted myself with the thought that this was over now, at least as far as I was concerned. I wanted back to my old life.

"You can keep that," I said, nodding towards the phone. "We've got copies."

I handed him my empty glass.

Then I turned and walked away.

CHAPTER FIFTY-FIVE

"Have some more to eat, Lawyer Lee," Mrs Lo ordered. "You need to put on weight. Too thin!"

Without asking, she loaded two more pork ribs into my bowl, already full with vegetable rice.

"I'll have some more, Ma." Tak Ming reached a tattooed arm across the table, going for the meat dish, but Mrs Lo was too fast for him, brutally tapping his chopsticks out of the way with her own. The preventive snap forced Tak Ming to retreat. The street enforcer pouted at his mother, but she remained unmoved.

"Let Lawyer Lee choose first. You too fat!"

"Really, Mrs Lo," I protested. "I've eaten enough to last me to the end of the month."

"See?" Tak Ming said. "And it's not me who is fat, Ma. It's that dog."

"Don't speak about Combo like that. Poor Combo!" She flicked some gristle onto the floor. Up until that point, I thought Combo had been either dead or asleep, he was so inert. But the speed at which that basset hound moved when he saw the food floating through the air, suggested the reactions of a Ninja assassin. After swallowing it in one bite, he waddled over, waggling his tail and thanked Mrs Lo by letting her scratch behind his pendulum ears. Then he went back over to his bed, turned three times, settled down and was back asleep in seconds.

"Is your neighbour giving you any more trouble about Combo, Mrs Lo?" I asked.

"Not since you and Tak Ming took care of it," she said. Remembering the part Tak Ming had played in saving Combo, she pushed the bowl of pork ribs his way.

It was Sunday lunch time.

A week had gone by since saving Terence Auyeung and things were almost back to normal. It had been some week, though.

On Wednesday, after two days of phoning in sick, I went into Gadgetech and handed in my resignation. I said it was due to a medical condition. Napoleon Wong didn't seem to care. He told me that his buy-out of Rufus Lam had stalled, but he was okay with that.

"Lam didn't want it proving a distraction from the election," Wong explained excitedly, swinging to and fro in his big leather chair behind his aircraft carrier desk. "But he promised me it would be first item on his agenda after the election is over. He reminded me of our strict obligation to keep everything confidential and," he stopped swinging and leaned forward, his piggy eyes sparkling, "he has dropped the asking price for his shares by fifteen percent. So the delay's worth it, don't you think?"

As soon as the election's over Lam's going to go back on his word and squeeze you until the pips squeak, you stupid, stupid man, Napoleon. That's what I had wanted to say. But instead I didn't answer, because the truth is I didn't care. My assessment of Napoleon Wong remained the same as on that first day I had met him in his office. He was a man with big ambitions and the arrogance to match. Only the talent and ability were lacking and that made him a pitiful figure.

Tabitha Yan took the news of my resignation with the professional equanimity I expected. She still held out hope that Terence Auyeung or Rufus Lam would turn up and save her from this hell-hole she was working in. I could have told her that the first wasn't coming back, and to be careful what she wished for with the second. But instead I wished her well, thanked her for all her help and got the hell out of there.

That afternoon, Phil Yip gave Tabitha a call, out of the blue, asking if she was interested in coming to work for Yip & Siu. I don't know how the interview went, or whether Tabitha would take the lifeboat being offered. I hoped she did.

I stayed at Phil's for a couple of days. Every day his wife Alison looked me over, treated my wounds and clicked her teeth at my refusal to go to hospital. His son Peter, my godson, taught me how to play a computer game, which involved a lot of shooting and driving at high speed. Phil's father, Old Man Yip, told me I should come back and work for the firm, said he had a number of contacts who needed a good litigator. For once Phil didn't argue with his father.

It was nice to have those few days at the Yips, pretending I was part of their family. But I moved back to my place on the Wednesday night and did my best to get my life back to what it was before. It was nothing much, but nothing much was what I needed right then. Time to figure out what came next in the life of Scott Lee.

Every day, I tried to ring Amy, but her mobile went straight to voice-mail. So did her landline. Every day I checked her blog for an update and my e-mail for news of where she was.

Every day I looked through the newspapers to see if she had broken a story. They were full of election coverage and that damn rally which was still going ahead on Sunday. Speculation was rife about how many would turn up, what the government reaction would be and whether there would be any violence.

But there was nothing from Amy. Nothing about Rufus Lam being a scuzz-bucket. And no reply from her to any of my messages.

I found out where she lived, went round there and spoke to the doorman. He told me she hadn't been seen for a week.

I did receive an e-mail from Mrs Lo, however. She had plenty of referrals for me, from other dog-owners facing the wrath of nasty landlords trying to evict their precious pooches. She invited me round for lunch that Sunday to talk about it, wouldn't take no for an answer. She even had Tak Ming phone me to make sure I accepted, then sent him round to pick me up.

So here I was, at Mrs Lo's, stuffed full with pork-rib, vegetable rice and sweet and sour soup, which had tasted so good it wouldn't have been out of place in an imperial feast. After lunch, we had coffee and watched some television. It was the day of the mass rally and two of the channels had dedicated their entire coverage to it.

Victoria Park and most of Causeway Bay were crammed full with people, according to the helicopter overhead-shots we were seeing. The place was a sea of umbrellas, the massive crowds paying tribute to the protests of the past.

Just like Rufus Lam would have wanted.

I felt my anger rising.

But after watching it for fifteen minutes, neither Mrs Lo nor Tak Ming were interested any more and neither was I, so we turned over to an old Stephen Chow movie on ATV.

"Wanna take Combo for a walk with me, Lawyer Lee?" Tak Ming asked me, when the film finished.

I had nothing better to do, so I followed the big lug and the fat dog out of the door.

Combo wasn't an easy dog to walk; basset-hounds never are. He's a pure sniffer-breed, you see, like an out of control hoover with his nose to the ground weaving this way and that, wherever the scent takes him. He cocked his leg a dozen times and Tak Ming sprayed water. He stopped for a poop which looked like it was his first for a week. Tak Ming shoveled up after him.

The street enforcer was also a perfect dog owner.

"Glad you could make it to lunch, Lawyer Lee," he said to me after dumping the newspaper-wrapped poop in the orange bin.

"No problem, Tak Ming. It was good of you to invite me."

"Ma wasn't kidding about other people needing your help. She keeps getting calls from people who want to meet you. In fact, here's one of them now."

She was leaning on a railing staring into the street as if watching the traffic go by. Only there was no traffic to watch. She wore a grey top, lycra tracksuit bottoms and running shoes. The hood on her top was up and tied under her chin.

From beneath the hood, Amy's face cracked a smile at me.

I wasn't sure which was the greater force to hit me right at that moment: the rush of relief, or the two-step my heart was doing on seeing her.

Tak Ming left me to it, said he would see me back at the flat.

I walked over, took her in my arms and just held her tight. I hugged her like I never wanted to let her go. We stayed that way for a while, not saying anything, letting the tidal wave of emotion work its way through.

Finally she drew back and looked at me, her face beautiful without make-up, just that dusting of freckles.

"Hi," I said. The experience of the last few weeks hadn't dented my knack for witty opening lines.

"Hi yourself."

We walked and talked. Amy told me she had been staying with a friend up in Tuen Muen, working out what to do. She hadn't contacted me because….well just because.

"You didn't publish the story," I said.

"No."

"Why?"

She shrugged. "I thought about it. Rufus Lam is a bastard. I hate him for what he did to my father, to my family. I always knew there was a story out there that would take him down. I always wanted it to be me that found it. And now I have done. But then…." She stopped, softly biting her lower lip and staring off into the distance.

"Amy?" I said.

"What is it they say? Be careful what you wish for? If I expose Rufus Lam, what does that do for Hong Kong. We get Jeremy Lau, another Beijing puppet who spends the next five years finding excuses to delay giving us a democratically elected Chief Executive. I don't expose him, sure they get a candidate controlled by Rufus Lam, but at least that candidate promises next time the Chief Executive will be directly elected."

"Beijing-controlled or tycoon-controlled," I said. "Doesn't that just sum it up! What is it they say? Better the devil you know than the devil you don't."

"It's bad, I agree," Amy said. "But there's something people still don't understand about this place."

"Yeah?"

"Beijing has always thought time was on its side with Hong Kong," she replied, "that as the years passed by following the Handover, Hong Kong would assimilate to Beijing's way of doing things. Resistance would erode and the demand for democracy would be blunted. But they've got that wrong, don't you see? As time passes, the demand only strengthens and matures. It's a yearning that is in our soul, and can't be controlled by anyone. Not by Beijing, not by the Hong Kong government and not by Rufus Lam. The hope will never die. Not with my generation, nor the next, nor the one after that."

After a pause, she pulled something out of her jacket pocket and handed it to me. "I saw this in today's paper."

I unfolded and read it. It was a corner piece, reporting on a murder scene at a condemned building where four dead bodies had been found. Three men and a woman. The bodies had yet to be identified.

Cherry Blossom and her entourage, I thought.

"If they trace that back to Rufus Lam, the scandal's there without my having to lift a finger," Amy said. "And there's more than enough to trace it back to him. The cars are registered to his company. It saves me from making a choice which isn't really mine to make."

"The election will be over by the time people find out Lam was involved," I said.

"So what if it is? Then you've got a tycoon-controlled candidate with the tycoon shrouded in scandal. If you were Elizabeth Leung what would you do in that situation?"

I thought about it for a second, then got where Amy was going. "Distance myself from Rufus Lam. The old political two-step. Take his money when I need it. Get rid of him, when I don't."

"And the best way of doing that is to focus on doing what you were appointed to do in the first place. Bring in full democratic elections for the CE. That would be some legacy for Elizabeth Leung. Like I said, the hope never dies"

The silence lay there a moment, apart from the constant hum of the traffic working its way in the distance. Hong Kong's sound-track, always on the move.

"A lot of 'ifs' need to fall into place for it to happen," I said.

"Isn't that always the case," she said. Then she turned her face towards me. "I'm going away, Scott."

At first I thought I didn't hear her right. Then I realized it was just wishful thinking. The disappointment thundered deep, but then so did the reality that it was the right thing for her to do, even though I didn't like it.

"Where to?" I asked.

"I don't know yet. May be to do some studying. May be to do some work. But I need to get out of Hong Kong for a bit."

"A bit?"

She hugged me then and it felt warm and good, how it was meant to be. And that made this all the more painful.

"You could come with me," she said.

I concentrated on the traffic sounds, on the logical factors I should be weighing up, in making the choice. On what my instinct was telling me. I'd been in Hong Kong a long time. I'd made it my home. I loved and hated the place in equal measure. It gave me permanency, but I had never put down roots, no-one in a city that moves at such velocity ever does. I had risen high and crashed low and risen again, such was the roller coaster life it offered. It was always changing and I hoped that would never change about the place.

As I told Amy my answer, deep down I knew it was the right one.

It was just a shame it didn't feel like it.

Life is full of contradictions, especially in a place like Hong Kong. But then again, sometimes the devil you know is better than the devil you don't.

THE END

ABOUT PROVERSE HONG KONG

Proverse Hong Kong is based in Hong Kong with strong regional and international connections.

Proverse has published novels, novellas, non-fiction (including autobiography, biography, history, memoirs, sport, travel narratives, fictionalized autobiography), single-author poetry and short-story collections, children's, teens / young adult and academic books. Other interests include diaries, and academic works in the humanities, social sciences, cultural studies, linguistics and education. Some Proverse books have accompanying audio texts. Some are translated into Chinese.

Proverse welcomes authors who have a story to tell, wisdom, perceptions or information to convey, a person they want to memorialize, a neglect they want to remedy, a record they want to correct, a strong interest that they want to share, skills they want to teach, and who consciously seek to make a contribution to society in an informative, interesting and well-written way. Proverse works with texts by non-native-speaker writers of English as well as by native English-speaking writers.

The name, "Proverse", combines the words "prose" and "verse" and is pronounced accordingly.

THE PROVERSE PRIZE

The Proverse Prize, an annual international competition for an unpublished book-length work of fiction, non-fiction, or poetry, was established in January 2008.

Its objectives are: to encourage excellence and / or excellence and usefulness in publishable written work in the English Language, which can, in varying degrees, "delight and instruct". Entries are invited from anywhere in the world.

Proverse Prize Winners / Joint-Winners whose work has already been published by Proverse Hong Kong

2009: Laura Solomon, Rebecca Jane Tomasis; 2010: Gillian Jones; 2011: David Diskin, Peter Gregoire; 2012: Sophronia Liu, Birgit Bunzel Linder; 2013: James McCarthy.

Summary Terms and Conditions
(for indication only & subject to revision)

The information below is for guidance only. Please refer to the year-specific Proverse Prize Entry Form & Terms & Conditions, which are uploaded, no later than 30 April each year, onto the Proverse Hong Kong website: <www.proversepublishing.com>.

The free Proverse e-Newsletter includes ongoing information about the Proverse Prize. To be put on the eNewsletter mailing-list, email: info@proversepublishing.com with your request.

The Prize
1) Publication by Proverse Hong Kong, with
2) Cash prize of HKD10,000 (HKD7.80 = approx. US$1.00)

Supplementary editing / publication grants may be made to selected other entrants for publication by Proverse Hong Kong.

Depending on the quality of the work in any year, the prize may be shared by at most two entrants or withheld, as recommended by the judges.

In 2014, the entry fee was: HKD220.00 OR GBP32.00.

Writers are eligible, who are at least eighteen on the date they sign The Proverse Prize entry documents. There is no nationality or residence restriction.

Each submitted work must be an unpublished publishable single-author work of non-fiction, fiction, poetry or a play, the original work of the entrant, and submitted in the English language. School textbooks are ineligible.

Translated work: If the work entered is a translation from a language other than English, both the original work and the translation should be previously unpublished. The submitted work will not be judged as a translation but as an original work.

Extent of the Manuscript: within the range of what is usual for the genre of the work submitted. However, it is advisable that novellas be in the range 35,000 to 50,000 words); other fiction (e.g. novels, short-story collections) and non-fiction (e.g. autobiographies,

biographies, diaries, letters, memoirs, essay collections, etc.) should be in the range, 80,000 to 110,000 words. Poetry collections should be in the range, 8,000 to 30,000 words. Other word-counts and mixed-genre submissions are not ruled out.

Writers may choose, if they wish, to obtain the services of an Editor in presenting their work, and should acknowledge this help and the nature and extent of this help in the Entry Form.

KEY DATES FOR THE PROVERSE PRIZE IN ANY YEAR
*(subject to confirmation and/or change)

Receipt of Entry Fees/Forms begins	14 April
Deadline for receipt of Entry Fees/ Entry Forms	31 May
Receipt of entered manuscripts begins	1 May
Deadline for receipt of entered manuscripts	30 June
Announcement of long-list	July-September of the year of entry*
Announcement of short-list	October-December of the year of entry*
Announcement of winner/max two joint winners	March / April of the year that follows the year of entry to November of the year that follows the year of entry*
Publication of winning book(s)	Within the period, beginning in November of the year that follows the year of entry*
Cash award made	At the same time as publication of the winning work(s)*

NOVELS, SHORT STORY COLLECTIONS
AND OTHER FICTION
Published by Proverse Hong Kong

Those who enjoy **The Devil You Know** by **Peter Gregoire** may also enjoy the following:

A Misted Mirror, by Gillian Jones. 2011.
A Painted Moment, by Jennifer Ching. 2010.
An Imitation of Life, by Laura Solomon. 2013.
Article 109, by Peter Gregoire. 2012.
Bao Bao's Odyssey: from Mao's Shanghai to Capitalist Hong Kong, by Paul Ting. 2012.
cemetery miss you, by Jason S Polley. 2011.
Death has a Thousand Doors, by Patricia Grey. 2011.
Hilary and David, by Laura Solomon. 2011.
Instant Messages, by Laura Solomon. 2010.
Man's Last Song, by James Tam. 2013.
Mishpacha – Family, by Rebecca Tomasis. 2010.
Odds and Sods, by Lawrence Gray. 2013.
Paranoia (the Walk and Talk with Angela), by Caleb Kavon. 2012.
Red Bird Summer, by Jan Pearson. 2014.
Revenge from Beyond, by Dennis Wong. 2011.
The Day They Came, by Gérard Louis Breissan. 2012.
The Monkey in Me: Confusion, Love and Hope under a Chinese Sky, by Caleb Kavon. 2009.
The Perilous Passage of Princess Petunia Peasant, by Victor Edward Apps. 2014.
The Reluctant Terrorist: in Search of the Jizo, by Caleb Kavon. 2011.
The Shingle Bar Sea Monster and Other Stories, by Laura Solomon. 2012.
The Village in the Mountains, by David Diskin. 2012.
Tightrope! A Bohemian Tale, by Olga Walló. Translated from Czech by Johanna Pokorny, Veronika Revická & others. 2010.
University Days, by Laura Solomon. 2014.
Vera Magpie, by Laura Solomon. 2013.

FIND OUT MORE ABOUT OUR AUTHORS
AND BOOKS

Website
<http://www.proversepublishing.com>.

Catalogue
Downloadable from the website.

Follow us on Twitter

Follow news and conversation: <twitter.com/Proversebooks>.
OR
Copy and paste the following to your browsing window and follow
the instructions. https://twitter.com/#!/ProverseBooks

Request our Newsletter

Send your request to info@proversepublishing.com

Availability

Most books are available in Hong Kong and world-wide
from our Hong Kong based Distributor,
The Chinese University Press of Hong Kong,
The Chinese University of Hong Kong, Shatin, NT,
Hong Kong SAR, China.
Email: cup-bus@cuhk.edu.hk
Website: <www.chineseupress.com>.

All books are available from Proverse Hong Kong
and the Proverse Hong Kong UK-based Distributor.